A SEASIDE MOURNING

An Inspector Abbs Mystery

John Bainbridge

GASLIGHT CRIME

First published in Great Britain in 2014 by Gaslight Crime

Copyright © John Bainbridge 2014

The right of John Bainbridge to be identified as the author of this work has been asserted by him in accordance with the Copyright, Designs and Patent Act 1988.

All rights reserved. No part of this publication may be reproduced, stored in or introduced into a retrieval system, or transmitted, in any form, or by any means (electronic, mechanical, photocopying, recording or otherwise) without the prior written permission of the author. Any person who does any unauthorised act in relation to this publication may be liable to criminal prosecution and civil claims for damages. Brief quotations for review purposes are an exemption to the above. This publication must not be circulated in any form of binding or cover other than that in which it is now published and without a similar condition including this condition being imposed on the subsequent purchaser.

All characters and places in this novel are fictitious and any resemblance to places or real persons, living or dead, is purely coincidental.

ISBN-13: 978-1496086129
ISBN-10: 1496086120

One

Devonshire 1873

Sergeant Reeve had seen enough of life to gaze relatively unmoved at knife wounds, flesh mashed by fists, maggots pulsing in the soft pulp of an old corpse, like the brown patch you'd toss away in an apple. He'd even once seen the ravages of a vitriol throwing and stomached it like a man. Seeing was one thing, it was the smells that got to him every time.

This one stank of river water, not so bad in itself but made a filthy brew by the gases rising from the poor bitch's stomach. Reeve did his best to breathe shallowly through his nose, while fixing his mind on the tankard of ale he'd have afterwards. He took a sideways glance at the inspector, who had requested the body be turned over and was studying the back.

'And these marks are?' He indicated the long scratches below the shoulders.

'Boat-hooks,' said the mortuary attendant. He paused to wipe the dew drop on his drooping grey moustache and continued in a bored tone.

'Post-mortem, no bleeding, see? From when they fished 'er out.'

Inspector Abbs grimaced. 'It all seems plain enough. She went in over the weir. No marks of violence other than what's to be expected from the body bumping about.'

He swallowed quietly. 'And the belly tells the tale.' He and Reeve looked at the unmistakable thickening around the middle.

'All right. You can cover her, I think we've seen enough. What are your thoughts, Sergeant?'

'Well sir, provided the doc doesn't come up with something unusual, I'd say there's nothing for us here. I don't reckon we'll ever find out who she was, even.'

'Probably not, if no one comes forward to enquire about her missing.'

They watched as the attendant flicked the rough sheet back over the corpse. The water had soaked away all trace of the young woman's visage and left a bloated mass.

'Most likely a dollymop thrown out by her employer,' said Reeve. 'Wonder if he knocked her up?'

'Who knows?' answered Abbs. 'Nobody cared.' He looked away at the drain in the floor, a hard set to his features. 'I agree she was most likely a servant. A common prostitute would have known where to go to deal with it.'

Belatedly Reeve remembered hearing some whisper about Abbs having lost a new-born child. It was when he'd joined the detective branch and Abbs had been pointed out to him as a stickler for paperwork. The inspector wasn't one to talk about himself and though he'd been put to work under him a few times lately, he knew nothing more than that.

'Thank you,' Abbs nodded at the attendant. 'Please tell Dr Chisholm we're satisfied, pending his report. Sorry we had to miss him.' He turned to the sergeant.

'We're done here. Let's get some air.'

Silently they climbed the basement steps, where the walls were hung with shiny white tiles like a urinal and as they emerged into the autumn sunshine, Reeve racked his thoughts for something to say.

'A bad business, sir. It isn't the first time we've seen it.'

'Nor the last, Reeve, nor the last.'

Adelaide Shaw swung her empty basket as she walked back along the esplanade. Her spirits rose in the sunshine, the first half of September having brought constant wind and rain. She picked her way between the puddles to save her hem and avoided the shingle thrown across the road. Pausing she watched the cart drawn up on the beach and the small boys stooping as they gathered seaweed. Inhaling deeply, she enjoyed the pungent reek of the glossy vegetation strewn in bottle green heaps.

The majority of Seaborough residents did not share her view. The local businessmen and town council in particular feared that the noxious smell would disbar their growing town from becoming a stylish resort where the fashionable would convalesce and send their children. Fortunately the seaweed was at its most powerful during spring and autumn tides. And after all, she thought, the farmers valued its goodness to improve their potato fields.

Turning away from the sea, she walked past the row of beeches on one side of Clarence Square, some leaves already turning orange among the green.

'Mornin' Miss.'

She nodded in acknowledgement as a workman with a length of wood under his arm, touched his cap and disappeared down the alley beside the town hall. The sound of hammering came from a door propped open. Few other people were about, though a dray was standing outside the *Crown and Cushion*, a pile of dung steaming. Across the street a maid could be seen, busily polishing an upstairs window.

Passing the municipal building reminded her that her father had to go out that evening. His standing in the town required him to take a seat on several of the committees that seemed to increase each year, Mr Halesworth generally taking the chair with his cronies at either side, no doubt. She knew that her father was considered a well-meaning eccentric in some circles, his concern for the poor indiscriminate, his kindness not confined to the sufficiently deserving.

Memory of a tiny incident from last spring still brought a livid flush to her sallow cheeks. She had been attending a musical evening, held as was customary at the town hall. Its purpose had been to raise funds for the hospital and she had been seeking the supper room during the interval. Weaving a path between wide skirts and cigar-smoke, clinking glasses and conversation, she had heard her own name spoken.

'Oh you know Shaw, he's bound to speak up for those wretches. He thinks his profession obliges him to.' A burst of hearty laughter greeted the remark. The broad back of the speaker was turned toward her and she could make out the bony profile of Mr Cox the druggist at his side. A group of businessmen were stationed by the supper table and she abandoned her thought of refreshment, returning instead to her seat. No, she did not care for Mr Alfred Halesworth, even though he had given her father a cheque for the orphans.

Further down the street she could see Mr Cox standing outside his shop and talking to Dr Avery. The doctor stood by his gig and was stowing a box on the seat, very likely collecting medicines for the hospital. He had been among the group listening to Mr Halesworth that evening but he had not been one of those who laughed. He had been most conscientious when her father had been laid low with bronchitis the previous winter. People sometimes thought his manner aloof but everyone agreed he was a clever doctor.

Reaching the vicarage, she unpinned her hat and picked up the second post lying on the hall table before following the spirited rendition of *Rock of Ages* coming from the back corridor. The kitchen smelt comfortingly of yeast and onion. A plump woman enveloped in a holland apron stood working at the deal table.

'There you are, Miss. Your father's been out in the garden this half hour nor more, standing on that soaking grass. You know what his chest's like. I told him, summer's long gone and there'll be colds to be had.' This was accompanied by an eloquent slam of the dough being kneaded.

'I'll fetch him in directly,' promised Adelaide. 'The Taylors were glad of your preserves.'

'You told them we've some clothes put aside for the little 'uns?'

'I did, Will Taylor will be up to collect them and now his leg's better, the boat can go out.' Adelaide reached forward and plunged her hand in the enamel bin, scooping out some currants.

'Be off with you, Miss. How's a body to get on, I'd like to know?'

'Sorry, Hannah. I can't resist them.'

'You never could,' the older woman's voice softened. 'Not since you had to climb on that stool to roll your little bit o' pastry, more than twenty years back.'

Her capable, flour-speckled arms gave the dough a final fold and tucked it in a basin. Pulling a cloth down from the airer, she draped it over the top and set it to rise near the range.

'Ah, Adelaide my dear.' Reverend Shaw straightened up from the rose bed when he saw his daughter appear in the arch of the straggly yew hedge. 'I fear *William Lobb* has fared badly with mildew these past months.'

'I'm sorry, Papa. I know it's one of your favourites.' Adelaide peered at the mossy bush her father was inspecting.

'We must hope that the frosts are not severe this year. In the meantime I shall ask Isaac to dig in some manure. You have a letter, I see.'

'I haven't opened it yet.' She did so and quickly scanned the short note written in neat copperplate. 'It's from Miss Chorley, inviting us to tea next week. Her nephew is paying her a visit at last and I suppose she wants to show him some company.'

'Is that so? I understood Miss Chorley to say she expected him before Christmas, not in September. He will like to tour our hospital, no doubt. He'll find it very different from his posting. From what I read in the newspapers, the military hospital at Netley is like a small town in itself. I shall enjoy conversing with him and meeting someone new will make a pleasant change for you.'

'It will be interesting to see him after all we've heard but I should think he'll find us dull fare after Hampshire.'

In the upper council chamber three men were hunched over a map, its top edges weighted by an ink well and a decanter. The gaslight popped, its familiar smell mingling unpleasantly with the faint tang of turpentine seeping up the stairs. On this floor no refurbishments had been deemed necessary, although the ceiling recorded two decades' meetings in an oily sheen of soot and tobacco. A meagre fire smouldered in the grate and the sudden shift of a coal made the bearded man start.

'What's the matter, Hicks? Nervous about your investment?'

'Not in the least, Halesworth. All I say is, there'll be none of your fat profit materialising unless we can get the doings. If Miss Chorley won't sell, we're finished before we've begun.'

'D... it, Hicks! You always look on the black side. Still, it's to be expected in your trade, I suppose.' Mr Halesworth strode over to the fireplace and added some more coal. Mr Hicks laughed and turned to their colleague. 'What say you, Avery?'

The doctor rubbed his hand thoughtfully over his chin. 'Could go either way. She has no real use for the land that I can see but neither does she need the money. I've found she can be stubborn when her mind's set on something.'

'She'll sell,' said Mr Halesworth, vigorously applying the poker. 'Poor bit of grazing like that, she can't make more than a pittance from it. It isn't as if it's anywhere near her house.' He tossed the tongs back in the scuttle and returned to the long table.

'Perhaps we've overlooked some suitable plot for our next venture,' Mr Hicks studied the map.

'We've been over all this,' exclaimed Mr Halesworth, standing between the others. 'The cliffs are unstable here, as any fool knows,' he tapped his finger to indicate where he meant. 'The strand's out, though it would make a prime site if that flea-pit were swept away.' He waved airily at the cots and passages of the original fishing village. 'And the land rising on both sides makes it uneconomic to build.' He traced an area beyond the streets. 'No, it has to be here. Flat and forms a natural extension to the town. A terrace of villas, quickly thrown up.' He rubbed his hands together, good humour restored. 'And a steady income for all of us.'

'They won't stand empty?' questioned Dr Avery.

'Certainly not. All those clerks and shop assistants looking to settle down. They'll be queuing up.'

'I think Halesworth's right,' contributed Mr Hicks. 'We saw a good return last time. It makes sense to think bigger.'

The doctor gazed at the wall as he considered. 'Salisbury-terrace was a shrewd investment granted, but we sold and collected our profit. These properties would remain on our hands. I'm not a rich man and cannot afford capital tied up without interest.'

'We're none of us rich,' said Mr Halesworth. 'But I for one, mean to be.' He slapped Dr Avery on the back. 'You've no cause to regret using your legacy. Well then, come in again and double your money in rents.'

A slow smile spread over the doctor's face. 'Very well, you've convinced me. I rather like a gamble if the odds are in my favour. Count me in.'

'That's the spirit, good man. Hicks, are you with us?'

Mr Hicks glanced up at the window as a spatter of rain hit the glass. 'It would be ideal,' he said. 'I pass there when I'm at the new cemetery. I'm in if we can get it.'

'You'll approach her on our behalf, then, Halesworth?' said Dr Avery.

'As soon as she'll see me. Never fear, I'll get the papers drawn up and we'll have the footings in before winter.' Mr Halesworth reached for a stack of papers at the far end of the table. 'Best look lively, the others will be here.' He threw himself into the chair and began to skim through the agenda as the others replaced the map.

Shortly after, a door banged, followed by a murmur of conversation and footfalls heard on the stairs.

'Good evening, gentlemen, though it's inclement weather again, I fear.' Reverend Shaw entered the room, shaking out his umbrella, followed immediately by the other committee members.

'Thank you, Mr Hicks. And you Mrs Lavis, you've both been very kind to me. And Mr Owen, he'll do a lovely service. I'm sure I never thought such a day would come, even though I took out the burial club.' The speaker broke off to dab her black-edged handkerchief to her eyes. Turning away a little she stopped to blow her nose. Mr Hicks and his assistant waited patiently by the door.

'I know it will all be done proper. You did everything very dignified for my sister's boy. You will be walking yourself, Mr Hicks?'

Mr Hicks inclined his head. 'Everything will be done exactly as you wish, Mrs Pardoe. The utmost reverence will be shown to your dear departed. I shall be following the hearse, accompanied by two mutes, as we agreed.'

'Oh I do like to see men in weepers, it shows proper respect. It's what my Albert deserved.' Mrs Pardoe peered short-sightedly at the undertaker, her round, worn face crumpled inside her mourning bonnet. 'He were in the best of health, 'part from indigestion, which he suffered something terrible. I never thought he'd be taken from us so soon.'

She looked, thought Mrs Lavis, like a timid mouse peering out of a nest in a children's picture book. Her employer showed the new widow off the premises and she replaced the drawer of cheap coffin ornaments.

'Bit of a waste on a Chapel service,' he commented, when they were alone. 'Still if it's what Mr Pardoe wanted.'

'I don't know,' replied Mrs Lavis, shaking her head. 'She's always been Chapel but he certainly didn't sign the pledge. Pity he didn't. I've seen Bert Pardoe a dozen times staggering home drunk from the Compass. And he used to beat her, Mr Hicks. She's had a black eye before now, the poor soul.'

'She's surely suffering even so. Poor woman indeed.' Mr Hicks regarded his assistant with something approaching affection. She was a great asset to his business with a good head for figure-work for a woman. And being a widow herself she showed a genuine sympathy to the newly bereaved.

'I shall take a turn outside.' Mr Hicks was quietly proud of his business, without doubt the leading undertaker's in the town. And if not quite a mourning warehouse, his funeral furnishings emporium endeavoured to meet every necessity for those afflicted by grief or required to make an outward show.

Shelves of crape and bombazine, drawers of mourning gloves, handkerchiefs, armbands, stationery, memorial cards and a case of best quality mourning jewellery made from Whitby jet lined the walls. Though the yard behind was where he felt most at home.

The smell of wood shavings from the workshop took him back to his start as apprentice to a cabinet-maker. The mare was out to hire but Samson in his stable whinnied as he recognised his footsteps. The lad was whistling *Maid and the soldier* as he cleaned the new hearse. It looked very stylish with its glass sides, the first to be seen in Seaborough.

Mr Hicks suppressed a smile before he spoke. 'Let gravity be your watchword on the premises, Bram.'

'S...sorry, Sir.' Bram clutched his cap, dropping the leather and stared at his employer. His whole figure looked tensed to flee, the faintest softening to his features.

Mr Hicks gentled his tone. 'It's all right, lad. You've done nothing wrong. Best not to whistle while you're here, though.'

Bram nodded. 'Right, Sir. I been polishing the flowers.' He pointed to the etched white pattern.

'So you have.'

'They're lilies, they are. Missus Lavis told me their name.'

'And you're doing a fine job.'

Two

After listening at the door, Miss Ada Geake moved lightly across the turkey carpet and tried the desk drawer. It had been locked which meant it contained something possibly of interest. Fortunately the key was in its customary hiding place. Reaching behind the glass case she ignored the shiny stare of the stuffed dog-fox posed among dried grasses, their colour long faded. Old Richard Chorley had played the country gentleman, though she had heard he was cold-shouldered by the real gentry of the county. For he was trade, having made his money from a silk and crape factory. She pulled a face at his full length portrait over the fireplace.

The desk was a flimsy piece with curved legs, designed for a lady's correspondence. Mr Chorley had picked up his furniture job-lot in country house sales and his daughter disliked change. In many ways the house was a shrine, she thought, with the jumble of walking canes still in the hall stand and the rack of pipes in the rarely used study. Miss Chorley lived according to her long dead father's edicts, which she quoted frequently, as though he had gone away and was expected back at any hour.

The contents of the drawer were soon examined. Miss Geake ignored the handsome red morocco diary, knowing from experience that its entries made dull reading. The interesting discovery was in fact an absence. The will had been removed which probably meant it had been taken to read at her bedside. That the unseen nephew was expected imminently could be no coincidence.

The sound of Miss Chorley's querulous tones made her hastily lock the drawer and return the key. The heavy tapping grew steadily nearer and by the time her employer turned the door knob, she was standing by the window, looking at the dimly outlined trees and rearranging a vase of bulrushes.

'Do stop fiddling with those, Ada.' Miss Chorley sank into the nearest chair, her hand resting on the ornate ivory handle of her cane. 'There is so much to be done. That foolish girl Sarah has made up the bed in my nephew's room with the wrong linen.'

'Yes, Miss Chorley. Would you like me to supervise Sarah?'

'No need, she knows what to do now. I want you to write a note for me and get William to take it round.'

'Certainly, ma'am. Will you dictate it now?'

'You may write it. It is to Mr Halesworth, the councillor. He asks for an interview with me, as soon as may be convenient.' Miss Chorley sighed, making her grey ringlets stir beneath their old-fashioned lace. 'And my nephew expected at any hour.'

'I understood Captain Selden was not expected until tomorrow?' asked Miss Geake.

'You may tell Mr Halesworth I shall receive him briefly in the forenoon. *Briefly,* mind. I cannot possibly imagine what he wishes to see me about. I hope he is not presuming on my acquaintance with his wife.'

'Perhaps he wishes to ask for a subscription?' ventured her companion. 'I hear he has been elected governor of the board school.'

Miss Chorley raised her hand wearily. 'You should not listen to gossip, Ada.'

'No, Miss Chorley.'

'I have a headache come on me and no wonder with so many calls on my time. This damp air oppresses me. You did tell Cook about the mutton? Gentlemen are always sure to be hungry after travelling.'

'I gave her your instructions.' Miss Geake unpinned the vinaigrette at her waist. 'Here you are, ma'am. Would you like one of your powders or should I send for Dr Avery?'

'This is sufficient, thank you, Ada. You are most kind.' Miss Chorley held the tiny flask beneath her nostrils. 'I shall rest here quietly for a time. Be so good as to pass me my book before you go.'

'I shall send William directly I have written.'

Miss Chorley opened her volume of Mr Keble's verse but shortly after being left alone, she rose and retrieved some items from her sewing box. Then she settled herself with the Ladies' Own Paper and a box of violet creams.

'It's quite a nasty cut but it won't need stitching.' Dr Avery dabbed gently as he cleaned the wound across his patient's palm.

'I wouldn't have bothered you except there could be glass in it.' The young man looked somewhat embarrassed.

'Come over to the window and I'll take a look.' Dr Avery took a magnifying glass from his desk and held his patient's splayed hand, tilting it to the light. The young man looked out of the window where privacy was achieved by a dense shrubbery of evergreens at the side of the house.

'I can reassure you that there is no glass present,' said the doctor as he straightened up.

'I'm much obliged to you.'

'I'll put some iodine on it against infection and bind it up. How did you come to do it?'

'A second's inattention. I was picking up the fragments of a broken phial and the light was dim.'

The doctor turned round from washing his hands and studied him. 'Phial, you say, then you're a druggist? No...wait, would you be the photographer who's set up in Charlotte-street?'

'I'm glad to hear the word is spreading, business has been decidedly slow,' the young man grinned. 'Winton's the name. Sorry I can't shake hands.'

The doctor nodded and twitched a brief smile. Mr Philip Winton thought the rather stern countenance looked younger for an instant. Somewhere in his early forties, Dr Avery had a haggard look to his clean-shaven face, the kind of fellow who would always be lean.

'Take a seat, I'll be with you in a second.' Winton sat on the worn leather chair and looked about him with interest.

The room held the usual paraphernalia to be expected in a doctor's surgery; a large, serviceable desk, a wooden folding couch and a glass-fronted bookcase full of reference books. The desk held a scarred blotter, ink well, pen tray and wipe with a wooden day calendar. Everything was cheap and functional. In contrast a handsome cane stood propped in the corner, its wooden handle carved as a horse's head. He hastily averted his gaze as the doctor stepped back in from the adjoining room.

'This is going to sting a little.'

'Your housekeeper said I'm fortunate to have found you at home?'

'I'm usually at the cottage hospital at this time of day but I called in to collect some papers.' Avery considered Winton's open face as he deftly held the wadding in place while weaving the bandage. 'It's possible I might be able to put some work your way.' Pausing, he reached for some scissors. 'We've been raising funds for a new wing, an isolation ward. The foundation stone is to be laid before Christmas and naturally there will be photographs taken to mark the occasion, our benefactors, the trustees and so forth. I see no reason why you shouldn't have the commission.'

'Really?' Winton looked delighted. 'I'd be honoured and most grateful to you, sir. I could submit some samples of my work.'

'Think nothing of it. See that you favour your hand for a while and don't let any of your chemicals near the cut as it heals.'

'Thank you, doctor. Now how much do I owe you?'

Mist had rolled in from the Channel overnight and crept through every street, hanging a damp shroud over the slate roof-tops. The morning sounds of hooves stamping, barrels rumbling, shop boys sweeping, the cries of street-sellers and the long, piercing train whistle were muffled and hollow. Mr Halesworth, impatient with the weather and the stink of seaweed was glad to climb the long hill that shook off Seaborough and wound inland.

As the land rose beyond the town, a thin sunlight was feebly attempting to pierce the clouds. Halesworth held the reins loosely and the gig rattled along at a steady pace, eventually approaching a crossroads where he slowed to turn off. An empty tollhouse stood at the corner, door and windows nailed up, its board torn down and the garden behind choked with nettles. He remembered the last family there, a widow and her seven children. He'd shared a schoolroom with two of the daughters. They both lay in the churchyard he would shortly pass, along with their father and a brother dead on a sea voyage. The damp saw off the lot of 'em.

The old church tower was coming into view above the trees, its masonry in a poor state. A woman in mourning was entering the lych-gate, carrying a basket of Michaelmas daisies. The click of the latch sent a flurry of rooks cawing and circling. Halesworth eased his pace as he heard the jangle of harness and a cart heavily laden with bricks came round the bend towards him. He nodded as the carter touched his hat to him.

Venning church, together with its rectory built in the last century, stood a little way aloof from the village. Then he was upon *The Roll Call* with its smoking chimneys. An elderly man was mopping and casting a pail of water through the open door. The main street consisted of a straggle of cottages, leaning into one another like a row of drunkards, their thatch for the most part ragged and streaked with moss. Here and there they were interspersed with later dwellings. At the end of the street stood a plain brick house with a spacious yard to one side in place of a garden. Halesworth turned in and drew to a halt.

Two workmen were engaged in conversation beside a long workshop. The ground near its entrance was littered with stone chippings and the men were gesturing towards a tall object shrouded in sacking.

They looked up and one clapped the other on the shoulder and handed him his mallet before strolling towards the gig.

'Jim,' he called and a young boy appeared from round the back. 'See to the horse, will you?'

'Good day, Caleb.'

'Mornin', Fred, we're honoured. Don't often see you out this way no more.'

'I'm a busy man.' Halesworth eyed the others. 'We need a word. Can we step inside where it's private?'

Caleb drew on his pipe before gesturing with the long stem. 'Best not, I'm waiting on a delivery of marble. Here will do.' They strolled over to the fence which separated the yard from an orchard, its trees laden with rosy fruit. 'A tidy crop, nothing like Crimson King for cider,' he remarked, resting his arms on the top.

'Never mind that,' snapped Halesworth. 'I came by way of Alma Villas. Seems to me you're well behind with the roof.'

'Rain set us back. No need to fret. We'll soon make up.'

'Well, see that you do. That isn't why I came though. It's Pardoe's accident. Tell me exactly what happened.'

Caleb shrugged and leant one boot on the bottom rung of the fence. 'Don't rightly know,' he considered. As he waited, drumming his fingers, Halesworth compared their appearance, the one in shirt-sleeves and worn moleskins, his own well-cut frock coat. Caleb's thinning, slightly greasy hair was in sharp contrast to his own thick head, which unlike his brother's, was as brown as ever. No one would think that he was the elder.

'He just fell,' continued Caleb, frowning. 'No one saw it, see. One minute he were tiling the roof, next thing was, we heard a cry. We come running, we were round the other side, but it were too late. There he was, lying on the ground.' He turned aside and spat, causing his brother to wince. 'It was awful, there was nothing we could do. He gave a sort of shudder and died.'

'Dreadful. So what did the police have to say?'

'We sent for them, directly, o' course. The sergeant came himself to see. Had a look at the scaffolding, it were fine. Nothing to be said. We were more concerned about someone telling his poor missus.'

'Had Pardoe been drinking?'

'No more than any of 'em. He were sober when he went up the ladder. I'd stake money on it.'

'Then there's no blame to be attached to us. Tancock was satisfied as to that?'

Caleb nodded. 'He must have slipped, poor sod.'

'There's to be no inquest. Still, that fat fool Tancock doesn't make work for himself. I think we're clear.' Halesworth brushed some specks of dirt from his sleeve. 'I'll be off then. We can't afford to have talk, especially in my position.'

Caleb yelled for the boy to make ready with the horse.

'It can be put behind us, then,' said Halesworth, drawing on his gloves.

'Mrs Pardoe won't be thinking like that.'

'Eh? No, quite right, Caleb. A sum of money, d'you think? As long as it's understood that it doesn't signify culpability. A good will hand-out for the widow. I shall see to it.'

'How's Rosa, by the way?'

'Spending my money,' said Halesworth as he mounted the step of his gig. 'I've another plan in mind that'll bring in all the work you can handle. You may need to take on.' He glanced at his old family home as he began to turn. 'I should get the go ahead tomorrow,' he called over his shoulder.

Three

Nathaniel Hicks hung his hat on the stand in his office and wandered back into the room where Biggs was unpacking his case. The latter was placing his equipment carefully in a certain order on a white cloth and naming each piece under his breath as he always did. Catching his employer's eye he cleared his throat and gave a small, self-conscious smile.

'I counted them at the house of course, Mr Hicks. It wouldn't do to leave anything behind and offend the family.'

'I know I can count on you, Biggs.'

'That is very gratifying.' Jabez Biggs held a long, flexible metal tube up to the light and breathed on it, before wiping a mark with a soft rag. Various bottles and jars were placed in a row, followed by scissors, darning needle, an enamel dish, several syringes and a large pump.

'More thread needed,' he muttered to himself. Collecting several of his instruments, he set about washing them in the sink before seeing that they were thoroughly dried. His large teeth and benign expression, the few strands of hair plastered evenly over his bald pate gave him the look of a benevolent grandpapa, considered Hicks. Few would guess that his clerk was a man of uncommon skill with the tools of his other trade.

Polishing to his satisfaction, Biggs coughed once more. 'I think I may venture, Mr Hicks, to say that our melancholy business was concluded most satisfactorily.' He began fitting his implements back in their compartments.

'It all went smoothly enough,' agreed Hicks.

'And due in no small part to young Mr Winton, if I may say so.'

Hicks nodded. 'He did well, discreet and efficient.' He glanced at the clock on the wall. 'It was his first time, you know?' Biggs went to the shelf and added a reel of thread to his wooden case.

'I rather had that impression, sir, although he covered it admirably. The family appreciated his manner.'

'Yes, I'm perfectly satisfied. We shall use him again.'

It had been Avery's thought that he might consider giving young Winton a try out. A few of them had been playing a hand at *The Marine* and the doctor was winning. Avery had been more relaxed than customary, the cares of his medical work tolled hard on him. He'd mentioned casually to the others that Draper's studio was shutting up shop, the old man was off to live with his daughter in the north of the county. Draper had been getting steadily more deaf and conversation had been awkward for the past year, being as undertaking required low voiced hints and murmured asides. Relatives in the next room didn't want to hear the nuts and bolts of the matter.

He had been uncertain about Winton's probable lack of experience but talking it over with Fanny, she agreed with Avery that the fellow should have his chance.

'After all, Nat,' she'd said, 'you had no experience when my father gave you your start.' And so he had paid Winton a visit, finding him a personable young chap and engaged him, after emphasising the need for tact and professionalism.

'You do see the necessity for getting it right first time? I know that isn't always easy in your line.'

'I understand, sir and am confident I can provide the service you require.' His manner was suitably dignified and grave. He'd not cared for probing about the man's private life but the question had to be asked.

'You have seen a dead body before? Forgive my asking but not everyone can remain impassive.' He'd wanted to kick himself, seeing the pain flare in Winton's eyes for an instant, like a struck vesta that went out.

'I have, Mr Hicks. My mother died a year ago and I was with her until the last. I should show no untoward emotion at the task.'

He had kept his word. The family portrait had been taken with the young daughter sitting comfortably on a chaise longue, her parents standing behind. No one would have guessed that narrow leather straps held the pose beneath the carefully arranged folds of her paisley shawl. Biggs's artistry had shaded roses in her cheeks, a healthy tint to her eyelids and her hair had been combed and fanned on her shoulders. The picture was that of a young girl who lay sleeping. And so she did. The photographer had needed little direction, seeming to go about his work instinctively, his demeanour solemn and unobtrusive. There was only one moment when Winton had faltered, his auburn head bent over the body had stilled for too long, his fingers clumsy as he arranged a locket. Fortunately the three of them were alone and Biggs and he had effected not to notice.

Another dry cough recalled his attention. Biggs had taken down the ledger and was fussily turning the pages. 'It did occur to me to wonder what brought Mr Winton to set up in our small town? His accent is not local and he does not appear to have relatives here.'

Hicks reached for an ashtray. 'I believe his mother died a while ago,' he remarked as he felt in his pockets. 'He may have no other family and Seaborough is on the up, after all. It's the right sort of place for a young chap to get on if he works hard.' Producing his case he proffered it to his clerk. 'Leave that until the morning. Have a smoke, Biggs, it'll lubricate your throat.'

The organ swelled to its last notes and was abruptly still. Adelaide Shaw listened attentively as her father gave the final blessing, though she was aware of an expectant shuffling of boots and stealthy gathering of handkerchiefs and hymnals. She stood waiting in the second pew for Miss Chorley at the front to lead the way down the aisle. Miss Geake accompanied her as usual, with downcast eyes and carrying a small, maroon case for prayer book and Bible, dangling on a cord handle. Bringing up the rear was Captain Selden.

Adelaide was intrigued to see him at last, his views on the royal family, the management of hospitals and many other matters being frequently quoted to Seaborough society. She had noticed that his pronouncements always coincided with his aunt's views, which were trenchantly expressed at every occasion. Her first impression was that he wore his uniform with a diffident stance, his posture tending to the round shouldered, rather than the erect, confident set associated with army officers. His sandy, somewhat faded hair and tentative moustache contributed to her impression, though she had been told only too often, that the Captain held an administrative position of some importance at the well-known military hospital in Hampshire. She knew he had returned from India but it was perhaps a long time since he had bellowed and stood before his men on a parade ground.

Now he halted and meeting her eye, smiled shyly and gestured for her to go before him. She inclined her head, returning his smile and joined the congregation flowing out behind her papa. As she left, Adelaide caught the clove fragrance from the pink carnation pinned on young Mrs Todd's fitted mantle. She leant on her husband's arm, together with her parents, Mr Jerrold and his wife as they waited by the porch door to speak to the vicar.

Hovering by a clipped yew, she watched the townsfolk with interest. Miss Chorley had taken her position by her papa as though they were joint hosts on a receiving line. Her nephew, his cap beneath his arm, shook hands with her father and stood politely aside for the Halesworths. Adelaide supressed a wry smile, she could tell that Rosa Halesworth was pricing Mrs Todd's beautifully-cut costume from head to foot. She'll be cutting out a pattern by the end of the week, she thought.

Mr Halesworth raised his hat, made a brief remark to her father and strode swiftly down the gravelled path without waiting for his wife. After the least possible acknowledgement, he had turned his shoulder from Miss Chorley. She did not think it could be unconscious. Certainly Mrs Halesworth looked surprised as she caught up with her husband by the open gate. Grasping his cane, he marched off without a backward glance, his wife scurrying to keep pace.

When the parishioners had departed and Reverend Shaw had had a word with his churchwarden, Adelaide and her papa crossed the churchyard path that led to the vicarage garden. It was Mr Shaw's habit to spend some time in his study between services, writing a fair copy of his sermon notes, reading and perhaps dozing a little before evensong. Hannah and their maid Betsey had their free afternoon, having already set out a cold collation.

Adelaide sat in the window seat and read the previous day's edition of her father's *Times*. Nothing was ever said but she knew that he left it deliberately on the dining table for her use, often folded at a particular page of interest. She knew it was not the sort of improving reading that Miss Chorley would think fitting on a Sunday and guessed that the day would hang heavily at Tower House.

'Thank you, Edwin. That will do very well.' Miss Chorley held up her hand and Captain Selden closed the heavy Bible from which he had been reading. 'Tell me, what did you think of our vicar's sermon this morning?'

The captain hesitated, 'he struck me as a good preacher. He looked a mild enough, old fellow and he certainly didn't thunder from the pulpit, yet his arguments were quietly compelling. He made you think.'

Miss Chorley sighed. 'The purpose of sermonising is not to make one think but to tell people how they must behave. The working classes need clear guidance.' Her heavily ringed fingers tapped on the knob of her cane. 'What did you think of the text, Ada?'

'It did seem to me that possibly the vicar's sentiments were a little too sympathetic towards sinners, Miss Chorley. Although of course, I am not qualified to judge.' Miss Geake turned to the captain. 'Our vicar is known for his charity.' Her hands were folded idly in her lap as her employer decreed that stitching was not permissible on the Sabbath.

'Quite so,' nodded Miss Chorley. 'Pity has its place but wrongdoers need to be shamed onto the path of righteousness. The vicar is a good man but too unworldly. I shall give him a hint when he is here tomorrow.'

'What was the full text?' Miss Geake quoted it softly. *'If we confess our sins, he is faithful and just and will forgive us our sins and purify us from all unrighteousness.'* She smiled sweetly at Captain Selden.

'Who was the dark-haired lady who slipped into the pew behind us?' he asked.

'Oh, you mean the vicar's daughter,' replied Miss Chorley. 'You will meet her when she comes to tea tomorrow. I have invited several people who will be esteemed to make your acquaintance and Miss Shaw is always useful to make up the numbers.'

'Miss Shaw teaches the Sabbath school and often gets to the service just in time,' murmured Miss Geake. 'She is a great help to her father about the parish.'

'Her duties are no excuse for tardiness,' pronounced Miss Chorley. 'Your grandpapa, Edwin, could not abide lax punctuality. I share his view.'

'I shall be pleased to meet your friends, Aunt Harriet. It's kind of you to arrange it.' Captain Selden shifted the Bible on his knees and looked about for somewhere he might put it down. Every surface was covered, there were vases and wax flowers under a glass dome, cases displaying a stuffed fox and an otter. His grandfather's collection of snuff boxes vied with shells, albums of pressed flowers and pieces of china.

'It is fortunate with your visit being brought forward that I have managed to arrange some entertainment for you. I wish the army could have spared you for longer but understand the importance of your duties. I have planned for you to tour your grandpapa's Memorial Hospital while you are with us. Though it hardly compares with Netley, we are very proud of its good work. I know you will be eager to see it and have improvements to suggest to Dr Avery. He is in charge of its management.'

Captain Selden looked somewhat alarmed. 'I shall enjoy visiting it of course, Aunt but I should hardly care to suggest changes. Medical matters are not my thing, as you know.'

'Nonsense, Edwin, you are too modest. You are an able administrator. Now tomorrow morning I intend that we visit a photographer's studio as I have no recent likeness of you.'

'Of course, if you wish it, Aunt.'

'We shall visit old friends of mine in Kempston, our nearest market town and take some drives out to view places of interest. On your last evening I am giving a dinner. I shall introduce you then to Mr Jerrold, my man of business.' The long-case clock in the hall began to chime the hour, echoing through the drawing-room.

'That is settled, then. Ada, kindly ring for tea.'

Four

Thunder rolled over the dark, drenched streets of Seaborough. Rain streamed relentlessly, gurgling along gutters, sleeking the sodden fur of scurrying rats. A weak, blurred glow shone from the window of the small police station off the Square and a constable's beat was measured in the regular creak of wet boots and the sway of his flickering lantern. The air stank of decaying scraps, seasoned with salt. Lightning sparked for an instant, out at sea.

Pulling her shawl more closely about her, Mrs Fayter looked at the fireguard and considered stirring up the dying coals. The small white dog on the hearth rug lifted his head and gave his tail a single thump. The doctor had told her not to wait up for him, he was a considerate employer but she had decided to sit on in her back parlour. When he returned he would be soaked and probably exhausted. He would be glad of hot soup. Her one concession to the lateness of the hour had been to unpin her hair ready for bed and it lay now, a loosely woven plait, still with some brown speckling the grey, across one shoulder.

However he might not return for hours. 'Infants will come when they've a mind to and not before,' the doctor was wont to say. The farmer up at Burrow had sent word earlier that evening to say his wife had started her confinement well before time. A year before, she'd had a breech birth and the poor mite had been delivered dead, despite all the doctor's endeavours. Now they were afeared it would happen again and Dr Avery had promised to be with her when her time came.

It was when she had decided to go up, it wanting only twenty minutes to midnight, that the knocking came. At first she thought the sounds were another clap of thunder. It made her jump but didn't discompose her right out of her senses like some. Plenty of her sex would rush around covering all the mirrors and crouching under the kitchen table until a storm passed. Gyp wasn't cowed by thunder either. He'd jumped to his feet and begun barking. When it came again she recognised the clap of the brass door knocker, immediately followed by a pounding of fist. Again, most of her kind would be terrified at this hour but in a doctor's household this was not unknown. Some poor soul was in great need of medical attention but she would have to send their messenger away.

'All right there, I'm a coming. I hear you,' she called. 'It's all right, Gyp. Stay there.' Shutting the kitchen door on the excited terrier, she hurried into the hall, where she undid the bolts and turned the key as swiftly as she could. When she opened the door and peered out, a great stream of rain cascaded down as though the gutter was blocked with leaves. A dark, hatless figure stood in the porch, his hair plastered to his head, one hand clutching the reins of his horse.

'At last. We need the doctor fetching at once. I've come from Tower House, Miss Chorley's taken badly.'

Mrs Fayter inclined her head towards him, struggling to hear over the storm. There was no mistaking the urgency about him. 'The doctor's not here. He's already been called away.'

'But what'll I do? We must have him, there's no time to be lost,' said the groom, raising his voice wildly. His mount shook his head and shifted his hooves.

'He might not be back for hours. You must try Dr Miller. Go!' urged Mrs Fayter as the man stood indecisively. As her words sunk in, he flung his leg over the saddle and the pale horse cantered away down the dark street.

Five

The contrast between the staid respectability of the cathedral precincts in Exeter and the teeming, foetid West Quarter always struck Josiah Abbs. The cool, emerald lawns overlooked by fine, old buildings, the dignified figures in black, clerical garb were not much more than a hop and a spit from one of the worst rookeries in the west of England. Within recent memory cholera had flared through the dog-leg streets and open sewers, killing a hundred or so poor devils, almost breaching the great, barred gates of the Close.

The old thoroughfare of Fore Street bisected the rookery, climbing from the Town Quay with its barques and barges, warehouses and tannery towards the municipal heart of the modern city. The rise up the hill was a succession of smells, he thought. The throat-catching stench from the tannery gave way to the brewery, its overpowering reek reminding him of meadowsweet along the lanes of boyhood. At close hand was the sourness of unwashed clothes and flesh, the fug emanating from the many flash houses and slops emptied from front room beer shops, fried fish, the occasional carcass of dog or cat and in winter the smoke from fires, all stewed together.

Then all of a sudden you moved into the order of watered streets, crossing-sweepers, hansoms, men of business, deacons and bells. It was his private opinion that the Bishop and clergy turned their back on the desperate wretches beyond their wall. Many were Irish, a generation after the ones who'd fled to England, escaping famine. Though better men than he couldn't make a start on clearing it. A cess-pit, his superintendent called it. It was a dangerous place when night fell and even in mid-afternoon a fellow had recently been assaulted while foolishly attempting to hand out temperance bills. Abbs was glad he had not been a constable there. His had been a village beat where he'd known every poacher and moucher. Reaching the corner of Queen Street, he glanced back at the cathedral towers, dominating the sky from both worlds then dismissing them from his mind, pushed open one side of the police station doors.

'Superintendent Nicholls wants to see you, Sir. The minute you come in, he said.'

'Understood, Sergeant. Any other messages for me?' replied Abbs, pausing by the desk sergeant's counter.

'Only that one, Sir.' The sergeant busied himself with sharpening a nib and studying the register before him. 'Whenever he deigns to return' was what the old man had actually said but no need to pass that on. Had Inspector Abbs generally been a bit more friendly like, he might have given him the nod. But Abbs, though pleasant enough, almost gentlemanly in his manner, wasn't one to josh and pass the time of day with you. Stiff as my gammy leg, that one. 'Now then, missus, what ails you?' He beckoned to a red-faced, elderly woman who sat clutching a bundle of linen.

Ignoring for the moment the corridor to Nicholls's office, Abbs entered his own small room. Several reports had appeared in the basket in his absence and the scattered crumbs he had left on the window sill for sparrows had gone. Just as he began to untie the top folder, someone tapped on the door and entered.

'Saw you come in, Sir,' announced the cheerful tones of Sergeant Reeve. 'There's nothing new there, just the night watchman's statement on the cracksman and the rest mostly need initialling.' Abbs nodded, removing his hat which the sergeant leaning forward on the desk was at risk of squashing.

'And the Super wants you, Sir. Word is, he's in a foul mood.'

'I daresay the Superintendent has a good deal on his mind,' murmured Abbs, austerely, placing an emphasis on the full title of their superior's rank. 'I'd best find out what.'

It was more than any officer dared to breeze into Nicholls's office after a perfunctory knock. Abbs waited patiently until the testy voice commanded 'Come.' Long enough for Inspector Martin to pull a commiserating face as he stepped smartly into the next office.

'At last. Where the devil have you been hiding yourself? No, don't bother,' blustered the Superintendent as Abbs opened his mouth to reply.

'Sit down, man. I haven't all day to waste.' Nicholls fiddled with his pen as the inspector complied, before dropping it on his blotter. He looked at Abbs then said abruptly, 'Ever been to Seaborough, have you?'

'Seaborough?' Abbs had to think where it was for a second; a small seaside town, closer to the neighbouring county than Exeter. 'No, Sir. I've never had cause to.'

Nicholls fingered his pen again, his small eyes fixed on his inspector. 'It's a shit- hole,' he announced with relish, enjoying the set look on the other's face. He knew perfectly well that Abbs found his turn of phrase distasteful. 'And that's where you're off.'

Fixing his gaze on the painting of Her Majesty behind Nicholls's head, Abbs breathed evenly. 'And the nature of the case, Sir?'

'Possible murder.' Nicholls consulted a sheet of paper.

'Someone of quality then to send for us,' said Abbs, thinking aloud. 'Possible, you say?'

'Local gentry, a female,' continued Nicholls. 'Taken ill suddenly in the night, dead shortly after. Might be nothing in it but the doctor refused to sign the death certificate.'

Abbs leant forward with interest. 'On what grounds, Sir?' The sheet wavered as the Superintendent narrowed his eyes to read his notes.

'Not her usual doctor so he hadn't been attending her. And it was unexpected. She hadn't been sickly until then, no more than any old woman with the vapours.'

'Do we take it the victim was well off?'

'I should say, enough money to endow the local hospital and other good works. She was a spinster, only living relative a nephew, who just happened to be staying with her. He's some sort of army officer. It sounds a thankless mess,' finished the Superintendent with satisfaction.

'I take it there was a post-mortem?'

'Naturally. Findings inconclusive. The deceased was a patient of the police-surgeon, name of Avery. The organs have been sent to the capital for detailed analysis, in other words looking for poison. We should hear in a day or two and some left-overs are being tested, from an afternoon tea, according to this.'

'The inquest was adjourned, presumably?'

'You presume correctly, Inspector.'

'What about the local station, Sir?'

Nicholls shrugged. 'The sergeant will brief you. He won't want to tread on any toes, he's got to live there. He won't have a constable to spare, I daresay, so take Reeve with you.'

'Very well, Sir. Shall I clear my desk first?'

'You're not indispensable, Abbs. Hand anything over and be on your way before nightfall.' He grinned without warmth. 'It's probably a mare's nest, some puffed up doctor wasting police time. But in case there's something in it, talk to the police-surgeon, interview the servants. Do some digging.' Abbs glanced at the clock on the mantelpiece. It was already five and twenty past three.

'It shouldn't take the pair of you more than a day or two so don't go thinking you're on holiday. You can return to present the medical evidence when the inquest reopens. If it does turn out to be foul play, I'll be expecting you to get a quick result. That's all.'

'Sir.' Abbs rose to his feet and was almost at the door when the Superintendent spoke again.

'Oh and Abbs, the victim had some folk to tea on the day she died. No need to bother the guests at this stage. I wouldn't go offending anyone who matters.' He paused to reach for the snuff box on his desk before looking up at him, a flicker of malice in his eyes. 'An official complaint could sink you.'

The back room at *The Marine Hotel* felt decidedly stuffy for September. Dr Avery would have liked to raise the sash and take in some sea air but the window overlooked the rear yard and carriage house. He leant against the mahogany bar, sipping his whisky and watching the others.

Halesworth gave a triumphant cry as he clicked the red object ball straight into the furthest pocket. 'My game. Come on, Hicks, pay up.'

Hicks added a coin to the two stacked on the rim of the billiard table. 'My mind's not on it tonight.'

'Nor mine though I still beat you hands down. Not playing tonight, Avery? Not like you.'

The doctor shook his head. Halesworth returned the three balls to their box and pocketed the coins. 'Go on then, put us out of our misery.'

'Not again, Halesworth. You know full well I cannot comment on the inquest. It would be grossly unprofessional.'

'But you examined the body. Surely you could tell what killed her?'

Dr Avery rubbed his forehead. 'It isn't always straightforward.'

'But you could hazard a guess?'

'Look, it's been a long day. I've been up since I don't know when. I simply called in for one quiet drink. You must wait until the town hears.'

'That won't take long, knowing Seaborough,' remarked Hicks, reaching between them for his glass.

'No, indeed,' sighed Avery.

'No one's talking of anything else,' continued Halesworth. 'But we need to know how this affects us. When the old woman sent me away with a flea in my ear, that was it. Now we're in with a chance again. Didn't I say something'll turn up?'

'Presumably you didn't finish off the old lady yourself?' asked Hicks.

'Didn't occur to me, old man. Maybe it was you drumming up custom?' They both laughed, heartily.

'Should we be talking like this?' said Dr Avery. 'Miss Chorley is dead, after all.'

'Exactly,' persisted Halesworth, 'and that changes everything. The nephew must get the lot. We need to get in quick and see if he'll sell the land to us. But if there was any funny business, the estate will be tied up for months. Jerrold will see to that.' Reaching in the pocket of his embroidered waistcoat he pulled out a cigar and proceeded to light it. 'What's more, if it turns out she was murdered,' he continued between puffs, 'Selden's bound to have done it. Who gets the estate then, eh?'

There was a short silence. Avery stared into his glass before draining it. Hicks pushed the bell on the counter. 'I think we could all do with another. You can't go around saying things like that, Halesworth. Miller's trying to make a name for himself. He's no friend of yours, is he, Avery?'

Dr Avery smiled faintly. 'I rather think he would like my position.'

'Exactly so. He wouldn't sign the certificate for your patient out of perverseness.'

Avery shook his head. 'I doubt Miller would go that far. He hadn't been attending Miss Chorley so he behaved correctly in the circumstances.'

Halesworth gave an exasperated sigh, 'where's Emily got to?'

'I should be on my way,' said Avery. The door opened and a man poked his head round, his eyes avid behind his wire spectacles.

'I say... have you heard?' he began. 'Oh Avery, you're here. Then you have heard,' his voice trailed off, crest-fallen.

'Heard what, Cox?' demanded Halesworth. 'Don't just stand there, come in and spit it out, man.'

'Well, if you insist. I had it direct from your clerk, Hicks, who's been talking to Tancock. Two detectives from Exeter are booked in at the Anchor and expected tonight.' He perched on the nearest stool and paused for effect. 'That proves it beyond a doubt. Miss Chorley was murdered, all right!'

By the time Abbs had spoken to Reeve, consulted *Bradshaw* and returned to his house to pack a case, the cathedral clock had struck five. They had arranged to meet by the bookstall and managed to obtain a second-class compartment to themselves.

'The evenings are beginning to draw in,' remarked Abbs as they sat down. 'You know, I can never take a train journey without thinking of the Briggs railway murder.'

'That was a rum do, sir. Just after I joined the Constabulary, that was. You'd think he would have been safe in first class.'

'I followed the case with interest. Talking of which, I see you've brought some reading matter, Sergeant. I shall follow your lead.'

'You didn't bring any sandwiches, did you sir? Only my landlady was out and I'm fair famished.'

'No, I'm afraid not. They'll give us something at the inn, I'm sure.'

'Unless we're too late.' Reeve jumped up again and leant out of the window. 'Wish I'd bought something on the platform.' The great purple brown engine gave a sudden lurch and whoosh of steam as the brakes creaked off.

'Too late now. Pull up the window, would you?'

Reaching up to extract the *Flying Post* sticking out of his bag, Reeve settled behind its pages and tried to ignore his rumbling guts. Abbs smiled to himself as he opened his copy of the *Fortnightly Review,* turning straight to the next chapter of Mr Trollope's serial. The train gathered speed above the ever-growing streets.

Three country stations later, having exhausted his periodical, Abbs placed it on the seat beside his billycock hat. Reeve was wiping the grimy glass and peering at the passing farmland. 'It's a long way between villages, Sir.'

'A lonely corner of the county,' agreed Abbs.

'Seaborough's a sleepy sort of place for murder, isn't it? I mean this isn't like a shiv in the guts down some alley.'

'Murders come in many shapes and sizes, not all confined to the working classes.'

'Do you know the place, Sir?'

'Not yet, Sergeant. I understand it's a growing town, looking to promote itself for the holiday trade.' He had made a brief enquiry of Martin when he passed on his files.

'The Bank holidays will make a difference to seaside towns, they say. D'you like the sea, Inspector?'

'I prefer not to be on it. I was taken on a boat trip once as a child and was sick over the side.' He hadn't thought of that in decades, a hot summer's day in Hunstanton. The family were abroad and the staff had been on their yearly outing. Squashed in a wagonette and confined in his too-tight collar, then stuffed full of oysters, he'd already been close to heaving before the sail on the Wash. The ignominy of being held over the rail by his mother and soundly scolded came back to him.

'I'll never forget the first time I saw the sea. My pa took us to Brighton. That's the place, better by far than anywhere in Devonshire. There's nowhere like it for pleasure. Streets of old houses like bride cakes, grand squares and fountains, even an Eastern palace, old King George's place.' Reeve grinned, the scenes passing before his mind like a magic lantern. 'The sea was full of little yachts bobbing and there were two fine piers to walk along, one just for catching boats and the other with every kind of entertainment and food you could think of.'

Watching his enthusiastic face, Abbs wondered what took his sergeant to Devonshire. His accent and indeed his whole demeanour revealed a boyhood spent in the capital. A certain sharpness of intellect, coupled with an easy, assured manner stood out among the placid, soft-voiced Devon men. They were both outsiders and it was no coincidence that Nicholls had started assigning Reeve to him, though he feared the association did his sergeant no good. He would not ask and encourage an intimacy awkward among men of different rank.

The sky was beginning to streak with rose pink weepers when they emerged from a tunnel and began to slow at last. Great heaps of slag and the looming shadow of a gasworks presented an ugly first impression of the seaside town. The landscape was seeping into dusk, soon darkness would fall as abruptly as a go-to-bed snuffed out. The jostle of Exeter felt a long way distant as they stepped down onto the empty platform. They had reached the end of the line and the locomotive stood hissing and belching, subsiding as the fireman jumped down from the footplate.

'We're to be met,' remarked Abbs as they looked about them. Only three other people left the train, vanishing through the door where the shadowy form of a ticket collector could be glimpsed. Then a stout figure, his stomach straining the buttons of a swallow-tail coat appeared in the doorway, hesitated and walked self-consciously towards them. He wiped the back of his hand across his moustache, dislodging a few pastry flakes before greeting them. Reeve felt like groaning.

'Reckon you'll be Inspector Abbs, Sir?'

The room was small, as the landlord's wife had apologetically mentioned, but it would do fine. The casement window set in the roof overlooked the bay and the furnishings were spotless. There was a good firm mattress and the paper had a cheerful sprigged flower pattern with a china plaque bearing the text *Thou God, seest all* over the bed. Abbs looked in the swivel mirror, noting the shadows beneath his eyes and the strained look they held.

Alone at last, he needed to make sense of all the jumbled impressions he had accumulated. It was a relief to be away from Nicholls and the feeling that he was walking a tightrope like an act on the halls. One mistake and his superior would delight in his fall. A man must work and he had no other skill save a certain facility for ferreting out the truth. There was no safety net. Removing his shirt and collar, he filled the ewer on the washstand and splashed his face with water.

Tancock had obtained a growler outside and their ride to the police station had only taken a few minutes. His impression had been that the town was only built thirty or forty years ago but he was wrong, for *The Anchor* dated back to the last century at least. It had probably been a village inn, he guessed and Seaborough developed from a settlement of fishing folk. The police station was modest, adjoining the sergeant's house and having only two cells. A constable had made them a pot of tea, nothing with it, though a toasting fork stood propped by a good fire. No matter, Reeve was provided for at last. Mrs Gaunt had kindly offered them a cold supper and a private parlour to eat it in.

Tancock had hovered between anxious deference and unease. He had wrongly assumed they would want to see their accommodation and make a start in the morning.

'Too much time has been lost already, Sergeant. That's unavoidable but we need to get started at once. It's vital to talk to people while their memories are still fresh. Preferably before they compare notes. But they will have done that.' Tancock didn't make eye contact as he listened, though he gave Reeve the once over.

'What do 'ee want to do first, Sir?'

'Tonight, I shall take the post-mortem report with me to study. I need to get a general picture of Miss Chorley's life. I'd like you to tell me all you can now and make two lists for me. First the members of her household, including every servant, and secondly, anyone she might have come in contact with, on the day she died. I need those first thing, if you will.'

Tancock had looked somewhat bemused, he thought. 'I'll do my best, Sir but I don't rightly know who she saw. She had some people to tea that day.'

'Give me a starting point and we can build on it later. Now, straight after breakfast I'd like you to conduct Sergeant Reeve and I to the house. I need to see where the death took place and we shall interview everyone between us.' He'd sounded authoritative, he knew but inside he felt tense with the need to overlook nothing. 'Then I shall need a word with the police doctor. Where do you suggest I see him?'

The sergeant had leant his bulk against the counter as he thought. 'He could come here, Sir, or you could go to the cottage hospital. I'll send word round to him.'

'We'll meet him at the hospital if you'll direct us in the morning. I'm sure he's a busy man. And make me an appointment with Miss Chorley's solicitor, for late tomorrow afternoon if possible, if you please.' The sergeant looked increasingly unhappy as he scribbled the instructions.

'Now Sergeant, tell us about Miss Chorley. As much detail as you can, did you know her to speak to?'

Abbs lay on the bed, his elbow leaning on the bolster. Feeling desperately tired and distracted by the sound of the sea, nevertheless he opened the post-mortem report and determined to concentrate.

Six

'I can't wait to be out of there, Hannah and that's the truth for you. Being there now makes my flesh crawl. I stick to the kitchen and scullery, at least there's bars on the windows. But going up to bed, well I don't mind telling you, I took the poker up last night.' The speaker swung her head emphatically and set her cup in the saucer with a clatter. 'Is there a drop more in the pot? It settles my nerves.'

'I'll make some fresh, Bessie. You stay there.' Hannah carefully set aside the spent leaves for Betsey to do the carpets and measured out some fresh tea from the caddy. 'Kettle won't be long. Now m'dear, you can't go on like this. There's no need to be feared in the house. You're not alone at night.'

Her companion sniffed and rammed a loose pin more firmly into her mousy hair. 'Sarah's neither use nor ornament, Jane's a silly goose. William's over the stables so he couldn't save us. I don't know if the murderer's lurking in the grounds, waiting for dark or...' She paused dramatically, 'if the danger's locked in with us. I hear *her* walking about at night, opening doors where she's no place to be. I say my prayers then I'm too frightened to sleep.'

'It sounds as though Miss Geake can't sleep either. The poor woman's entitled to open a door without you thinking you'll be murdered in your bed.' Hannah stirred the brown teapot and picked up the strainer. 'Why should you suspect her? She's to be pitied. She's lost her home and no possible reference, though I daresay Mr Jerrold will write a line for her. But some will think she's under a cloud. It won't be easy. I should say she's frightened herself.'

'Not that one. You think too well of folk, bound to, being in a vicarage family. Oh, she was always *butter wouldn't melt* in front of Miss Chorley. Spoke very proper to us below stairs on the surface but a tongue dipped in lemon juice, all the same. A regular cat, she is. I can't abide the things, I wouldn't hurt one but they're sly creatures, slinking about and Ada Geake's the same. I'm certain sure she had Mary dismissed.'

'It may be so,' said Hannah thoughtfully as she sipped her tea. 'You'd know her better than most but I can't believe she'd hurt her mistress. That doctor Miller must have got it wrong.'

Bessie shook her head. 'The police believe him. They've searched all the bedrooms, you know, even been through the linen cupboard, rumpling the lot. And I've had bobbies all over my kitchen this morning, their great boots traipsing in my larder. That inspector wanted to know everything about the mistress's meals on the day she was gathered, God rest her soul. They asked about the scraps an' had anyone else been ill? He seemed interested in the mushrooms I gave them for breakfast, along with best devilled kidneys. I told them and I'll say to anyone, if the mistress was poisoned, it wasn't from my cooking.

Ten year I've been at Tower House and always given satisfaction.'

'Don't take on so, you'll give yourself a seizure,' Hannah patted her friend's arm. 'What were the detectives like?'

'Not from these parts, both London men, I'd say. The one in charge was quite genteel for a policeman. They came to the front door, bold as you like. Miss Chorley would have had something to say about that.' Sighing she helped herself to more sugar. 'He looked ordinary enough, not very dark nor fair. Quiet, but he had a way of looking right through you. Put me in mind of a schoolmaster. The sergeant was a young fellow, well set up despite his affliction and Sarah was making eyes at him. *She* was all sweetness and light, offering them tea.'

Bessie gathered her shawl about her shoulders. 'No, my mind's made up, I've a bit put by. I shall ask Mr Jerrold to let me have my wages and I'm off to my sister's. You must write to me, Hannah. I'm sorry I'm sure if it's letting Captain Selden down but I don't want to spend another night in that house.' She leant closer, 'if Miss Geake didn't finish off the mistress, then who did? Answer me that.'

'Good day, Mrs Watkins. May I know the question?'

Bessie started guiltily as she looked up to find Reverend Shaw standing in the doorway, a concerned look on his face and a tea cup balanced on a plate in his hand.

A long cart with *Halesworth General Builders and Plumbing* on the side was standing near the entrance of the cottage hospital with a man on the rear handing down a sack to his mate. They looked up as the two detectives passed. Inside, they followed the corridor as directed by the porter until they reached a small open ward. A tall man in a frock-coat with his back to them, clearly the doctor, was standing by the bed of an elderly woman, while a nurse held back the bedclothes. As they approached he looked round, murmured a word to his patient and came towards them.

'Inspector Abbs?' He looked keenly at them both and Abbs felt that this man could tell a malingerer at a glance. 'Avery. How d'you do,' he held out his hand and shook briefly with a firm grip before turning to Reeve.

'Doctor, this is Sergeant Reeve.' Dr Avery nodded pleasantly at Reeve and shook his hand.

'Shall we go to my office?' Without waiting for a reply the doctor set off further along the corridor as they followed.

'It's quieter here than I expected,' commented Abbs as he caught up with Avery.

'Well, we've the builders back today but you mean medically. It varies, the commotion's first thing in the morning when the sick turn up at the reception room. Not all need to be admitted of course. Most receive advice and something from the dispensary. The woman I was with has come in today.' Avery winced, 'an ulcerated leg that won't heal, very painful.' He drew up at a door which he unlocked and ushered them in. 'It's poverty at the root of it. Plentiful good food and coal would help. We do what we can. At least thanks to Miss Chorley they no longer have to find their way half across the county for help.' As he spoke he swept some newspapers off a chair, mostly the pink sheets of *Bell's Sporting Life* Abbs noticed, and carried it over to the desk before taking up a stand by the window. 'Do take a seat, both of you.'

Unusual, thought Abbs not to assume his chair behind the desk and dominate the proceedings. But then doctors had a natural authority and Avery in treating Reeve as an equal, seemed to have a refreshing lack of pomposity.

'We noticed the hospital name.' They had read the lettering carved into the stone lintel above the red brick, *The Chorley Memorial Cottage Hospital.* 'So if Miss Chorley had a lot to do with the hospital and you were her doctor, you would have met frequently and known her well?'

Dr Avery frowned in thought. 'Certainly I knew her fairly well as her medical practitioner and she did send for me quite often. She took a great interest in the hospital naturally but as you'd expect, she had nothing to do with its daily management.' Reeve licked his pencil and wrote a brief note. As he sat with bent head, Abbs noticed Avery give a brief appraising glance to the port-wine stain that disfigured the edge of Reeve's face, bleeding like a spilt glass from the side of his temple into his hair.

The doctor leant against the wall between the window and a door to the grounds, its upper portion glazed. 'Miss Chorley gave this land for a hospital six years ago in memory of her father and the building was funded by public subscription. We have twenty beds at present. The town in fact has just finished raising the money to extend the hospital with an isolation wing. A pity she didn't live to see it built.'

'I've read the post-mortem report and know there was no obvious cause to suggest unnatural death. Could you talk us through the symptoms as you've been told them? I realise you weren't at the scene at all.'

'No, it's all hearsay. But before I go on, can I offer you gentlemen any refreshment? It's been remiss of me, I can ring for a nurse if you'd care for some tea?'

'No thank you, sir,' said Reeve, a trifle gloomily. Abbs smiled inwardly, 'that's very civil of you, Doctor but we had some at Tower House.'

'In that case I'll continue. You'll have heard from Sergeant Tancock that Miss Chorley's manservant called at my home at about twenty minutes before midnight. Unfortunately I was absent, attending an expected breech birth at a farm some miles distant so my housekeeper advised the man to seek out Dr Miller.'

'And he reached Tower House shortly after midnight. Now the sergeant interviewed Miss Chorley's household in your presence the following day?'

'That's correct. Miss Geake, Miss Chorley's companion stated that her mistress first complained of feeling unwell at some time after eight o'clock. She mentioned a severe headache and retired to her room, afterwards sending for a glass of brandy. About an hour later she rang for Miss Geake, complaining of nausea, feeling hot and stomach pains. She vomited copiously and had recurrent diarrhoea. Initially as I understand it, she refused suggestions to send for me as she felt increasingly drowsy. She thought the worst was over after she'd vomited and simply wanted to sleep. Miss Geake sat with her. Miss Chorley seemed to doze but later became in such distress with further vomiting and diarrhoea that her nephew was told and he took the decision to send for medical aid.'

Dr Avery paused to allow Reeve time to write, then went on. 'Apparently by the time Miller arrived she was semi-conscious with laboured breathing and there was nothing he could do. He pronounced life extinct shortly after.'

'Thank you, that's very clear.' Abbs looked steadily at Avery. 'Tell me, Doctor, would you have signed the death certificate?'

Avery sighed, 'in all honesty, Inspector, having attended Miss Chorley regularly, I would have had no reason not to do so. The symptoms as described to me are consistent with a sudden onset gastric fever or food poisoning. I would have questioned those present about what they'd had to eat that day and I believe, would have been perfectly satisfied.'

Reeve looked up as though keen, thought Abbs, to ask something. 'Go on, Sergeant.'

'What about the fact that no one else in the house was taken ill, sir?'

'That wouldn't be unusual. I learned subsequently that they had mushrooms at breakfast and potted shrimps were served at afternoon tea. It would only need one shrimp to be contaminated or one poisonous mushroom to be picked by mistake. Such things are far from unknown.'

'Thank you, sir.'

'And the post-mortem showed nothing untoward, your report says?'

'No indeed. There were faint traces of vomit in the mouth and throat, a slight swelling to the female organs which would be consistent with diarrhoea. I had no reason to doubt the truth of the symptoms described.'

Clearing his throat, Abbs worded his next question with care. 'Sergeant Tancock suggested that Dr Miller might have been over-cautious due to some element of professional rivalry?'

Avery's face, rather stern in repose, looked wryly amused. 'All professions include an element of professional rivalry, do they not? You must ask Dr Miller about that.' He shrugged and as Abbs remained silent, appeared to think some further comment necessary. 'There was some slight ill-feeling soon after I came to Seaborough, it must be eight years ago. A young boy was failing to improve under Dr Miller's care. The family consulted me and our opinions differed over treatment. Medical men do disagree, detectives too on occasion, perhaps?'

Abbs grimaced, 'It isn't unknown.' He glanced at the clock on the wall which hung above a safe. 'We won't keep you much longer, Doctor. Can you tell us why Miss Chorley was in the habit of consulting you and what if anything, you prescribed?'

'Certainly. In layman's terms she was something of a hypochondriac. She was in fact in reasonable health for someone of her age, which I would estimate in the mid-sixties. However she had too much time on her hands and she enjoyed being the centre of attention.' He shifted his position slightly as he thought. 'That may sound harsh but it's all too common among elderly ladies with money. A working class woman has no time to spare in dwelling on imagined ailments. Miss Chorley suffered from periodic indigestion due to over-indulgence in rich food and headaches, which were probably due to boredom or constipation.'

Abbs felt rather than saw Reeve suppress a grin. 'She sounds like a lady who would have expected some medicine to take?'

'She did of course. I made up some headache powders, distilled from willow and also something to ease her digestion. They were little more than cornflour, sugar and peppermint. A charcoal biscuit would have sufficed. No powder could help her as well as a little more abstinence at the dinner table.'

'I think that covers everything. Thank you for your time, Doctor, you've been most helpful.' Abbs rose and the others followed.

'I'll ring for a nurse and have you shown out.'

'No need, we can find our way.' At the door, Abbs paused, his hand on the jamb. 'One last thing, Doctor Avery. Do you think it likely that Miss Chorley could have been murdered?'

'The whole town's talking of nothing else but the idea seems preposterous. Who would do such a terrible thing and why?'

'Why indeed? When I was a green young constable, a wise old sergeant used to say that murder's often done to keep things staying the same. I didn't understand then but he was right.'

'If it was murder,' said Avery slowly, 'then someone's been exceedingly clever.'

'By the way did you meet Captain Selden when he was here?'

'Only briefly. Miss Chorley introduced us after church on the Sunday. You surely don't think...?'

'I'm just gathering information for the Coroner. Until we get those analysis results, it's too soon to think anything yet,' said Abbs.

The afternoon silence in the room was broken only by the lessening cries of a pie seller in the street outside. Reeve knew better than to interrupt the old man when he was reading. He waited quietly as Abbs turned through his notebook, idly looking round the sergeant's office at the police station. Tancock had made himself comfortable. The horsehair chair in which he was sitting occupied the chimney corner. A small table alongside held a brass ashtray and on the mantelpiece, incongruous in such a place, stood a small, shiny pink jug emblazoned with the motto *A Present From Margate*. Behind the inspector was the customary row of ledgers, Snowden's *Police Officers and Constables Guide* and bound *Police Gazettes*. It was a curious blend of officialdom and parlour.

'Two ps in opportunity,' murmured his superior.

'Righto, Sir.'

Abbs closed the notebook, tossing it lightly on the desk next to his own. The remnants of a late lunch, a plate of cold lamb sandwiches provided by Mrs Tancock, lay beside them. 'Clear and methodical, Reeve.'

The sergeant grinned, taking this as high praise. 'Nothing seemed irregular to me. I can't see any of the servants polishing off the old lady, can you, Sir?'

'Not on the face of it, no, Sergeant. What did you make of the lady's companion?'

'She was rattled but most people are when we come calling. She didn't strike me as stupid enough to commit murder when she'd be a likely suspect, besides what would she get out of it? She'd lose her home.'

'People kill for all sorts of reasons. They may seem trivial to anyone else but it matters to them, d'you see? It's finding what matters to them, Reeve.' Reeve nodded, his brow creased in thought.

'Though I agree, no one at Tower House seems an obvious prospect. We shall see if Miss Geake gets a mention in the will. I doubt there'd be a legacy worth risking a secure position for, let alone the rope but she could have hated her employer and snapped. That's what I mean. Murder's been done before now because a party continually cracked their knuckles or picked their teeth when they'd eaten.' Reeve thought better of scratching his ear again and lowered his hand.

'I thought this Captain Selden would have remained at the house,' he remarked. 'Surely he knew we'd want to see him?'

'I'm not best pleased, he's the most important witness. But until we hear it's foul play, our authority is limited. He spoke to the coroner and he was due back from his leave. Perhaps he couldn't bear to stay on at Tower House, we don't know how fond he was of his aunt. At any rate he'll have to return, army or no, when the inquest reopens.'

'When do you think we'll hear from London, Sir?'

'Shortly I hope. Toxicology tests take time but they'll have priority. We can expect the telegraph at any hour. It's still perfectly possible that Miss Chorley died of natural causes but Superintendent Nicholls directed us here and you and I, Reeve must do the job before us.' Rising to his feet, the inspector opened his watch. 'Nearly time we were on our way. If you wouldn't mind taking the tray back to Mrs Tancock, I'll wait outside.'

The police station was in a short street lying just off a square, the bottom of which lay open to the sea. It was a sprightly sort of day with the tide coming in and sunlight glinting on the water. A few people were strolling along the seafront, two women pushing perambulators with a small child running ahead, an elderly gent carrying a newspaper and someone was pushing a well-wrapped figure in a bath chair. Abbs paused on the corner as Reeve caught up with him, plunging his bowler on his springy hair and wrinkling his nose.

'Phew, what's that? It was hanging around last night.'

'Decaying seaweed.' Abbs pointed towards the beach with his rosewood cane. 'It's going over, much worse a month ago apparently. Mrs Gaunt told me, she was quite apologetic about it.'

'I'm not surprised. Enough to put anyone off staying here.' Reeve peered seaward. 'No pier, I suppose?'

'They don't go in for them much in Devonshire,' replied Abbs. 'This way I believe.' The two men made their way across the square. Two sides were edged by a row of beeches, their leaves turning. Several gardeners were at work in the flower borders, digging up the dying carpet bedding. In the centre stood a rather ugly drinking fountain. Abbs halted briefly to read the plaque, stating that it was installed by public subscription to commemorate Her Majesty's silver jubilee. The buildings edging the modest square were the usual sort found in any town in England. A town hall dominated the north side, though a miniature of its city counterparts. It had fresh paintwork of Brunswick green and a squat tower, not unlike the one at Miss Chorley's house, though this was faced with a clock. There were two solidly imposing banks and on the corner nearest the sea stood *The Marine Hotel*, where the swells stayed by the look of it.

A scruffy fellow was playing a tin whistle beside the town hall, rather well in Abbs's opinion. He didn't recognise the air, which perhaps had an Irish lilt to it. Its jaunty melody was at odds with the man's unhappy appearance. His beard was as ragged as his trousers and one leg was thrust stiffly forward from his stool at an awkward angle. As they waited to cross the road, a well-dressed man finishing a cigar came out of the town hall and swept swiftly down the steps. He touched his hat to two ladies then went up to the whistle player. He was obviously sending the other on his way for the fellow picked up his stool and cap and set off along the street. A discharged soldier, decided Abbs, watching the man's erect back and pronounced limp.

'According to Sergeant Tancock, Mr Jerrold's office is along here,' said the inspector as they crossed the junction behind a grocer's van. A row of limes bordered both sides of the street of distinguished bay-fronted terraces.

'Lawyers always do themselves well,' commented Reeve.

Seven

The best chair was by unspoken agreement left empty. From time to time one of the ladies glanced up at it as though seeing a living occupant. Their voices were unusually subdued as they bent over their work and yet, thought Adelaide Shaw, there was an air of suppressed excitement in Mrs Jerrold's drawing-room.

'I don't know how we will ever grow accustomed to these meetings without Miss Chorley's presence. It is very strange without her,' remarked their hostess.

'It is remarkable how suddenly things can change,' said Adelaide. 'Life goes on in the same way year after year, a little dull perhaps but familiar and comforting. Then in an instant, everything habitual is gone. Hannah calls it the devil giving the pot a stir.' When no one spoke, she coloured and examined the runner she was embroidering.

'We shall have to decide who will now head our society,' remarked Mrs Frances Hicks, having fetched some scissors from the ladies at the other end of the room. 'None of us can keep our minds on our work this afternoon. The rumours circulating are too horrible to contemplate.' Sitting down again she turned to her neighbour, Mrs Todd. 'Let us think of happier matters, my dear. How is your little one?'

'She is teething at present, ma'am, and disturbing the household with her cries.'

'It must be a trying time, hearing the poor lamb suffer. I remember it well with my own. If a ring won't soothe her, you must try a spoonful of *Godfrey's*. There is nothing like it for making an infant sleep.'

'Thank you, I shall mention it to my nursery maid.'

'If that doesn't work, you must take your Edie to be looked over by Dr Avery.' Mrs Hicks turned more fully towards Mrs Todd, her sewing forgotten on her lap. She lowered her voice confidentially.

'If only he had seen Miss Chorley, she may be with us still. Mr Hicks and I will never cease to bless him for pulling our Thomas through the diphtheria. We had all but resigned ourselves to losing him but the doctor never gave up. All night long he sat with Tom until the fever broke. I lost two of mine, you know.' The younger woman watched her hand stray to a large mourning broach pinned on her saxe blue bodice. The customary good humour in Mrs Hicks's placid face faltered momentarily.

'James was gathered with the measles when he was seven and my Blanche, she is with the angels now. Taken from us at ten months by a chill.' She sighed softly. 'She looked like a perfect doll in her white coffin. We laid her in her christening gown and placed a posy of snowdrops in her tiny hand. We lost her in the new year and that's all the flowers there were.' Mrs Hicks picked up her thread work, her fingers puckering the cloth.

'I am very sorry to hear of your troubles, Mrs Hicks.'

'Bless you, dear, my tongue has run away with me, as usual.'

Mrs Halesworth leant forward from her corner of the sofa. 'Has Mr Jerrold met the policemen yet?'

'We really should not be discussing this,' pleaded their hostess. 'Our purpose here is not for idle gossip.'

'But we all want to know what's going on,' replied Mrs Halesworth. 'There's no point in denying it.'

'Did not you say Papa was seeing them today, Mama?' asked Mrs Todd.

'Hush, Beatrice. You should not mention matters of business.'

'My husband never discusses his business affairs with me,' said Mrs Halesworth.

'As is proper,' said Mrs Jerrold, approvingly.

'So I make it my business to find out.'

'You may as well tell us anything you know, Mama.'

Mrs Jerrold bowed to pressure. 'Well,' she looked around the circle of ladies, confident she had their attention. 'Mr Jerrold did happen to say that he is seeing the detective from Exeter this very afternoon.' Glances were exchanged in a satisfying response.

'Finding out what's in the will,' said Mrs Halesworth, rummaging in her work basket.

'I don't think Mr Jerrold will tell him the terms before it's read,' said his wife. 'His duty is to Captain

Seldon now. He wasn't pleased that the police want to see him, not at all,' she muttered with feeling. He had been quite short with Ann when she brought in his eggs and bacon.

'What will happen to poor Miss Geake, I wonder?' contributed Adelaide.

'She'll have to enquire at a domestic employment agency, I suppose,' Mrs Halesworth shrugged. 'Assuming that is, she's...'

'Ladies, please,' begged Mrs Jerrold. 'We should speculate no more. And we ought to discuss the arrangements for our sale of work. I shall ring for Ann as I'm sure we're all ready for some tea.'

'I can't help recalling the last time we had tea together, Adelaide,' said Mrs Hicks as they settled themselves again. 'Thank you, Ann, is that seedy cake, I see?' She paused as the parlour-maid helped her from a cake stand.

'I've been thinking a lot about that day,' admitted Adelaide. She accepted a sponge finger and began to break off pieces absently, her gaze on the Jerrolds' piano, draped in buff velvet and covered in silver frames. 'No one else was unwell, that I've heard.'

'Miss Chorley wasn't taken ill for some hours afterwards, I know because Mr Hicks was there after us. This really is delicious. I must get Cook to enquire for the receipt.'

Adelaide glanced at her companion in surprise. The older matron's soft, features still retained sufficient trace of the pretty, young girl she had once been. She swallowed her mouthful and continued. 'He wanted some exercise and walked up the hill to escort me home but we had already left. Captain Selden invited him in for a drink, most cordially. I expect he was glad of some masculine company.' Adelaide nodded thoughtfully as she picked up her tea cup.

'According to Nathaniel, Miss Chorley had retired to her room but not a word was said about ill health and surely he wouldn't have been invited in, if she was taken poorly?'

'It does seem to have happened suddenly,' said Adelaide. 'I know Papa is worried about all the rumour-mongering in the town. I have a feeling he believes Miss Chorley was murdered.'

Abbs opened his watch, wondering if Mr Jerrold was engaged or if keeping them waiting was a deliberate ploy, aimed at reminding them of their place. An elderly clerk with a fringe of white hair remaining about his head had shown them into a waiting-room, his manner stiff with disapproval. That was a quarter-hour ago. Reeve sat slumped on a wooden chair opposite, from time to time filling his cheeks with air and blowing, a habit of his when forcibly inactive. Abbs knew his sergeant preferred to be up and doing. For his part he had flicked through the *Transactions of the Devonshire Association* on the table between them and examined the watercolour of Dartmoor over the fireplace, thus exhausting the room's entertainment. He wondered if the very act of requesting an interview had offended the lawyer and would lead to a complaint landing on the desk of Superintendent Nicholls. An investigation like this could feel like tip-toeing through a covert without setting off spring-guns. The door knob turned silently and the clerk entered.

'Mr Jerrold senior will see you now if you'll come this way.' They followed him to a panelled door at the rear of the inner hallway. He tapped softly and a voice bade them come in. The man behind the handsome walnut partners desk half-rose as they entered and lowered himself again. He was not about to shake hands.

'Good day to you, Inspector,' Mr Jerrold looked through the spectacles on the end of his nose at a sheet of paper, in a manner somewhat reminiscent of Nicholls. 'Abbs. An unusual name, not from these parts, I should say? Sit down.'

Abbs took the other chair. 'Thank you, sir. My name is not uncommon in Norfolk, which was the county of my birth.' He was aware of Reeve looking around for somewhere to sit. 'I wonder if my sergeant might bring a chair closer. I should like him to take notes.'

'If you deem it necessary, though there is little I am in a position to tell you.' The attorney waited while

Reeve carried an upright chair from before a bureau and set it down slightly behind the inspector. 'I can give you a few minutes.' He looked self-important and inclined to be irritable, judged Abbs. He didn't care for the way Mr Jerrold ignored the sergeant but they were inured to it. Reeve certainly did not regard himself as an invisible servant as evidenced by the way he opened his notebook with a flourish, pencil at the ready and looked around the room with unashamed interest.

It was expensively furnished with an old-fashioned marble fireplace and a bracket clock on the mantelpiece. A large glass-fronted bookcase with cupboard dominated one wall and a side table held a rosewood and silver tantalus. A pair of elaborate silver inkwells sat on the desk next to a satinwood humidor. The window behind looked onto a neat garden of trim hollies and gravel. Abbs frowned as he debated how to begin.

'I'm sure you appreciate that ours is a difficult position, sir. We are required by the coroner to investigate the circumstances of Miss Chorley's demise while awaiting further medical evidence. We have no wish to give offence to her friends and neighbours, who no doubt are grieving...'

Mr Jerrold settled back in his chair. 'I do see your present difficulty, Inspector. Your sentiments do you credit. Naturally I'm prepared to aid you with any information within my power to disclose.' His silver grey head was tilted to one side and he steepled his fingers together, displaying his well-manicured nails.

'Perhaps you could begin by giving me your impressions of Miss Chorley. I need to get an overview of her life, the position she held in the community. I should think her legal advisor would be an ideal person to give an unbiased account.'

'You have come to the right person, Inspector. I was Miss Chorley's solicitor for many years and indeed my father acted for her father Mr Richard Chorley. Our firm handled all the family's legal affairs, land transactions, wills and so forth.'

'Miss Chorley was unmarried, I know. Did she have much family living?'

'None at all apart from her nephew Captain Edwin Selden. Her parents died back in my father's time. She was the eldest of three surviving children, her only brother pre-deceased her, hence leaving her to inherit the family home, that is Tower House and her father's entire estate. Without going into detail I may say that this was considerable in terms of assets and capital. Old Richard Chorley made his money in commerce, a silk and crape factory to be precise. He was a shrewd investor, a warm man as they say.'

'Where exactly does Captain Selden fit in?'

'He's the son of Miss Chorley's sister, Caroline who married a Mr Selden. Neither of them are living. Captain Selden's mother died of smallpox, I believe. Miss Chorley was anxious that her nephew should go into the army, following the footsteps of his uncle. Her brother James Chorley died at Inkerman, he was unmarried.'

'So am I right in assuming that Captain Selden is Miss Chorley's heir?'

Mr Jerrold took a visible moment to consider. 'Strictly speaking, Inspector, I am not at liberty to reveal the contents of my late client's will before it is read. I too find myself in an awkward position while there is this, what can I say... uncertainty regarding the manner of Miss Chorley's death.' Abbs waited, one of his maxims was that if you let a silence alone, the other person will fill it.'

'I believe I may say that you would be correct in your assumption.'

'Thank you, sir.' Behind him, Reeve scribbled a brief note. 'And Miss Geake, the companion. Can you tell me if she is a legatee?'

'I should neither confirm nor deny, Inspector. Shall we say that Miss Chorley behaved very properly as an employer?'

'Would that be an unusually large sum, sir?'

Mr Jerrold pursed his lips. 'Miss Chorley was a prudent lady, I would not say that she was unusually generous, no. She left various charitable bequests and the customary legacies to those in her employ at the time of her death.'

'So you wouldn't say the will contained any surprises then, sir?'

'I would not.' Hesitating, Mr Jerrold continued, 'my client was in the habit of sending for me from time to time to draw up a new will. This is by no means unusual with old ladies, you understand. However it was mostly the sums that varied. On occasion one person or another was omitted but this never applied to Captain Selden. Miss Chorley had a great sense of what was due to family. I have now said all I can on the subject.'

'Thank you, sir. Could you tell us more about Miss Chorley's life in Seaborough?'

'I am a very busy man, Inspector,' Mr Jerrold sighed heavily. 'Very well, she was one of the town's most prominent personages, sitting on various committees and known for her charitable works. In fact there wasn't much she didn't take an interest in.'

'Could you expound on that, please?'

'Miss Chorley was a pious lady and naturally involved in the parish church. The vicar, Reverend Shaw can tell you more about that. I know she gave quite a lot of money for various gifts, she provided an organ for instance. She was particularly involved in the cottage hospital, as she had it built as a memorial to her father. She led the subscriptions to raise money for a new wing. Dr Avery is the one to talk to there. He's the visiting doctor and has a practice in the town.'

'Yes, We've spoken earlier today as he's also the police-surgeon.'

'I don't know what more I can tell you. Miss Chorley was in charge of the Ladies Society as we call it, *The Ladies' Society for the Relief of Indigent Widows and Orphans* to give it its full title. My wife is a committee member and they are meeting in my own home at this very hour. They are one of the leading charities in Seaborough.' Mr Jerrold smiled thinly, 'they do good works and it provides a suitable interest for the ladies.'

Eight

'They've buggered off back to Exeter and good riddance to 'em, say I.' Sergeant Tancock raised his tankard in a mock salute before taking a great swallow. 'Said something about they'd done all they could here and the inspector had to report back to his superior. Furriners, what do they know?'

His companion rightly interpreted this as meaning not Devonshire men or possibly being from the north of the county. 'Where were they from, in your opinion?'

Tancock wiped the back of his mouth and abundant whiskers with a clean handkerchief before answering. 'London,' he pronounced, 'leastways the sergeant, chirpy as a Cockney sparrow. Must've been made up to sergeant young,' he added reflectively. 'Still there's more opportunity to show your worth in a big place. Not so easy here.'

'You could always bring the murderer to justice,' suggested his companion. Tancock preened himself momentarily then his face fell. 'Not likely is it, they wouldn't let me do any interviews. You wouldn't be making fun with me I hope, Mr Biggs?'

'Certainly not, Sergeant.'

Jabez Biggs took a tiny sip of his own ale, pulling a face as he did. 'It seems to me that local knowledge will be what's needed to solve this terrible crime.'

'You may be right there. Now the inspector, he may've been from London or somewhere else. He weren't from these parts, that I do know. There was a something in his voice.'

'Welsh perhaps or Scotch?' asked Biggs with interest.

'No, I know those. Northerner maybe,' Tancock downed some more of his drink, ' who cares? Not I, he's a starchy so-and-so. Talks to you all polite but eyes everywhere. I saw him through the winder, blowing dust off my private files, looking like he had a week-old dead cat under his nose. Told me to do up my buttons, b---- cheek!'

'It would pay then, if I might suggest Sergeant Tancock, to ensure everything is in immaculate order before the detectives return for the inquest.'

'I know that,' growled the sergeant. 'Your round.' He set down his tankard with a thump.

'Same again for the sergeant, if you please, miss.' Biggs produced a shilling and slid it across the bar.

'Will you be giving evidence yourself, Mr Tancock?' he asked when he had seated himself again.

'That I will. I was the one Doctor Miller sent for, weren't I?'

'I should like to see that. I shall endeavour to attend, work permitting of course.'

'Well your customers will wait, won't they?'

Tancock looked round the crowded room as he spoke, from the old men playing dominoes in the corner to the young clerks and shop assistants quaffing at the bar. The landlord of the *Dewdrop Inn* was no fool, they were clustered round the buxom barmaid like horseflies on fresh dung.

'Anyroad,' he said absently, 'you won't have long to wait. No sooner got rid of them and they'll be back. Inquest date's been set.'

A sharp intake of breath as Mr Biggs leant forward. 'You did say it was murder, Mr Tancock?' he asked quietly.

'I never said nothing,' retorted Tancock. 'More than my job's worth. I suppose Hicks will be hoping to bury Miss Chorley?'

Mr Biggs flushed and gave his single dry cough. 'I scarcely think the heir would want less than the foremost undertaker's in Seaborough. Economy would hardly be fitting.'

'You'll have your work cut out, I know that much. If you take my meaning.' Tancock grinned and took another swig of his ale. 'She weren't pretty when she were alive and the doctor's taken a knife and fork to her. What with her insides being in a jar, I doubt there'll be much left.'

'We should not speak disrespectfully of the departed, Mr Tancock. For such is the fate as will befall us all.' Mr Biggs flexed his fingers as he spoke. 'Oh I do love a challenge.' He got to his feet and pulled on his gloves. 'I shall bid you goodnight, sergeant.' As he eased past the table he noticed a young man with his back to them, slide out from the next settle and make his way to the door. 'That's surely young Mr Winton,' he said to himself. A burst of piano music came from the taproom as the fellow pushed through the crowded public and reached the porch door.

'I say, Mr Winton,' called Biggs as he stepped into the street. The other turned reluctantly, he thought and raised his hat.

'Good evening, Mr Biggs. I beg your pardon, I didn't see you in there.'

'How are you settling in with us? I trust our small town is to your liking?'

'Oh, quite well, thank you. Yes, I'm finding it very pleasant here.' The young man's face was pale in the dusk.

'Business good, I trust?'

'Slow but steady.'

Mr Biggs coughed discreetly. 'Perhaps we'll have the pleasure of working together again soon. I enjoyed our last association, melancholy though it was.'

'Er yes, indeed. Perhaps we shall. Good night.' Winton bowed and set off rapidly towards the square.

Mr Biggs stood looking after him a while. As the lamplighter appeared on the corner, he watched him reach up to the lever with his long pole. In no hurry to return to his modest home and solitary chop, he waited while first one then a string of tiny flares and pools of soft light spun along the street. As the workman's footsteps drew near, he turned away. 'Yes, I do love a challenge,' he murmured softly as he thought over what he had learned.

Nine

The makeshift public gallery was as densely packed as a match-safe. Seaborough being too small a town for its own assizes, the coroner's court was taking place in the ballroom of *The Marine Hotel*. One by one the witnesses had taken the stand, Captain Selden, grave-faced with a mild manner, Miss Geake, demure beneath a black veil. The two doctors were as contrasting as Jack Sprat and his wife, Miller, short in stature and portly, swaying on his heels with self-importance, Avery, tall, lean and composed. Then came the servants, over-awed and nervy but they struck Abbs as truthful. He had been aware of the craning of necks as he gave his evidence, could almost sense the furrowed brows take in the medical terms as he read them out.

Casually easing forward a little, he let his gaze drift along the row where the witnesses resumed their seats. Selden was sitting with an elderly man in clerical dress. Unremarkable of appearance, Abbs had nonetheless noticed him following each statement with close attention. Behind him Mr Jerrold the attorney leaned over to say a word to them both.

Whispering and rustlings suddenly ceased as the door opened at the end of the long room and the twelve jurors filed back in. Abbs watched their self-conscious faces, trying to guess their occupations, shopkeepers, saddlers, carpenters and clerks. Colonel Osborne requested the foreman to give their verdict and the fellow stood stiffly in his best suit, swallowing; his voice when it came as cracked as his well-polished boot leather.

Wilful murder by person or persons unknown.

The resultant gasps and blatant asides caused the coroner to rap his gavel on the table before him. Captain Selden sank forward, nibbling one of his nails. Though Miss Geake's expression was impossible to see, Abbs did not miss her gloved fingers clenched on the black-edged handkerchief she held; the sole outward expression of grief to be seen. Avery was shaking his head in disbelief, Dr Miller seemed almost elated, turning instantly to his neighbour. A man in the front row of the public gallery whispered urgently to his dark-bearded companion. The quick movement of his head with its thick brown waves, set Abbs wondering where he'd seen him before. Then he had it, outside the town hall, the man admonishing the whistle-player. Beside him Sergeant Tancock shifted his fat thighs on the hard bench, his tall hat held on his knees.

When the room was silent again, Colonel Osborne spoke for the last time. Florid-faced, with the appearance of a man who'd rather be exercising his hunter on his estate, the coroner discharged the jury and formally released custody of the deceased's body back to the care of the sole relative.

The hotel lobby was thronged with people in no hurry to leave. Abbs pushed past their backs in Tancock's wake. The strain of giving succinct evidence and the press of voices were bringing on one of his headaches. A dull beat was beginning on one side of his forehead like a lightly tapped hammer, regular as a blacksmith. The intensity of the blow would gradually strengthen until the only recourse was to lie down in dim light and above all, quiet. Such an antidote was rarely possible for a working man. Fresh air and solitude could suffice if taken early.

'Let's get out of here, Sergeant.'

'I reckon the doctor wants a word, sir.' Tancock indicated Dr Avery making his way towards them. He paused briefly as a benevolent-looking older man halted his progress, stepping in his way with a husky cough and consoling expression. At the foot of the stairs the other doctor, Miller was at the centre of a small group, two of whom turned to stare at Avery as he passed. He caught up with them as they paused by the front entrance.

'Do you mind if we talk outside, Doctor?'

'I'd prefer it, Inspector. I suppose I must get used to being taken for a fool.' Avery halted on the pavement and shook his head again. 'I can't understand it,' he said slowly, half to himself. 'I've been going over the post-mortem in my mind since you told me, Sergeant, retracing the steps. I don't know what I could have done differently. It's a methodical process,' he said, turning to Abbs.

'It wasn't your fault, Doctor,' said Tancock awkwardly. 'The coroner said so. Doctor Miller would've done the same.' The three men stepped against the wall to allow a lady to pass. She ushered a small boy in front of her, a red balloon bobbing on a string from his hand.

'That's so, Doctor. Colonel Osborne underlined the fact that your findings were perfectly correct. As I understand it, a less conscientious doctor would not have called them inconclusive but would have signed the certificate as natural causes.'

Avery looked thoughtful. 'Thank you, both of you. I know medically you're correct, I examined the stomach contents carefully. There was no sign of anything unusual.' He rubbed his chin as he considered. 'Forgive me, it makes unpleasant listening. No, I had no reason to conduct the Marsh test which is the only reliable indicator of arsenic in a recent cadaver. But that won't stop people thinking me a poor doctor,' he added, his voice hardening.

'S'cuse me, sir,' broke in Tancock. 'He's a reporter,' jerking a thumb at a man marching determinedly towards them. 'Shall I see to him?'

'Please do,' murmured Abbs. 'I'll see you back at the station.' They saw Tancock bar the pavement, placing a beefy hand on the reporter's shoulder as they turned away.

'It's irrational but I can't rid myself of the feeling that I've let down Miss Chorley. She was in many ways my benefactress,' continued Dr Avery. 'Without her I should not have my position at the hospital.'

'Your feelings do you credit but there's only one person to blame and they'll answer for this at the end of a rope.'

'The results of the food analysed were clear, you said?'

'That's correct. No arsenic found but of course most of the tea had been consumed.'

Avery glanced curiously at Abbs as they walked. 'Are you unwell, Inspector? You grow more pale.'

'A slight headache, nothing more. It was airless in the hotel.'

'In that case the sea breeze should help. Is your own sergeant not back with you?'

'He was needed elsewhere but he's on his way.'

'You'll have much to do and I have patients to attend, if they still trust me, so I'll bid you good day.' Raising his hat, Avery tucked his cane under his arm and strode purposefully in front of a waiting carriage.'

Crossing the street, Abbs wandered along the promenade and leaned against the sea wall separating it from the beach. It was all stone and shingle apart from a narrow strip of sand along the seaweed-heaped frill left by the tide. That was a curious reddish brown hue and looked grubby and unappealing. Inspector Martin was right. Although a pleasant enough town, Seaborough did not look to have the attributes desirable in a resort: no pier, pierrot or Punch and Judy here.

A small tan and white dog came racing along the beach, his owner pottering behind, from time to time looking down and poking among the pebbles with his stick. Taking in some deep breaths of the briny air, Abbs watched the contented pair and felt his tension begin to uncoil. He was surprised to find himself aware of Reeve's absence. They were short-handed at the station and Nicholls had sent him knocking on doors, hunting witnesses to a foul case of housebreaking. The owner had been beaten about the head with his own life-preserver. The superintendent had grudgingly said that Reeve could follow on since it was now a murder inquiry. A sudden burst of raucous, plaintive cries erupted as a few seagulls soared across the sky. As he idly watched, two fellows reached the bathing-machines and began to push and wheel the first one, bumping it up the beach.

Supper had been a sorry affair from the moment Papa had finished saying grace, thought Adelaide. He had toyed with his beef, his thoughts clearly elsewhere and even Hannah's stewed blackberries with a thick crust of cream had failed to revive his absent spirits. Rising from the table, she went to the sideboard.

'May I fetch you some cheese, Papa?' She waited patiently for him to look up.

'What is it you say, my dear? Ah, some Stilton, no, I think not, tonight. I fear I have little appetite.'

'You usually love blackberries and this was the last of them, it's almost Michaelmas.'

Her father looked down at his bowl as if wondering how it came there. 'I'm sorry to waste Hannah's labours.'

'Never mind, Papa, shall we sit and be cosy by the fire?' The vicar smiled gratefully at his daughter.

'I should like that, Adelaide.'

When they were settled on either side of the fireplace, Adelaide took up her embroidery and appeared intent on deciding which colour silk to use next. Her father took his tobacco jar from the mantelpiece and set it on the small table by his chair. His pipe lay in his hand as though there were comfort in holding its shape though he made no attempt to fill it. The coal blazed steadily, its flames reflecting in the fire-dogs, the bottle green velvet curtains were left open to catch the last vestige of light and to an onlooker the vicarage drawing-room presented an inviting scene. After a short time the vicar began to speak.

'The inquest was a great ordeal for Captain Selden.'

Adelaide looked up instantly. 'I suppose none of us can imagine his feelings, the horror of having a relative murdered.'

'Quite so. It has come as a terrible shock to the poor fellow. He had seen very little of his aunt for some years but one always thinks there is time.' Her father was gazing into the fire, then his eyes met hers. 'This cannot be said to be God's will, Adelaide, and I wish I could believe it the work of a stranger but I cannot.' He grasped the stem of his pipe. 'Someone among us has done this appalling deed.'

Setting aside all pretence of industry, Adelaide considered her father's words. 'You don't think Captain Selden then...?' She felt unable to be any more direct. Removing the lid of the tobacco jar, Samuel Shaw began trailing the mixture through his fingers, before packing a little into the bowl of his pipe.

'He seems a perfectly nice man but people are saying... well we don't really know him.'

'I know what people are saying,' said Mr Shaw. 'No, I don't believe Captain Selden came visiting his aunt, supplied with arsenic. No one in their senses would do something so likely to throw them under suspicion.'

'But Papa, surely whoever did this has lost their senses. Won't they be insane?' interrupted Adelaide. 'Someone has quietly lost their mind, without anyone noticing.'

'In the meaning that they've lost all sense of right and wrong, I agree, my dear.' said Mr Shaw between puffs. 'But as a man of God, I would make a distinction between insanity and evil. It seems to me that Miss Chorley's murder has been carefully planned and quite possibly in such a way as to lay suspicion on the Captain.'

There was a silence while Adelaide considered this. 'I can't believe it to be one of the servants, we know them all,' she said. 'Nor Miss Geake, she's been with Miss Chorley for years. Companions don't kill their mistress because they've been bored or a little condescended to.'

'The police will surely focus their attention on her and that will be a most unpleasant experience. I shall offer her my support tomorrow and any constructive help I can give, such as writing a character reference,' said Mr Shaw.

'You are going to Tower House, Papa?'

'Captain Selden wishes to discuss the funeral service. Because of the circumstances he thinks it proper that it be less elaborate than one would usually expect.' The vicar shook his head sadly. 'He went to make the arrangements with Mr Hicks after the inquest. Because there's already been a great delay it must take place with all urgency. It is to be in three days' time. Miss Chorley will be interred with her father of course.'

Adelaide nodded, Richard Chorley was laid to rest in a large square plot surmounted by a tall marble cross. 'Your diary is free, fortunately, Papa.'

Her father looked warmly at her. 'I do not know what I should do without you, Adelaide. The Captain has been given leave of absence until the funeral, then he talks of having the house shut up. I don't know his plans thereafter, but it doesn't sound as though he intends to make his future home in Seaborough.'

'I suppose the policemen from Exeter will question him first?'

'The detective inspector spoke to him before the inquest. He wishes to call on the Captain and Miss Geake in the morning.' Mr Shaw knocked out his pipe on the grate. 'Even tobacco will not comfort me this evening. I must give a great deal of thought to my sermon this week.' He glanced up at the window. 'Darkness has fallen, will you shut out the night, my dear?'

'Of course, Papa.' As she did every evening, Adelaide looked across at the low spire, rising like a finger pointing heavenwards between the line of holm oaks which separated the vicarage garden from the churchyard. The moon was a thin sliver and the garden looked faintly sinister with shapes of ink-black darkness and chess-piece shadows. She told herself not to be so foolish, knowing full well that morning would return them to sundial, yew hedge, monkey puzzle and fir.

'Have you met the detectives, Papa?' she enquired as she drew the curtains.

'Not yet, I saw the inspector give his evidence to Colonel Osborne. You will have to prepare to meet them yourself, Adelaide. No doubt the police will wish to question us both in due course.'

She spun round in surprise. 'But we cannot help them, we know nothing.'

'We knew Miss Chorley and we were present on that last day. Don't look so alarmed, my dear. The police can only work by talking to everyone and piecing information together. We will all of us have a little to tell.'

Ten

One of the traits Abbs was beginning to like in Reeve was his enthusiasm for his work. Most subordinates waited passively for orders whereas Reeve was full of questions and keen to play his part in solving their inquiry. He was minded to allow him to speak to the servants again by himself.

'Which door this time, sir?'

Abbs looked up at the house with its regular sash windows and half-drawn curtains. It had stood, if he was any judge, before the town was built and been remodelled in the present century with the eponymous square tower at one end and a large pillared porch. An ugly pile, its additions sprouting like warts on an old face.

'The front.'

The knocker was still bound with crape and its muffled thuds brought a young parlour-maid wearing black ribbon in her cap to admit them. 'Captain Selden's expecting you, sir. He said to show you into the library. Shall I take your things?' She tapped on a door further along the tiled hall and entered.

'If you please, sir. It's the policemen.' Eyeing the two men with open curiosity, she bobbed a curtsey and withdrew. The room was dominated by a large oil painting hanging above the fireplace. Its hazy gun carriages, smoke and patchy red figures caught the eye before the man who moved forward to greet them.

'Good morning, Inspector Abbs.'

Abbs introduced Reeve and the three of them sat on a pair of sofas arranged near the window. 'We're sorry to disturb you at such a distressing time, Captain, but you'll understand the urgency. A good deal of time has been lost.'

Captain Selden inclined his head. 'Of course, Inspector. I'll answer your questions as well as I can. Naturally I want my aunt's murderer caught.' He swept his hand, indicating helplessness. 'Though frankly, I don't see what use I can be.'

In Abbs's opinion, witnesses who prefaced their statement with *frankly* rarely were so. *To be honest* was another warning sign, usually accompanied by a disingenuous smile. However, innocent people were often nervous when interviewed by the police. He decided to keep an open mind for the moment.

'It's a question of taking statements from everyone in Miss Chorley's life, looking for discrepancies or anything odd. Each person adds information to build an overall picture. Then it comes down to finding someone with motive, means and opportunity.'

The Captain was examining his nails which were badly bitten. His hands were on the small side for a man and lightly freckled. His head jerked up as Abbs finished speaking. 'But couldn't there be more than one person with all three?'

'That's possible. It's my job to build a watertight case, then it's up to judge and jury.'

Captain Selden nodded. 'What can I tell you?'

'I have to ask you, sir, do you have any knowledge of a motive for this crime? Did your aunt speak of anyone with a grudge against her or a quarrel in her private life or business?'

After hesitating slightly, Selden shook his head. 'I can think of nothing, Inspector and I've thought of little else. I still believe my aunt's death could have been an accident, nothing else makes sense.'

'You heard the medical evidence at the inquest, sir. I'm afraid that's been ruled out. While ladies do use arsenic for cosmetic reasons, it's extremely unlikely that anyone would take such a hefty dose.'

Selden's fore-finger picked at the side of his thumbnail as he listened. 'Very well, I accept what you say.'

'The solution will lie somewhere in Miss Chorley's character. Forgive me but would you say she was a lady likely to make enemies?'

'You must understand that I have not seen my aunt for several years. Until a little under a year ago, my regiment was in India. Since my return to this country I've been settling into an administrative post. My aunt had invited me to visit her and this was the first chance to do so.'

'Nothing comes to mind that Miss Chorley mentioned in a letter, an incident that sounded trivial at the time, perhaps?'

'Not that I recall.' Selden watched Reeve busily scribbling. 'I have almost no knowledge of my aunt's circle. She wrote at regular intervals and mentioned her charity work, the local hospital, orphans and so on. I know she took a great interest in the church but I didn't pay a great deal of attention. It all seemed a very long way off.' His gaze fell on the large brown-shaded globe standing in an alcove.

'To be honest, Inspector, my aunt was of a somewhat forceful disposition. She meant well, had people's best interests at heart and all that but she always thought she knew better than they did. She pushed me into the army at a young age solely because her brother had served in the North Gloucesters. My father gave way to her and I had no say in the matter.'

Couldn't stand up to her, thought Abbs. Selden was settling into his stride, nerves forgotten and his soft voice taking on an increasingly hard-done-by tone. 'I certainly don't mean to speak ill of the dead, Inspector.'

'That's understood, sir.'

'Thinking about it, I suppose it's possible that my aunt unwittingly got someone's back up.' Selden shrugged and fell silent.

'Your candour is much appreciated, Captain. Moving on, Miss Geake kindly made us a list of everyone invited to tea here on the day Miss Chorley died. D'you have it, sergeant?' Reeve handed him an inked sheet of paper.

'My aunt wanted me to meet some of her acquaintances. There were three ladies, all involved with her charity work I believe, as well as her neighbour, an elderly gentleman on the hospital board and the vicar.'

'You saw nothing unusual throughout the afternoon? With hindsight, no one behaving suspiciously near Miss Chorley's food or drink?'

'No, but one doesn't pay attention to such things. The maid passed her plates and the cake stand. Miss Geake poured tea several times I think.'

Abbs nodded. 'You didn't see a guest anywhere in the house they shouldn't be?'

Captain Selden touched his neat moustache with the back of a knuckle as he considered. 'I saw nothing out of the ordinary, people did move about. The ladies went off to the conservatory to look at plants and I suppose to wash their hands and so forth.' Reeve cleared his throat as he bent further over his notebook.

'To your knowledge did Miss Chorley see anyone else that day?'

'As a matter of fact, yes. I escorted her to a photographer's studio in the morning. She wanted a recent likeness taken of me in uniform.'

Abbs and Reeve exchanged glances. 'Miss Geake didn't mention this.'

'I daresay it slipped her mind. She didn't accompany us.'

'Where was this, Captain Selden?'

'Just off the high street, I don't recall the name. The photographer was a young chap, not long in business I think my aunt said.'

'We'll find him. Were you offered any refreshment?'

'By Jove yes. Now you mention it, my aunt accepted a cup of tea and a biscuit while she watched, but she didn't even know the man.'

'Just routine. We'd be failing in our duty if we didn't account for all the food and drink Miss Chorley had on her last day.'

'Quite so. There's one more thing. I had a drink early that evening with a gentleman called Hicks. His wife was a guest that afternoon and he called to collect her but she'd already gone. I invited him in but he didn't even see my aunt.'

'What time was this?'

'About six, I should say. My aunt was upstairs and unaware that Mr Hicks was in the house. We had a whisky and soda in here.' Selden smiled at the inspector. 'Fact is, I was glad of some masculine company.'

'Had you met Mr Hicks previously?'

'We were introduced briefly after church. He expressed an interest in India.'

'And did Mr Hicks leave your presence while he was here?'

'He didn't leave this room but I did for a short time. I went to my bedroom to fetch a map to show him. He stayed around a half-hour and my aunt wasn't taken ill until eight or thereabouts.'

'The maid said Miss Chorley rang for a glass of brandy after she went to her bedroom. Would that have been obtained from the tantalus in here, sir?'

'It's the only one I've seen. Yes, I suppose it would.'

'And this was after Mr Hicks left?'

'Yes, though I don't see where this is leading.'

Abbs rose to his feet, Reeve immediately following his lead. 'You've been very patient, Captain, thank you.'

'I hope I've been of some use.' Selden paused by the fireplace where Reeve was gazing at the painting. 'Inkerman, Sergeant. My uncle lost his life there in the fog. That's his regiment, the 28th Foot. My grandfather had it done.'

'Mr Jerrold mentioned you'd be having the house closed up after the funeral, sir? 'said Abbs.

'I've changed my mind,' replied Selden as he rang the bell. 'I've asked Miss Geake if she'd be willing to stay on for a while until everything is resolved. It makes sense as she'll need time to enquire after a new position. I shall return to Hampshire straight after the funeral. When this nightmare's finally over, I shall sell.'

'Perhaps Sergeant Reeve could have another word with the servants while I see Miss Geake?'

'She was in here, sir,' said the maid uncertainly, then her face cleared as she saw the door ajar. 'She must have stepped outside.'

'Don't worry, I'll find her,' replied Abbs. 'It's Sarah, isn't it?'

'Yes, sir.' The young woman looked gratified that he remembered.

'Would you take the sergeant to see Mrs Watkins, please? He'd like to ask you all a few more questions. Nothing to worry about,' he added. Sarah nodded and turned on her heel, the sway of her apron indicating she was aware of Reeve following behind her.

Left alone, Abbs looked around the conservatory with interest. Sunlight through the upper glass was reflecting red, yellow and blue lights across the flagged floor. They seemed to quiver fractionally and move as he did. Maidenhair fern, mother-in-law's tongue and ivies spilled from clay pots along the wide window-sill. He halted before a Wardian case, thinking there was something unpleasant about the way the plants were trapped. The smell of watered compost took him momentarily back to boyhood, in the melon house at the Hall with his father. Pushing away the past he circumvented the iron seat and table to leave by the garden door.

Miss Geake was standing before a flower border, a thin, black figure in a paramatta dress with scissors in her hand and a flat basket at her feet. She watched him walk towards her along the brick path, a spray of bronze flowers raised to her face.

'Do you care for chrysanthemums, Inspector? What could be more appropriate for a house of mourning? I always think they smell of death.'

Country folk said they smelt like cats' piss. He knew what she meant, they were the cemetery flower. In autumn he always purchased a bunch from the old woman selling outside the gates, perhaps it was because they lasted well.

'Good day, Miss Geake. I can't say I've given it any thought,' he lied.

'Ah, a ladies' companion has plenty of time to think, you see.' She turned away from him as she laid the stems in her basket.

'I don't doubt you've been thinking about Miss Chorley's death.'

'Of course.' She selected a stem and cut it, discarding a spent bloom. 'Really, the gardeners have become lax,' she remarked, 'but then they are no longer admonished.' She smiled archly at him as though she were pouring tea.

'They don't live on the premises and they weren't here the day Miss Chorley died,' murmured Abbs, recalling his earlier visit. Sergeant Tancock's men had spoken to them.

'We wouldn't want them looking in the window at their betters.' Miss Geake gave a vicious snip to another stem.

Abbs sighed inwardly. 'Miss Geake, your employer was murdered. I need to know if you can think of any motive, or any unusual event in Miss Chorley's life in the last weeks, however trivial?'

'I believe I can, Inspector,' she said.

'Perhaps you'd care to sit?' said Abbs, gesturing to a nearby wooden seat. He picked up her basket. 'This is a pleasant, sheltered corner.' He waited until she had arranged her skirt and began to speak again.

'Have you encountered Mr Alfred Halesworth?' she enquired.

He shook his head. 'I have not, though the name is familiar. A Mrs Alfred Halesworth was a guest here on the day Miss Chorley died.'

'His wife.' Snip, went the scissors as she began to trim the ends of the stalks. 'He's a councillor and regards himself as one of the leading men in Seaborough.'

'Was he a friend of Miss Chorley?' asked Abbs, noting the *regards himself*.

Miss Geake made a small snort, indicative of amused contempt, he thought. 'He would like to have been. No, she thought him a parvenu. And she would know,' she remarked in an aside. 'She saw Mrs

Halesworth often through the *Ladies' Society*, hence the invitation. That's where the comfortably-off ladies of Seaborough meet to gossip and interfere in the lives of their inferiors. I was required to attend to thread Miss Chorley's needle and carry her workbox.'

Abbs wondered about the change in Miss Geake's demeanour since their first meeting. He glanced discreetly at her face, handsome, though with too strong a nose to be considered a desirable specimen of womanhood. They were much of an age, he estimated. Her eyes sparkled with malice and a fierce intelligence. Was it the knowledge that a legacy was coming and a few weeks' respite from seeking a new position? Surely she did not expect enough money to set her free?

'About a week before Miss Chorley died, she asked me to write a note to Mr Halesworth, agreeing to his request for an interview.'

'Do you know what this interview was about?'

'I do not. At first I thought he was after a subscription.'

'Please go on.'

'He came the following day on the morning before Captain Selden's arrival. I was not asked to be present and overheard nothing,' added Miss Geake, turning to him. 'But I happened to be entering the hall when Mr Halesworth left.' She paused again before continuing. 'He thrust past me, ignoring my greeting. Then he grabbed his stick so hurriedly he almost upended the stand and wrenched the door open without waiting to be shown out. I think he would have slammed it had he dared, he was furious.' She sat back in unmistakable satisfaction.

'Thank you for telling me,' said Abbs. He reached into his coat and took out his notebook.

'Something else you should know, Inspector.' Miss Geake was clearly enjoying herself. He could understand that it was a relief to say what she thought without picking her words, though he did not care for the relish. 'A parlour-maid was dismissed a few weeks ago for stealing. No doubt she bore a grudge against Miss Chorley.'

'What were the circumstances?'

'She stole a garnet ring from her mistress, probably thinking it a valuable ruby. It was missed and a general search made. It was found hidden in her possessions and she was dismissed at once.'

'Were the police called?'

'No,' Miss Geake looked sideways at Abbs and smiled. 'Miss Chorley did not care to have the Constabulary in the house. Mary was sent back to her family without a character.'

'Surely she could have had no access to this house afterwards?'

'You might think that but I happened to see her in the lane just the day before Miss Chorley died. If she had nerve enough to steal, she could have been visiting one of the servants. She was friendly with them, I daresay.'

'Where might I find this Mary?'

'Her father keeps a small farm beyond Venning. That's the nearest village if you continue past the house.' Abbs made a brief note.

'And did you also happen to see Mr Nathaniel Hicks call on the day of the tea party?' he asked.

'No, I did not,' said Miss Geake in a surprised tone. 'Are you sure about that, Inspector? He was not invited, unlike his wife. She's a good-natured, vapid creature who never stops talking.' Abbs remained silent.

'Nathaniel Hicks you'll find is close friend to Mr Halesworth.'

'One thing more,' said Abbs 'and I won't take up your time any longer. To your knowledge has arsenic ever been purchased for this household, for the gardener or groom for instance or for Miss Chorley herself?'

'For her complexion, you mean? Not for the stables as far as I know. I've never heard tell of rats here but you'd best ask William. As for Miss Chorley, it's not something she ever confided in me but she was vain enough.' Leaning forward, Miss Geake picked up her basket, setting it on her lap, preparatory to moving. 'Her hair was thinning and she wore a false piece though she'd die rather than admit it and she preened herself when Mr Emerson sat by her at the tea-table, though he's past seventy. He had ample opportunity to poison her,' she remarked.

Abbs recalled Miss Chorley's dressing-table with its ivory-inlaid brushes and hand mirror. Among the trinket trays and scent bottles there'd been a china hair-holder with some long grey hairs saved. He found such intimate sights both distasteful and sad. Murder had many consequences, loss of dignity for the victim was just one of them. Many a small secret would be laid bare before he and Reeve were done.

'You'll find many things about Miss Chorley were false.' said Miss Geake. 'You saw the library, shelf upon shelf of books in their fine bindings. All for show! Her father bought them to impress callers with his learning. They've never been read and I daresay never will be. I was not permitted to borrow any.' Her voice shook with suppressed anger.

She stood up abruptly and faced Abbs, still clasping her basket as he rose. She snipped each word in the same way she'd wielded the scissors. 'And the brother, the distinguished hero of Inkerman. She was always vague about exactly how he died. No medals ever mentioned and believe me, they would have been. I should enquire of Captain Selden, it's my belief his father died of the flux.'

'I'm grateful for your candour, madam.' Abbs followed Miss Geake inside, her flare of temper seemingly snuffed out. She sounded subdued as she turned to him in the conservatory. 'I must get these in water, I'll bid you good day, Inspector. The maid will show you out.'

Reeve, waiting in the hall was studying a stag's head mounted over a door. Abbs minded of Miss Geake's scornful outburst, doubted it had been shot by a Chorley. He had elected to walk back, knowing that Nicholls would never countenance many cab fares on expenses. It would give them a chance to get the measure of the town. When they were a few yards from the gates, a modest carriage slowed past them and turned in, affording a glimpse of the clerical gentleman he'd seen at the inquest.

'Shame you weren't in the kitchen, sir,' continued Reeve. 'Mrs Watkins insisted I try her lardy cake.'

'So you're confident nothing new emerged since we were here previously?'

'Yes, sir. The cook's still livid that someone put poison in her food and the scullery maid's terrified we think it was her, that's the gist of it.'

Abbs nodded, deep in thought. 'Miss Geake on the other hand was fulsome in her fresh information.'

He described what he'd been told about Mr Halesworth as they walked along the hedgerows, clusters of ripe elderberries bending over their heads. A woman in a donkey cart passed them, then they reached a wagon so laden with hay that it was having difficulty turning from a side lane. A fellow had jumped down and was gesturing encouragement at the horse and driver. As they turned into a bend,

Seaborough lay spread out below them; grey slate rooftops with drifting smoke, a cemetery with a chapel and its headstones bunched in a corner, the drum of a small gasworks with heaps of coal, a church spire, the town hall square and the dirty-looking beach nibbled by the sea. The two men began the long descent into the residential streets, the hollow, damp hoot of a train sounding as it chugged on its way.

'So we'll have to talk to Mr Halesworth, the question is how? We can't very well ask him bluntly why he quarrelled with Miss Chorley, he'll only deny it. Then there's the photographer to be seen, the undertaker and the guests at afternoon tea. Plenty to keep us busy.'

'What about the maid who was dismissed, sir?'

'I shall send you to talk to her, Sergeant. She might be more forthcoming with someone nearer her own age.'

'Righto, sir,' said Reeve, grinning with pleasure. 'You think I'll know if she's lying?'

'Trust your instincts, Reeve.' They had reached a hump-backed bridge and both instinctively paused to look over the parapet at the railway line beneath, before continuing on. 'We'll head back to the station now and find out where this photographer has his place of business. His name's Winton. Sergeant Tancock is sure to know. We'll call on him this afternoon but I could do with a cup of tea first.'

'I wouldn't say no to stopping off for a pie along the way, sir. This sea air's giving me an appetite.'

Eleven

It was a most ordinary street in a fair-sized market town and that was the beauty of it. Small enough to be a pleasant place for a young widow to settle, yet large enough for her to make a modest living and above all to be anonymous. One of the more useful amenities of this ancient settlement with its coaching inns and crumbling butter cross was a station. In a westerly direction the line eventually ran to Exeter but long before that, a line branched off to the small seaside town of Seaborough.

Mr Alfred Halesworth had quite forgotten it was market day in Kempston and found that when he stepped onto the platform, a good many people followed suit from the inferior carriages. He had himself elected to wear sober attire and carried a stick with a derby handle of plain cow horn as befits a shop manager or clerk, rather than the fine cane with a silver pommel he usually favoured. Though his appearance was unobtrusive, his spirits were good, his confident stride and jaunty air still caught the eye of more than one young woman.

Perceval-street was conveniently near the station. Its houses were small and respectable, spotless cream or ecru lace hung from every bay despite the proximity of soot. The entrance to an alley lay between each short terrace, the earthen paths free from weeds and rubbish. The thoroughfare was empty though Mr

Halesworth still glanced back before extracting a house key from his coat pocket. Two paces on the tiled path took him to the front door of one particular house which had gay scarlet geraniums in the diamond-shaped flower-bed of its diminutive front garden. In the scullery a woman at the sink caught the sound of a key scratching in the lock. Hastily drying her hands on a cloth, she unfolded her cuffs and smoothed the wisps of her fair hair as she hurried to the front door.

'Oh Fred, it's you,' she exclaimed, her complexion warm with pleasure. 'It isn't your day, there's nothing's wrong, is there?'

'Nothing at all. Some council business was postponed and I fancied getting away. Aren't you pleased to see me?' he teased as he hung his hat and coat on a peg. The hall was so narrow that a person could touch both walls, leaving no space for a stand. An oak barometer hung to one side, its round edge decorated with carved leaves and acorns. Opposite hung a small looking-glass, below which a slender shelf, hardly more than a ledge, served for letters.

'Oh, Fred. You must know how pleased I am. It's only, imagine what would I do if I had a pupil?'

Halesworth chuckled and caught at the strings of the young woman's apron. 'Luckily you're alone and can devote your time to me, Nelly.'

'The fire's lit, go through, Fred and I'll bring us some tea.' Nelly folded her apron as she spoke and ushered him through the half-open door, before disappearing to set the kettle on the range.

In the front parlour everything was trim and welcoming. The piano took pride of place with its twin stools and tidy pile of sheet music on top. Some sort of fern stood in a brown glazed bowl on the table in the window and tobacco-coloured button-back chairs were arranged invitingly by the hearth. Looking about in satisfaction, Halesworth idly wondered why he always felt so at home in the unassuming room. He sat back, closing his eyes for a moment, soothed by the sounds of a teapot being warmed and the rattle of china.

'How are Miss Violet and little Myrtle?' enquired Nelly when they were sipping their tea.

Halesworth grunted, 'they're off having their photograph taken to mark Violet's birthday on Sunday.'

'How lovely for them. And does she still practise?'

'Their mother sees to that sort of thing, I don't see much of them. Let's not talk of Seaborough. How's the boy doing?'

'Very well. He's in good health and working hard at school. Can you stay to see him? He would love to see his uncle.'

'I don't see why not. I'm glad to hear he's getting on. He's a bright boy, a credit to you. Does he need anything?'

'No thank you. You're very kind but I'm managing. Alfred wants for nothing.'

'Come now, no false pride. You would say, Nelly? I don't want the lad going to school in tight boots.'

'Truly, we're doing all right. You're already so good to us and I don't want to take advantage.' Nelly smiled fondly at him. 'You look tired, Fred, you work so hard for all of us.'

He felt touched by the concern on her pretty face. What a contrast to Rosa and her never-ending list of things needed for herself, the house and their daughters. Only that morning she'd ruined his breakfast by prattling on about the wretched photographer. Never mind that Cook had overdone his chop and a chap liked to read *The Times* in peace.'

'I do have a lot of concerns at present,' he agreed, setting his saucer on the hearth and stretching. How pleasant it was to put his cup where he liked, without his missus objecting. 'Still, one obstacle's recently been removed. I always get what I want, one way or another.' He patted his lap invitingly. 'Come sit by me, Nelly.'

P. Winton Portrait and Landscape Photographic Artist was inscribed in freshly painted lettering. The window held three large photographs displayed on stands, against a maroon curtain. Two of them were conventional portraits, a single gentleman standing and a family group seated. The other was more interesting in Abbs's eyes. It depicted a stream tumbling down a rocky chasm in woodland with the pattern of dappled sunlight on the leaves. A selection of *cartes de visite* were laid out in a fan shape and a notice of terms completed the display.

'Negatives carefully kept. Copies can be had at any time. Charges extra for children,' commented Reeve, 'because of keeping them still, I suppose.'

'I imagine so,' agreed Abbs. 'I daresay spoiling the plates comes expensive.' A bell jangled as he pushed open the door and they entered a cramped office which seemed full of people. A smartly dressed matron was seated by a desk where a young man in a morning coat was scribbling something. He looked up with rather a harassed expression. A young girl was sitting against the wall, together with a nursemaid who was attending to a much younger child. The girl threw them an indifferent glance and turned away.

'Good afternoon, gentlemen. Please take a seat and I'll be with you in one moment,' said the young man.

'Put your arms through, Miss Myrtle, that's right,' murmured the maid as she bent over the wriggling child and attempted to button her into a small jacket. Although there were two empty chairs, Abbs and Reeve elected to remain apart from the family group.

'You'll send them round before Sunday, Mr Winton,' said the customer, with her erect back to them. Her firm tone was an underlining rather than an enquiry.

'Certainly, Mrs Halesworth.' Abbs raised his eyebrows at Reeve who grinned back. 'You'll have the cabinet prints in good time for your daughter's birthday. And these are the measurements you require for the frames.' He handed her a folded slip of paper. 'Thank you for your custom, it has been a pleasure to work with such charming sitters.'

'I trust you don't charge extra for flannel, young man,' replied Mrs Halesworth as she rose, tucking the paper into her reticule. 'Come along, Violet.' The older girl stood, wearing a bored expression. Abbs removed his hat and stepped forward.

'Excuse me, madam, Inspector Abbs of the Exeter City Police,' he bowed and Mr Winton looked up abruptly. 'This is a fortuitous meeting, I wonder if I might speak to you concerning recent events at Tower House?'

Mrs Halesworth looked him up and down, ignoring Sergeant Reeve. 'I presume you're speaking to everyone, Inspector? You've no particular grounds for seeking me out, I trust?'

'That is so, madam, it's a matter of routine. We're seeing everyone who saw Miss Chorley on the day of her demise.'

'Well I can be of no help. No one buttered the sandwiches in my presence. It was a perfectly normal social occasion, rather dull, if you want the truth.'

Abbs summoned his considerable reserves of patience. 'I'd still like to hear your impressions in more detail, ma'am, if I might? Perhaps when you've had more time to recall them?'

She gave an abrupt nod, setting her pendant earrings moving. 'Very well. I can see you tomorrow in the morning. I believe my husband will wish to be present.'

'Thank you, Mrs Halesworth, I'm much obliged.'

'Ten o'clock will suit. Come along, Jessie. Mr Winton will let you have our address,' she added, pulling on her gloves. Reeve jumped to hold the door as Mrs Halesworth swept out with her elder daughter. The nursemaid followed more slowly, encouraging the child.

Reeve suddenly darted over to the chairs and retrieved something, calling after the young woman. 'Excuse me, miss, the little girl left this.' He held out a piece of fawn, woollen cloth.

'It's her scrap of shawl, she will take it everywhere.' Reeve stooped and held it out to the child. She regarded him with a solemn expression then suddenly chuckled with glee as she took the cloth and held it to her cheek. Reeve hastily composed his features and the nursemaid smiled her thanks before hurrying out to the waiting carriage.

'Now, sir, perhaps we can have a word with you?' asked Abbs.

'Certainly. Inspector, you said? I'll just put the catch over the door,' said Mr Winton, turning his sign to *Closed*. 'Now, how can I be of assistance to you, gentlemen?'

'You'll have heard what I said to Mrs Halesworth. Do I take it you're aware of the death of Miss Harriet Chorley and the circumstances surrounding it?'

Mr Winton nodded soberly. 'It was reported at length in the local paper. You'll want to ask me about her visit here? I recall it well.'

'Good. What can you tell us about it?'

The photographer moved behind his desk and produced a ledger from a drawer. 'She came in late morning, accompanied by a gentleman in army uniform. He was to sit for the photograph. I believe he addressed her as *Aunt*.' Turning back a page he found an entry. 'Yes, here's the order.' He rotated the book and indicated the line.

'Two copies. Is that customary?'

'Not always, but I recall Miss Chorley saying that the gentleman should have another for himself. I understood that the photograph was for her to keep.' He looked from one man to the other. 'Is there anything else you'd like to know?'

'Did Miss Chorley take anything to eat or drink while she was here?'

'Yes, she drank a cup of tea and I think she may have had a biscuit with it.' His voice trailed away and he waited for Abbs to speak again.

'Is that customary, to offer refreshments?'

Mr Winton shook his head. 'Not to everyone but better-off customers rather expect the attention. Mrs Halesworth had a cup of tea while she watched her daughters. I had the idea from the studio where I was apprenticed. Sitters often bring someone with them and it's quite a long wait. First there's a discussion about the requirements, then the sitter's posed and so on. Would you like to see?'

'If you please, we'd be interested to see where you work.'

'Through here.'

They followed Mr Winton into a large studio which held a haphazard assortment of furnishings and articles, perhaps resembling the backstage of a theatre, thought Abbs. Skirting his tripod and camera apparatus which stood in the centre of the room, he led them to a corner where a sofa and armchairs were grouped by a side-table. It held a tea tray with a single cup and a plate of arrowroot biscuits. The nursemaid presumably had not been thirsty.

'There's a small kitchen at the back and I've converted the scullery to my darkroom. Would you like to see?'

'No need, thank you. I take it the chemicals are all safely stored?'

'Oh certainly.' Mr Winton looked alarmed. 'There's no possibility of a mishap.'

Reeve wondered over to inspect the varied props. A velvet-upholstered chair had been positioned in line with the camera and a rocking horse stood at a little distance. A large screen painted to suggest a garden stood against the wall, together with a wooden pillar and a section of balustrade made to resemble stone. An ornate wooden chair was by a rattan plant stand displaying potted ferns and a chaise longue sat next to a reading desk.

'That looks like an instrument of medieval torture,' he remarked, eyeing a wooden neck clamp with a heavy base.

Mr Winton laughed nervously. 'They can be uncomfortable, I'm told but they're often necessary. The ladies can find it difficult to hold a pose for very long.'

'Can you recall what Miss Chorley and her nephew talked about, while they were here, sir?'

'I don't consciously listen to the conversation of clients and besides the person sitting cannot speak. I'm sorry I can't recall anything significant. Miss Chorley was deciding on the pose her nephew should take. She wanted a three-quarter stance.' Mr Winton rested an index finger on his moustache as he thought. 'I had the impression that Captain Selden was not keen on being here. He had no real enthusiasm for having his likeness taken, it was to oblige his aunt.'

'How did you get the little girl to keep still?' enquired Reeve with genuine interest. Mr Winton turned to him, his features relaxing. 'Oh, that's easy, her sister stood right by the chair, the child stood on the fur and her sister had an arm around her waist. Sometimes I pose them with a hand on a pile of books. It all depends on what the mother wants. I have albums to show them and they pick out the type of setting they like.'

'It sounds as though you could do with an assistant,' continued Reeve. 'You've a lot to do with fetching tea and arranging props.'

Mr Winton picked up a child's riding crop which lay on the floor, tucking it into a box. 'It is a great deal to organise, there's my darkroom of course and accounts to be done. I hope to be able to employ an assistant in the future. I should like to advertise more, although word of mouth is the best recommendation.'

'I like the landscape you have displayed in the window,' said Abbs. The young man's face lit up.

'Do you really? You're the first person to mention it.'

'Where was it taken?'

'In Derbyshire, I was experimenting with light effects.'

'You're a long way from home then,' said Reeve.

'No, I was on a walking tour.'

'I didn't think you had a north country accent,' said Abbs pleasantly. 'Though I believe someone mentioned you hadn't been long in Seaborough?'

'No, I moved here from the next county.'

'What made you come here?' enquired Abbs. The photographer bent over his camera, his face hidden.

'Seaborough is a growing town and I read in a paper that a studio was closing. I'd been looking to set up on my own for a while.'

'Do you live on the premises?'

'Yes, I have two rooms upstairs. If that's all, I'll write down the Halesworths' address for you, Inspector.'

Handing Abbs the direction, Mr Winton hesitated. 'Mr Halesworth is a prominent person in the town. He's my landlord, genial enough but best to keep on the right side of him, so they say.'

The evening train was already in when Mr Halesworth hastened through the ticket office and across the platform. The smell of cinders was in the air and the engine steamed like an impatient dray-horse, the guard blew his whistle just as he flung open a door in a first class carriage and clambered swiftly aboard. The compartment he lurched into was empty save for a fellow sprawled behind the open pages of the *Flying Post*.

Catching his breath, he lowered himself into the opposite corner seat and shook open his own copy, bought on the way to the station. It was fortunate he had not missed the train and had a long wait, but events did tend to arrange themselves as he wished. The day had been a rewarding one and there was the pleasant feeling of having played truant. The lad and his mother had both been gratifyingly pleased to see him, far more so than his elder daughter and her mama. However life couldn't be all play and with these considerations Mr Halesworth dismissed the day from his mind and gave his attention to the stock prices.

It was only when they had passed the Venning tunnel and the train began to slow for the terminus that Mr Halesworth put aside his paper and took the slightest notice of his fellow passenger. He had been vaguely aware that the figure had slumped lower in his seat, snoozing beneath his broadsheet. Getting to his feet, he felt the other man seemed little inclined to leave the compartment. Glancing curiously at him, Halesworth suddenly saw the other's face reflected in the glass, lit by the last rays of the evening sun.

'Good grief, Avery. What the devil are you doing hiding yourself away there?'

The doctor lowered his paper and reluctantly met his gaze. Outside the lamps were being lit on the platform and above the sound of doors being heaved open, the voice of a porter could be heard. *'.... at Seaborough. This train terminates here.'*

'Halesworth,' said Dr Avery in a tone of resignation. 'You must excuse me, I was dozing and didn't realise it was you. I little thought to see you here.'

'Nor I you, what's the matter with your face?' Halesworth stared curiously at Avery and the angry red bruise across the side of his jaw. The doctor brushed it with his fingertips as if surprised to feel it there.

'It's nothing, I was asked to attend someone who turned out to be a drunk. In his stupor he lashed out and accidentally caught me. We had better get out,' he indicated at the porter who opened their door, touching his cap to Mr Halesworth.

'Where's your bag of tricks?'

'What?' said Dr Avery. He got awkwardly to his feet as Mr Halesworth stepped down.

'Your stethoscope and so on?' Halesworth waited on the platform as the doctor climbed down, wincing and holding a hand to his side.

'I don't take my bag everywhere. I wasn't expecting to see a patient,' answered Dr Avery. 'I'm extremely tired and not in the mood for an inquisition, Halesworth.'

'Steady on, old man, you look as though you fell down a flight of steps as well. That's what comes of trying to do someone a good turn, eh?' They walked towards the way out, Mr Halesworth slowing his pace. 'You didn't bring your cane either, I see.'

Dr Avery ignored him.

'Well, I can see you've had a rough day of it. I won't enquire what you've been up to.'

'Decent of you but I've nothing to hide. Nor have you, I'm sure.

'No need for the sarcasm, Avery. I've been to see someone on a bit of business, that's all. I'd as soon as it wasn't bandied about.'

'No one will hear anything from me,' said Dr Avery, coldly.

'Obliged to you.' They reached the station forecourt and halted on the corner beside *The Railway Arms*. 'Care to share a cab?'

'Thank you, no. We go in opposite directions.'

'Then I'll bid you goodnight, I'm for my supper.' Avery looked on while Mr Halesworth climbed into the waiting cab, giving his direction to the driver. As the sound of hooves receded, he leant against the wall, cursing inwardly. A knife-thrust of pain met his breathing and his brow felt clammy despite the cool evening. Halesworth was as great a gossip as the washer-women at the hospital. This meeting would be regaled and embellished to Hicks and anyone calling in at the billiard room of *the Marine,* were it not that Halesworth had obviously been on some dubious enterprise. There was no other cab and Dr Avery set about the slow, painful walk to his house, where he would bind up his ribs and attempt to disguise his condition from the concern of his kindly housekeeper.

Twelve

'So now you've slept on it, Reeve, does anything strike you about the witnesses we interviewed yesterday?'

Scratching his ear, Reeve felt his way cautiously. In his experience it wasn't common for an inspector to ask his subordinate's opinion. Generally they stuck to giving orders without explaining their thinking. Abbs was an exception, you felt he was training you up. And something more, that he was prepared to listen to what you said, was interested even. He found he didn't want to say anything foolish.

'Well, sir, about Mr Winton. I might be wrong...'

'Go on.' Abbs waited without showing impatience, which was one of the things that made him good at questioning people. Reeve had noticed that people responded well to that quiet, gentleman-like way of his. He let them talk and tell him things, like the solicitor who reeled off the important points in the will while saying he couldn't comment. He didn't bluster like Superintendent Nicholls nor crawl to his betters, though he'd seen Abbs flatter witnesses to disarm them.

'I thought he seemed uneasy the whole time. That's common enough when talking to us but it got worse when you asked him where he came from and why he moved here.'

Having stuck his neck out, Reeve waited anxiously for the response. There was little room in the small office Sergeant Tancock had given them and the air smelt musty. It was used as a repository for the usual files, lost property and equipment found in every station. They still had a few of the old-style larger rattles on a shelf, together with truncheons painted with the initial of the old king.

'I thought so too.' Aware that a pleased grin illumined Reeve's face, Abbs continued. 'Our Mr Winton struck me as evasive about his background and his reason for setting up shop in Seaborough.' He frowned in thought, then came to a decision. 'We'll leave it there for the moment, we've plenty of people still to see. There may be nothing in it. People have all sorts of secrets which are nothing to do with murder but we'll bear it in mind.' Glancing up at the small casement, Abbs saw that the rain showed no sign of lessening.

'One thing more, I was curious as to why Captain Selden has changed his mind about shutting up the house. You recall he said he intends leaving Miss Geake in charge?'

'Could it be simple kindness, sir? So she has a roof over her head while she obtains her next employment?'

Abbs shook his head slowly. 'It's a thought but I don't believe so. No employer shows that kind of consideration for their staff, inherited staff too. He's had no long contact with them, they're strangers. We know now that Tower House isn't his childhood home so he can have no sentiment about it. He told us he does intend to sell.' He paused to drain the cooling dregs of his tea. 'Why incur unnecessary wages? It would be more usual to pay off the servants and shut up the house until it can be sold.'

'Whatever his reason, it's a help to Miss Geake.'

'Yes, it is, I've a notion that lady is quick to turn events to her advantage. I'm afraid we shall both get wet, Reeve. You know your way?'

'I do, sir. Sergeant Tancock gave me directions.'

'Then I'll see you back here.'

Mr Hicks was privately of the opinion that every funeral he had orchestrated had been a dress rehearsal for this one. Miss Chorley's cortege would be the most prestigious he had presided over. He regretted that the dreadful circumstances dictated a smaller scale than would have been expected. Nevertheless there was an air of expectancy about his premises and the lists on his desk put him in mind of a general conducting a campaign. The outlay was considerable, from the hire of extra horses to the provision of four mutes to lead the procession. Then there was the necessary call at the hospital mortuary. The long delay since death rendered the customary lying of an open coffin at the deceased's home quite impossible. Now everything was ready and at short notice too.

'But how magnificent it will be, sir. I should say the finest cortege seen in Seaborough. What a feather in our cap.' Mr Biggs clapped his hands together, his eyes twinkling.

'I'd like the weather to look up,' said Mr Hicks. 'It'll be a shame if the mourners get soaked at the grave-side and the plumes bedraggled.'

Mr Biggs nodded, his expression solemn in an instant. 'Alas, that is beyond our control, though sunshine would seem equally inappropriate. A grey day would be best, sombre yet dry.' He indulged in his dry cough once more as Mrs Lavis manoeuvred through the door with a laden tray. 'Ah, a veritable angel.' He cleared a space on the desk by moving a box of black sealing wax and a torn open package from the stationers.

'Thank you, Mrs Lavis, that's very welcome,' said Mr Hicks. 'What do you think of this?' He handed her a stiff, black edged card.

'Shall I be mother?' enquired Mr Biggs and proceeded to pour.

'That does look fine quality,' replied Mrs Lavis as she examined the wording.

'Very dignified,' added Mr Biggs, peering over her shoulder. 'And a fitting sentiment. 'She'll be sadly missed, I don't doubt.' Mrs Lavis and Mr Hicks exchanged glances. 'Though only one family carriage needed and a single family mourner. One could wish for more. May I?' He took the card and studied it, running a long fingernail over the raised flower engraved to one edge. 'And the border, which flower did you decide on, Mr Hicks?'

'It's coltsfoot. Seemed the most appropriate for murder.'

'Ah yes,' murmured Mr Biggs. *Justice shall be done.*' A small silence fell. Mrs Lavis looked through the smeared office window at the yellowed leaves of the plane tree, hanging like limp handkerchiefs in the rain. Mr Hicks helped himself to a piece of shortbread.

A discreet cough broke the lull. 'Changing the subject, Mrs Lavis, have you seen Mrs Pardoe lately?'

'It's funny you should ask that. I did see her in the street this week and she seemed quite light-hearted. She was telling me she's ordered her winter coal, I don't know how. She's been the length of the alley asking to borrow a bucketful before now and I happened to see both her lads were wearing new boots. I'll be glad if the poor body has had some good fortune come to her at last.'

'An inheritance, do you think?' asked Mr Biggs with interest.

'I wouldn't have thought so. Bert Pardoe spent most of his wages in The Compass. She often had to fetch his suit out of hock. I can't think he had anything to leave her and I don't believe she has any family of her own.'

Mr Biggs slurped his tea noisily and set down his cup. 'Now that I come to think of it, Mrs Pardoe was wearing a new bonnet, trimmed with jet at Chapel last Sunday. Not one of ours, from a milliner's. Could she have earned something extra, I wonder?'

'Well, not by washing sheets at the hospital.'

'I daresay Caleb Halesworth has given her something.'

Mr Biggs turned round to his employer. 'I believe you've hit on it, Mr Hicks. That's one small puzzle solved. I do like to get to the bottom of things.'

As he waited, rain trickling down the back of his shirt collar, Inspector Abbs reflected on how much time he spent on door-steps. That and the writing up of notes and reports were the mainstay of his work. He had woken from a disturbed sleep filled with repetitive dreams as though he were awake and working. All the strangers he had recently met blurred together and the night hours became a treadmill of questions, sifting words and watching faces. Desperately trying to find a discrepancy or a lie, the loose end of a thread that followed would lead to the truth about Miss Chorley's murder. He awoke too with a fading thought that there was something he should have registered, a look on a face, a gesture?

He could not grasp at the lost impression, nor could he afford to fail.

He forced himself to concentrate by studying the Halesworths' home. It was a prosperous house, built within the last few years. The spacious front garden still had a raw look to it, the row of holm oaks behind the boundary wall were young and spindly. It would be a long time before they did justice to the name *Oakhurst*, inscribed on one of the brick pillars at the gate. The roof was many-gabled, edged with heavily ornamented barge boards and the red bricks were decorated with diamond patterns of contrasting grey. It was a house intended to impress.

The middle-aged parlour-maid looked pointedly at his damp boots as he entered and followed her down the hallway. Through an open door he glimpsed a highly polished dining table with a ruby glass lustre at its centre.

'The policeman, sir.'

The maid stood back for him to enter what was probably a morning room, situated as it was on the east side of the house. The man standing by the fireplace, ostentatiously consulting a gold watch as though he were in a tableau was the one he had noticed at the inquest, in the front row of the public. Mrs Halesworth was not present.

'You're on time, at least. I can only spare a few minutes. I'm Councillor Halesworth, my wife'll be along presently.'

'Inspector Abbs, sir, of the Exeter City police.'

'Sit if you like,' Mr Halesworth waved at a chair.

'Thank you, sir, you know why I'm here?'

'To hear what my wife has to say about who murdered Miss Chorley?'

Abbs smiled faintly at the other's directness.

'I doubt you'll get anything useful out of her. Women aren't observant, to my mind, not unless it's another woman's hat and so forth.' Mr Halesworth grinned suddenly and Abbs could see how people would find him charming when he cared to take the trouble.

'I daresay you're right, sir. I do see that it's distasteful for the ladies to be questioned, but in your position you'll understand that I have to see everybody who visited the house on that last day.'

Visibly relaxing, Halesworth straddled the hearth-rug, one thumb planted in his fob chain, from which a small seal dangled. Looking, Abbs thought, as though he were posing for his official portrait.

'Quite so, you have your duty, Inspector.'

'Perhaps you can tell me more about Miss Chorley, Councillor Halesworth. Did you know the lady well?'

'You'd better understand, Inspector, that this is a small town. Everyone in the same position in society knows one another. I wasn't a close friend of Miss Chorley but we encountered one another often enough. Though we may be small, we pride ourselves on our activities here in Seaborough, charitable works, concerts, and so on. I'm called to serve on so many committees, I need never spend an evening at home.'

Abbs nodded, deeming it best to keep his notebook in his pocket. 'I imagine that you can shed no light on Miss Chorley's death at all?'

Mr Halesworth spread his hands before him. 'It's baffling. She was an innocuous old lady. I suppose in such cases you always look to see who benefits? *Cui bono*, Inspector. That's my advice.'

'Thank you, sir. One of the servants at Tower House mentioned that you called a week before Miss Chorley died.'

Discreetly studying Halesworth's reaction, Abbs decided that most women would find him very nearly handsome with his thick brown hair and soft moustache but his countenance was unbalanced by a thin mouth, which hardened for an instant into a straight gash.

'Now I come to think of it, so I did.' There came a slight pause which Abbs did not intend to fill. 'It was of no account. I merely called in connection with the orphans, a request for a subscription.'

The door opened and Mrs Halesworth came in. 'There you are, Rosa. Inspector, you've already met my wife.'

Ignoring the armchairs Mrs Halesworth perched on a chair by a davenport in the corner. When Abbs resumed his seat, she looked up at him, her hands folded in her lap.

'What is it you wish to ask me, Inspector?' She in her turn glanced down at the watch pinned to her bodice. Abbs had the distinct feeling that he didn't have long, so decided to plunge in.

'You were a guest at Miss Chorley's house on the day she died. May I ask what time you arrived and left, Mrs Halesworth?'

'I was there shortly after three, that was the time specified.' Abbs nodded, encouragingly. 'It would have been acceptable to call later but these occasions are best at the beginning, if you ask me, when people are fresh.'

'Otherwise the tea and the gossip are stewed, eh?' remarked Mr Halesworth, by the window. His wife threw him an irritated glance.

'I was the first lady there, apart from Miss Geake, of course, who doesn't count. Old Mr Emerson was already installed at the tea table and Mrs Hicks came just after me.'

'Thank you, that's very helpful. So you were in a position to observe each of the guests as they arrived?'

'You could say so, though I don't make it my business to watch other people.'

'I think the inspector means to imply that not much gets past you, my dear,' said Halesworth.'

Mrs Halesworth sniffed.

'I know what you're going to ask me next and I can save you the time. You'll want to know if I saw anyone behaving out of the ordinary, being somewhere they shouldn't be?'

'You're absolutely right, madam.'

'Well, you're in luck, Inspector. Thinking it over after I met you yesterday, I did remember something of use to you. I saw Miss Shaw, that's the vicar's daughter slipping through the door that leads to the servants' quarters...' Mrs Halesworth paused briefly, 'and the kitchen.'

The stink of the seaweed had not been left behind in the town but seemed to linger in the fields thereabouts. It had been a single stop on the railway but a long, wet trudge from the station. The place was smaller than he expected, more of a smallholding than a farm. It seemed to consist of a few scruffy fields carved out from wild common of furze and a scattering of low scrub.

He didn't hate the countryside or even dislike it, decided Ned Reeve. It was more that it wasn't his world. His first ten years had been spent in the jostling streets of St Pancras where sellers cried their wares on every corner and working people of all description, Irish, Jews and Continentals lived in tall, cheap lodging-houses cheek by jowl with small businesses. His father's had been among them and helping with the cab-horse and peering through the railings of the Regent's Park had been the nearest to the countryside he'd ever known.

Even when his Pa died and his Ma followed within months, after he'd been fetched by his uncle to Exeter, he'd rarely ventured out of the city. There were vast areas of Devonshire he'd never seen, including until recently this lonely corner, which didn't have much to commend it. There was an emptiness to the country that made him feel uneasy and vaguely discontented, unlike himself. Though he'd been in many a tight spot, alleys and wharves where you didn't venture after nightfall and didn't linger by day, still he understood their lurking menace and knew how to defend himself. Wide open spaces made him feel the mark of invisible watchers.

Burrow Farm appeared to be mostly laid to vegetables with rows of thick leafy stalks growing on long ridges of the claggy red earth. He didn't know what they were. The fields nearest the track had been recently harvested, the soil churned up and littered with yellow leaves and stems. Near the buildings he could see signs of life, a single cow of the same red as the land and bedraggled brown hens. The place had a dismal aspect in the rain. It had lessened to what he had learned to call mizzle, the soft, wet west country mist that you scarcely noticed, though it soaked you through. No dog barked on his approach. There were nettles growing in the corners of the yard and a few tiles slipping on the mossy roof gave the place a slightly run-down look.

As he neared the outbuildings, the farmhouse door opened and a woman of indeterminate age stood waiting. Her scraped-back hair and sun-browned complexion gave her a harsh appearance but when he reached her, Reeve could see it was made up of fortitude and tiredness.

'Would you be the policeman?'

'That's me, Sergeant Reeve. You'll be Mrs Tucker?' He smiled in a way he hoped would disarm her, for at close quarters he could see the anxious expression on her face.

'The constable told us to wait on your coming, only I thought you'd be in uniform.'

'I'm with the detective branch, ma'am. There aren't that many of us in the county, as yet.' After nigh on nine years, he still enjoyed saying that. He did not announce as he could have done, that he was the youngest sergeant in the County Police and made up before his ten year service on account of a particular incident.

'You'd best come in, only...' Instead of standing aside, Mrs Tucker took a step into the yard, drawing the door half-to behind her and lowering her voice. 'Only I'd take it kindly if you'd keep your voice down. My man's upstairs, he's laid up with his chest. Our Mary's a good girl and not the sort to bring the police to our door. Her father's not best pleased about you coming and he's in no fit state to come downstairs. Everything's been said and he don't want it gone over again.' Her fingers kneaded a fistful of her apron as she spoke.

He hastened to set her fears at rest, speaking quietly. 'Miss Tucker isn't in any trouble, I assure you. Because of Miss Chorley's murder, Inspector Abbs, my superior needs to know of everything that happened at Tower House in recent weeks, especially any unusual occurrence. Let her tell me about her dismissal and that will be an end to it. It's just routine,' he ended, reassuringly.

Mrs Tucker looked earnestly at him and held back the door, waiting while he used the boot scraper. Stooping beneath the lintel, Reeve followed her into a dark passage with an uneven, flagged floor. A steep boxed staircase rose from one side. Motioning him through a door on the right, Mrs Tucker shut it quietly behind them. A young woman got to her feet, scarcely more than a girl and smoothed down her skirt. He explained again, speaking quietly. Mary Tucker gave him a pleasant smile and invited him to sit.

'Let me take your wet jacket, Sergeant and my mother will make you some tea.'

'That's very good of you both, though I don't want to give any trouble.'

'It's no trouble, we have it ready. It only wants the water.' She busied herself arranging his things over the back of a chair before the hearth while Mrs Tucker left them. There was an awkward silence which Reeve spent looking round the room. They had shown him into the parlour which smelt of polish and had a chilly, unused feeling with the fire but recently lit. On the mantelpiece with its crocheted scarf, two silver-coloured shells caught his eye. They were like the two halves of a giant oyster and stood at either end behind a candlestick.

Mrs Tucker returned directly with a tea-pot. He guessed it was their best china, taken from the corner cabinet. Gratefully accepting a cup, he swallowed a scalding mouthful before retrieving his notebook and looking at the two faces waiting expectantly.

'Miss Tucker, can you tell me how it came about that you lost your position with Miss Chorley?' The young woman didn't answer immediately, so he tried again. 'No need to be embarrassed, Miss. You wouldn't believe the things I've heard. Just tell how it was in your own words.'

A hint of anger flashed in her eyes, though she began to speak in a self-possessed manner. 'Beg pardon, sir, I'm not embarrassed. It makes me furious to think of it and I was just wondering how to begin.'

'Mary... best not make trouble,' said her mother, placing a hand on her daughter's arm.

'No, ma, I shall tell the truth.' Mary turned back to Reeve, looking at him directly. 'I was dismissed for stealing a valuable ring, sir, only I never did such a wicked thing. I was happy at Miss Chorley's house and my parents raised me to be honest. It's true, when a search was made of the servants' quarters, the ring was found in my drawer...' She drew herself up straighter and continued in a firm voice, 'but I never put it there. I've sworn on our Bible there and I'll do it again for you.'

'You're not in court, Miss. I shall write down your words and show them to my inspector.' Reeve took several hearty gulps of tea while he worked out what Abbs would likely ask next. 'Do you have any ideas on who did put it in your room?'

'I do, sir.' She shushed her mother with a gesture. 'I'm not feared to say it under this roof. I believe Miss Ada Geake, the companion did it to get me disgraced.'

'Why do you think that, Miss?'

'Because I knew she'd been looking in the mistress's desk. The ring was missed later that very day and I was packed off by nightfall.'

'I see,' said Reeve, busily scribbling. The old man was going to find this very interesting. He was glad to have something of significance to report back. 'So, let me get this right, you happened upon Miss Geake opening the desk, did you?'

'Not exactly. I went to the drawing-room to dust and I was deliberately trying to walk quietly because Miss Chorley had gone to lie down with a bad head.

She'd already reprimanded Sarah, that's the other maid, for making too much noise when she was brushing the stairs. The mistress was very sensitive to the slightest sound. Am I going too fast for you?'

'No, do go on,' Reeve smiled at her. Sitting side by side, he could see that Mary resembled her mother, only young and pretty at present. It was sad that women came to look careworn and pinched. Looking at Mrs Tucker's calloused hands he could understand why a position as parlour-maid in a fine house would seem an easier situation.

'When I entered the room Miss Geake was reaching up behind the case with a stuffed fox in. I saw her not directly, but in the mirror. Well, I wondered what she was about. At first I thought she was wiping her finger to check for dust, that's what the mistress would do. But it was a strange action so when Miss Geake had left, I felt there myself...' A burst of hoarse coughing erupted suddenly from somewhere on the upper floor.' The two women exchanged anxious looks.

'Father's awake. Shall I go to him?' They listened but the sounds subsided.

'I'll see to him presently. Finish your tale.'

'I pulled out a small key and knew it to be for Miss Chorley's desk drawer. I'd seen her fit it in the lock often enough but not where she kept it, so I knew what Miss Geake had been doing.'

'How did she know she'd been rumbled?' asked Reeve.

'I don't know. And I couldn't prove she planted the ruby ring from Miss Chorley's porcupine box but I know she did.'

'Did you tell Miss Chorley any of this?' Reeve found himself believing the girl.

'What would have been the point? There was the ring tucked among my nightgowns,' she blushed and went on. 'Miss Chorley saw it found herself. She was disgusted with me, after she'd given me my chance. She was always talking about honesty and moral rectitude.' Mary looked down at her lap, her voice fading away.

'Hush now, you know your father and I believe you,' murmured Mrs Tucker, patting her daughter's arm.

'Miss Geake was too clever to be there when the search was made. Mrs Watkins who's cook-housekeeper had to do it and she begged Miss Chorley to send me home without calling the police. Otherwise I'd be in Exeter gaol but I am innocent of all wrong-doing,' she finished.

'You won't do anything to my daughter, now she's told you this?' asked Mrs Tucker.

'Don't worry, ma'am,' replied Reeve cheerfully. 'Even if Miss Chorley were alive to lodge the complaint, there's no evidence. It's your word against theirs after the event. Try to put it behind you, I'd say.'

Mrs Tucker nodded, 'that's for the best.'

'But what about justice?' Mary's voice rose in a burst.

'Hush, girl, remember what I said.' Her mother gestured towards the ceiling. 'Justice don't put food on the table.'

Reeve got to his feet and picked up his things. 'Thanks for being so frank, Miss.'

'We won't have to have anyone else here, will we?' asked Mrs Tucker.

He dared not speak for Abbs, just in case he wished to see Mary himself. 'I can't give you an assurance, it isn't within my power. Anyways the inspector's a decent sort. If he does want to see you, there's nothing to worry over but I reckon he won't need to.' A sudden thought struck him, just in time. 'By the way, Miss, were you in the vicinity of Tower House at any time since you left?'

Mary looked evenly at him. 'I have to pass there, it's the lane down to Seaborough. Once I waited for Sarah, the other maid on her afternoon off. But I've never set foot in the grounds of the house since, no matter what anyone's said.'

The coughing started again as though someone were bent double, trying to rid their guts of a blockage. It was painful to hear and each effort more feeble.

'I'll have to go up, Mary will show you out.' Mrs Tucker hurried to the door.

'Many thanks for the tea.' They followed more slowly, Reeve carrying his damp bowler. Mary took a step in the yard with the door half-pulled just as her mother had done.

'The rain's stopped at last.'

'I'm glad of it. Is it just you and your parents here?' he asked.

She shook her head, 'I've a brother and sister at the school in the village. And my eldest brother went to sea.'

'What will you do now?'

'My father won't get better. I'm needed here now.' Her arms folded against the chill, Mary Tucker gazed at the long years across the empty fields.

Nodding clumsily, Reeve turned away. There was no more to be said.

Thirteen

'Reeve's not back yet, I presume?'

Sergeant Tancock cursed under his breath as his nib spattered ink on the ledger he was filling in. 'No, sir, it's a good walk from the station the other end.' Dabbing with blotting paper, he looked up at the inspector who had put his head round the office door. 'Can I be of assistance, sir?'

As Abbs came into the room and pulled out the other chair, he noticed the sour tang of pickles on the sergeant's breath and a greasy screw of waxed paper in the basket under the desk. He had called back at *The Anchor* for a quick dinner of bread and cheese while he mulled over his meeting with the Halesworths.

'I'd like you to send one of your constables round all the chemists to check their poison registers. Have them copy out the names for the last three months, if you please. We'll see if anyone familiar turns up.'

'I'll get someone onto it straight away, sir.' Sergeant Tancock made to get up but Abbs motioned him to stay.

'In a moment will do, Sergeant. Tell me, what do you know of Councillor Alfred Halesworth?'

The sergeant lowered his ample buttocks and pursed his lips thoughtfully. 'Bit of a mixture really, sir. He's a big man in these parts, fingers in lots of pies. Likes to think he practically runs the town.

You'll find a lot of folk'll speak well of him. He's generous with money for the needy and quite a favourite with the ladies, so I've heard, and he's full of energy, a great one for getting things done.'

Abbs waited but Tancock seemed to be finished. 'And the others? Those that don't speak well,' he prompted.

The sergeant grimaced, 'Well, sir, Mr Halesworth is all for change. He talks of building up Seaborough to be a smart resort. Why not, he says? Now we've the railway to bring more people in. We've only had the line two year, you see. Afore that you had to go by road from Kempston Junction.' He broke off to belch discreetly. 'Anyway, says he, We've the sea like Weymouth and Brighton and any fine place. He talks of building smart hotels, we've only a few, and The Marine's the only one you could call select. Then he thinks of pulling down the old town, that's beyond where you're staying and even building a pier.'

Thinking of Reeve's expressed fondness for lively seaside entertainment, Abbs suppressed a smile. 'And this is upsetting some residents?' Especially those poor devils whose abode is the old town, he thought.

Tancock leant back in his chair, more relaxed than he'd been since their return. 'People don't like change, do they sir? The thing is it's all very well to talk of investment and how it will help shopkeepers, hotel-owners and the like. Fact is it will help those already rich, don't everything?'

'I agree with you about people disliking change. I daresay many residents like Seaborough the way it is?'

The sergeant nodded emphatically. 'That's it. There's a lot to be said for a quiet life. Why, imagine the crime it'd bring.'

'Tell about Mr Halesworth's background, if you know.'

'He were a local boy. Come from Venning, the nearest village north-west of the town. That's where Sergeant Reeve took the railway to, this morning. His father were a small-time builder and that's where the money comes from. Alfred Halesworth and his brother built it up and up. Now his brother, Caleb that is, runs the business and Councillor Halesworth keeps his distance. He'll never climb a ladder again, not in his fancy weskets.'

Abbs was beginning to be amused by Sergeant Tancock's pictorial way of describing things. He had noticed that Mr Halesworth was sporting a slightly loud waistcoat for the morning. 'So if he's part-owner of a building business, that does explain why he's so keen to expand Seaborough.'

'He's quite the landlord too, buys up empty shops and they built a row of small villas near the church. I did hear Colonel Osborne's agent purchased some to lease out.'

'I interviewed one of his tenants yesterday, Mr Winton, a photographer.'

'I don't know him but I'd heard someone had taken over the premises in Charlotte-street. Mr Halesworth is known as a hard man in business, a bit quick to evict, you might say.'

'A person of contradictions,' said Abbs, 'though I suppose that can be said of most of us.'

'The doctor might be able to tell you more, sir. He's quite well acquainted with Mr Halesworth I believe.'

'That's useful to know.'

'He's joined some council committee or other on account of public health, I've heard him mention it. Mr Halesworth's closest crony is Nathaniel Hicks, the principal undertaker in the town, him that's burying Miss Chorley tomorrow.'

Abbs cast his mind back to the inquest. 'Is he by any chance a broad-shouldered man with a black beard?'

'That's him. He's well-liked and of a cheery disposition for all his calling. There's none looks more solemn when he's leading a procession. His wife's a pleasant lady, my brother's girl does the rough work in their house and she speaks well of the household. Mrs Hicks interviewed her herself and spoke kindly to her.'

'Does everyone in Seaborough know one another?'

'It sometimes do seem like it. The worthies of the town all congregate in the back room at the Marine. They say there's more committee work decided there than at the town hall.' Sergeant Tancock unbent so far as to scratch his belly as he reflected.

A sudden thought struck Abbs. 'Do you happen to know if Miss Chorley owned any land in the town, an empty parcel or dilapidated building?'

The sergeant shook his head. 'Afraid I've no idea, sir.'

'No matter, I'll look into it.' He stood up, yawning, 'I must get back. Thank you, Sergeant, that's been most helpful. Can you also point me in the right direction for the vicarage?'

'Certainly, sir.' The sergeant crossed the office and explained on the street map pinned to the wall. 'Now Reverend Shaw's a different kettle of fish. You won't find any to say a bad word about him, particularly not among the poor.'

'I think it's time I consulted the wisdom of the church.'

As Abbs walked briskly across the square he decided that his opinion of Sergeant Tancock's perspicacity was somewhat improved. He and Reeve would be required back in Exeter soon enough and Superintendent Nicholls would expect the murderer found. The answer would lie in sifting some fact of background knowledge. He needed to coax people to tell him that which they did not even know was relevant. Tancock's understanding of the suspects could be invaluable.

He couldn't resist taking a look at the church before calling at the vicarage. Though they would be there on the morrow to watch the interment from a distance, it would be impossible to view the interior. He had a liking for old churchyards with their higgledy sloping stones and ancient yews, they were peaceful places. Cemeteries were very different. They were desolate towns of the dead with their neatly laid-out avenues and walks, the chapel, their park-like railings, benches and lodge, their visitors dutifully attending the departed populace.

The parish church of Seaborough was a disappointment. It was to be found in the majority of English towns, built in blocks of modern grey stone with the addition of a short spire. Pausing, he read the board, St Edward the Confessor then entered the wrought-ironwork gates. The churchyard was not very large and seemed crammed with plots. He recalled seeing a cemetery as he and Reeve walked down the hill into the town. To one side a path led off to a gate in the hedge and he could see what were probably the eaves of the vicarage through the trees. Rising from the midst of a row of headstones was a prominent white marble cross. The shingle in the large plot before it had been heaped on the turf and sacking stretched across an open grave, weighed down with bricks.

The rain had stopped while he was writing up his notes but the darkening clouds overhead looked about to burst with another downpour. Jackdaws were strutting about the tombs, making their curious harsh call, their grey heads always putting him in mind of judges' wigs. A woman emerged from the church porch with an armful of golden-rod. She waited for him and smiled shyly as he drew near.

'Good afternoon, do you wish to look over the church?'

Abbs touched his hat. 'Good afternoon, madam. I should like to do so if it's convenient but I'm looking for Reverend Shaw.'

Her look became concerned. She had an expressive face, one which would make it difficult to conceal her thoughts. 'He is presently at home, sir, I'm his daughter. May I be of any help to you?'

'I believe so. My name is Abbs, I'm an inspector with Exeter City Police, here to investigate the demise of Miss Harriet Chorley.'

'I see.' Her face became pensive. 'Of course, my father said you would wish to speak to us both.'

He nodded pleasantly. 'Perhaps I might speak with you now, Miss Shaw? It shouldn't take long.'

'Excuse me if I just throw these away, then I'll take you to the vicarage.' He followed her a few paces until she tossed the stems on a heap by the wall. 'They would have lasted a little longer but they aren't suitable for a funeral service. Too cheerful,' she added, half to herself. 'We had the harvest thanksgiving on Sunday, this is a sad contrast. I came to make sure nothing has been overlooked.' He glanced up as fat drops of rain began to patter down. By unspoken consent they took cover in the porch.

'Are you in a great hurry, Inspector or shall we talk here? You said you would like to look over the church?'

'I should think this shower will pass over soon enough. It seems more like April than late September. Perhaps we could wait inside while you finish what you were doing, Miss Shaw.' He stood aside courteously, carrying his hat as she led the way inside.

'I know you and your father were among the guests at Tower House on the day Miss Chorley died, so I take it you knew her well?'

She stopped by the table bearing hymn-books and turned back to him. 'I'd known her since childhood and I met her often socially but I don't really believe I ever knew her well.' She obviously thought more explanation was required and went on, hesitantly.

'I was so much younger than Miss Chorley. She talked a great deal when we met but we were never intimate and she said simply what was expected of a lady of her age and class.' Miss Shaw coloured, 'excuse me, Inspector, I've said too much and find myself rambling without answering your question.'

'No, no,' Abbs motioned with his hand. 'I know exactly what you mean, Miss Shaw. What sort of things did Miss Chorley talk about?'

'The royal family, Mr Gladstone, the responsibility of the poor for their own plight. If there was any gossip at the meetings of our charitable ladies' society, she would have decided views on that. And she often spoke of her nephew when he was in India. She was very proud of his achievements in the army.'

'I've been told that Miss Chorley took a keen interest in the church?'

'She did, sometimes my father would have preferred it to be a little less, I think. And there was the hospital of course. I should say that the church and the poor were her most frequent subjects of conversation.'

Miss Shaw wandered a few paces towards the rear of the church. 'What I was trying to say, I suppose was that I don't know what she truly felt about other things. I sometimes think that we ladies meet and exchange a variety of accustomed responses; the weather, who was at a social occasion, concern for the needy. There is rarely anything fresh and none of us are saying what we really think. It would not be proper.'

'I believe it to be the same with men,' said Abbs. 'Perhaps only the working-class have the luxury of saying what they mean.'

'If that's so, it's the only one they have,' said Miss Shaw, soberly. 'Would you like a moment to look round by yourself, Inspector? I said I would check that all is ready for my father in the vestry.'

'Thank you, Miss Shaw, please take all the time you require.'

'I shall only need a moment.'

Abbs paced slowly about the nave, his footfalls echoing on tiles patterned with fleur de lys. An ornate crucifix stood on the altar, above which St Edward was depicted in richly patterned glass. An enormous organ dominated the wall nearby and the air held a lingering whiff of brass polish. That composite odour he rather liked in old churches, made up of damp hymnals, mice and the mustiness of centuries was absent.

'I'm afraid we have no treasures to show you,' remarked Miss Shaw, echoing his thoughts as she rejoined him. 'What you see here is largely Miss Chorley's doing. She gave the organ as well as the crucifix. My father would have preferred a plain cross.'

Abbs recalled the books by the bedside, ones she evidently did read. 'Miss Chorley was a devotee of Pusey and the high church movement?'

'She was. I think my father secretly wishes he had an ancient church with medieval brasses and a Crusader's tomb. He has an interest in antiquities.'

'I can understand that,' replied Abbs.

'Then he will enjoy talking with you. He rarely meets anyone new who shares his interests.' Miss Shaw's enthusiasm was suddenly displaced by an embarrassed expression. 'I was forgetting, Inspector, you are here on quite different business. What would you like to ask me?' She sank into the nearest pew and Abbs joined her, leaving space between them.

'Perhaps you could cast your mind back to the afternoon tea you attended on the day Miss Chorley died. Did anything unusual strike you about the occasion?'

'Only that it was most unusual for us to meet Captain Selden. Most of us had never seen him before and we were curious, I confess.'

'Did you like him?' asked Abbs. Miss Shaw seemed to have a lively insight which looked beyond social pleasantries.

'Yes, I did, he seemed a kind man, most attentive to his aunt, but he did not say a great deal. Miss Chorley was very... dominant in her ways. She often answered remarks intended for someone else. Captain Selden was quieter than I'd imagined an army officer. I had the impression he was more at ease conversing with Mr Emerson and my father.'

While he considered this, Miss Shaw turned her head and looked up at a memorial beneath the nearest window. Following her gaze Abbs saw that it was dedicated to the memory of Miss Chorley's brother James, *fought bravely at the Battle of Inkerman, died of his wounds 6th November 1854.* The day after the battle if he remembered rightly, *aged 32 years.*

'He was quite a lot younger than his sister,' she said. 'I believe Captain Selden's mother Caroline was a year younger than Miss Chorley. The Seldens come from somewhere in the north.'

'He did not visit his aunt as a young man, do you know?'

'Not at all, I think. I suppose he was away at school then the army. I have heard that his mama died when he was quite young so perhaps the connection was not closely kept up. I have lived in Seaborough since I can remember and do not believe he has been here. Miss Chorley would stay in London every year so they may have met there.'

Abbs found himself studying her face. Miss Shaw was past her youth and a little older than Reeve, perhaps just past thirty, he thought. While she would not be considered handsome by many, he found her countenance agreeable. He wondered irrelevantly if she was contented in her lot.

'Did any of the guests leave the drawing-room at any time?'

'All we ladies did at one time or another. After we'd eaten, Mrs Halesworth expressed a wish to see Miss Chorley's fern collection so she escorted us to the conservatory. The gentlemen stayed behind and come to think of it, Miss Geake returned before the rest of us. She was at the rear of the party and I recall seeing her slip out. There's nothing to be read into that,' said Miss Shaw hastily, turning to Abbs. 'She probably had a headache. I think her life was not always easy with Miss Chorley. I mean she was treated kindly but it must be tiring to be continually at another's beck and call.'

'Please go on.'

'Is this really useful, Inspector?'

'I know it can feel distasteful to be questioned about your friends and neighbours but an old lady has been murdered. I'm afraid it is necessary,' replied Abbs.

'It's so hard to believe that someone among us could be a murderer. Someone we see every week, who smiles and discusses the weather.' She was silent for a moment then fixed her serious gaze on him. 'May I ask you a question?'

'By all means though it may not be possible to answer.'

'Do you think one of us present on that afternoon poisoned Miss Chorley?'

Before he could speak, Abbs spun round as a sudden harsh sound reverberated in the church like gunshot. Miss Shaw flinched and looked over her shoulder. The door latch had been lifted and a woman stood, holding an umbrella and silhouetted against the porch.

'Adelaide, my dear, your papa sent me to fetch you. It's stopped raining.' She called out with a Devonshire accent soft as cream as she negotiated the single step, holding her wide skirt. 'Beg pardon, I thought you were alone.'

Miss Shaw slipped out of the other end of the pew. 'Inspector, may I present Mrs Nathaniel Hicks.'

'I'm glad to make your acquaintance, madam.'

Mrs Hicks returned the inspector's gaze with warm interest as though she had happened upon an unexpected treat. 'And I you, sir. Though the good Lord knows it's a terrible thing that's brought you to us.' Mrs Hicks glared meaningfully at the altar as though the Almighty should have known better. 'One occasionally hears of these dreadful things of course, but not in Seaborough.'

'I had intended to call on you, Mrs Hicks. Miss Shaw has been describing to me the tea you attended at Miss Chorley's house on the ....'

'Day she died,' broke in the newcomer. 'Don't let me interrupt you, sir. I shall sit here and wait, if I may.'

'I think Inspector Abbs needs to question us all,' said Miss Shaw, smiling warmly at her friend.

'Yes, to be sure he will. It is like one of Mrs Braddon's novels.' The cherries on Mrs Hick's bonnet bobbed in agreement as she sat.

'I was just relating how we went to see the conservatory,' resumed Miss Shaw.

'You want to know who had the means to poison the food and drink, Inspector? Of course we are all suspects,' said Mrs Hicks with relish. 'There was ample opportunity for someone to have poisoned Miss Chorley. When we returned from the conservatory the drawing-room was quite unattended and plenty of food still laid out. Do not you recall, Adelaide?'

'Yes,' said Miss Shaw, a shade reluctantly, Abbs thought. 'The gentlemen had gone to look over something in the library.'

'An atlas. Captain Selden had been telling them about his time in India. Is that the sort of thing you want to know, Inspector?'

'It is, thank you, Mrs Hicks. Where was Miss Geake at this time?'

'She came in from the terrace, saying something about feeling stifled and needing a breath of fresh air. Miss Chorley always had early fires, she liked her comforts. Mind you, Miss Geake could have put something in the food before any of us returned.'

Miss Shaw looked horrified and was about to protest. 'I know what you are going to say, my dear but there it is,' Mrs Hicks continued.

'I went to the kitchen myself,' said Miss Shaw. 'Our cook, Hannah asked me to speak to Mrs Watkins and enquire whether she wanted any plums for Miss Chorley. We've had a great many and they don't last.'

'It's the wasps,' said Mrs Hicks. 'They are still around and they do love plums.'

Abbs smiled politely and mentally dismissed one query.

'Is there anything else you can add, Mrs Hicks? Have you any suspicions regarding Miss Chorley's death?'

Shaking her head, Mrs Hicks looked regretful. 'I wish I could help you, Inspector but it is a great mystery. Somebody must have regarded Miss Chorley as an enemy but no one can work out who or why. We have all thought of nothing else.'

Not quite true, thought Abbs as he thanked the ladies. One person among you knows. Though they were not necessarily among the guests on that day.

'Shall you come and meet my father now?' asked Miss Shaw as they made their way to the door.

'I should like to, if he can see me. I imagine he will not be free at all tomorrow.'

'After the service in the morning he is going to Tower House. Mr Jerrold has asked my father to attend the reading of the will, which means Miss Chorley has left a bequest to the church. Come with us now and he will help you in any way he can.'

Both the vicarage and its incumbent were welcoming. The outer door of the former stood comfortably open to all callers. In its way the house was as ecclesiastical as the church with leaded glass and lancet windows but inside were all the appurtenances of a much-loved home. Following the two ladies, his quick eye had an impression of crimson turkey carpet, walls hung with water-colours and a rich, inviting aroma of something like mutton stew. Little Mrs Hicks replaced her furled umbrella in the hall-stand as though she were an accustomed visitor to the house and greeted the housemaid who took their things.

'You are most welcome, Inspector, Abbs... correct me if I'm wrong but does not that name hail from eastern England?'

'You're quite right, sir. My family came from Norfolk.'

The Reverend Samuel Shaw's face lit up. 'The locality of some of the finest churches in England. As a young man I once had the privilege of a few days walking tour there. I have never forgotten those wide skies with their church towers and windmills on a low horizon.'

'Would you care for some tea, Inspector?' enquired Miss Shaw. She rang the bell and cleared some space on a low table, her arms full of books.

'Thank you, Miss Shaw, I'd be most grateful.' Abbs took an ineffectual step forward to help but they were deposited on the window-seat before they toppled. He found the room unexpectedly disarming. How pleasant it would be to sink into one of the padded wing chairs with a cushion behind his head and eat hot buttered muffins by the fire. To sit in good company and talk of books or nothing at all, to be still and watch the flames. Mentally shaking himself he found the vicar watching him. His eyes behind his wire spectacles held a solicitous expression.

'We'll have tea now if you please, Betsey.' The young servant stared wide-eyed at him as she left the room. He was beginning to feel an object of curiosity to everyone in Seaborough.

'I suggest we retreat to my study and leave the ladies to their conversation,' said Mr Shaw. 'Through here, Inspector.'

The window of the study overlooked a rose garden to the side of the house, sheltered by a yew hedge. The vicar busied himself removing the fireguard and rattling the coals into a good blaze, enabling Abbs to look discreetly around. It had become instinctive over the years to make a swift survey of rooms to get the measure of their owner, a unpleasant trait, he thought.

A large oak bookcase held the obvious Bibles, collected sermons and other devotional works, along with several shelves of histories of Devonshire, its antiquities, geology and flora. There was also an extensive selection of poetry. A pipe-rack stood on the desk next to a volume of Mr Tennyson. A sheaf of inked papers were held down by an uncommonly shaped flint.

'Ah, I see my axe-head has taken your eye. It is remarkably fine, don't you think?' Mr Shaw handed the stone to Abbs who examined it with interest, tracing an edge with his index finger. 'See how well it was worked, it displays craftsmanship as skilled as any we have in our industrial age.'

'I agree, sir. Where did you find it?'

'A mile back from the cliff there is a hill-fort, from which in part Seaborough derives its name. It's a favourite tramp of mine when trying to tease out a sermon. You must view my small collection of arrow-heads and other knapped flints, for I can see your enthusiasm is genuine rather than simply courtesy.'

Leading Abbs to a cabinet, he pulled out a shallow drawer and they bent over the exhibits together. 'This one is particularly good. I am indebted to the rabbits who excavate the earth around their burrows, though I fear that does not stop me enjoying their meat. However I digress, I hear the sound of our tea coming, then you must ask me your questions.'

A cursory knock on the door was followed instantly by the entrance not of the same housemaid but a plump, grey-haired female bearing a tray.

'Thank you, Hannah, that's very welcome.'

'Thank' ee, sir, I can manage. You sit yourself there in the warm.' Abbs sat meekly in the armchair she indicated, while a cup of steaming tea was placed at his elbow, together with a plate of slices of fruit cake.

'You're most kind, that looks delicious.'

'You're very welcome, sir. Now Reverend, you won't forget to eat some? You'll see that he does, sir?' Fixing them both with a stern look, Hannah gave a satisfied nod and left them.

'Hannah has been with us for many years,' said Mr Shaw. 'Help yourself to sugar. We are very fortunate to have her devoted service. She is much more to us than cook.'

'I do appreciate your hospitality, sir.'

'It's the least we can do, Inspector. You come to restore order to our shattered community. How may I assist you?' Gone was the absent-minded air of a kindly, provincial minister, the vicar looked intently at the detective, a steely resolve in his quiet voice. Abbs felt he was catching a glimpse of how this unworldly-seeming man held his congregation from the pulpit.

'You've known your parishioners here for many years?'

The vicar nodded, 'that is correct. At least insofar as they allow me to know them.'

'Miss Shaw said something similar when I asked if she knew Miss Chorley well.'

'My daughter has a shrewd mind for a young woman. *Still waters run deep* as the saying has it.'

'I don't quite know what it is I come to ask of you, sir.' Abbs replaced his saucer and leant forward earnestly. 'There is no obvious motive for Miss Chorley's murder. You were of her circle and I want to ask if you can shed any light from your long observation of your parishioners, I suppose.'

A moment's silence and the vicar spoke again. 'On rare occasions someone in my position may gradually notice a troubled soul among our midst. There are small acts of malice perhaps, a word dropped into the wrong ear in seeming innocence. Someone who seems perfectly ordinary but in truth stands apart, manipulating for their own ends.'

'And you are saying that you know such a person? Someone in Miss Chorley's circle?'

'Ours is not a confessional church, of course,' replied the vicar in a gentle tone. 'But even so, if someone had confided in me something which could be construed as a motive, I could not simply repeat it to you, Inspector. That would be a breach of trust. By the same token I cannot give you the name of a parishioner whom I fear may have a warped character. I could be quite mistaken. Judgement is the prerogative of the Almighty, you see.'

'I do understand your position, sir. And that this is your home. My sergeant and I will be long gone when the repercussions of Miss Chorley's murder still linger.'

'Sadly, that is so.' The vicar looked away at last and gazed blankly at the glowing coals. 'I see you understand human nature very well, sir.'

'No death brings more loss than murder. There is not even a... a clean sort of grief for the mourners. One of the losses is privacy. I must come in and must sort through people's lives, turning over their secrets and all the small matters they prefer to keep hidden, like a scavenger sifting through a dust-heap.' Abbs took a mouthful of tea as though to swill the bitter self-distaste he heard in his voice.

'Your work must be extremely difficult and receive little gratitude but you are the instrument of justice, Inspector. No man should feel apologetic about his honest work.'

'I don't know about justice, Reverend Shaw. I leave that to the courts. I'm here to catch a murderer.'

'Of course.' The vicar added some sugar cubes to his cup and stirred his tea slowly as he thought. 'You mentioned grief. One of the saddest things that occurs to me is the lack of mourners for Miss Chorley's death. She never married and had no family left apart from Captain Selden.'

'And he had seen little of his aunt over the years. I do get the impression that Miss Chorley had long acquaintance rather than close friends.'

The vicar bowed his head in agreement. 'You have not spoken to Mr Emerson yet, I think? He was her nearest neighbour and knew the family well for many years.'

'Not yet, I intend visiting him at some point, after the funeral.'

'To answer your question, Inspector, I have no one in mind who could have perpetrated this terrible act. To take another's life – except it be judicial – is to risk salvation for one's soul. There may be some redemption for a desperate wretch who murdered in a second, in a brawl say. But surely this poisoning was a premeditated act?'

'Yes. The poison may have been carried around awaiting an opportunity but the decision to kill had to be planned.'

'Be assured, Inspector, if I knew of someone I thought capable of such an act, I would tell you.'

'Thank you, sir. It is useful to be able to speak frankly with you.'

'Is it possible that it was an act of revenge, think you?'

'There's nothing to suggest that,' answered Abbs.

'Then if the motive was not pecuniary, I wonder if the murderer was not in some kind of danger from Miss Chorley?'

'Danger... You mean because of something she knew? It's an interesting thought.'

'We are admonished not to think ill of the dead, Inspector. Miss Chorley did much good for the poor and sick. We owe our cottage hospital to her charity. However she was apt to differentiate between the deserving and the undeserving poor, if you follow me?'

Abbs winced, 'I do but that's a common feeling, surely.'

'One you share?'

'I've seen enough misery and despair in the backstreets of Exeter to know that the poor need decent food and lodging. How they came to that fix is immaterial.'

Mr Shaw smiled warmly at him. 'I hope you'll come and see us again, Mr Abbs if you wish to talk by the fire. The vicarage door is always open. Now please try Hannah's fruit cake or she will never forgive me.'

'Thank you,' said Abbs simply.

His expression growing grave once more, the vicar spoke again. 'There is only one pointer I can give you. Miss Chorley was a righteous woman. If she knew a damaging fact about another person... she would not temper earthly justice with mercy.'

Fourteen

A weak sunlight was seeping through the branches of the sycamores above the stable wall. There was a chance now that the rain had done that the morning would bring a fine day for the funeral. But if she knew Seaborough and she did, the damp with a mild air would bring fog. The seaweed hung outside the kitchen door had predicted the great sweep of rain and the old stick barometer in the hall said *change* when she'd rapped it earlier. It had been too much to resist, Miss Chorley had allowed no one else to touch it. She stood looking out of the window for this was the quiet hour of late afternoon when Jane had prepared the vegetables and it was not yet time to set the dinner on.

The Master and Miss Geake had both ordered a tray again, seeming to avoid one another's company. He spent every evening shut away in the library, the tantalus always within reach, smoking and going through old papers. Sarah had reported the state of the ashes with burnt fragments fallen in the hearth. Miss Geake had taken to having a tray in her room and she spent the evenings in the drawing-room, in her dead mistress's old place on the sofa. She'd even had the sauce to sit openly at Miss Chorley's desk and rummage through her stationery.

She looked around her domain, reflecting that she would never cook dinner for the mistress again. Ten years had woven grey threads among her hair and thickened her waist but there was vigour in her yet. She was luckier than most for never again would she have to take herself to an agency and plead to strangers that she was a good plain cook and careful with her accounts. Louisa had assured her that she only took a very genteel sort of boarder in Tunbridge. There were streets of fine shops to see and theatricals and entertainments of every kind. She'd see a bit of life and be more or less her own mistress at last. There was even the prospect held out of seeing London. Tunbridge had three stations and a trip to the capital could easily be had in a day. Well, she supposed she didn't regret Mr Jerrold persuading her to stay on another month. The extra wages were welcome but she would be glad to go to her sister, all the same. Good riddance to Seaborough and she wouldn't miss the sea at all.

Through the open scullery door Jane could be seen scouring one of the copper pans, the sink reeking of vinegar. Funny to think she'd normally be putting up jellies and preserves at this time of year. What would happen to all the utensils she'd used year in year out, which felt very like her own possessions? The china on the dresser made her think of the big tureens in the cupboard beneath. She'd always loved that navy blue pattern and wouldn't they be going begging? Miss Geake hardly came into the kitchen, no further than hovering in the doorway when she passed on her orders. Even she would have more to think about than china. The best service was kept in the dining-room sideboard and that would be accounted for.

Deciding regretfully that she could hardly have them packed up with her boxes, she dismissed the idea. She'd always coveted the lovely set of silver fish knives and they'd been forgotten in one of the sideboard drawers for a year at least, Miss Chorley having given up fish after she'd choked on a bone. Ada Geake would never think of those and surely she was entitled to a little present to send her on her way? And that happy thought led to a ripple of excited anticipation turning in her belly. She was to attend the reading of the will. Captain Selden had come into the kitchen, looking embarrassed and told her himself. And that meant Miss Chorley had remembered her or her name wasn't Bessie Watkins.

There was little to be done for the morning. In the circumstances Captain Selden was not receiving the mourners at the house after the funeral. Only those summoned to the reading of the will would be offered refreshment and little enough at that. Miss Chorley who had prided herself on keeping a good table would be turning in her grave. Her poor spirit would surely have no rest until the murderer were found. Captain Selden had been to the cellar himself to bring up the port and sherry. The funeral biscuits lay ready in the larder.

Entering the kitchen with a rustle of her black bombazine skirt, Sarah came to an indignant halt by the table, putting an end to her wool-gathering. 'Imagine what Miss Geake's doing now, Mrs Watkins.'

'I don't begin to guess, Sarah. It could be anything with that one. Tell us then.' Jane had come to the scullery door to listen, red-faced with a strand of damp hair stuck unbecomingly across her brow.

'The master rang from the Tower Room and it fair gave me a fright to see that bell jangle. When I got up there he's just inside the door and Miss Geake's standing in the middle of the carpet, looking pleased with herself. You know that tiny smile she does?'

'I've seen it often enough behind the mistress's back.'

'Well, you wouldn't credit it, the master told her to go through Miss Chorley's things and box them. *Take any garments you wish, Miss Geake,* he said. *I have no use for them.*' Sarah looked from Mrs Watkins to Jane to savour the full effect of her news.

The cook folded her arms to her bosom. 'It isn't even as though she were a ladies' maid, though I doubt Captain Selden would know how things should be done. She's a bit taller, though she can sell the dresses for a good sum and there's plenty she can wear. Did he include gloves and bonnets and such like?'

'I don't know, I'm sure,' replied Sarah, pulling out a chair. 'Everything I shouldn't wonder. He'll want it all gone.'

'Fill the kettle, Jane,' said Mrs Watkins, taking her place at the head of the scarred, deal table. No, she wouldn't miss the seaside at all and some real silver flatware would look a treat on Louisa's walnut sideboard.

'Commercial travellers,' murmured the publican's wife as she removed their supper plates. 'They're in good voice tonight. I hope they aren't bothering you, sir. I can ask them to keep the noise down.'

'Let them be, Mrs Gaunt, they aren't disturbing us.' Abbs smiled up at the publican's wife, seeming in unusually good spirits, thought Reeve.

'There's baked apple to follow or cheese if you prefer.'

'I've had sufficient, thank you. What about you, Reeve?' The sergeant brightened a little as he asked hastily for pudding. The inspector didn't often appreciate the importance of sustenance, having a poor appetite himself. He'd been on tenterhooks in case Abbs had suggested they leave the table and talk in his room. Though the inspector wasn't one to invite you into his private quarters, Mrs Gaunt had explained apologetically on their return that there was no spare parlour for them this time. He had eaten his beefsteak like a starving man and mopped up the

176

gravy until the plate was polished with the last of Abbs's bread.

Reeve was feeling thoroughly disgruntled with Seaborough, Inspector Abbs and their fellow diners. Their work was done for the day and they had nothing better to do than get steadily corned and exchange convivial stories. They had pushed two tables together in the middle of the room and were now calling to the waiter for more port. Earlier a couple of them had nudged one another and turned quite openly as he and Abbs had taken their seats.

It had been a long trudge in still-damp clothes to catch the train back after interviewing Mary Tucker, then a bone-rattling on the hard benches in third and a further walk back from the station. He'd missed his dinner and Abbs was off interviewing the vicar without him. He'd felt obliged to fall in with Sergeant Tancock's suggestion that he accompany a constable round the druggists, which meant more tramping in wet boots. Now his feet were smarting and the old man didn't seem as interested in his report about Miss Geake as he'd expected. Abbs hadn't even enquired about the poison register yet. The jug of hot custard that accompanied his bowl brought a small comfort, were he allowed to eat in peace. Pouring it liberally over his apple, Reeve listened gloomily as the inspector, after glancing at their companions, spoke again in a low voice.

'I was saying, it suddenly occurred to me that Mr Halesworth may have been proposing some kind of business deal with Miss Chorley. He may have an eye on a parcel of land she owned in the town. Alternatively, do you recall the doctor mentioning that the hospital is to be extended? I wonder if the builders have been appointed? That's a contract the Halesworth brothers would like to get their hands on, surely.'

'We know she sent him away with a flea in his ear, at any rate,' answered Reeve, indistinctly. 'It doesn't sound like a motive for....' Watching the worsted check backs at the other table, he tailed off, 'You know, sir.'

'I agree but we need to clear away anything unexplained, then the hope is that the solution will be left in plain sight. I intend a further word with the attorney in the morning. He'll soon be able to tell us if there's anything in my theory.'

'Won't he be busy all day with the reading of the will in the afternoon?'

'Undoubtedly but I'll catch him before he leaves for the funeral. It won't take long.'

'So do you reckon the servant girl's cleared away then, sir? I explained about the father.'

'Oh I should think so. Most of what we find will be irrelevant but it will take us nearer, Reeve. We mustn't be downhearted. Think of it as holding a thread in a labyrinth, we follow it to daylight.'

'Right, sir,' said the sergeant. There were times when Abbs had a curious way of talking. His head down, he concentrated on scraping the remains of his custard.

'We've achieved a lot in three days,' continued Abbs, his fingers tapping idly on his napkin. 'Only two more people to interview. First though, we'll have to get the funeral out of the way.'

'That reminds me, sir.' Pushing aside his bowl Reeve felt in his jacket pocket. 'You haven't seen the list compiled from the druggists', yet.'

'Ah, yes. Were there many premises to visit?' Taking the proffered paper, Abbs unfolded it as he asked.

'Only three. One in the High Street, Fore Street,' Reeve corrected himself. 'Another just off it and the third was a poky place in a back street. That's where I found a name we recognise.' Abbs raised his eyebrows and folded the paper again.

'He'll have an explanation, sir, like the vicar's daughter. They're all respectable as can be,' Reeve sighed heavily.

'One of them isn't,' replied Abbs. 'We shall enquire of the undertaker soon enough.'

The gas flickered and dipped behind its glass shade before casting its fan-shaped luminescence on the patch of ceiling above where Miss Geake sat. She was not given to superstitious fancies but this was no ordinary evening and, when a door shut overhead, she found her ears straining in expectation of the familiar footfall and tap of the cane. The mirror on the wall behind her was covered with black crape and the long-case clock in the hall was stopped. It felt as though the house was waiting. She had taken to usurping her erstwhile employer's corner of the sofa, the best-lit place in the room for reading. At first she had felt that the upholstery still bore the imprint of Miss Chorley's form, like the mustard-brown velvet worn shiny along the arm where her thin sleeve had rested and the bent old fingers fidgeted.

When the door opened slowly, she did not admit to relief to see Captain Selden step just inside the drawing-room. He brushed a finger across his moustache and spoke distantly, looking somewhere to her left.

'I have your reference, Miss Geake.' He held out an envelope with its flap unsealed. 'I've written what you wanted.'

'Thank you. You can leave it on the desk.' She enjoyed speaking coolly and watching him do as she wished. He returned to the door before hesitating.

'Was there something else, Captain?'

'Do you have any idea when it will suit you to leave here? I shall return to my post the day after tomorrow and Mr Jerrold tells me the cook is anxious to be gone.'

'I do not think I shall need accommodating for much longer,' said Miss Geake, thoughtfully. 'I have made all the enquiries I can about a new post and am waiting to hear any day.'

With a look of relief, Captain Selden stiffly bade her good night.

Miss Geake sat on, deep in thought. An owl hooted several times, each sound more distant as though a ghostly echo of itself. The coals sizzled and burnt low. Eventually she rose and began to pace the length of the room. Holding aside a curtain, she stared out. The night sky was clouded. Finally she sat at the desk and pushed away the envelope on the blotter without reading it. Placing a sheet of black-bordered paper before her, she dipped her pen in the ink and began swiftly to write.

Fifteen

When Abbs emerged from the front door of *The Anchor* he found that the sea opposite was gone, shrouded in fog. Somewhere nearby a muffin seller was ringing his hand-bell and his cry, vanishing down a side-street, sounded oddly discordant as though the fog were swallowing his voice. The herring-gulls usually raucous at breakfast time were silent.

It was the morning of Miss Chorley's funeral and at various places in and around the town, the society of Seaborough would be making their preparations to attend. As would he and Reeve, though in their case from a distance. First though, there was Mr Jerrold to be consulted. As he stood, he could hear the water washing steadily into the shore, a curious sensation when it could not be seen.

A seaside mourning, thought the inspector whimsically, as he recalled his conversation with the vicar. A sad business with the majority of mourners present only to show respect and no one truly grieving. Though perhaps that was as well, grief was not to be wished on anyone. Abbs turned his back on the coast, able to see a few yards ahead though the end of the street was lost in mist. As he walked cautiously, he wondered how the murderer was feeling that morning. Did they feel safe or did they live in fear of him and his powers of deduction? He could not afford to fail. And if he did, Reeve would be tainted by association with him.

Guessing that Mr Daniel Jerrold was unlikely to call at his place of business on such a morning, Abbs followed the directions he had been given to his home. At the junction with a busier street, he saw that a carriage and pair emerging through the fog had almost collided with a grocer's van, both drivers exchanging insults as they steadied the horses. He took a wrong turning and found himself in a quiet road of large detached villas. The pavements were empty apart from the footsteps of an elderly person somewhere behind him. They were guiding themselves with a cane which tap-tapped on every railing with the regularity of a blind man.

When at last he found Navarino-road his pace was slowed still further as he kept stopping to make out the name on a pillar. *Ivydene* had the solidly prosperous appearance he expected; an enormous monkey-puzzle dominating the front garden, its stiff branches reaching towards the upper sash windows. The door was opened swiftly by a pretty parlour-maid in a smart uniform. On explaining who he was and asking to see her master, she shook her head doubtfully.

'I'll enquire but I doubt Mr Jerrold is at home to visitors.' The front door was left ajar and waiting under the porch, Abbs, who possessed excellent hearing, could catch the dismissive tone of the attorney's response.

'I'm sorry, sir, it's as I thought. Mr Jerrold cannot see anyone today. He says you're to make an appointment to see him at his office.'

'Please tell him that I regret disturbing him at this hour but need to speak with him on police business. It will take only a moment.' As the maid vanished again, Abbs wondered if he had been unwise to press the matter. There was no more time for reflection as the door opened wide enough to admit him and he was shown into the inner hall.

'Who was that, Ann?' called a voice on the stairs. Looking up, Abbs saw a grey-haired matron, dressed in a dark plaid, poised with one hand on the bannister. 'Do try to keep the damp air out.' Before the maid could answer, a door to the right opened and Mr Jerrold came out.

'It's nothing for you to concern yourself about, Alice,' he said testily before turning his back on the speaker. The woman's eyes met Abbs's for an instant with a hint of sympathy before she retraced her footsteps and disappeared along the landing. Mr Jerrold frowned dismissively at the hovering maid who bobbed and escaped into the rear of the house.

'What is the meaning of this intrusion, Inspector? Anything you wish to say can wait until this day is over. Where is your respect, sir?' Knowing he trod on suddenly shifting ground, Abbs hesitated a second too long in selecting his reply.

'Well? Have you nothing to say for yourself, now you've thrust your way in at the *front door* of my private dwelling?'

'I apologised for presenting myself here but you know my business, Mr Jerrold, I'm trying to catch a murderer. I cannot interview anyone today and we can't afford to waste time. I must do what I can to further my enquiries.' The detective's reasoned tone failed to pacify the attorney. He was already wearing a black necktie, noted Abbs and his silk mourning scarf hung from the hall-stand by his frock coat and top hat.

Deliberately consulting the lantern clock, Jerrold eyed the inspector as though a street-urchin were oozing mud on his carpet. 'Five minutes, Inspector. And I strongly object to your manner. I hardly need reminding that my late client has departed this life at the hands of a ....' glancing behind him, 'of another,' he hissed.

'I won't waste any more of your time, sir. What I need to know is this, did Miss Chorley own any other property in Seaborough?'

The attorney stared at him. 'Property, is that all?' As Abbs waited in silence, he continued in a chilly tone. 'She owned several small cottages in the old town, which were inherited from her father. When the railway came a few years ago and new adjacent streets were laid out, I purchased a few terraced houses on her behalf. This was in my capacity of managing her investments. In addition Miss Chorley also owned various small properties in Exeter. Does that answer your vital question, Inspector?'

'Partly, thank you. Did she own any parcels of land in the town that are not built on?'

'There is one such as you describe on the edge of the town, it is presently let to a farmer for rough grazing.'

'Would this be on a long lease?'

Mr Jerrold gave an exasperated sigh. 'My son Arthur dealt with it. Without consulting our records... no, I believe it is let by the half-year.'

'I've only one further question for you, sir. Would Miss Chorley in your opinion have been likely to sell any of her holdings?'

'On no account. She lived on her rents and never touched capital. She believed there was no greater security than property.'

'I see, thank you for your time, Mr Jerrold. I'd be obliged if you would arrange to have a copy of the will left at the police station after it's been read.'

'Your officer may collect one from my clerk this afternoon.'

'As you wish, sir. Then I'll bid you good morning.' Abbs bowed and turned to leave.

'One moment.' The attorney waited until Abbs had swung round. 'I am dissatisfied with the manner in which you conduct your investigation. Instead of enquiring after strangers, you appear to spend all your time questioning Miss Chorley's own acquaintances and troubling highly respectable people such as Councillor Halesworth. I think you forget your place and take too much on yourself. You are a public servant, man. I wish to take the name of your superior officer.'

The cortege had made its stately way along Fore Street, moving at slow walking pace and passing the lowered shop blinds beneath their sagging awnings. People stopped to watch the procession, falling silent, the men pulling off their caps and bowing their heads as it drew near. The featherman carrying his staff of swaying black-dyed ostrich plumes led the way, followed by the town's principal undertaker carrying his black wand. Four solemn mutes walked behind him, two by two, their weepers streaming down from their top hats. The hearse was a sombre spectacle, led by two pairs of gleaming black horses, their feathers dipping and nodding as they moved under the direction of the coachman, his whip decorated with black ribbon bows. It was an unusual hearse with etched glass sides through which the oak coffin could be seen, its lid heaped with silk flowers.

As the cortege looming out of the fog reached the church gates, a single bell began to toll insistently above the slowing of mourning coach-wheels. The chief mourner descended first and was led into the church by Reverend Shaw. The others followed, Mr Jerrold close to Captain Selden, Colonel Osborne the Coroner, Dr Avery, among many others they could not know. Sergeant Tancock represented the Constabulary in his best uniform. Their dark garb put Abbs in mind of a straggling line of crows.

'You probably reckon this as really bad, sir. But it's not, you know, nothing like.'

'What?' said Abbs belatedly as Reeve's words sunk in. He turned to look at his companion who was leaning against a tomb and stuffing his hands in his pockets.

'The fog. This is absolutely nothing compared to a real London particular. For a start it's mostly from the sea, isn't it?'

With an effort Abbs dragged his unproductive thoughts back to where he was, aware once more of the distant notes of the church organ, 'Yes, mostly a natural phenomenon, though the fires don't help.'

'Nor that gas. If you ask me sir, Seaborough stinks something rotten.'

'Best not to air that at the station, Reeve,' murmured Abbs dryly, 'though I have some sympathy with your view.'

'Oh no, course not, sir. I wouldn't go carping at a man's home and they're all very decent coves. I'm only saying this don't compare with the fogs I mind from boyhood. You could pass within a yard of your own mother and never know. Folk stumbled along clutching at walls else you'd find yourself run down. This is bad for Devonshire, mind,' conceded Reeve generously. He paused to scrape some mud off his boot along the kerbstone of the grave beside him.

He was right at that. The sickly stench emanating from the *Seaborough Gaslight and Coke Company* permeated the fog and crept into Abbs's throat, making him choke. A weak yellow light shone through the fog behind the cross on the church spire.

'Feeling better?' he enquired. The discourse on the weather had been delivered in his sergeant's accustomed light tone. Reeve looked at him with a sheepish grin. Abbs gave him a rare, brief smile before turning away into a companionable silence.

He had been wrestling with the matter of Mr Jerrold. Trying to work out whether the man's dignity would be assuaged by his parting remarks or if he would complain to Superintendent Nicholls. Even if Jerrold did not act on his veiled threat, he did not expect them to be allowed much more time in Seaborough. On one thing he was determined, if he had to defend his conduct of the case to Nicholls, he wanted to keep young Reeve out of it. Though Nicholls would have to think hard before dismissing an officer with a commendation for bravery, there was a danger the sergeant could find himself out of the detective branch and a beat constable once more.

'Here they come, sir.' Reverend Shaw, wearing his funeral surplice was emerging from the porch and leading those of the mourners who wished to follow behind the coffin to the grave. The undertaker's men pushed the bier along the shingle path as far as they could before carrying the elaborate coffin to the edge of the waiting hole. From their position discreetly hidden by an evergreen oak, the two detectives should have had a good view of most of the churchyard, were the scene not partly obscured by the shifting fog.

The mourners stood with bent heads as the vicar spoke the final words. One of the undertaker's men stood behind Captain Selden with the customary box of earth to be scattered on the coffin. Suddenly Reeve turned to Abbs and whispered rapidly. 'Over there, sir. Do you see behind that angel? Someone else is watching.' Abbs looked to see a muffled figure crouching behind a winged stone figure. Male certainly but the mist made it impossible to tell if the person was someone they had met.

'See if you can get round the other side and find out if it's anyone we know,' Abbs instructed in a whisper. 'But whatever you do, don't let the funeral party see.'

With a swift nod, Reeve moved off silently, taking a wide circuit. Abbs watched tensely, one eye on the sergeant and the other on the mourners. Thankfully their attention was on the coffin now being lowered into the grave. Reeve had disappeared from sight, making his way behind the church. When Abbs peered again a second later, the figure had vanished. There was no point in staying where he was any longer so he made his way to the gate and prepared to lurk unobtrusively behind the last carriage.

It was shortly after that the first members of the funeral party began to leave the churchyard. Abbs stepped back, not wanting to run into Mr Jerrold. He saw no one he recognised, Captain Selden was probably receiving condolences and talking to the vicar. Then he saw a face he knew, a gentleman was saying goodbye to Dr Avery. The doctor turned to step into a carriage and as he did so, Abbs noticed an ugly bruise spread along his jaw.

He was alone again, the first conveyances having moved off when Reeve appeared, red-faced and panting with his exertions. 'Sorry, sir, I lost him. He saw me and made himself scarce. Went and bolted through a gate in the hedge and down someone's drive.'

'The vicarage,' said Abbs while Reeve straightened up.

'I followed him but I went and tripped over. Time I got to the street, he'd disappeared. He didn't come this way?'

Abbs shook his head. 'That's a pity but not your fault, this wretched weather.'

'It doesn't matter, sir. I know where to find him, I recognised him.' His breathing returning to normal, Reeve looked pleased with himself. 'It was the photographer chap, Mr Winton.'

When she finally heard the rattle of carriage wheels, Adelaide quickly put down her sewing and hurried to the window. The fog had cleared by late afternoon and the night sky was scattered with stars as she watched her father set down, in the light spilled from the open door. By the time she reached the hall, Isaac was already turning on his way to the stable and Betsey had taken an armful of rug from the vicar. Adelaide watched approvingly as she helped him off with his travelling coat and collected hat and gloves. She was a good willing girl and coming along nicely under Hannah's tuition. Adelaide herself was helping Betsey with her lettering and fine stitching. She was filling out at last with plentiful good food, her face losing the pinched look she had when she came to them.

'That will be all for tonight, thank you, Betsey. I'll see to it if we need anything else.' Adelaide dismissed the girl, knowing she had little enough time to herself. Although she hoped theirs was not an arduous household, Betsey would still be up at six to see to the fires. At least she would have an easier time with them than straining her eyesight in a factory.

She watched her father fondly as he replaced his town stick, as he called it, in the hall stand. He was very attached to his handsome partridge wood cane with its silver collar, an inscribed present from the congregation of his first parish, on the occasion of his leaving. It lived beside the sturdier blackthorn he used on his country walks.

'Would you care for some refreshment, Papa?'

'Nothing, thank you, my dear. Captain Selden and I dined very well. I am glad to be at home though, the nights are turning chilly.' Mr Shaw held out his hands to the drawing-room fire as Adelaide resumed her seat.

'That feels better. The rooms at Tower House are of such proportions as to be draughty away from the hearth. Despite its grand furnishings, it is not a comfortable house.'

'Nor can the occasion have been, I should think? It was kind of you to keep the Captain company.'

Mr Shaw took his tobacco jar from the mantelpiece and began to fill his pipe. 'It was the least I could do. He's most anxious to return to his home in Hampshire and resume his post for the time being, at least. Whether he intends to leave the army, I know not. He is now very comfortably off but he is adamant that he will sell the house. It is good of him to keep it open until Miss Geake can leave.' Pausing while he opened the match-safe, Mr Shaw continued. 'He is away in the morning and it is probable we shall not meet him again. What a tragic end to his long-promised visit.'

'Indeed but at least he saw his aunt once more. Had he not brought forward his visit, he would not even have had that. He knows that seeing him made her last days happy.' Stooping to add some extra coal, Adelaide looked questioningly at her father when he did not answer. 'Papa? Are you very tired?'

Mr Shaw smiled gently at his daughter's solicitous expression. 'It has been a long day,' he admitted. 'I hope you are right, my dear, but it occurs to me that Miss Chorley may have been murdered *because* of the Captain's visit.' He fingered the bowl of his pipe absently, 'though it makes no sense at all.'

'Unless he was intended to be blamed,' said Adelaide slowly. 'A kind of scapegoat,' she shivered and drew nearer the fire. 'Do you think Inspector Abbs will find out the truth?'

'He struck me as a very intelligent man,' replied Mr Shaw. 'Sensitive too, which must make his work more difficult, I should think.'

'He had rather a sad face, I thought, but then I suppose a policeman would be with all the awful things they see.' Picking up her thread-work, Adelaide resumed with a brisk voice. 'How was Miss Geake this evening?'

'She did not join us at dinner, saying she had a headache. She told me beforehand that she has heard from a prospective employer only this morning, a widowed lady living in Guildford.'

'I hope she gets the position and that the lady is congenial. It must be a worrying time for her.'

'Yes, with a detective less acute than Inspector Abbs, she could even have been arrested.'

'Do you really think so?' said Adelaide. 'I only meant it must be alarming to lose her home and have to suit a new employer,'

'The poor lady has had a most unhappy time.' The vicar drew on his pipe, hesitated and went on. 'I know I can trust your discretion, Adelaide. Miss Geake has received a legacy but it is not large. I think it may have been smaller than she was expecting.'

Adelaide nodded but did not comment. Privately she was not surprised. Miss Chorley had been generous with her funds for charitable endeavours but she had noticed long since that petty economies were practised on her household. She had more than once seen Miss Geake dispatched on a trivial errand on foot in the wettest weather and heard Miss Chorley remark that the exercise would do Ada good. She had also had an unpleasant habit of speaking about Miss Geake as though she were not present. Hannah too had often reported that Mrs Watkins was instructed to be less extravagant with the servants' food.

'However,' added Mr Shaw, his expression brightening, 'Miss Chorley has left an extremely generous sum for the Church, one hundred pounds!'

'Oh Papa, that is a huge amount. You must be so pleased.'

'It is a chance to do some real good. Miss Chorley has left a similar sum for provision for the hospital. Some of the legacy is to be used on charitable works as I see fit and part has been set aside for the erection of a lych-gate in her memory. It will be a handsome addition to the churchyard and of practical benefit in poor weather. We shall make sure it has benches. It cannot be constructed yet, of course.' He looked gravely at his daughter. 'It would not be fitting until justice has been done.'

It had been a long, tedious day. The work of a police officer necessitated hanging around for lengthy spells of time but at least as a uniformed constable he had been moving at his own pace. A change to the detective branch had involved learning to follow criminals; the skills of loitering seemingly aimlessly, observing the suspect through shop windows, dodging into alleys to avoid being seen, trailing someone through a crowd, watching all the while for flimps and fine-wirers, waiting outside shady lurks, all without being spotted and with an eye to your back. With promotion came longer hours at a desk and finding ways to interview the quality without giving offence. It seemed he had failed dismally at the latter.

Turning over and thumping his pillow again, Abbs flung himself on his back and stared into the darkness, gradually making out the shapes of curtain, chest of drawers and wash-stand. His head was too peopled for sleep to come. Jerrold was a pompous fool and probably would enjoy writing a letter of complaint to Superintendent Nicholls. He had a couple of days' grace before any summons back to Exeter to explain himself. Even then there was a fair chance he would be allowed to continue, there being only four detectives of his rank in the county. It depended on what criminal activity was taking place elsewhere. He would resent being taken away from this case. It presented a great puzzle but there was a solution and he meant to find it.

Which led back to Philip Winton. He had spent part of the afternoon reading back through his notes. What was it the photographer had said? *I grew up in the next county.* He had been careful not to name it, let alone mention a town or parish. There was little point in speaking to him again at present, he still felt. Reeve, like an eager terrier with his tail a-quiver had been all for going straight to the studio but he had pointed out that curiosity was no crime. If Winton had some stronger reason for watching the burial, he was unlikely to tell them. Best to leave him unsure whether Reeve had recognised him. Frustrated, Abbs wished he could recall whatever was knocking at the edge of his memory. There was some tiny fact he had noticed when they visited the photographer's studio, but try as he might he could not retrieve it. Nor was it to be found in the careful memoranda he had made after their meeting.

Life had seemed much simpler in his early days in the force, he thought. First working his beat in a small market town, then being appointed constable in a strung-out village much like the one where he had grown up. He could name every poacher and the gypsies who visited the district each year. A useful life but he had been keen to get on. Promotion and transfer to the county's fledgling detective branch came in the same year, encouraged by his own inspector who brought him forward. Later came a further step in rank, meeting Ellen and her not wanting to give up her Devonshire home for him. Abbs slammed shut the door on his past and determined to compose himself for sleep, turning again and shrugging the eiderdown about his shoulders. Though it was a long while before his breathing slowed in rhythm with the susurration of the waves.

Sixteen

There was no one on the desk and the empty outer office resounded with yells and cursing coming from the short corridor that led to the pair of cells. Beneath it all came a repeated groaning.

'What the devil's going on?' muttered Abbs. He had slept badly and sent Reeve on ahead, saying he wanted a word with the landlord.

'S'cuse me, sir,' said a young constable, emerging from the other door. He passed Abbs with a tray bearing several tin mugs of tea. 'Got the cells full to bursting. There was an affray outside The Compass last night and we had to arrest five of them. It's been like Bedlam here since dawn, this might quieten them down. Honestly you'd think they'd have slept it off by now. Two of them's Irish, you see.' He rolled his eyes and made for the passage, slopping the hot liquid as he went.

'Is Sergeant Reeve about?' asked Abbs.

'He's gone for the doctor, sir,' called the constable. 'Seems now one of them reckons he's broken his arm. Sergeant Tancock's in there with him.' Abbs followed to see for himself. The floor of the corridor had a large recently cleaned patch and a mop and bucket stood propped against the wall. A pungent reek of tar soap overlaid but did not conceal the sour taint of vomit.

'Give it to me,' he took the tray from the constable while the latter reached for the key hanging beside the door and unlocked it.

'Thank you, sir. Now then Paddy, pipe down. The Inspector's here and he doesn't want to hear your foul language. Drink this and shut up, begging your pardon, sir,' he added.

Abbs looked in at a sorry sight. The dishevelled rough who'd been making all the racket was already grasping the mug and gulping down his tea. One of his eyes was blacked and half-closed, his knuckles were scraped raw and there were blood stains on his ripped sleeve but he seemed none the worse for it, grinning at him and revealing several brown, crooked teeth as he wiped his hand across his mouth and belched in satisfaction. His mate lay across the narrow cot, his arms behind his head, after an indifferent glance silently ignoring them and the tea set down beside him. Dried blood was caked about his nose and had dripped down his waistcoat. Abbs guessed that his assailant had come off worse.

'It's Constable Dean, isn't it?' he asked when they were back in the cramped passage. 'You took Sergeant Reeve around the druggists'.'

'That's right, sir.' Eager-eyed, keen to oblige and a door-knocker beard, Abbs had noticed him about the station. The other cell door was ajar and Sergeant Tancock eased himself through as they spoke.

'Mornin' Inspector. If you're wanting your sergeant, he offered to fetch Dr Avery. The doctor shouldn't have left for the hospital yet so they'll be back soon. Sorry about all the row,' he finished awkwardly.

'Not your fault, sergeant. How's the injured prisoner?' Abbs peered into the crowded cell where one of the men crouched by another who was sitting on the cot and nursing his right arm, white-faced. A third, older with white stubble was slumped against the wall behind the door.

'He'll be all right. He were fairly quiet for most of the night but now he's been complaining fit to wake the dead. Best to let the doctor see him, I thought. I'm a man down after arresting them, he's gone off duty with sore ribs and the others are out on the beat.'

'D'you often get this kind of trouble?'

Sergeant Tancock yawned copiously as they moved back to the entrance.

'Every now and then. It'll be quiet for months then suddenly there'll be a rumpus in one of the lowest pubs. Often it's between the fishermen like, but this lot are labourers for Halesworth's. They'll have had their pay and tempers flare when there's strong drink taken, as you know, sir.'

'Not so long ago they had a death at their building site,' added Constable Dean as he joined them. 'One of them fell from scaffolding, he was a regular customer of ours for being disorderly.'

'Was his death an accident?' enquired Abbs.

'Oh yes, sir,' replied Tancock. 'I looked in to it, myself. He wasn't drunk and no one was near him when he fell. E'd been feeling ill, according to several accounts, his widow and others, complaining of dizziness like. He probably shouldn't have been up there but no one could say it was Caleb Halesworth's fault. Bert Pardoe wouldn't have said anything. No one can afford to be sent home or laid off.' Abbs grunted, sympathetically. Losing your work was the path to ruin.

'Get you a cup of tea, sir?' enquired Dean.

'Not now, thanks. I'll step out for a bit.' Another hot drink would have been welcome but fresh air would do more to clear his head. There was no sign of the others as he looked along the street. A quiet, grey morning when the day seemed as little awake as he felt himself but at least it was dry and clear. He had reached the bottom of the square and was strolling past one of the imposing bank premises when he heard his name hailed. A carriage was pulling in to the kerb and Captain Selden had his head out of the window.

'Inspector Abbs, I was on my way to see you.' He stepped down, glancing up at the coachman. 'I won't be a moment, William.'

'I'm glad you caught me, Captain. What can I do for you?'

'It's nothing like that, I thought I should inform you that I'm returning to Hampshire. I'm on my way to the station now.'

'I see. Thank you for letting me know, sir.'

'The staff are on notice but the house won't be closed up until Miss Geake leaves for her next post. By all means call if you need to see anything again or talk to the servants. Mr Jerrold will see to paying them off and having the place sold.'

Abbs noted the stony face of Miss Chorley's man William sitting on the box, the reins held loosely in his lap. 'That's good of you, sir. On behalf of the Constabulary I should like to offer our condolences again and give assurance that we are doing our utmost to solve the crime. We shall not give up, Captain, and you will be kept informed.'

Flushing slightly, Selden looked at his boots and rubbed a finger across his moustache before meeting the inspector's gaze. 'Thank you, Inspector, your remarks are appreciated.' He looked around at the esplanade and the line of beeches behind him. 'It's all been well... terrible. Frankly Abbs, I shall be glad to get out of Seaborough and never see nor hear of this benighted place again.'

'That's understandable, sir. I wish you a good journey.' Nodding sadly, Selden turned away and got back in, rapping on the roof with his cane when he was seated. Abbs stood watching as William set off along the foot of the square and across the far side. A few russet leaves drifted down in their wake.

'What's been going on here? I thought the outside was all finished?' The workman who'd been tunelessly humming through closed teeth, jumped at the sound of a voice at his shoulder. Carefully setting down the pane of glass he'd been holding up, he turned to answer. The sarcastic reply died unspoken as he saw it was Councillor Halesworth.

'A pane got cracked last night. Won't take a minute to whip out,' he offered. Mr Halesworth looked the fellow up and down, from the stub of pencil behind one ear to the scuffs on his boots. 'Mind you do a neat job, then. I shall inspect it when I leave and I'll be having words with Sergeant Tancock about this.' With a self-satisfied nod he dismissed the workman from his mind and entered the town hall. Even so, his good mood was not sullied. While an assault on what he almost considered his private fiefdom was an outrage, he would rather relish giving the policeman a verbal leathering. Public order was a serious matter. He grinned to think how expertly he could have handled the putty and replaced the glass himself. How astonished the fellow would be. The man was not one of brother Caleb's labourers. He could not be seen to hand a contract for refurbishing the town hall to a business he part-owned, more's the pity.

A small pile of letters had been placed on his desk, together with the minutes of the previous meeting of the sanitation committee. Halesworth grimaced as he poked a cursory finger through the opened letters. Nothing of interest there and an evening's talk of drainage to look forward to. Avery, who'd only been appointed for his medical knowledge would side with the vicar and they'd all be forced to listen to a boring discourse on how the poor needed an adequate water supply.

Let the poor get off their arses and work harder if they wanted homes like their betters. He'd had to. The truth and this the vicar would not see, was that the poor were perfectly happy as they were. He was all for town improvements, no man more but you couldn't try to raise a man's station in life for him. Why, it went against the natural order of things. Fact is, there were two kinds of men in the world, those who had ambition and those who had none, take brother Caleb for instance.

Turning to the window Halesworth stood looking out at a view that never failed to give him satisfaction. Clarence Square was the heart of Seaborough, home of its municipal buildings, banks, post office and superior hotel, all dominated by the town hall. The streets were filling up with carriers and people were constantly crossing the public garden and greeting each other on the pavements. As he gazed beyond them at the grey line of sea, his mind's eye saw fine pier buildings on girders straddling the waves and eager holiday-makers queuing for a pleasure steamer. He had added a comfortable gentlemen's club with rooms for billiards, smoking and coffee-drinking, when the clock above him striking the half-hour recalled him to the present.

Taking up his official correspondence, he revealed an envelope which had remained unopened by his clerk. Addressed to him in a neat hand, it was marked *Strictly Private*. Slitting it with his letter opener, Halesworth dropped into his chair and extracted a single sheet. As he read the contents, he felt his kidneys turn to ice. Crumpling the paper in a ball, he hurled it ineffectually at the empty grate. Fumbling for his box of vestas, he intended to destroy the letter, only to retrieve it seconds later, smooth out the sheet, fold it and place it in his pocket-book. While his lower regions still felt icy, a vein throbbed in his forehead as though at risk of apoplexy. A knock at the door made him jolt.

'Come in.'

'Good morning, sir. Some letters for you to sign, if you please.' Timmins the clerk bent deferentially over him as he laid the papers on the blotter.

'Leave them, I'll do them later.'

'As you wish, Mr Halesworth. But if you could see your way to signing them now, they could catch the post.'

'Oh, have it your own way. Give 'em here.'

'Not so bad today, sir. The fog seems to have left us.' Halesworth glared up at the man, whose pallor looked as colourless as his whiskers.

'Get out of my light, will you?' He strived for a normal tone to his voice but as he reached for his pen, the pier and its projected theatre seemed to collapse in to the sea.

Handing a coin to the news seller, Abbs took a paper and retraced his course back to the police station. A gig now stood outside with a lad holding its brown horse. Behind the front desk Constable Dean was in patient conversation with two women, one young, the other of middle years and both wearing anxious expressions. Abbs escaped in search of Reeve and found him in the end cell with Dr Avery. The other two men had been removed and the remaining space taken by Sergeant Tancock.

'Be steady, man, how can I aid you if you won't let me examine your arm? Help me remove his jacket, will you?' asked Avery. Reeve pulled the garment off the labourer's good arm and they gently eased the fustian off his other shoulder, releasing the sleeve. The fellow groaned heavily, cradling his right arm again. Avery sat next to him and gently straightened the injured limb, flexing it cautiously.

'It isn't broken,' he said at once. Catching Abbs's eye, he nodded at him. 'Good day, Inspector.' Abbs returned his greeting, watching him at work with interest.

'If it ain't broke, it's a fracture, Doctor. I'm in agony, I ain't puttin' it on.' The workman screwed up his face as Avery felt his wrist.

'No one said you were,' he remarked mildly.

''E did,' said his patient, shooting a vicious look at Sergeant Tancock. The sergeant sniffed and shifted himself.

'I'll see you outside when you've finished, Doctor.'

'Does the pain run the length of your arm to your fingers?' asked Avery.

'Too right it does, like red-hot pokers.' Avery nodded and began probing his shoulder while manipulating his upper arm to see the movement.

'Ow, watch what you're doing, will yer.'

'I thought as much,' said Avery straightening up. 'It isn't your arm at all, it's your shoulder. Fall on it, did you?'

'Landed on it like a sack of taters with me mate on top of me. But 'ow can it be me shoulder? It does 'urt but not as bad as me arm. I told yer it's in agony. Call yourself a doctor?'

'You have what's called a rotating cuff sprain,' said Avery. 'During the fight you were in, you tore the muscles round the shoulder joint, probably when you fell. You're experiencing received pain, that is, pain running from the injured muscles along the nerve endings in your arm. Such pain is often worse than at the source.' The fellow greeted this information in sullen silence.

'A sling will help and I'll give you something for the pain,' continued Avery, 'but there's nothing else I can do. Time will heal it and rest will help.' He stood up, moving stiffly himself and his mouth tightened as though in discomfort. At close quarters the bruise along his jaw that Abbs had noticed the previous day was turning from indigo to yellow. He rummaged in his medical bag and with a jerk of his head, Abbs indicated to Reeve that they should leave the doctor to his patient.

Back in the reception area Sergeant Tancock was leaning on the counter, talking to the constable.

'Inspector Abbs,' said Dean, 'message just come for you, sir.' There was a second when Abbs tensed, expecting to see a telegram from Superintendent Nicholls, until he handed him a folded sheet of paper.

'Thank you, Constable.' Rapidly reading the few sentences, he turned to Reeve. 'This is useful. It's from Mr Emerson. He says he presumes we'll need to speak to him and he invites us to call this afternoon, if convenient. If so, he's offered to send us back in his carriage. Very decent of him.'

'So we'll see Mr Hicks this morning, sir?' asked Reeve.

'Yes, we'll be off there now.'

'Did I hear you propose calling on Hicks?' asked Avery as he joined them. 'Only I happen to know he's away today.'

'Is that so, doctor? Thanks for letting us know.'

'He mentioned yesterday that he's travelling to Exeter to see a supplier. Mrs Hicks is accompanying him and they won't be back before nightfall.'

'Very well, he'll keep until tomorrow.'

'Mr Emerson isn't actually a suspect, I take it, sir?' contributed Sergeant Tancock 'not with him being a retired JP?'

'No, I need to see him as he was at Miss Chorley's tea,' replied Abbs. 'I've been told he knew the family for many years.'

'I've patched up your man as best I can,' said Dr Avery to the sergeant. 'At least his arm isn't broken, the injury's in his shoulder. It will heal in a few weeks but I hope he has some savings, he cannot do physical work until it does. Are you going to charge him?' he asked abruptly.

Sergeant Tancock shrugged. 'Ought to by rights, he were part of an affray.'

'Surely he's suffered enough? He clearly came off worst and I doubt he can afford a fine.'

'What do you think, sir?'

Abbs held up his hands. 'It's out of my jurisdiction, Sergeant. You must use your discretion.'

'I suppose it'd cut down on paperwork. We're charging the Irish, specially the one who did for Constable Prowse. You look like you've been in the wars yourself, doctor,' commented the sergeant.

'So everyone keeps saying,' said Dr Avery. 'If you must know, I fell down a flight of stairs, thanks to a loose rod.' He snapped shut his bag. 'I must be at the hospital. If that's all, I'll bid you good morning, gentlemen.'

'Funny, that,' said Sergeant Tancock when the door had swung to behind him. 'I overheard him telling someone at the funeral that he'd attended a drunk collapsed in the street and caught a flailing fist from him.'

'That bruise looks like it came from a fist,' said Reeve. Looking over the frosted half of the window, Abbs watched the doctor climb gingerly into his gig. The lad started down the street, hands in pockets and Avery moved off with a flick of his reins. Abbs gazed thoughtfully after them.

Seventeen

'Laetus House, wonder what it means?' said Reeve as they approached the gate-post.

'Happy,' replied Abbs automatically, 'or glad, if I remember rightly.' He stopped to catch his breath, looking round at the deepening autumnal colours of the lane they had climbed. The home of Mr Emerson was further on than Miss Chorley's house and its only near neighbour. From where they were standing, a wide sweep of the bay could be seen. A small cargo vessel was making its way down the Channel, perhaps heading for the ship canal at Exeter, though trade there was declining.

Reeve glanced at Abbs in surprise. 'Did you study Latin then, sir?'

'For a while,' said Abbs as they began walking along the drive. He felt some explanation was necessary and added. 'I grew up in a servant's cottage on an estate. For a time I studied with the local rector's pupils.'

Laetus House was built, he thought at the end of the previous century and unlike its neighbour had not been ruined. Its rows of sash windows were three storeys high and its fawn-coloured stucco was mostly hidden by the fiery red leaves of a Virginia creeper.

'You'd need plenty of rhino to keep this up,' muttered Reeve just before the door was opened. Abbs agreed silently, wondering if the house lived up to its name. The person who greeted them was a surprise. A stocky man of about fifty with a battered face and in his shirt-sleeves took their things. His features did not quite seem to agree somehow, as though his bulbous nose wanted to look in a different direction from his chin. His small, sharp dark eyes darted everywhere. They agreed on comparing notes later that he could have been anything dubious from a prize-fighter to a peter-man in his youth.

'Mr Emerson's seeing you in the smoking room. Down here,' said the unusual servant in a gravelly Scotch accent. They followed as he led them to the rear of the house, gave a cursory knock and put his head round a door. 'The police for you,' he announced, pronouncing it *pollis*. 'Two o' them.'

'Bring them in,' said a light, refined voice. Its owner was sitting in a high-backed armchair by the fire with a rug over his knees. Mr Emerson was probably in his seventies and had an elegant appearance with neatly brushed thin grey hair. He wore an old-fashioned wing-collar above a maroon smoking-jacket. His breathing was noticeably shallow and noisy, his head back on a cushion. Despite his unhealthy pallor, his eyes were bright and his smile warm.

'Excuse my not rising, gentlemen,' he said when Abbs had made their names known. 'Please make yourselves comfortable.'

Thanking him, the two detectives took their places on the sofa, Reeve immediately taking out his notebook.

'Can I offer you both some madeira and a biscuit?'

'Not on duty, sir, thank you.'

'It's good of you to visit me here, Inspector. I'm afraid I can get out little these days, Miss Chorley's invitation to tea being a rare exception. I'm that tiresome article, an invalid, most frustrating.' As if in illustration Mr Emerson broke off in a fit of coughing. The manservant who'd been hovering in the doorway, moved quickly to his master's side.

Abbs looked discreetly at their surroundings, which revealed so much about a person while Reeve, a picture of healthy youth, lowered his eyes in embarrassed sympathy to his empty page. They were in a wholly masculine room with dark-panelled walls hung with political caricatures. A table held a revolving bookstand and bound copies of periodicals. A second table against the opposite wall was laid out with humidor, pipe rack, tobacco jars, vesta case and a silver cigarette box, its open lid showing the contents divided into compartments.

Though not indulging himself, he recognised the slim, dark smokes which came from Russia and the fat, creamy-papered Turkish variety. It was a regular tobacconist's emporium. A pair of tall windows overlooked the garden, in one of them the window-seat was replaced by an inset wash-basin and taps. Though the brass ashtray on the small table by Mr Emerson was empty, the room was heavy with the trapped odour of stale cigarette smoke. There could be no doubt, even to a blind man of its purpose.

As his coughing died away, his man held a glass of water to Mr Emerson's lips and helped him sit upright again, his muscular arms raising him effortlessly.

'Forgive me for that unedifying exhibition. Thank you, Logan, I'll be all right now.'

'Don't be letting them tire you out, sir,' said the manservant. He gave the detectives a stern glare as he left the room.

Mr Emerson looked at them both with some amusement. 'You are wondering how Logan came to be here? The Scots always seem to wander far from home. We encountered each other long ago in the course of my tenure as a J.P. I have taken an interest in recidivism and prison reform. I trust that does not put us at odds, Inspector?'

'It does not, sir,' said Abbs. 'I'm for anything that brings us fewer customers.'

'How about you, Sergeant? Do you believe that regular employment can reform a rogue?'

'I don't see why not, sir,' replied Reeve. 'Depends on the man. There's some wicked just for the pleasure of it, 'cause they're made that way. But most criminals want to keep body and soul together and to give their families decent things... same as the rich.'

'Well said,' Mr Emerson nodded in agreement. Reeve contrived to look both surprised and pleased.

'Logan decided on a change of career, I'm pleased to say. He's proved loyal and a great help to me but he's a little uncomfortable around officers of the law.' They all smiled.

'Now, Inspector,' said their host, leaning forward. 'I knew you'd want to question me at some point about Miss Chorley's last afternoon but my old friend Sam Shaw suggested I invite you here. He seemed to think you might find it useful to hear more about the family background.'

Abbs raised his eyebrows. 'That was very kind of Mr Shaw and you, sir. I'd be glad of anything you can tell us. To begin with, did anything seem odd or out of place to you during the tea party?'

'I've gone over the events of that afternoon many times and I can think of nothing, no possible indication of what was to come. Harriet, Miss Chorley was particularly animated, delighted of course to have her nephew there.' He paused to take a slow breath and sip some water. 'She was in her element parading him before friends and neighbours but Captain Selden was rather diffident. An uncomfortable trait for an army officer but he was a shy little fellow as a boy.'

'Did you know him well, Mr Emerson?' asked Abbs.

'Not at all, I saw him two or three times when his mother brought him to stay. Caroline, Mrs Selden was Miss Harriet Chorley's younger sister, though they were close in age.' He smiled reminiscently. 'She was a pretty, lively girl, quite unlike Harriet. Our families knew one another well as the only near neighbours. Their parents weren't accepted fully by the best families hereabouts, the Osbornes and others, new money, you see.'

'Ridiculous snobbery,' he continued, 'but my own parents were fairly new to the area themselves so the families struck up an acquaintance. Then when Caroline Chorley married a chap from the north, her father wasn't well pleased so she visited without her husband. Selden was in business and old Richard wanted her to marry gentry and improve the family. Poor Caroline, she was dead from the smallpox by her early thirties. Now you mustn't let me bore you, Inspector. I spend too much of my time in the past. It seems closer than the days before me.'

'Please continue, if you will, it's most interesting. If I can understand Miss Chorley I believe it will help to solve her murder.'

Mr Emerson looked keenly at Abbs. 'You theorise that the victim's character will reveal the motive?'

Abbs thought for a moment. 'Yes, I think so, in a domestic case like this.'

'You may well be right.' Stopping once more to take several long, ragged breaths, Mr Emerson turned over his memories. 'Harriet worshipped her father but sadly it wasn't reciprocated. She was quite passed over in favour of Caroline and James. Harriet was plain, not to put too fine a point on it and she lacked social graces. Richard Chorley would have liked a son first of course. After Caroline's birth they had probably resigned themselves to no more, until along came James ten years after.' Tilting his head back again, Mr Emerson breathed long and evenly, each effort making a soft wheezing sound.

'Can I get you anything, sir?' asked Reeve. Mr Emerson held up a hand until he felt able to speak again.

'I lack nothing, thank you, Sergeant.' He gestured at his side table. 'I can ring if need be. There is nothing Dr Miller can offer me apart from some pills at prescribed times and an insistence on rest. I would consult Dr Avery if I thought it would make any difference. I know Miss Chorley thought highly of him.' Abbs looked at the paraphernalia of an invalid, the water glass and jug, folded kerchief, inlaid pill box and hand bell. A pocket volume of Mr Borrow's *Wild Wales* lay close at hand as well as a small cigarette case and matches. Mr Emerson reached for them as he watched.

'This will help me more than any physic.' The detectives both declined as he proffered the case. 'No? I hope you don't mind if I do.' Waving the spent match he placed it in the ashtray. 'Ah, that's better.' Exhaling smoke which drifted above the fireplace, their host spoke again. 'Where was I? Yes, James Chorley, I can't claim to have known him intimately, you understand. I was so much older, several years senior to the girls. But I remember he was, not unnaturally, his father's pride and joy after giving up hope of a male heir. Every good thing was lavished on him. Fortunately Harriet adored her little brother too. It could so easily have gone a different way.'

Abbs was as interested as in a novel. He had seen their portraits and could imagine the Chorleys and Tower House as a busy family home. It must, he thought, have been a sad husk of its former life when Miss Chorley lived there alone with Miss Geake. 'What happened to Mrs Chorley, sir?'

'She died a year or so after James's birth. I think she never recovered properly from her confinement. Harriet soon became a little woman and gradually took on the duties of running the household. Caroline eventually married Mr Selden and left, Harriet was passed over.' Removing a shred of tobacco from his teeth, Mr Emerson shook his head sadly. 'It's unfortunate when a woman does not have a marriage and children on which to focus her energies. Harriet was of an energetic disposition, though wearied in recent years. She threw herself into charitable works and particularly the cottage hospital. You know she established that in her father's memory?'

'Yes, we met Dr Avery there. It's an impressive place.'

'Of course, he's police surgeon also. What else can I tell you? James went in for the army and lost his life at Inkerman. He was a young blade, sowed plenty of wild oats in his youth. Much later, Harriet, Miss Chorley, encouraged Mr Selden to buy her nephew a commission, but I don't believe he ever had the same taste for military life as his uncle. I had the impression that the Paymaster's office suits him better than campaigning.'

'Service in India wouldn't suit everyone,' remarked Abbs. 'I don't believe I could stand the heat.'

'I'm with you,' said Mr Emerson, 'though Captain Selden was describing summers at the hill stations which did sound more congenial. I understand the social life was very good. Miss Chorley was most interested, wanting to know every detail. It's a blessing that Selden was able to bring forward his visit. At least she saw her only family again, after so long.'

Abbs shifted his position. 'So Captain Selden was expected later in the year?' he said, casually. 'I didn't realise that.'

'I don't suppose it occurred to him to mention it,' replied Mr Emerson. 'I remember hearing he was due in the weeks preceding Christmas. Miss Chorley had hopes of his spending the festive season here. Then she said the army wanted him to take his leave this month.'

It was painful to watch the poor gentleman, thought Abbs as he extinguished the fag end of his cigarette and sank back, his breathing becoming more laboured, like machinery in want of grease.

'You've been extremely helpful, Mr Emerson. Thank you for inviting us to your home. We mustn't take up any more of your time.'

'On the contrary, Inspector, it's you and your sergeant who have been indulgent to an old man. It's pleasant to relive times long gone. I should not, I daresay, enquire how your investigation fares?'

'I believe,' said Abbs as he rose to his feet, 'we may finally be getting somewhere. We have one or two leads to pursue.' Reeve looked sideways at him as he stood.

Mr Emerson reached up to clasp the detective's hand. 'Poor Harriet didn't deserve to be poisoned in her bed.' His hoarse voice was little stronger than a whisper. 'Find whoever did this, Abbs.'

'We will, Mr Emerson,' he promised.

There was far less seaweed on the beach and in consequence the stench was fading. Abbs leant on the railings as he considered his next course. Reeve had been invited to take a drink with one of the constables when he came off duty and he sought the open air again. If Jerrold had acted on his implied threat to contact Superintendent Nicholls, he was likely to hear on the morrow. He felt as though a storm were about to break over him.

While they were walking to Laetus House he had suddenly remembered what he had seen at Philip Winton's studio and Mr Emerson had indirectly made his suspicion seem more likely. The question was how best to find confirmation? It would be better to find proof before confronting Winton, in case he gave them a flat denial. The answer lay in the capital, he thought. When he returned to the police station he would compose a telegram requesting the services of Scotland Yard.

Nevertheless he was not wholly convinced that Philip Winton was their murderer. Mr Emerson had set him thinking on a quite different line, though he did not know what it meant. Idly watching a line of seagulls as they flew beyond the oldest quarter of Seaborough, Abbs recognised the slight figure of Miss Shaw walking towards him. Raising his hat, she smiled in recognition as he wished her good afternoon.

'Thank you, Inspector Abbs,' she surrendered her empty basket which he offered to carry. 'I didn't expect to see you here, are you exploring?'

He looked down at her, some wisps of dark hair escaping from her bonnet and lifting in the breeze. 'Yes and escaping my temporary office. I find I think better outside.'

'My father says the same but in that case I mustn't disturb you.' Miss Shaw held a hand towards her basket.

'Not at all, I'm glad to see you. I've been visiting Mr Emerson this afternoon and found it was arranged by your father's forethought.'

'They're old friends. My father visits him every week for a game of chess.'

'Will you please convey my thanks to him? I appreciate his help.'

'Of course but you can thank him when next you meet. He would like to see you again, I know.'

'You're most kind, I enjoyed talking to your father very much.' Miss Shaw smiled at him, clearly pleased by a compliment to her parent.

'It must be difficult to leave your home and stay in a strange town, unless you are used to it in your work?'

Abbs thought of the small, dreary house he rented. 'No, it's rare for a case to require staying somewhere but I don't mind too much where I am as long as I've something to read.'

'Books are the best of companions. I've just come from talking to a family and trying to persuade them to send their children to the new board school. It's hard for people with no money to spare.' She turned and looked back at the tiny cottages beyond where the esplanade ended.

'They say basic schooling will be made compulsory in a few years,' remarked Abbs.

'A good thing.' Miss Shaw nodded in agreement.

'Is it mostly fishermen who live down there?' He gestured towards the huddled buildings. In front of them two women were sitting on the pebbles mending nets.

'Yes, although some of the families have little work. As you can see, the men can only launch small boats from here.'

'The town could do with a harbour then.'

'You sound like Mr Halesworth,' said Miss Shaw. 'There was one here in the last century when Seaborough was a village. The harbour wall was swept away one night in a great storm and it's been silted ever since.'

'And now the town seems to be developing in another way.'

'I suppose it was inevitable once we had the railway.' Turning their back on Seaborough's past, they began strolling towards the centre of the town. Abbs found Miss Shaw's company unexpectedly restful. Unlike most women she seemed content to remain silent. Perversely he found himself wanting to converse further.

'Do you enjoy living in Seaborough, Miss Shaw?' he asked curiously.

'I do, our friends are here, my father is contented and I have never known anywhere else.' She glanced at him, her face serious. He had noticed that she did not prattle the first thing that came into her head. 'But part of me would like to have that freshness of beginning anew instead of life being dull and always knowing what's ahead.' A wistfulness faded in her voice. 'I forgot about Miss Chorley for a moment. Life here will never feel predictable again.'

He was at a loss what to say to her. Any words of reassurance would sound hollow and trite. Though from what he knew of human nature, most people were not sensitive. They would carry on much as before and Harriet Chorley would be a worn name on a memorial, unread and forgotten.

'How about you, Inspector? Do you enjoy living in Devonshire?' He was still searching for the right words and to his dismay did not hear himself uttering the polite, meaningless remarks he would have said to anyone else.

'I've never really become used to it,' he confessed. 'The topography is very different from where I grew up.' A pull of longing for his Norfolk home tugged almost physically in his chest. Miss Shaw looked quietly sympathetic as they walked on and he was grateful that she said no more.

Eighteen

'Mr Hicks, I think you'd better come. It's Bram, he's worked himself up like a top and I... beg pardon, I didn't know anyone was with you.' The woman hurrying in from the rear of the shop, her words tumbling before her, stopped abruptly as she saw the two men standing with her employer and Mr Biggs. Dressed in dark blue merino, with her hair a tweedy mixture of grey and brown, she had a kind face which told of a placid disposition.

'This is Mrs Lavis, my assistant,' Mr Hicks turned back to her. 'These gentlemen are police officers.'

'Good morning to you, ma'am.' Returning their greeting, the lady stood deferentially with her hands folded.

'What's the matter with Bram? He's the lad who helps with the horses and suchlike,' explained Mr Hicks to Abbs.

'He's in with Samson now and won't come out. He's got it in his head that he saw a ghost in the churchyard last evening and Joe's been teasing him. Mr Biggs and I can see to him. I wouldn't have called you if I'd known you had visitors.'

Pulling out his watch, Mr Hicks compared the time with the large wall clock. 'Joe should have taken Delilah down to Towser's by now. Sorry about this, Inspector. We hire out the horses when they're not needed. Towser's are a removal firm.'

'He's just left, sir,' said Mrs Lavis.

'Good, then shall we go to my office?'

'Actually sir,' said Abbs, 'I should like to hear the lad's tale.'

'In that case I'll show you the stables, though I must warn you Bram's perhaps not the most reliable witness.'

Mr Hicks's clerk had been silently studying the detectives with his head tilted to one side. Like a thrush watching a juicy worm, thought Abbs. He recognised him as the featherman who'd led the funeral procession and he'd approached Dr Avery after the inquest. Mr Biggs gave a slight, hollow cough, preparatory to speaking and tapped the edge of his forehead with a forefinger. 'The boy's touched.' He held out an arm, ushering them after his employer, 'this way, if you please.' Abbs and Reeve followed the two men behind the counter and through a short passage, leaving Mrs Lavis in the shop.

Emerging in a good-sized yard they saw a stable, coach house and a workshop built across the end wall. High wooden gates gave on to the street. Through the open door of the workshop could be seen a coffin on trestles, a plane resting on the lid. Reeve wandered over to the occupied loose box and spoke softly to the horse looking out at them, Mr Hicks joined him.

'He's a fine beast, sir.'

The undertaker smiled appreciatively, through his thick beard. 'Isn't he, just? This is Samson, he knows I've usually a sugar lump about me,' he felt in his waistcoat pocket. 'Here we are, care to give it to him?' Reeve held out his palm for the stallion, patting his head while the offering vanished. 'He's in peak condition, isn't he? Glossy coat and black as night.'

'Yes, they have to be, of course and a good, steady temperament. I wish you could see the mare, they're perfectly matched. Quite hard to come by, so many have a white blaze.' Samson nuzzled Reeve's head, showing a large set of teeth, not unlike Mr Biggs, decided Abbs.

'You obviously like horses, Sergeant.'

'I grew up around them, sir. My pa was a cabman.'

'He knows you like him. I'd better see if I can winkle Bram out.' Mr Hicks leant over the door of the other stall, peering in the shadows. 'Bram, come on out, will you? Joe didn't mean any harm.' There was a few seconds' silence. 'Come on, lad.' A rustling of straw and a figure shuffled out of the end door, his arms hanging limp by his sides. He was a tow-haired, gangly youth with a slight but unmistakeable looseness in his features. Abbs felt a sad pity as he caught sight of Bram's face. Life was hard enough without being marked out.

'So what's all this about, Bram? Tell us what you told Joe.' Mr Hicks leant against the stable wall. He spoke kindly, absent-mindedly rubbing Samson's head as he looked at the youth. Bram gave a quick, nervous glance at the two strangers before staring at his boots.

'Now then, cat got your tongue?' said Mr Biggs, stepping forward. 'This gentleman's an important policeman. He'll lock you up if you keep him waiting.' His jocular tone, probably intended to be kind, would have terrified a child. Abbs threw him a sour glance of dislike. Bram twitched and his fingers picked at his hands, Abbs noticed they had reddened patches with raised spots.

'No one's going to lock anyone up,' he said quietly. 'We've come for a talk with Mr Hicks, Bram and we're interested to hear what you saw. There's nothing to worry about. Will you tell us?' Bram jerked his head and edged nearer, stopping by Reeve.

'I see to Samson,' he announced.

'He's a credit to you.'

Appearing mollified, the youth began again.

'I was goin' by the churchyard last night and I saw her.'

'Who did you see?' asked Reeve in a friendly tone.

'That old lady, the one we buried. It were her ghost, all in grey she were. I was walkin' past the wall and I saw her. Joe wouldn't believe me but I did.' His voice wavering, Bram peered at each face in turn.

'What was the lady doing?' asked Abbs, lightly.

'Flittin' between the graves. She'd risen and she was going to the church. I ran afore she saw me and tried to take me with her.'

'Do you have a watch, Bram?'

The youth shook his head.

'Was it dark when you saw her?'

'Dusky. I bin to Liddlow's for some scrag end for my ma. He lets you have it cheap when he's closing. Liddlow's fat boy was sweeping out the sawdust. I don't like him.'

'Ahem, surely it was someone cutting through the churchyard?' said Mr Biggs. 'Miss Shaw, perhaps, she's the vicar's daughter.'

Bram shook his head vehemently. 'T'wasn't Miss Adelaide, she wouldn't frighten me.'

'Bram attends Miss Shaw's Sabbath school,' murmured Mr Hicks. 'He would recognise her, I think.'

'Have you any particular reason to be interested, Inspector?' Mr Biggs looked avidly at the detective.

Abbs shook his head, 'Idle curiosity.' Dismissing the matter, he turned to the undertaker. 'Perhaps we could have that word now, sir?'

'Of course. Off you go and see Mrs Lavis, Bram.' Mr Hicks led them back inside to his office with his clerk bringing up the rear. Abbs was determined that Biggs be firmly shut out, though he wouldn't be surprised to catch him listening at the door.

'Would you care for some tea?' asked Mr Hicks over his shoulder.

'Thank you, no,' replied Abbs. 'Too soon after breakfast for us, isn't it, Sergeant?'

'Yes sir,' said Reeve in a voice that lacked conviction.

There were already two comfortable chairs drawn up to the undertaker's desk. Abbs spared a passing thought for all the unhappy individuals who had taken them. No miasma of grief hung in the air, though, rather there was a pleasant whiff of cherry pie from the small jug of heliotrope on the desk. Their mauve shade was appropriate for mourning. Abbs wondered if that was intentional. The room itself was subdued and arranged in discreet good taste with drab, grey-green paper and furnishings.

Mr Hicks leant back in his chair. 'How can I help you?'

'I understand you purchased some arsenic several weeks ago,' began Abbs. 'Can you begin by telling us why you needed it?'

Mr Hicks laughed, 'By Jove, I hope you don't have me in mind as the Seaborough poisoner.' Abbs waited, his face revealing nothing. 'It was for the rats, every now and then you'll always get a problem with stables. You'll know this, Sergeant.' Reeve nodded. 'We could do with a cat but people will drown kittens as soon as they're born. My wife has asked around if someone will keep one back for us. I know you met my wife with the Shaws.' Abbs inclined his head, making no comment while he studied the undertaker, intent on weighing up his character.

'I see, sir,' he said. 'Could you tell us about your calling at Tower House on the evening Miss Chorley died?'

'There's little to say,' Mr Hicks shrugged. 'It was looking like rain, there was a tremendous storm later that evening, I recall. My wife had been invited to afternoon tea, as you know. I decided to call and escort her home.'

'But she'd already left?'

'That's right. I was shown in to Captain Selden and he invited me to stay for a peg or two. I didn't see Miss Chorley but it must have been before she was taken ill, or surely I wouldn't have been asked in?'

'Quite so. And did you have any ulterior motive for trying to see Captain Selden?'

The undertaker looked puzzled, 'I don't follow you, Inspector.'

'Perhaps you should know that I've spoken to Mr Halesworth, sir,' said Abbs. 'I'd just like you to confirm matters.'

Mr Hicks grinned again. He toyed with the glass paperweight on his blotter, his hands perfectly relaxed. 'Very well, you're quite right, Inspector. I did have an ulterior motive.' Reeve made a brief note and looked up.

'I don't know how much Halesworth told you but he, Avery and I are hoping to put together a deal, building some houses to rent. Halesworth approached Miss Chorley as she had a parcel of land that was ideal and little used. Seaborough needs to expand but there's limited building land with the topography. The old lady declined to sell, her prerogative of course. I thought there was no harm in sounding out Selden in case he was amenable to using his influence. It seemed to me that Halesworth might have rubbed her up the wrong way, you see.'

'And did you ask him, Mr Hicks?'

'I didn't in fact. I started to skirt round the subject but the right opening didn't arise. Selden was tired, he'd had a long afternoon making small-talk. I think he was glad to relax with a drink and another chap. I suppose I thought I'd laid some groundwork, no pun intended and there'd be another time.'

'And now there's every likelihood that Captain Selden will sell to your consortium,' said Abbs, pleasantly.

'Steady on, Inspector, we're hardly that. Halesworth has a building business. We're simply three professional men clubbing together to make a modest investment. We didn't murder an elderly lady for it, the idea's outrageous.'

'No, sir. I don't believe you did,' replied Abbs. 'But we need be in possession of all the relevant facts. I hope you see that.'

'That's reasonable enough in the circumstances,' said Mr Hicks. 'I'm surprised Halesworth told you. Or was it Avery? Though he plays his cards close to his chest.'

'We didn't know Dr Avery had business dealings with you. Actually Mr Hicks, Councillor Halesworth didn't mention any of this when we interviewed him. We pieced together what we thought was a likely scenario.' Mr Hicks stared at him for a moment before breaking into a rueful laugh.

'Do you have any arsenic left?'

'No, it was all laid down. Under strict supervision, what with the horses and we had a pile of dead rats to show for it.'

'I believe you were left alone for a few minutes in the library at Tower House?'

'Look, am I a suspect, Inspector Abbs?' Mr Hicks was beginning to sound alarmed.

'Please answer the question, sir, it's simply routine.'

'You already know by the sound of it. Selden slipped out of the room to fetch a map. I must have been alone for a few minutes. I looked out of the windows, examined the curios in a display table and glanced at a few book titles.' He smiled boyishly. 'It was the first time I'd been inside the house.'

Abbs glanced at Reeve, indicating they were finished. 'We've all done it, sir.'

'I'd watch it, Sarge,' said Constable Dean. 'Your inspector's had a telegram and he didn't look too happy when I went in.'

'Righto, thanks for the tip off,' said Reeve.

'What's it like in the detective branch?' The constable shut his ledger and leaned confidentially over the counter. 'A sight more exciting than dealing with drunks and strayed horses, I bet.'

Reeve sauntered over, his hands in his pockets. 'It's not all murders, you know. Mostly it's thieving, house-breaking and serious assault. Bit of forgery,' he added, 'this sort of case is a rarity.'

'Have you worked on one like this before?' Dean's attention hung on every word.

'Not exactly like this,' admitted Reeve. 'I've done a murder or two among the criminal class. They're straightforward enough, most times you don't have far to look for the culprit. This is really something to get your teeth into.'

'Reckon your inspector will find who done it?'

'Course he will. It's a tricky case but Inspector Abbs is known in Exeter for his perspicacity. He's one of the very best in the force.'

'Is he a hard man to work for?'

Reeve considered, 'he works you hard, expects you to be thinking about the case all the time and have your notes tidy. There's no taking it easy but he's straight. He wouldn't do the dirty on you, like take credit for your idea.' He scratched his head as he thought. 'He actually asks what you think and then listens when you tell him.'

'Sergeant Tancock 'ud never do that,' said Constable Dean. 'Anyways, Inspector Abbs asked for a *Bradshaw*.'

'I'd best see what's afoot.' Giving a cursory rap on the door, in case the old man was in one of his stickler moods, Reeve entered their temporary office to find Abbs at his desk. The inspector looked up and broke off his scribbling.

'Ah, Sergeant, there you are. Good. I've been summoned back to Queen Street. Superintendent Nicholls requires a report of our progress or otherwise.' Getting up, Abbs shut the door fast and hesitated, then made up his mind. 'Actually that's not really it. The Superintendent does want a report but I've been summoned to account for a complaint made by Mr Jerrold. I told you what passed between us.'

'Yes, sir.' Reeve frowned, that was a bad turn.

'There you have it. I shall leave at once and either stay away overnight or possibly return this evening. Failing that, I won't be required to return to Seaborough at all. I'll grab a bag now and have a word with the Gaunts about my room.'

'Am I not to accompany you, sir?'

Abbs shook his head. 'It hasn't been mentioned so I think it's best you're out of harm's way. It's me

Jerrold has found fault with. I shall tell the Superintendent that you are not involved in any way.'

'It's not that, sir,' protested Reeve. 'What if the Superintendent does pull us off the case? I mean... no offence intended, sir.'

The Inspector pulled a face. 'If another officer returns, it will be up to you to brief him and hand over our findings. I hope it won't come to that, I should like to see this through but we must abide by the Superintendent's decision.'

Reeve opened his mouth to argue and catching Abbs's eye, thought better of it. 'Sir,' he muttered. 'What shall I do while you're away?'

'Expect the telegram from the Yard. I stressed the urgency so it could come at any time. Read it of course but don't act on it. I hope we can see Mr Winton together. While you're waiting you can go over everything we've written down, see if anything fresh occurs to you. And have some time to yourself, Lord knows, we get little enough. Now I'll be on my way.' Opening his watch, Abbs picked up his coat. 'There's a train at half-past midday I can catch.'

Reeve accompanied him to the entrance and stood watching the inspector as he hurried down the steps and along the street. Giving way to an old lady who still wore a wide crinoline and swerving round a couple of stooping children playing marbles in the gutter, his long stride scattered a swept pile of blown leaves and his lone figure was swiftly lost to view.

Reverend Septimus Owen's knees were remarkably uncomfortable on the hard wooden floor as he tried unsuccessfully to concentrate. He rested his clasped knuckles against his forehead, his elbows supported on the edge of the front pew as he began again to intercede with his Maker. Unfortunately the next thought that floated across his consciousness was that perhaps he had been too hasty in rejecting the suggestion of hassocks. At the time they had seemed too comfortable, effete even, typical of all that was complacent about the well to do Church of England goers. No doubt Samuel Shaw never knelt on a hard floor. Mr Owen sighed and thought again how much he needed a helpmeet. If only the Almighty would see fit to send him one who would support him in his work. She who would gratefully receive his guidance and provide the small comforts that his home lacked. His thoughts were straying onto precisely what form those comforts might take when he heard the outer door swing open.

He waited just long enough to hear someone step inside the chapel and see him at prayer, a female footfall he judged, before rising gracefully as though unaware he was no longer alone. It was with a slight sense of disappointment that he beheld the dumpy figure of Mrs Bertha Pardoe, a familiar member of his congregation. Surely the Almighty did not mean to send her to his aid? The fact that she was at least ten years his senior would not in itself deter him, if a lady were suitable in other respects. A new widow in her unbecoming bombazine, she was neither prosperous nor pretty, in addition being burdened with two strapping boys. A man in his position deserved to meet a lady of quality, someone sweetly submissive who was called to serve her Maker by assisting his humble minister. She would preside equally well over hearth and tea urn, pantry and pamphlet, untiringly devoted to easing his labours.

'Mrs Pardoe. And what brings you here at this hour? Have I mistook the ladies' cleaning day?' Bestowing a brief though gracious smile, Mr Owen strolled over to the blackboard and, consulting a jotting in his pocket-book, proceeded to chalk some hymn numbers.

'Oh no, sir, that's Monday.' The widow Pardoe watched the minister's back for a moment, the only sound being the dashing of the chalk. 'Your washing's by the door, Mr Owen.'

Irritated by her information and reminded anew of his uncomfortable domestic situation, he frowned as he dusted off his hands. Really, had the woman no sense of propriety? Such trivial, earthly matters had no place in His house. Was he so little valued that he could be accosted by any washer-woman?

'My thanks to you. Perhaps in future you could take it to my door, rather than our place of worship?'

'Yes sir. I was on my way there, only being as I was passing, I thought I'd look in and see.'

'Very well. I trust we shall see you at the temperance meeting next week?'

'I'll be there, sir, along with my boys. I don't want them to go the way of their poor father.' Mr Owen turned away hastily as tears glistened in her eyes. Effecting to check the marker in the Bible on his reading-desk, he hoped she would leave. But it was not to be.

'Was there something else?' he enquired resignedly. The little woman had stopped dabbing her eyes at last, yet still lingered by the side door.

'The truth is, I was wanting a word with you, sir.' At a stand-still again, she peered at him. He recalled seeing her wear wire spectacles when she sang from her hymn-book, most unbecoming in a woman.

'What is it you wish to say to me?'

'I don't rightly know where to start, Reverend. I'm in that much of a dilemma and it's been hanging over me for weeks. At first, I was that pleased... I thought the Good Lord Almighty had answered my prayers, for when my Albert was first took from us, I didn't know how we were going to manage. My wages from the hospital wouldn't provide for the rent and feed us, you see. Two shillings a day I get. And with two lads always growing out of their trousers ...'

'Mrs Pardoe, please desist,' said Mr Owen. 'Do not distress yourself so, good lady. Sit down and tell me clearly what is your problem. Do I understand that you wish to ask my advice?'

Sinking on to the nearest bench, Mrs Pardoe looked up at him gratefully. 'Yes please, sir. I must have your guidance. Only I don't want to be a thief. Poor but honest, my family have always been. Well,' she amended, 'not wanting to tell a falsehood in the house of God, my Albert had been light-fingered in his time, but not since we were wed. He promised me and it does say in the Bible that each of us is tempted. My poor Albert always did say I told a tale backwards.'

'Am I to believe that you have acted dishonestly, Mrs Pardoe?' Remaining standing, the minister looked sternly down at her. 'Tell me at once how you have sinned. No more shilly-shallying and remember that the Almighty is listening.'

Mrs Pardoe sat up straight. 'It's like this, sir. I always knew my husband had a hiding-place beneath a loose floorboard in our room. After he died so sudden, it was a while before I thought about it. Mr Hicks's burial club paid out for his funeral, thank the Good Lord and the tiny bit I had put by went on rent and mourning clothes, though I couldn't afford to get it all from Hicks's.'

'Yes, yes, so you looked in your husband's hidey-hole? What did you find?'

'Twelve pound, seven and eight,' said Mrs Pardoe. 'I couldn't believe it, Mr Owen. I came over all weak and had to sit on the rug for a time. It didn't seem real. Then I counted it and hid it in my hat box, where I keep my mother's topaz brooch, pinned to a piece of flannel. I had to keep it there or I fear Albert would have pawned it.' Mrs Pardoe looked up at the minister. 'He was a good man, sir, for all he'd never come to Chapel but strong drink was his weakness. I never wore my brooch but I liked to think it was there. My mother had it from her own mother on her wedding day.'

Mr Owen frowned. 'I really am at a loss to know why you are telling me all this, Mrs Pardoe. You don't know how your late husband came by this money and you believe he stole it, is that it?'

Flinching as though she'd been struck, Mrs Pardoe nodded. 'It truly did seem like a miracle at first. I paid the grocer and got our coal in, the cellar's full to bursting, bought new boots for young Bert and John. But as the weeks have gone by, it's been on my conscience, growing and growing like a carbuncle.' She shook her head sadly. 'I've thought so hard, sir, until my head nearly bursts and I don't know how my husband could have come by that money honestly.'

'It's a strange sum,' said Mr Owen, thoughtfully. 'I should think it had started out a round amount and been broken in to.'

'Them's my thoughts, too, sir,' agreed Mrs Pardoe as she tucked her handkerchief into her glove.

'And had Mr Pardoe been spending extra money in his last weeks?'

'He'd been spending more time in The Compass and he seemed real pleased with himself, like he had a secret but he wouldn't say what.' Mrs Pardoe touched her side as she thought back. 'He didn't give me any extra, no, sir. What do I do, Mr Owen? Should I go to the police with what's left?'

'No, Mrs Pardoe,' said the minister. 'You cannot. You have nothing to tell them, no knowledge of any criminal act. Can you truly think of no one who could have given your husband a sum of money? Could he perhaps have done some work for someone or applied to a relative for a loan?'

'There's no one and Albert couldn't have done any extra work without my knowing. There aren't the hours, sir.'

'In that case I believe you may never know how he came by it.' A sudden ray of sunlight shone through one of the clear latticed windows illuminating them both. It occurred to Mr Owen in passing, what a fine painting they would make; the Wesleyan Methodist minister gravely giving counsel to his sister in Christ, as she gazed, beseechingly at him. He half-turned and pointed dramatically towards the cross. 'Only One-who-sees-all knows the truth of it.' Drawing himself up, he looked down at Mrs Pardoe. 'You are innocent of all wrong-doing, dear lady. You have done the right thing in telling me. Let your conscience be eased.'

Mrs Pardoe's face brightened, 'you don't know how thankful I am, Mr Owen. You've properly set my mind at rest. I feel so much better for coming to you.' Gathering her skirts, she rose to her feet, shuffling awkwardly out of the pew. As the minister stepped aside and she made her way to the door, a thought struck her and she halted. 'So, in your opinion, Mr Owen, it's all right for me to spend what's left?'

Pursing his lips, Mr Owen struck a further pose with his hand slipped in his frock coat. 'That I did not say, Mrs Pardoe. While there is doubt in your heart that the money could be ill-gotten gains it is surely tainted. The only way it can be cleansed is to give it to some worthy cause. To those whose need is far greater than your own.' Flinging out his arm, he gestured meaningfully at the poor-box.

Mrs Pardoe faltered, the pleasure drained from her face once more. 'Oh... If you think that's right, sir ...' There was a small, desperate hesitation, then submission. 'I shall do as you say.' She sighed and began to undo her worn reticule.

Nineteen

Left alone, Abbs remained seated before Nicholls's desk for a few minutes. Their meeting had scarcely begun before the superintendent had been called away by a grizzled sergeant, a generation older than Reeve. Nicholls had been unusually subdued, he thought, seeming about to get down to business without a sarcastic preface. The reason was plain to see. His gravelly voice had been a dried husk of itself and a tin of menthol and eucalyptus lozenges lay on the desk.

Stretching, he stood and moved to the window, a good hour in the train carriage had made him want to loosen his limbs. He looked out at pigeons shifting on the window-sills and elaborate ledges of the Albert Memorial Institution. The splendid building which was said to rival the great museums of the capital, dominated the corner of two streets with its warm sandstone and vast arched windows. It was intended, according to the press to be a cathedral of learning. A steady flow of visitors were entering, those with sketch-books beneath their arms doubtless bound for the School of Art. There was also a School of Science. He'd been to tour the museum once when it opened three or four years ago, admiring the collection of antiquities. Had Mr Shaw studied them, perhaps corresponding with other learned gentlemen there? The best of the place, he considered was the free lending-library and reading-room though not everyone agreed with its charity, the Superintendent among them.

It was another of those grey, nondescript days in Exeter. Looking down on the crowded roofs of carriages and the piled loads of open carriers, a shrimp of a crossing-sweeper expertly leaping clear at the last second, an errand boy dodging between passers-by, Abbs felt strange to be back there. In the space of a week the quieter streets of Seaborough and the changing light on the sea had become familiar. Hearing a door bang and footsteps along the corridor, he returned to the chair.

When the door opened, a constable came first, bearing two cups of tea. That is, a flowered china cup and saucer set on the superintendent's side of the desk and Abbs was amused to see a tin mug for him. Nicholls seated himself heavily and took up his cup, wincing as he swallowed.

'We're all run off our feet here while you're taking the waters at the seaside.' The cup crashed carelessly back in the saucer. That was more like the Nicholls they knew, thought Abbs. He really shouldn't rise to it.

'We're hardly there for our health, sir.'

The superintendent grunted. 'Don't talk to me about health. I should be at home in bed, it being Friday but I'll be stuck here all weekend. The place won't run itself. This cold's laying men down like ninepins then to cap it all, Martin's broken his ankle. Though I'm beggared if I know why he isn't back working at his desk with it.'

'I'm sorry to hear that. How did it happen?'

'B..... fool fell through a rotten stair. He was after seeing a suspect in a crib.' Nicholls jerked his thumb at the wall which Abbs interpreted to mean in the rookery of the West Quarter. 'Just as well he had two men with him or he'd have been dumped in an alley minus his clothes and watch.' He poured a little of his tea in his saucer and blew on it, before raising it to his lips. Abbs set down his mug without drinking.

'Now then, you were saying afore we were interrupted, you've interviewed every suspect?'

'That's correct, sir, everyone Miss Chorley saw on the day she died, servants, guests and a photographer whom she visited in the morning. We've also ruled out a visitor who called at the house in early evening and didn't see Miss Chorley.'

'So who's your money on?'

'Difficult to say, sir, it's a baffling case,' Abbs paused to take up his tea again.

'You're not paid to be baffled, Abbs. This wasn't some old woman in a slum, her murderer must be brought to justice.' The superintendent sneezed and produced a large cambric handkerchief.

'Miss Chorley's position is irrelevant,' said Abbs. 'I hope I'd be just as eager if the victim were impoverished. I was about to say that the photographer Philip Winton has drawn our attention. I have certain suspicions and await confirmation before interviewing him again. Sergeant Reeve has remained in Seaborough on my orders, waiting to hear from Scotland Yard.'

Sniffing and loosening his collar, Nicholls's small dark eyes looked sharply at Abbs. 'If this Winton's your man, that cocky young sod Reeve had better not let him scarper.'

'He won't, sir, Reeve's very competent and Mr Winton has no idea we're looking at him. I don't say he's our man but his actions need explaining.'

'What are these suspicions? And who said you could contact the Yard on your own authority? I don't want them poking their long noses in, thinking we can't cope in the provinces.'

'I agree, sir but they're on the spot to visit Somerset House. I did think of sending Reeve to London but knew you'd be mindful of the expense,' replied Abbs, innocently. He proceeded to explain his theory about the young photographer.

'So what it amounts to, you could be right or could be talking out of your arse,' croaked the superintendent when Abbs had finished. 'Lot to pin on what could have been a trick of the light.'

'It was no trick of the light, they had the same gesture,' repeated Abbs. Reserves of patience were needed when negotiating a meeting with Nicholls, fortunately he possessed them. 'Something was nagging at me when I met Mr Winton, some thought I couldn't catch hold of. Then meeting Captain Selden again as he was leaving must have jolted my memory. Later that day it came to me. Both men have a way of holding a finger to their top lip when they're thinking. And once that set me wondering, there's a faint likeness if you know to look for it, it isn't obvious. And they both have reddish hair. Again, you don't notice any similarity because the Captain's was sandy and is now greying and Mr Winton has a sort of chestnut shade. I'm sure they're somehow related. Add to that the way he was watching Miss Chorley's funeral but didn't intend to be seen doing so openly.'

'Well you'll look a fine fool if it comes to nothing,' muttered Nicholls. He flicked through the remainder of Abbs's report. 'Mind you keep me informed. Anyone else a possibility?'

Hesitating, Abbs shook his head. 'There are one or two anomalies but that's always the way. I'd like to get this matter cleared up first.'

Sneezing again and sending a fine spray of droplets over the paper, Nicholls wiped his nose. 'Poison's generally a woman's weapon.' He helped himself to a lozenge. 'Though when you think of the Road murder...'

'Point taken,' agreed Abbs. The savage murder of the infant child of a prosperous family had shocked the entire country, over a decade earlier. The gory details were poured over by everyone who could read and the obscure Wiltshire village of Road had become known to all. The victim's own sister had been suspected from the start though it had taken five years to bring her to justice after she had suddenly confessed to the killing. In the summer of 1860 he had been a young constable and had followed the case with interest. The family, he now recalled, had once lived on the Devonshire coast at Sidmouth, some miles west of Seaborough.

'You'd best stop wasting time and get yourself back there,' said the superintendent.

'I'll do that, sir.' Concealing his surprise, Abbs picked up his hat, preparing to rise.

'Not so fast. I've had a letter of complaint about you.' Abbs made no comment. 'Didn't take you long to get someone's back up, I warned you.' Nicholls pulled open a drawer and tossed a long envelope on the blotter. It lay between them, Abbs glanced at it and let his gaze flick away.

'It never pays to get on the wrong side of an attorney. Can't stand 'em, myself,' said Nicholls. 'Pompous swine, thinks he can tell me how to do my job.' Picking up the envelope he threw it back in his drawer. 'I couldn't give a tinker's cuss how much you offend him if you nail this murderer, Abbs. This attorney wants you replaced but I don't dance to his jig. Anyways there's no one of rank to spare. He can have you back and lump it.' Head bent forward, his voice cracking and mopping with the white handkerchief like a flag of surrender, Nicholls waved his hand irritably at him to leave.

When Abbs let himself in through his front door, everything seemed smaller, odd and diminished as home always does after even a few days' absence. Not that he thought of it as home. Since his wife's death it was simply a place where he slept and kept his things. A letter was on the mat and he recognised his sister's hand, pocketing it to read on the train. The terraced house was tiny and a few paces led to the scullery at the rear. He stood at the sink, where the dish cloth hung curled and stiff from a nail and a sifting of dust filmed the wooden draining board. A rusty stain bled towards the plug hole where the tap had dripped. He already regretted the eel pie he'd consumed at a coffee stall before walking the short distance to Sidwell. For the first time he wondered in which neighbourhood did Reeve live? He had no knowledge of his life beyond their work.

The window looked out on a back wall with a bolted gate to a narrow alley and the roof-tops of the street behind. A hundred chimneys puffed soot across the oyster-shell sky. The small yard was empty. Nothing survived of Ellen's attempts to make a garden. That had blackened beneath his neglect and the ashes he'd dumped on the single earth bed. The only greenery was a hideous spotted laurel, which had been there when they came. He had always hated the blotched leaves which had thrived in the darkest corner beside the coal shed. Perhaps when the case was over, he would dig it out.

Taking the stairs with a new determination, he entered the back bedroom with its single bed, found some clean linen and set about returning to Seaborough with all speed. Outside the railway station a legless newseller propped on a miniature cart was decrying the headlines. In the capital there'd been an 'orrible slaying and Mr Gladstone had after all managed to reform the government.

'Thank 'ee, mister Abbs.' Though run together in one breath, presumably the two facts were not linked, he reflected as he nodded at the speaker and added a coin to the hat.

'How are you, Micah? No grandson today?'

'Gorn ter school,' the old man replied simply, pride evident in his voice. 'Took yer advice.'

'Glad to hear it.'

It had rained in Seaborough and Abbs could catch a waft of damp earth in front gardens as he walked through the streets. The sun had come out with the soft light of October, low in the sky. He had noticed before how at the end of a drab day there would sometimes be an unexpectedly lovely hour in early evening. His meeting with Nicholls behind him, he felt as free as... as a lad let out of the schoolroom. He smiled to himself as he passed the Board school with its entrance at either end, *Boys* and *Girls* carved in the stonework. A new built school-house stood across the puddled yard and a young woman was opening the downstairs window. He sometimes wondered about the lives of people he glimpsed for an instant and never saw again, perhaps that was in the nature of a detective.

The tap room of *The Anchor* was half-empty though Reeve was there, talking to the landlord with his back to the open door. Next to him at the bar Abbs recognised the undertaker's clerk. Quite why he should be sinister when his appearance was benign and respectable, Abbs didn't know. Partly his calling, no doubt and something more, the way he kept utterly still as he listened and watched with barely-suppressed inquisitiveness. He had his large eyes fixed on Reeve's face now as the latter picked up his tankard. Mr Gaunt caught his eye just as Reeve saw him in the mirror behind the bar.

'Evenin', Mr Abbs. You've come back to us, then.' Reeve and Jabez Biggs both swung round.

'Yes, my business in Exeter was concluded earlier than I expected.' Abbs nodded to his sergeant who was grinning broadly.

'Will you be wantin' a bite of supper? I'll tell the missus. Your room's all ready and waiting for you.'

'Thank you, Mr Gaunt. I'll dine with the sergeant as usual, if it's no trouble.'

'None at all, sir, I'll let Sally know.' The landlord put down his cloth and disappeared in to the back.

'It's roast pork and hot mustard,' announced Reeve. Mr Biggs gave what the sergeant described as his graveyard cough, preparatory to speaking. Abbs raised his eyebrows at the sergeant, who managed to convey encouragement by a slight nod and cheerful expression, while trying to evade the gaze of Mr Biggs.

'You've been all the way back to Exeter then, Inspector?'

'That's right,' said Abbs, pleasantly.

'Urgent police business, no doubt?'

'No doubt at all.'

'I don't suppose you can give a hint as to the progress of your investigation?' persisted Mr Biggs. 'Only people are naturally fearful with a murderer among us.'

'I'm sure you appreciate that I cannot comment on the matter, sir. Only to say that the townsfolk have no need to be afraid.'

'You've been to report to your superior. I should like to have been a fly on the wall, Inspector.' Mr Biggs smiled into his sherry at his small pleasantry.

Nicholls would have soon swatted you, if you were, thought Abbs. He smiled, weak as watered milk.

'How about a turn outside, Sergeant? I could do with some fresh air after being cooped up in the train.'

'Good idea, sir,' said Reeve, promptly sliding off his stool. 'Just the thing before supper.' They escaped before Mr Biggs could suggest accompanying them.

'I thought I'd never shake him off. It's good to see you back, sir.'

Abbs nodded in acknowledgement. 'Let's go further down, I wouldn't put it past our Mr Biggs to follow.' He gestured across the street and crossing, they strolled along the esplanade.

'He was telling me he's not just a clerk, he does the laying-out and embalming,' Reeve grimaced. 'He started going on about how he pumps fluid through the veins and how he removes stuff. Can you imagine the stench? He's a strange cove. You can tell he loves his work, artistry he calls it.' Reeve gave a sepulchral cough and produced a fair impression of Mr Biggs's sombre tones. Abbs suppressed a smile.

'The telegram's come?'

'It has, sir, I don't know what you'll make of it.'

'Then tell me,' demanded Abbs.

'Righto,' said Reeve, leaning against the sea wall. 'It's back at the station of course but I copied it in my notebook in case you returned.' Removing the small cloth-bound book from his pocket, he began turning the pages. 'Here we are, though I know it off by heart, anyways.' Clearing his throat he began to read. 'Born on 24th March 1847 at an address in Gloucester, county of Gloucestershire. That makes him in his twenty-seventh year,' added Reeve in an aside. 'Mother Margaret Winton.'

'Go on,' said Abbs as the sergeant paused. 'And the father?'

'Father unknown.'

'Poor woman,' muttered Abbs, sparing a thought for the ignominy she must have felt in registering her son's birth, though it was hardly uncommon. 'That's it, then? A dead end.' Dismayed for a second, the inspector suddenly stared at Reeve. 'Hang on, you looked pleased with yourself.'

Grinning, Reeve flourished his notebook. 'I saved the best till last. You were dead right, sir. Name... Philip Chorley.'

Abbs gave a low whistle. 'Philip Chorley Winton. So what do we have? The mother didn't dare give the father's name on the certificate but she *did* bestow it on his son as a middle name.' He clapped a hand to his forehead, 'What's more if my memory serves me correctly, Captain Selden mentioned that his uncle served in the North Gloucesters. Our Mr Winton has to be Selden's cousin.'

'Which gives him quite a motive for Miss Chorley's murder,' continued Reeve. 'By all accounts she wouldn't have been the type to acknowledge him but Captain Selden might take a kinder view if Winton makes the relationship known to him.' Clenching his fist with excitement, Reeve hurried on. 'We've got him, sir. He can't have much money and the Captain could set him up for life, now he's inherited. He'll be planning to leave a decent interval before he contacts him, no doubt. I bet he has something up his sleeve, family documents he uncovers, something like that.' He shook his head, 'he seemed a regular sort of chap.'

'Hold your horses,' said Abbs gently. 'We'll see what he has to say in the morning.'

Puzzled, Reeve looked up at the inspector. 'Don't you think it's him, sir?'

'Let's keep an open mind. Either way, it's a big part of this mess cleared up, I fancy.'

'Leastways, we're back on the case, are we, sir? Er.. everything's all right?'

'We're back on the case, Sergeant. And it seems we're not the only ones.' Abbs indicated Mr Biggs who was emerging from *The Anchor*. He peered in both directions, shielding his eyes with a hand before heading purposefully towards them.

Twenty

As it turned out, Reeve had to contain his impatience a while longer. Waking in the small hours, Abbs found his light-hearted relief had vanished and in its place the kind of headache that brought with it debilitating pain and nausea. Falling into an uneasy sleep around dawn, he awoke feeling no better with a dry mouth and an aversion to daylight. He had managed to stumble to the bathroom by the landing in the night and rinse out Mrs Gaunt's china washing bowl, he remembered. Dragging himself to his feet and dressing, he knocked at Reeve's door and explained that this malady came upon him on occasion. It would be impossible for him to continue that day. Refusing his offer to send for the doctor, Abbs sought refuge back in bed, where he sank in and out of shallow, nonsensical dreams for much of the day.

The next day saw Abbs still pale but able to join Reeve for breakfast, where he found himself unusually hungry. Their landlady had been very kind, bringing him soup in the evening. The sergeant had looked in but he knew that the only remedy was quiet and the curtains drawn. In late afternoon he had tried to read a little. He was relieved it was Sunday and could turn away Reeve's enquiry about visiting Mr Winton.

'He'll keep until the morrow, after all, he may be at church. I shall go for a walk today. Fresh air will help set me right.' And so in truth, would solitude.

After the recent rain it was a muddy climb up to the site of the hill-fort. The claggy earth gave off a strong reek in a way particular to autumn. Abbs knew that the sticky red clay of east Devonshire would soon make roads treacherous and the old ways nigh on impassable. The coming of the branch line must have been a boon to Seaborough, though perhaps it had given the town what his mother would have called ideas above its station in life. He had not intended the pun. Words were a strange business and the wrong ones could even hang a man. He did not think that Philip Winton was their murderer but much depended on his answers. Sufficient evidence was piled against the young man. If he were taken off the case, another inspector might seek no further, especially with Superintendent Nicholls at his shoulder.

And if Winton was innocent, where should they look next? Reeve would be asking him on his return and as yet he had no answer. He could think of nothing he had neglected to do. Yet in spite of his anxiety, his spirits lifted somewhat as he neared the top of the incline. His head pain had quite gone. Sergeant Tancock had readily supplied directions to the hill-fort though confessing it were many a year since he'd been up that way. The enclosed land left behind, the narrow path between hedgerows had opened onto rough heath. Abbs noticed the countless cobwebs that were draped among the browning bracken, made unusually visible by the heavy dew.

He idled away a pleasant half-hour tracing the sloping ramparts of the ancient fortification, banks thickly strewn with mouldering leaves and a ditch at their foot. Pines grew around the perimeter, their shapes twisted by the wind. The breeze soughed through their tops and their trunks creaked ominously. The sound of church bells reached him from Seaborough and the villages across the distant vale. The grassy middle lay bare and to the south, the sea shone like polished pewter. When he reluctantly stepped down the far bank, Abbs decided to find his way back to the town by a circular route. He was tired of being cooped up in other people's rooms. A steady tramp in the open air was conducive to thinking. After a mile or so the way steadily descended towards a lane with farmland beyond, autumnal shades making a rag rug of the landscape.

As he reached the road he became aware of dogs barking. Several traps and a few gigs were drawn up on the wide verge, their tethered horses placidly grazing and oblivious to the retreating sounds. A group of men were walking along a track towards a large barn. It had a dilapidated air with slates slipping and brambles encroaching on the blank rear wall.

Some of the men looked like farmers or estate workers but some despite their old clothes had a prosperous air and Mr Halesworth, Dr Avery and Mr Hicks were among them.

They were just too far off to make out what they were saying though he could tell the party was in good spirits. The doctor in the fore of the group was more animated than he had seen him previously, laughing heartily at something said by one of his companions and gesturing with a stout, country stick. He and several others were accompanied by excited terriers, alert and yapping, straining ahead on tangled leashes. Abbs watched them from the shadow of a great elm. There was no one else he recognised. So, he thought, the three of them were not only speculative builders on the side, they were ratting gents.

It was not a sport that had ever appealed to him though it was a favourite pastime in his native Norfolk countryside, more so than in Devonshire perhaps for they stored more grain. Though wherever men were gathered, there would always be wagers. All he could think of to do was to retrace his steps and speak to Miss Geake again. He wondered why Captain Selden had changed his mind about shutting up Tower House immediately? The vicar had hinted there was someone among his parishioners who made him uneasy, though who could say if that had any connection to the murder? It would be pleasant to sit by his fireside again and discuss the case with him but despite the invitation, he felt reluctant to impose.

As the edge of the town came in sight, the lane led through a water-splash, affording him the chance to knock the mud from his boots. Though he had enjoyed the exercise and topography, Abbs felt the walk had been unsatisfactory in its purpose of deciding his next course. He could only hope the fresh air would help him sleep and the following day he'd discern the truth about Mr Winton.

Twenty-one

Rosa wanted something, no doubt about it. For one thing she couldn't sit still, hands fidgeting at the cruet, jumping up to adjust the curtain so the sun didn't fade the furnishings, never mind him trying to read the paper. Then she was watching him surreptitiously, gauging his mood, angling the best line to take. Well she would find he was no pike to be played. And then, this being the real clincher, there was her meek tone of voice and air of solicitude for his comfort. Before his eggs and ham, Cook had sent in kippers. Rosa usually made a fuss about ordering kippers, his favourite, complaining about the lingering odour, but oh no, nothing was too much trouble for him this morning.

The instant he set down his knife and pushed aside the plate, she jumped up and tugged the bell pull. Mr Halesworth watched her in return, his attention seemingly fixed on his folded copy of *The Times*.

'Was the ham to your liking, Fred?'

'So-so,' he murmured, one eye on a report about interest rates. There was talk in the capital that a financial crisis was on the way and they wouldn't hold at their present nine per cent.

'I bought the kippers myself, knowing how you like them.' No answer, as he turned the page. It amused him to see her eyes narrow as she bit back some tart remark. The dining-room door opened and the girl came in with his toast. Rosa had finished toying with her meagre breakfast and generally left him alone, after running through all the errands she had to do. Another sign that she was after something.

'Thank you, Liddy. Tell Cook that the master enjoyed his kippers.'

'Yes 'm,' the girl dumped the toast rack, slumped her shoulders in what passed for a bob and shut the door. She was a pinched little thing, all bones and no meat but that was Rosa's choosing. His missus though mindful of the convention that a handsome parlour-maid reflected the status of the family, took good care to pick ones who were past their youth or on the plain side.

'Marmalade, Fred?' She was at it again, passing the dish of Dundee, that only he liked, though it were within easy reach. Next she was fiddling with her napkin ring, tapping the ivory lightly on the damask tablecloth. Wait for it, any moment now, he reckoned as he scraped butter and preserve lavishly on his slice and crammed a corner in his mouth.

'Fred,' she made two syllables of his name, drawn out in a wheedling voice. 'I've been thinking...'

'Eh?' he grunted. Setting down his half-eaten toast, he unfolded his paper and shook open the full pages.

'Oh Fred, don't disappear behind that when I want to talk to you.'

'Can't it wait?'

'You're hardly at home these days. No, it can't wait or we'll lose it.'

Might as well swallow the medicine, see how much it was going to cost him. His mind flicked to the great crisis hanging over his head. All women wanted from a fellow was his money, one way or another. 'How much, this time?'

'What's that you say, I don't follow you?' Her brow furrowed unbecomingly and spying round the page, he could see her mother on her face. Fortunately the effect wiped away as though rubbed from a slate. He scowled to think that one day the likeness may be permanent.

'New dresses, is it? Something else for the girls?'

'I don't know why you should take such a tone, Fred Halesworth. The girls and I hardly ask for anything new.'

That's more like it, he grinned to himself. She was bridling now in her customary manner.

'Riding habit for Violet, not a month since.' He rustled the page to indicate that the conversation was at an end.

Rosa sniffed in that way women had. 'Most men would take a pride in their wife and daughters being well turned-out. Perhaps you'd rather your daughters were a laughing stock? Anyway it's not as if we can't afford it.'

She was right, he thought, that in the general way of things he was careless of what she ordered from her dressmaker. He liked to be known as a generous fellow and it did look well of him that his females were the best dressed in the town. And she was not to know he had the expense of keeping up two establishments.

'Order what you want, within reason.' He turned a page noisily, hoping having gained her victory, she would leave him to finish his breakfast in peace. 'Any more coffee?'

'Let me pour it for you.' She set the cup by his hand and he reached for it by feel. 'That's very cordial of you, Fred but it isn't garments I want to talk to you about.' Swallowing his coffee as he tried to read, he effected not to hear. 'It's something much more important. Do put that down and listen.'

Reluctantly, Mr Halesworth lowered his paper. 'Let's have it then. I've to be off, soon.'

His wife took a deep breath. 'I've been thinking for some time now that we're a mite cramped in this house. It isn't anywhere near as convenient as I thought it would be and it seems to me we'd all be much happier if we packed our boxes and moved.'

'Eh?' said Mr Halesworth, after a few seconds' silence. 'What the devil's got in to your head now, woman?'

'Getting on, Fred Halesworth, that's what's got in to my head. Something I thought you were all for. And no gentleman would speak to his lawful wedded wife in such a way.' Mrs Halesworth jerked her head in emphasis as she finished speaking and sat back with her arms folded. Her husband knew that look of old, the opening round in a skirmish had been fired.

'But we did take a great step up when we moved here,' said her husband with a baffled air. 'We haven't been in this house two year. Why, you had that put in this autumn.' He glanced up at the elaborate gasolier above their heads. 'Cost me a pretty penny that did. It isn't even tarnished yet.'

'We can have it done again. Tower House will need improvements, I'm sure.'

'Tower House! Have you taken leave of your senses?'

'Don't shout, Fred, the servants will hear. Now just stop and consider it.' The wheedling manner was back. 'You're head of the council, one of Seaborough's foremost citizens. You should have the right setting to take you still further. Background matters, you know it does.'

'Don't go getting above yourself, Rosa. You didn't marry a gentleman but the son of a village builder, if you remember. And your background's a tuppenny ha'penny beer shop with a Ma who could add up all right but scarcely sign her name.'

His missus slammed down the salt cellar, fit to crack it. 'My mother ran a small brew-house, as well you know. And she saved enough to give you a good start when you took it. I know that's the only reason you married me.' The words hung in the air but were not taken up and refuted.

The door opened and the girl appeared again with the post on a tray. 'Your letters, sir, ma'm.'

Glad of the distraction, perhaps he had gone too far, Mr Halesworth quickly flicked through the four envelopes. A cold relief pooled in his chest. Any day could bring a communication to the house. He couldn't possibly be at home for every post. 'One for you, my dear.' He tossed an envelope bearing the name of a milliner's towards his wife. They waited in leaden silence while the maid removed the chafing-dishes from the sideboard and left with her stacked tray.

'What's brought this on?' asked Mr Halesworth in a more reasoned tone. 'I thought you liked this house?'

'I did but don't you see it, Fred?' his wife leaned forward eagerly. 'Tower House is one of the very best properties in Seaborough. 'What would living there say about you?'

'That I didn't know the end of my money.'

'It has such an air of distinction.'

'True. I'll grant you that, I suppose.' Mr Halesworth thought back to the day in September when he and his business proposal been dismissed by Miss Chorley. He'd admired the fine architecture when he'd been waiting at the front entrance. Just for an instant he saw himself drawing up to that portico in a smart, new carriage. His wife saw the softening of his expression.

'That long drive adds a lot to the property and you wouldn't say garden, it would be grounds, stables to the rear, outbuildings. It's almost like an estate in miniature. Think what a good marriage Violet could make from a home like that.'

Shaking his head, Mr Halesworth looked thoughtful. 'I don't say you're wrong, Rosa, but it would stretch us too far. I doubt we could afford it.'

'Mrs Jerrold told me that Captain Selden wants it on the market any day. Miss Geake's leaving and the servants are on notice. Mr Jerrold thinks he'll take a fair price for a quick sale. You did make yourself known to him at the funeral, did you not?'

'Jerrold introduced us, I made sure of it. Hicks, Avery and I want to buy some land from Selden as it is.'

'It's too good a chance to miss,' declared his wife. She lay her hand on his sleeve. 'Fred, at least think it over, do.'

'I suppose there's no harm in enquiring what Selden wants for it,' said her devoted husband. Giving up on his paper, Mr Halesworth drained his cup and stood up. 'I'm off to the town hall.'

'Is there anything in particular you fancy for supper?'

'Don't wait for me. I may look in at the Marine this evening and get a bite there.' He waited for a sharp comment but she smiled sweetly. 'Celebrate my winnings from yesterday,' he added. He held up a hand as she opened her mouth to say something. 'I shall be seeing our Caleb later. No more nagging and I just might find time to look at some figures and mention it to him.'

Breakfast had been a hasty affair, both having been too keyed up to speak over much. Though as Abbs remarked, Mr Winton may have a photographic sitting booked first thing and they couldn't interrupt that in all decency.

'After all, he has to live here. No need to make him the talking point of the town. He has a living to make as well.'

'You really don't think he did it, do you, Inspector?' asked Reeve when they were out of hearing in the police station. Abbs, who had been enquiring if there were any messages from Exeter, turned to give Reeve his full attention.

'I think what we've found would be enough to hang him, he had motive and opportunity. Anyone could purchase the means. I know it would please our superiors if this case were wrapped up quickly. But as I'm not in the murdering business myself, I require something more than circumstantial evidence. We'll give him a chance to convince us of his innocence.'

Waving the sergeant ahead of him, he resumed when they were in their office. 'I'll just see the telegram for myself and we'll be off. No, I don't see our Mr Winton as a cold-blooded poisoner, I must confess I rather liked him. Thank you.' Taking the paper which Reeve found for him in the drawer, he studied it carefully. 'It's a delicate subject, I doubt he will care to discuss his mother with us but there's no way round it.'

The studio door was locked with the closed sign turned to the fore. All that could be seen of the dim interior was a chair, the curtained door to the studio and a hat stand. Stepping back, Abbs looked up at the two sash windows belonging to the premises. Their faded curtains were drawn back unevenly and in one of them, a fly-paper could be seen hanging. He had the same problem himself at this time of year, when they came in houses to grow sluggish against the glass and perish. The business next door was a boot & shoe maker's and beyond that a linen-draper.

'There he is,' exclaimed Reeve. Mr Winton had turned the corner and was walking swiftly towards them, holding a loaf under one arm and a paper bag besides. On seeing them he faltered, a dismayed look upon his face, then continued slowly up to his door.

'You're seeking me, gentlemen?' More a statement than a question and said with resignation. Mr Winton stood between them, the paper bag he held was sticking to its contents and a crimson stain already seeping through. Seeing Reeve eye it, the photographer held it aloft. 'Oxtail,' he announced. 'My supper for the next few nights. What is it you want with me? I've already told you all I can.'

'Not out here, sir,' murmured Abbs. Though the side street was quiet, they were attracting glances from the few passers-by and the shoe maker was standing in his doorway. Mr Winton produced his key and led them inside.

'I'll just get rid of this.' The two detectives followed him through the studio and into a kitchen. Ignoring them, the photographer put down his loaf and took an enamel plate from the rack over the sink. Placing the butcher's bag on it, he deposited it on the slate shelf in his small larder. Washing his hands, he dried them on a cloth and turned to face them. 'I can fetch another chair from the studio,' he said reluctantly.

'We can manage, thanks,' said Abbs. He leant against the table, indicating Reeve to take the chair. 'Perhaps you'd like to sit down.' The photographer sank onto the Windsor chair by the range.

'You look alarmed, Mr Winton,' began Abbs. 'Are you quite sure there isn't something more you would like to tell us?' The young man looked up at him, then at Reeve, busy folding back his notebook. He licked his lips as though to speak and said nothing. They waited until he felt obliged to fill the silence.

'I told you, I know nothing about Miss Chorley's death. Why won't you believe me?' His voice wavered like a candle flame in a draught.

'Perhaps if you'd been honest with us from the start?' said Abbs evenly. 'It would have saved us some effort inquiring into your background.'

'You have no right.' Whey-faced, the photographer half-rose.

'We have every right in the name of Her Majesty. Sit down, Mr Winton,' said Abbs, his voice hardening. 'Why were you hiding in the churchyard and watching Miss Chorley's funeral?'

'I did no such thing. You must be mistaken.'

Abbs glanced at the sergeant. 'You were there all right,' said Reeve, indignantly. 'You ran for it when you saw me. I gave chase and would have caught you but for the fog. You scarpered down the vicarage drive, no point denying it.'

'What if I was there? I've done some work for Mr Hicks the undertaker. It's natural I should take an interest in such a spectacle.'

'Quite so,' said Abbs. 'Many people watched on the pavements. No one else felt the need to skulk behind a grave memorial.' He watched the photographer redden with embarrassment he felt, rather than anger. 'Let us stop wasting one another's time. We know what is written on your birth certificate.'

Their suspect put his hands over his face. Abbs studied the cramped room where the window gave onto a brick wall and another fly-paper hung from a meat hook on a beam overhead. It occurred to him that a patient person could soak them to extract the arsenic but he did not believe that had happened in this shabby room with its painstaking efforts at homeliness. The rag rug and cushions were some years old, he thought, though clean and carefully sewn. There were times when he greatly disliked his work.

As they waited, somewhere nearby the chimes of a deep, echoing clock began to sound the hour. Mr Winton gave a shuddering sigh, smoothed his fingers over his hair and sat up. 'It's the town hall,' he said, 'it used to wake me at first but you get used to it. You get used to anything.' He looked straight at Abbs. 'You know then that I'm a Chorley by birth if not legality. I'll answer your questions and I regret not being frank with you but I did not murder Miss Chorley, you have to believe me.'

'Tell us if you will, the background to your connection with the Chorley family and why you came to Seaborough.'

Mr Winton looked away, his hands on his knees. 'My mother had...' He hesitated and went on, low-voiced. 'An affair of the heart with a young army officer. She met him at a regimental dance in her home town. Gloucester,' he added. 'My mother was... a respectable girl, the daughter of a clerk. She was not given to such behaviour but she was very young and blinded by love. In a just world no blame should attach to her. The young man was the one at fault. It was the old story.' The bitterness seeping in his tone reminded Abbs of Miss Geake as she described the Chorley family.

'Her seducer promised marriage but he was of good family and a coward. When he was told that the inevitable had happened, my mother never saw him again. The regiment left thereafter and she was sent away to relatives to hide her shame.' Gazing unseeingly at the range, Mr Winton continued in fits and starts. 'My mother spoke well of him all her life, she laid any blame on her not being good enough for his family. She understood, she was a gentle creature, the best of women.' At this he looked angrily at the two men as though they would refute his claim.

Reeve was, Abbs knew, tense with excitement as the truth was revealed. Quite without malice but he was young enough to enjoy the chase. He had not been at the game long enough to know how the necessity of harrying a man left a sour taste in one's mouth.

'Would you like a glass of water?' he enquired.

The photographer swallowed and nodded, 'please.' Reeve got up and looked about. 'In the corner cupboard.' They waited while the sergeant ran the tap and handed him the glass. 'Thank you,' he gulped several mouthfuls and wiped the back of his fingers across his soft moustache. 'Sorry about that, where was I?'

'You were coming to where Miss Chorley fits in, I think,' said Abbs.

'My father was James Chorley, her younger brother.'

'Forgive me, did you always know his name?'

'Yes, as I said, my mother would speak of him. Not frequently but often enough over the years. She had obtained from him a lock of his hair and this she kept in a locket with her own likeness. He died at the battle of Inkerman, serving under Major-General Bentinck. She was told this by my grandfather, who made it his business to find out and she would tell all she knew to me in order to instil a filial pride.' Mr Winton grimaced in distaste. 'As a b..... growing up without a name or father, I saw things differently.'

'Did you and your mother return to Gloucester?' asked Abbs. The photographer shook his head. 'My grandfather didn't want us in the town, I only saw him once. No, we remained in Bristol. My mother lost her home and family as well. She made a living as a dressmaker though her health was never strong and we were always poor.'

'And your decision to move to Seaborough?'

A shadow of sadness passed over Mr Winton's face. 'My mother died about a year ago. She'd developed a weakness of her heart. I'd managed to save a little money from my work as a photographer's assistant. With the sum my mother had put by there was just sufficient to rent premises and try setting up on my own. I knew my father's family home was at Seaborough. When the opportunity arose, I decided to come here.' Pausing, he took another few gulps of water, 'It was as good a place as any for a fresh start. There was nothing to keep me in Bristol and I prefer a smaller town.'

Reeve shifted on his chair and Abbs raised his eyebrows at him, tacitly inviting him to take over. 'You can't expect us to believe that's all there was to it. Wasn't it your intention to approach Miss Chorley for help?'

'No, I .... I don't know what I intended,' said Mr Winton, his voice rising in agitation. 'Until I came here, I didn't even know if there were any Chorleys still alive. Of course I was curious about my father's family but how could I make myself known to them? I can't prove any claim to kinship and there's no legal claim on the estate now. To be illegitimate is to have no name.'

'That wouldn't stop Miss Chorley helping you if she wished,' said Reeve. 'Or paying you off in order to protect her dead brother's reputation. By all accounts she thought a lot of him. From what we've discovered of her, she wouldn't want the Chorley name covered in scandal. She wanted it known for charitable works like the cottage hospital. And now she is dead, Captain Selden may be easier to tap.'

Mr Winton looked about him, beads of sweat glistening on his forehead, although the day was cool. 'I don't deny I have very little money, my business is not flourishing as I had hoped. But how could I apply to Captain Selden with his aunt murdered? Would not that make me the chief suspect immediately?'

'Not if you left it for a year, then concocted a good story,' answered Reeve. 'He would perhaps settle with you to avoid loss of reputation or give you a lump sum out of decency.'

'I swear to you, I am innocent. Please. You must believe me.'

Studying him, Abbs decided it was time to intervene again. 'Thank you for telling us this. It cannot have been easy to speak of it.'

Shrugging, Mr Winton looked away again. 'In some ways it's a relief. There's never been anyone to tell.'

'That is everything? You can think of nothing that would help us discover who murdered your aunt?'

'Nothing. I wish there were.'

'Then we'll leave it there,' said Abbs. Reeve catching his eye, rose to his feet.

'You aren't going to arrest me?' enquired Mr Winton.

'No, sir, you've answered our questions satisfactorily.'

At the door Abbs swung round as he was leaving. 'Take heart, Mr Winton, I hope your business picks up soon.'

'Sir?' Reeve looked questioningly at him as they walked along the shabby street. 'Do you think I was too hard on him?'

Abbs sighed, 'No, Sergeant, it's the nature of our job.'

Twenty-two

'He isn't fit to do more than sit by the fire and sip beef tea. He mustn't even think of going outside today and I made sure I told him so.' Using her arm, Hannah brushed a lank lock of hair off her forehead and glared at Adelaide who was drying the breakfast dishes. The range was alight and the kitchen warm and damp with the odour of lye on linen brought in from the wash-house.

'There's no need to be so fierce, Hannah. I agree with you. Papa would be best off in bed but go he will not. At least he's warm and can doze in his chair. He won't hear of sending for the doctor.'

'I reckon he's right there, miss. There's no physician can do more for the Reverend than we can. We knows his chest, goose grease, rest and good food's the best medicine.'

'His appetite is very poor, though. And I wonder if you should call at the druggist and get something made up to ease his cough?'

'Best thing for that's an onion with a dollop of honey,' said Hannah. 'My beef tea'll soothe his throat and we've some calves foot jelly left in the larder. That's a blessing the way you hand it out to all and sundry.' She smiled affectionately at her companion as she emptied the greasy water. 'Nothing like it for strengthening an invalid and it's easy to take when you've no appetite.'

'I must go over and open the church, Papa will fret terribly if that isn't done. Then I shall keep him company if he wishes.'

'And I must just see how far on Betsey is, afore I'm away to the grocer's.' Unpinning her apron and taking her basket, Hannah went in search of the maid, muttering to herself all the while.

It had rained again the previous evening and a blowy night had brought down more leaves, making the path to the churchyard slippery. Adelaide paused as she always did on reaching the grave of her mama. Green lichen was spotting across the white marble, obscuring the first line of lettering, *Grace, dearly beloved wife* and her father's name below. The two of them would clean it with a stiff brush again in the spring. It was pointless to try before winter when the staining would return, spreading like mould through cheese. She wished she could remember her mother. She knew of her only through the portrait in the drawing-room, the unaccustomed softness in Hannah's voice when she spoke of her and the precisely lettered inscriptions in books. Come the new year the grey-green spears of snowdrops would cover her grassy mound, then celandines, the yellow stars of spring. Adelaide shivered as she thought of her Papa's weak chest and a sudden breeze gusted, lifting the fragile leaves.

When she rounded the corner of the church, her immediate impression was that a bundle of grey clothing lay blocking the entrance to the porch. As she looked, she knew it was a woman's body lying on the ground, half out of the open archway. She ran the few yards, not waiting to pick up her skirt and treading on the hem. It would be some poor creature weak with hunger and please God, it was not yet cold enough for someone to die of exposure.

As she went to kneel by the woman, her eyes took in the matted hair, hidden as she'd approached by the bonnet which was dislodged but still held by its ribbons. As her mind struggled to make sense of what lay before her, Adelaide started and something between a choke and a gasp emerged from her throat. A wave of nausea swayed her but she stayed on her feet. Much later she was quietly glad that she had not disgraced herself by screaming.

There was no possible hope that the woman could be roused and taken into the warm. She was long gone from that place. An area on the side of her head had been shattered like an egg shell with a teaspoon. Amid the dark, clotted blood, more black than red, she glimpsed horrifying flecks of white before tearing her gaze away. Though before she did, Adelaide saw enough to recognise the face.

'So what do you think?' finished Abbs. 'Have we missed anything? Don't be afraid to say, I'd welcome any suggestions.' Usually someone who sat still, he fiddled with a pencil as he spoke, a measure of his frustration. Reeve opened his mouth to say something just as the door was thrown open.

'What is it, Sergeant?'

'You'd best come quick, sir. Both of you. Word's just come from the vicarage. There's been another murder.'

'Who is it? Who's been killed?' Reeve's chair went over backwards with a crash as he leapt to his feet. Abbs stood more slowly, his mind racing. He stared at Sergeant Tancock's red-veined face, his throat dry.

'It's Miss Chorley's companion, they found her at the church.'

'Miss Geake,' Reeve's eyes were lit with excitement. 'How was she killed?'

'Head bashed in.'

'Is anyone else hurt?' asked Abbs.

'Don't think so, sir, Isaac didn't say. Isaac May, that is, he's the vicar's groom.'

'Let's get over there,' said Abbs crisply. 'We'll take him back with us. We'll need you as well, Sergeant. Send a constable for Dr Avery and ask him to meet us at the church and organise transport from the hospital to get the body moved to the mortuary. I want to view the corpse as it was found then back here to notify my superintendent and send word to Colonel Osborne. Got all that?'

'Yes Sir.' Sergeant Tancock hurried out.

'Blimey, sir, we didn't see that one coming,' said Reeve as they strode into the front office.

'We should have done,' muttered Abbs, grim-voiced. The groom was being attended to by an older constable he knew only by sight. Isaac May was in his fifties, a sturdy, balding man of middling height. He stepped forward as the constable explained who Abbs was.

'I know who you are, sir. I saw you from the garden when you called on Mr Shaw.'

'Who found the body?'

'Why it was Miss Adelaide, sir. She came haring up the path and saw me first. She'd been across to unlock the church. White as marble she was.'

'Was she unharmed? Did she see anyone else?'

'She's not hurt, sir but shocked, I'd say. I don't believe she saw anyone or she'd have said. Miss Adelaide's strong-minded. She's often sat with the dying and helped to lay them out but not like this.'

'Have you seen the body yourself, Isaac?' He shook his head decisively. 'Not I, sir. The mistress said it was important you knew just as soon as could be. It was quicker to go on foot than get the carriage harnessed.'

'She was quite right. We'll accompany you back now. Is anyone waiting with the body, do you know?'

'Miss Adelaide was going right back, soon as she ran in to tell Mr Shaw and he's laid up poorly. She said she had to prevent anyone else seeing the body. Once the vicar knows, he'll be there, sir, sick or not. He'll say it's his duty.'

Sergeant Tancock, puffing, came back through the front entrance. 'Ready when you are, sir. I've flagged down a carter.'

'Good thinking, Sergeant.'

'Thank 'ee, sir. I'm leaving you in charge 'til I get back, Prowse, so keep your wits about you. Lord knows when any of us'll get off duty now,' he added.

As they hurried up the main path through the churchyard, Miss Shaw and the vicar stood waiting for them, partially blocking a view of the corpse. As they both stepped forward to meet the policemen, Abbs saw for the first time the sprawled figure on the gravel. Isaac moved awkwardly to the vicar's side, peering behind him at the body and dragging off his cap.

'Inspector, thank you for coming so swiftly. We have touched nothing and fortunately no one has approached the churchyard.' Mr Shaw did look unwell, thought Abbs. His features were drawn and the clerical cape hung heavily about his shoulders.

'Thank you, sir. We appreciate your remaining here until we arrived. If you'd like to take Miss Shaw back to the vicarage, I'll join you as soon as I can.' He turned to the vicar's daughter, despite her pallor she appeared to be composed. 'I'm sorry that I'll have to speak to you presently, Miss Shaw but you'll understand the urgency.'

'Of course, Inspector,' she murmured and placed her arm through her father's. 'Come, Papa, let us get you out of the cold.'

Sergeant Reeve slid unobtrusively past the group and approached the body. Standing well back, his eyes searched the vicinity as he'd been taught. There were no marks in the gravel which would indicate a struggle. Tancock joined him with a sharp intake of breath and a stifled curse as he saw the smashed skull.

'No, my dear.' Patting his daughter's sleeve, Mr Shaw took a determined step away from her. 'I shall remain here.'

'Please, Papa, you're not well enough to stay out here,' said Miss Shaw. 'There's nothing you can do.'

'You are mistaken, my dear,' replied Mr Shaw, gently. 'I shall endeavour to keep out of your way, gentlemen but I must wait with the body, Inspector. Miss Geake was one of my parishioners.'

Abbs knew when he was beaten. 'As you wish, sir.' He turned to Isaac. 'Would you take Miss Shaw into the house?'

'Gladly, sir.' The groom looked pleased to have a purpose.

'Adelaide,' called the vicar, when they were a few yards off. 'Keep Hannah away when she returns.' His daughter nodded in acknowledgement but did not speak. Abbs could see that she was apprehensive about her father. Their eyes met and she immediately turned away to follow Isaac, her back rigid.

Joining Reeve who was now crouching by the corpse, Abbs inspected the wound. Sergeant Tancock hovered by them, clutching his notebook. 'First impressions, Sergeant?'

Reeve scratched his head, unconsciously touching the same area as that of the broken skull. 'The blow's to one side and nearer the temple, so as she was turned away, I'd say. Someone standing behind and on her right side. Right-handed? That's most of the population, so no help at all.'

'Any information helps. I agree, so the first question is, did she see her attacker? Was it someone she knew or an assault by a stranger?'

'Someone she knew,' said Reeve promptly. 'The same person who murdered Miss Chorley. She wouldn't let a stranger get that close. And she didn't think she was in any danger or she wouldn't have turned her back on them.'

'Sound reasoning,' said Abbs. 'Is this path used other than for visiting the church? A short-cut perhaps?' He looked up at Tancock, who shook his head.

'No, sir, the only other way out's through the vicarage garden.'

'Ah, yes.' Abbs recalled waiting there on the day of the previous victim's funeral. Mr Winton had used the same gate. 'And we know Miss Geake had no family buried here. Is it possible she was visiting Miss Chorley's grave, I wonder?'

'Possible, sir but she didn't seem to like her much,' said Reeve. 'And there's no fresh flowers.' The others turned to look across to where dead wreaths were placed on the raw earth.

'Quite right.' Abbs studied the corpse, carefully lifting the right hand an inch. 'No visible clues then. No unusual button or scrap of paper clutched in the palm to aid us, as there undoubtedly would be in a sensation novel.' He looked meaningfully at Sergeant Tancock, who coloured and looked away. Abbs had found a well-thumbed copy of a volume by Mr Wilkie Collins in his temporary desk drawer on his first day. Glancing at Mr Shaw's bent head he then felt ashamed of his levity. He wished he could explain that a gallows humour was the detective's defence in the presence of violent death. The vicar's folded hands suggested that he had his own defences.

'There's no sign of a lady's reticule, sir,' said Reeve, suddenly. 'They mostly carry something for money and handkerchief, don't they?'

'You're right, well spotted, Sergeant.' Abbs scanned the grass and nearby graves without finding anything. The sound of clattering hooves distracted him and the three policemen watched an ambulance van draw up by the gate. Soon after the tall figure of Dr Avery came crunching along the path with Constable Dean at his side, the latter carrying a stretcher.

'Thank you for coming, Doctor,'

'My job, Inspector.' Dr Avery stared down at the corpse. 'A bad business.'

'Indeed, I'd be glad of anything you can tell us now.'

'Give me a moment.' The doctor squatted in his turn and examined the wound, his fingers delicately probing round its broken edges. Then he lifted the outstretched arm, as stiff as a branch. The other arm caught beneath the body was bent at an unnatural angle. Finally he felt one of the legs through the grey wool skirt, again gauging its rigidity.' Looking up, he caught Constable Dean's face suffused with embarrassment. 'A necessity, Constable,' he said, austerely. 'It's to determine rigor.'

Straightening up, he dusted his handkerchief over his fingertips and directed himself to Abbs. 'There were at least two blows, possibly more, delivered with some considerable force.'

'Does that rule out a woman?'

Dr Avery hesitated while he considered. Abbs had noticed how the doctor was a man who measured his words. Not perhaps a physician with an easy, jovial manner at the bedside but one whose medical opinion, he felt, could be trusted implicitly.

'No, a woman could have struck them but would have had to be as tall as Miss Geake. The angle of the blows is downward and they would have been carried out with the arm raised.'

'What about if Miss Geake was bending?' said Reeve. 'Suppose she was stooping to pick something up and the murderer seized their chance?'

'It's possible.'

'Can you make any guess at the weapon, Doctor?' continued Abbs.

His brow wrinkled, the doctor continued to gaze upon the corpse. 'Something rounded, no sharp edges. There could be a splinter impacted when I examine her on the table.' Dean winced and Sergeant Tancock wandering a little away, spat in the grass and dashed the back of his hand across his mouth.

'Something like the pommel of a cane?' asked Abbs.

'That sort of thing or a life preserver, perhaps.'

'How about the time of death?'

'Tricky when the body's been outside.' The doctor pushed the toe of his boot in the gravel, tracing lines as he worked it out. 'Rigor mortis is fully established. As I presume you know, that takes half a day, say twelve, thirteen hours or thereabouts, not less.'

Pulling out his watch, Abbs calculated aloud. 'It's almost ten now so that gives us ten o'clock last evening or an hour or two earlier. Would you agree with that, Doctor?'

'I would, as I say it's impossible to be completely accurate. For one thing the temperature of an October night would slow the onset of rigor.'

'Long after dark at any rate. She certainly wasn't visiting the church. We might be able to narrow it down once we know when Miss Geake was last seen alive.'

'She didn't die at once,' continued Dr Avery.

'Really, even with the skull smashed like that?' Abbs and Reeve both bent closer.

'It is remarkable how the body can survive for a short time after severe trauma. I'm no detective but it appears to me the poor woman began to crawl, probably only a foot or two. You see the bloodstains here? Then she would have lost consciousness and mercifully known no more.'

'Maybe the murderer was disturbed?' ventured Constable Dean.

'Could have been,' replied Abbs. 'No one's come forward to report anything but someone could have disturbed the attack without being aware, I suppose. You can enquire at all the houses nearby and the public house on the corner, Constable. Someone may have seen something. Miss Geake arriving or the murderer leaving if we're fortunate.'

'Sir. Shall I get on to that as soon as we've moved the body?'

'There'll be someone to help at the hospital,' said the doctor. 'If you could help load the stretcher, I can manage.'

'I think we're almost ready,' said Abbs. 'Yes, Constable. One of the problems with a murder enquiry is that everything needs doing at once. People's memories fade quickly. We also need the surrounding area searched in case the weapon was discarded.' He felt the sleeve of the mantle as he spoke. 'Damp and the ground beneath the body is dry. Does anyone know what time the rain started last night?'

They shook their heads but Mr Shaw came over to them. 'I looked out of the window at about five and twenty past seven. It wasn't raining then but it started a few minutes later. I can be sure as it was soon after the church clock sounding the half hour.'

'Thank you, Mr Shaw. that helps with the timing.'

'You don't look well, sir,' said Dr Avery. 'I should recommend you go indoors and take a glass of wine.'

'You are very kind, Doctor. But I cannot abandon my vigil.' There was a quiet dignity about Mr Shaw which befitted his calling.

'Miss Geake's remains will be taken up now, sir. When will you be able to perform the post-mortem, Doctor?'

'With all urgency I presume?' Dr Avery consulted his watch, 'It shall be done this afternoon if Mr Biggs is free. Do you wish to be present?'

'Hang on, Mr Biggs?' said Abbs, frowning.

'He's clerk to Hicks, the undertaker.'

'We've met.' Reeve and Abbs exchanged glances.

'He's acted as my assistant on occasion. We have no need for a full-time mortuary attendant in a place like Seaborough,' explained Dr Avery, thinking Abbs baffled. 'He's very useful.'

'We don't need to be present if you'll give us a verbal summary.'

'Then shall we say four? I'll aim to be finishing then. The porter will direct you.'

'Until then, doctor. Would you lend a hand, please, Sergeant?'

Stepping back, Mr Shaw made the sign of the cross as Sergeant Tancock and the constable carefully lifted the corpse on the stretcher. They shuffled down the path with the doctor walking behind. One arm stuck out incongruously as though in a theatrical gesture. The actress had finally left the stage.

'I shall return to the vicarage,' said Mr Shaw. 'We are at your disposal, Inspector. The door will be open. Please come straight in when you are ready.' He sounded both weary and sad.

'Mr Biggs again,' commented Reeve as they waited for the Sergeant and Dean to return.

'If he tries to listen in, eject him,' replied Abbs, savagely. 'Arrest him if needs be.'

'What do you want doing now, sir?' Sergeant Tancock was breathing heavily as he came to a standstill before them. Constable Dean looked decidedly more enthusiastic about the tasks that lay ahead.

'Set your men to searching for the weapon and a lady's reticule and don't forget the vicarage drive, as I recall it has a dense shrubbery.'

'What exactly do we look for with the weapon, like?'

'You heard the doctor, something rounded and weighty. Obviously with an end long enough to be wielded. If it were a cane, the murderer will still have it, so look for a life preserver or a cudgel. And use your imagination, keep an eye out for a likely length of wood or a branch even. It could be some distance away or flung in a garden.'

Tancock nodded unhappily.

'Then knock on doors. You're asking did anyone see Miss Geake or anyone else before half-past seven last evening? Not just entering or leaving the churchyard or the vicarage drive but in the street. If they saw anyone, get times. Remember our murderer would have been trying to blend in.' A thought struck Abbs. 'Talk to the gas company when you can. Find out which lamp-lighter worked this street and question them, then find the beat constable.'

The sergeant chewed his lip. 'Do I take men off the beat, Inspector?'

'Certainly, this takes priority, Sergeant. Reeve and I are going to speak to the Shaws then I must call on

Colonel Osborne. You sent someone to inform him as I asked?'

'I did, sir.'

'Good, as coroner he'll expect me to report to him in person. I'd imagine he'll call an inquest and adjourn tomorrow. I believe he lives some distance away. Can you get hold of a conveyance to take me out there?'

'There's a fellow hires his pony and trap by the railway station, I'll get him to take you. Colonel Osborne's estate is out Venning way, on the road past the Chorley residence.'

'Thank you, have him wait at the police house in about an hour. Dean, you can go to Tower House with Sergeant Reeve later. He'll meet you back at the station when Sergeant Tancock's finished with you here.'

Dean's spirits rose as visibly as his superior's sank. 'Yes, sir.'

'It will be good experience for you.'

'Excuse me, sir,' protested Tancock. 'This is goin' to take hours. People won't be in and we'll have to keep going back.'

'Best get to it then, Sergeant. Shifts will end when the work's done and not before.'

Reeve followed Abbs along the path where he had chased Mr Winton on the day of the funeral. If he felt some sympathy for Sergeant Tancock who was reeling with instructions, he was wise enough not to show it. He had seen the old man in this mood before.

'I doubt there's much the Shaws can tell us,' remarked Abbs, 'so this shouldn't take long. I should like to go with you to the Chorley house but we need to get it searched before the servants touch the deceased's effects and the coroner takes priority. I know you won't miss anything.'

'Do my best not to, sir. Dean looks very gratified to be singled out.'

'He seems keen and you mentioned he might like to transfer to our side of the fence. I shall return to the station and telegraph to Exeter when we're done here. Superintendent Nicholls must be told there's been another murder.' Abbs's voice was carefully neutral. 'You might see how Sergeant Tancock and his constables are faring on your way back. Diplomatically,' he added.

Reeve grinned, 'they have it easy in a country place like this. They wouldn't know what hit 'em in a big town.'

'Ah well, I'm a countryman myself, Sergeant,' said Abbs 'and we wouldn't wish the rookeries on these good people.' He paused as he reached the gate in the wall. 'I've another job for you when we leave here. Mr Jerrold must be informed. Call at his place of business and leave an urgent message with his clerk if he's not there. If you see him, tell him you're on your way to Tower House and if he objects, remind him this is a murder enquiry and refer him to me.'

'I'll do that, sir,' said Reeve. The outer door of the vicarage was open as before and a stout figure could be glimpsed waiting for them as they crossed the wet lawn.

'Come away in, sir.' The housekeeper greeted them in a greatly subdued manner compared to their previous meeting.

'Thank you, it's Hannah, isn't it?'

'That's me, sir. The vicar and Miss Adelaide are waiting for you in the parlour.' Looking down at Reeve's boots, she sniffed as she took their hats.'

'Did you know Miss Geake, Hannah?'

'Only by sight. You get to know most people that way in Seaborough, when you've lived here as long as I have. But I saw her when she called here the day afore yesterday. Whoever would have believed the poor body were in mortal peril? I had no foreboding when I rose this morning or ...'

'Thank you, Hannah,' said a quiet, sonorous voice. Miss Shaw held open the drawing-room door, 'please come in.'

'Thanks, miss.' Abbs followed the sergeant into the warm. Miss Shaw's composure appeared to him as thin as ice on a puddle and would bear as little weight. He pushed away his picture of the shattered depression on Miss Geake's head.

'This is Sergeant Reeve, with me from Exeter.' Rising from his chair, the vicar invited them to take the sofa drawn up near the fire.

'May we offer you any refreshment?'

'Thank you, no. it's very good of you, Mr Shaw, but we'll take up as little of your time as possible.'

'Of course, Inspector. We mustn't delay you.'

Abbs turned to Miss Shaw. 'I'm sorry you've been subjected to such an ordeal and for having to ask you about it.'

'It's quite all right, Inspector, really. Nothing matters except the work you have to do.'

'It's only a couple of questions for you both. What time did you go to the church, Miss Shaw?'

'About ten minutes after nine. I saw the kitchen clock as I left.'

'And at what time is the church usually locked?' Miss Shaw turned to her father, who leant forward.

'Soon after four in the afternoon on a weekday, on Sundays we have evensong of course. I believe the house of God should be open for prayer as long as possible but in practice people would not come to us any later.'

'You didn't by any chance pick up anything from near the body?' enquired Abbs. 'A purse or bag, for instance. You might have done it without thinking.'

Miss Shaw shook her head, keeping her gaze on him. 'No, I touched nothing. I went to put my hand on her arm, I didn't know she was dead you see and then ... I saw the head.' He watched the blood drain from her face and her hands tighten. Hands were always revealing when a person was being interviewed. It took a skilled dissembler to keep them loose when they were lying. Someone as genial as Mr Hicks, he thought. Halesworth would more likely bluster and lose his temper, Winton would look embarrassed. Miss Shaw would lie only to avoid hurting someone and then she would make a poor fist of it.

Turning instead to Reeve, she continued. 'I couldn't take it in at once. When I first saw the body I thought it was a bundle of old clothes and someone had placed a bonnet on top. I feel dreadful that I could have been so stupid. People do sometimes leave things for the poor you see, though usually here or at the church hall.'

'You mustn't be hard on yourself, miss,' said Reeve. 'You've had a bad shock, no lady should ever see what you've had to.'

Miss Shaw smiled sadly at him.

'Do you think it possible that Miss Geake was on her way to visit you, Mr Shaw?' asked Abbs. 'If she was coming from the direction of the square, might she walk through the churchyard and use the gate to the vicarage?'

'I don't believe so, Inspector. No one uses that gate except our household. No, she would carry on past the church and up the drive. If her purse is missing, could she not have been attacked for money?'

'Do you really believe that, Mr Shaw?'

'You do not, Inspector Abbs, then.' He sank back, diminished in his winged chair. 'No, you are right, of course. I am an old man who does not want to acknowledge the evil in our midst. To murder someone on consecrated ground...'

'Papa,' Miss Shaw reached out impulsively to her father but let her hand fall away. Breaking the small silence that followed, some embers collapsed, dislodging a hot coal on the edge of the hearth. Reeve quickly grabbed the tongs and lobbed the lump back in the flames.

'We are obliged to you, Sergeant Reeve,' said the vicar.

'Your housekeeper said that Miss Geake did call on you two days since?'

'That is so, she came to tell me she'd obtained a new post and thank me for her reference. She seemed...' Mr Shaw thought back. 'Light-hearted. She told me she was off to Surrey in three days and she was glad to be leaving Devonshire and Seaborough in particular, I fear. I am sorry she was unhappy among us.'

'Did you see her, Miss Shaw?'

'No, I was out visiting. I hadn't seen Miss Geake since the day Miss Chorley died. She stopped coming to the *Ladies' Society*. She was in mourning of course but I don't think she liked coming very much and only did because Miss Chorley expected it.'

'And did Miss Geake say any more to you about her plans, sir? Or anything else at all?'

'I'm afraid not, she only stayed a few minutes. She was saying good-bye.' The vicar cast a wistful glance at the mantelpiece and Abbs guessed he was seeking his pipe. 'Do you recall when we met, Inspector? You asked me if there were anyone who... troubled me, shall we say, among my congregation?'

'I remember, sir.'

'And I admitted that there was one person who gave me cause for disquiet?' Mr Shaw looked steadily at Abbs. 'I felt unable to be more specific at that time. I regret to say that the person was Miss Geake.'

Twenty-three

Reeve carefully avoided looking at Dean as Mrs Watkins raised her handkerchief to her eyes again. Try as she might, it was still perfectly dry. The two maids were true to their feelings. Sarah, the pretty one looked quite indifferent as she sipped her mahogany-brown tea. Whereas Jane, who did the rough work stared at them with eyes like chapel hat pegs.

Attempting a choked sob, Mrs Watkins settled for shaking her head from side to side. 'Who'd of thought it, foul murder going on while decent folk were abed. Thinking she was safe upstairs and all the while that poor creature was lying in the churchyard in a pool of her own blood.'

'Have some more tea, Mrs W,' said practical Sarah, lifting the pot nearer her. 'We none of us liked her.'

'Hold your tongue, miss, you're so sharp you'll cut yourself,' exclaimed the cook, rounding on her. 'It don't do to speak ill of the dead.'

'You spoke plenty when she was here. No sense in denying it.' Sarah smiled at the policemen, revealing a gap in her lower teeth. 'These two want the truth not gammon. You do, don't you?'

'Yes, miss, that's what we're here for,' answered Reeve. 'So none of you had any idea that Miss Geake was missing until she didn't come down for breakfast?'

'That's right,' said Sarah, watching him scribble.

'Didn't you take her early morning tea?'

Sarah and the cook exchanged glances.

'Not since the master left.'

'Nothing's been what you might call normal here since Miss Chorley died,' said Mrs Watkins. 'Miss Geake couldn't expect to be waited on same as when the mistress were alive. She'd nothing to do with herself all day, after all. We've been waiting to shut up the house and go our separate ways. I don't mind telling you, I leave this house tomorrow. There's been two murders at this door and I've no intention of making the third.'

'What'll I do, Mrs Watkins?' said the kitchen maid, speaking for the first time.

'Go back to your family, you silly girl. Your mother'll take you back, won't she?' Jane nodded, her expression uncertain.

'Are you fixed up all right?' Reeve enquired of Sarah.

She tossed her head, making her cap-ribbons swing. 'It's all the same to me. I'm to be married in the spring so I can go home for a while.'

'What did you think when you saw Miss Geake's bed hadn't been slept in?' Reeve returned his attention to the matter in hand.

'We didn't know what to think,' said Mrs Watkins. 'Since the master left, she'd taken to going out walking, leastways she didn't ask William for the carriage but she'd never gone missing all night afore. I'd 'ave said she'd just upped and gone but her things were still in her room.'

'She always did like to go for a walk,' said Sarah, 'when Miss Chorley was resting. Aren't you going to write what I say?'

'Not necessary,' replied Reeve shortly. 'At what time did Miss Geake leave the house yesterday?'

Sarah turned to the older woman. 'It's no good looking at me,' said Mrs Watkins, 'I was having my lie down.'

'She rang for tea in the library at four o'clock,' said Sarah. 'I didn't see her go out.'

'Was she there when you went back to take it away?'

'No, but I saw her on the stairs when I went into the hall.'

'So she could have been getting ready to go out?'

'Maybe but she might have been doing anything.'

'Didn't she order dinner?'

'No, I forgot. She said when I brought the tea that she wouldn't require a tray. She'd taken to having a tray in her room instead of sitting at that long table by herself.'

'You didn't think it odd that she didn't want any supper?'

Sarah shrugged, 'not my place to. I suppose I thought she had a headache. We were glad of less work.'

'What about you, miss?'

Addressed directly, Jane shook her head. 'I wouldn't see anything from the kitchen.' She put her head down like a startled rabbit when Constable Dean smiled at her.

'We'll see Miss Geake's room now,' announced Reeve, standing up.

'You take them up, Sarah,' said Mrs Watkins. 'I'm sure I'm too afflicted by the shock.'

'What she means,' confided Sarah when they were on the galleried landing, 'is she'll help herself to some brandy for her nerves.'

'Aren't the spirits locked away?' enquired Constable Dean.

Sarah glanced at him, scornfully. 'There's brandy and sherry kept in the pantry for cooking. Don't you know anything?' The constable's ears reddened and taking pity on him, Reeve broke in.

'It's this end room, isn't it? You can leave us to it.'

'I'll keep you company. After all, you might pinch something.' Following them through the door, Sarah plumped down on the edge of the bed.

Reeve stood in the middle of the bedroom, deciding where to start, Dean waiting beside him for his lead. The sergeant was rather enjoying himself with an audience. It was a good-sized corner room with a pair of windows overlooking the front lawn and furnishings in a chilly, peacock blue. In the middle of the carpet stood a large trunk with an open lid.

Taking a look inside he saw it was part-filled with layers of neatly folded clothing interspersed with paper.

'She'd started to pack for leaving,' said Sarah. She got up again and wandered over to stand behind him. 'Didn't get very far.' Moving to the dressing-table she tilted the looking-glass, admiring her reflection. 'The wardrobe's still full of Miss Chorley's things that Captain Selden gave her.'

'That was decent of him,' said Constable Dean, for the sake of something to say.

'Was it, though?' said Sarah, carelessly, watching Reeve in the glass.

'What's that supposed to mean?' he replied. 'If you have any information, just spit it out. We're in a hurry.' Sarah smiled sweetly at him and wetting her finger, wound a curl in her front-knot. 'Or would you rather tell the Inspector?'

'I don't know anything,' she admitted 'but I wouldn't be surprised if Miss Geake had something on the Captain.'

Reeve decided not to take out his notebook for the moment nor show how interested he was. 'Go on.'

'Even before Miss Chorley died, it struck me he was funny with her. That is, he didn't like to stay alone in a room with her.'

'Sounds like he was keen on her and a bit shy to me.'

'Well you're wrong there. Though he was on the shy side, that made him pleasant to everyone. Anxious to please he was with the mistress. It was more like he was half-scared of Miss Geake.'

Leaning against a tall chest of drawers, Reeve regarded Sarah as she perched on the dressing-table stool then turned his attention to his colleague. Constable Dean was standing self-consciously by a window, his hands clasped behind his back. 'Make a start on the wardrobe, Dean. Feel in all the pockets, check for inside ones and don't forget the hat-boxes on top.'

'Right away, sarge,' said the constable eagerly.

'You seemed to have noticed a lot, miss. Surely you didn't see that much of them?'

'When the mistress was alive, I was constantly in and out of the drawing-room, fetching and carrying. As well as serving them at meals.'

'If that's all you can tell us, we'll get on,' said Reeve in a bored tone.

'I've not finished yet,' interrupted Sarah. 'Why did Captain Selden change his mind about shutting the house up, directly after the funeral?' It was almost word for word the question Abbs had asked.

'Well? Do you know why or not?'

'Something Miss Geake said to him. It was the last time they dined together. When I took in the main course they were making polite remarks to one another. But time I came back to clear before bringing in pudding, you could cut the air with a knife. He was white as whey and she sat there looking pleased with herself. Then he got up, blurted out something about not being hungry and left the room. It was the next morning he sent for Mrs Watkins and said about keeping the house open a while. He asked us to stay on until Miss Geake left.'

Sarah smiled pertly at Reeve, ensuring her profile was displayed to best advantage. 'I heard you interviewed Mary, so you know what Miss Geake done to her.'

'Cut along then, if that's all,' said Reeve. 'We've work to do if you haven't.'

Tossing her head, Sarah flounced from the room, wringing the door-knob and banging the door.

'She's a saucy one,' commented Dean. 'There's nothing here. Where now?'

'I don't envy her betrothed,' said Reeve. 'Try these drawers. I'll take the dressing-table. Take out any writing, letters, lists and so forth. She may have kept a diary though that might be in there.' He indicated a writing box and tried the lid. 'Locked, keep an eye out for a key. Oh and if you come across any books, shake 'em out.'

'Are you walking out with anyone, sarge?' asked Dean, his face hidden as he stooped over a drawer.

'No one in particular, I'm too fly to be caught yet awhile,' said Reeve, loftily.

Peering between the slices of bread Abbs eyed the lamb with its white frill of congealed fat and lump of gristle. It was no good, he couldn't face sandwiches before a post-mortem, even though they didn't intend to be present at the carving-up. No doubt young Reeve would oblige by disposing of them, lest they gave offence to Mrs Tancock. Pulling a sheet of paper towards him, he dipped his pen in the ink and began to make a list. Some twenty minutes later he heard familiar footsteps and the sergeant's breezy countenance appeared in the door, followed by Constable Prowse with two cups of tea.

'How did you get on?' asked Abbs when they were alone again.

Looking pleased, Reeve laid two banknotes on the blotter with a flourish. 'These were in the deceased's writing box, sir. It was locked but Dean managed to find the key.'

'Where was it?' asked Abbs with interest.

'Shoved in the toe of a boot and wedged with a handkerchief.'

'Good work. I suppose she didn't want to carry it with her. Did you ask about Miss Geake having a door key?'

'I did, in the general run of things she'd ring to be let in, as you said. They locked up and bolted all the doors before dark, no specific time, except for a side door on the terrace. Apparently Miss Geake was in the habit of strolling out there for a breath of air before turning in. So it would be locked but she would bolt it before she went to bed. The keys were kept hanging in the corridor off the kitchen and when I got the cook to check, the one for the side door was missing.'

'So Miss Geake must have had it with her and probably intended to slip back without any of the servants knowing she'd been out? Her mantle didn't have pockets as far as I could see. She must have carried a reticule. Sergeant Tancock and the others aren't back yet.'

'The cook noticed the side door wasn't bolted this morning but thought Miss Geake had forgotten,' said Reeve. 'They're doing as little as possible, I'd say with no one to watch over them. That Mrs Watkins was adamant she's leaving tomorrow though she was saying that when we first went up there.'

'They'll all go now. Captain Selden won't want to pay their wages any longer.'

'The maid Sarah had something interesting to say about that.' Taking a seat, Reeve proceeded to repeat her conversation.

'Now that is useful,' said Abbs when he had finished. 'She might not have told that to me. You've done well, Sergeant. How did you find Constable Dean?'

'Keen to learn, sir. He took his searching diligently.'

'You over-saw him though, I take it?'

'Yes, sir, there was nothing else of interest. The only papers were this small notebook she seemed to use for recording expenses and a letter stating the terms of her new post,' said Reeve, producing them from his pocket and placing them next to the money. 'Sad, really. The coachman confirmed he was taking her trunk to the station.'

Abbs began to leaf through the slim notebook and scanned the letter. 'I suppose a diary or journal was too much to hope for.'

'It's a fair amount of money,' said Reeve 'do you think it came from the legacy Miss Chorley left her, sir?'

'Definitely not,' said Abbs, 'probate won't have been granted yet. It is a tidy sum for a companion to have lying around. Though we don't know what savings she had and she would have needed cash for her travelling arrangements. The bank manager will tell us in the circumstances.' Without pausing, Abbs proffered the plate. Reeve accepted a sandwich gratefully.

'Did you see Mr Jerrold?'

The answer came indistinctly while Reeve hastily swallowed his chewy mouthful. 'He wasn't there as it turned out. These are good. I saw that same snooty clerk and told him. He didn't turn a hair.'

Abbs nodded, thinking that the attorney would doubtless feel he hadn't been treated with due deference. 'Colonel Osborne was available. The inquest's being called tomorrow afternoon and will be adjourned as soon as the formalities are done. I've also contacted the Hampshire force. I want someone to discreetly check that Captain Selden is back at work in Netley.'

'D'you reckon he could have sneaked back and killed her, sir? It's a long way to travel.'

'But he's had sufficient time to get back here and do it. It all depends on the motive for Miss Geake's murder. I agree it's a long shot but we can't afford to overlook anything. We'd need to work out if he had sufficient time to return to Hampshire. There's been so much to get underway since this morning, I've barely had time to formulate any theories yet.' Cradling his cup, Abbs drained the last of his tea. 'I don't know, Sergeant. It has to be checked, and with any luck we'll hear from them by nightfall. Eat up and we'll be on our way again.'

A large horse chestnut overhung the street from the garden of the house next to the hospital. The pavement was lavishly strewn with spiky bright green seed cases. Some had burst, revealing glossy conkers which were being picked over by three small boys. A coalman's cart stood near the entrance, the blinkered horses waiting patiently and a great rumbling as of coals down a chute was coming from the side of the building.

A young nurse opened the door as a thickset man in porter's uniform hurried round the corner to catch them. 'Sorry to keep you waiting, Inspector, had to see the coal in. The sacks all have to be counted. S'allright, nurse, I'll show them the way. It's easiest if I take you, it's right down the back.'

His waxed grey moustache and straight back giving him the look of an old army man, the porter laid them down a right-angled corridor at a swift pace. They passed a small ward on either side, their occupants and a nurse's desk open to view. Although similar this was not the way Dr Avery had taken them on their previous visit. Through other doors they glimpsed a dispensary, outsized sinks and a latrine. The tiles on wall and floor gleamed with disinfectant and overlaying that as they reached the end double doors was a reek of carbolic and chemical.

'Straight through there. The doctor's expecting you.' They both recognised the dark odour familiar from the Exeter mortuary.

'Good afternoon to you both.' Dr Avery was in his linen and unfolding his sleeves as he turned to greet them. Mr Jabez Biggs was holding out the doctor's dark frock coat for him to put on. 'Well timed, as you see, we're done here.'

The body lay on the table in the middle of the room, beneath a large gas bracket. It was decently covered by a sheet from which the bare feet protruded. At the upper body, the breasts were covered and a raw red line was scored between them, reaching almost to the bottom of the neck and held together with fresh stitching. It always reminded Reeve of a fish skeleton and he noticed that the stitches were neater than those he'd seen on other corpses.

Mr Biggs hovered discreetly at Dr Avery's elbow, his eyes downcast and features composed so solemnly that the sergeant had an urge to laugh. He concentrated instead on a workbench along the back of the room and a large glass jar containing something like tripe.

'You're both all right in here, I take it? Not likely to keel over?'

'We've seen our share of post-mortems,' said Abbs evenly.

'I don't mind what I see, Doctor, it's the stench,' said Reeve.

'In that case I wouldn't venture too close to that,' said Dr Avery, gesturing at a kidney-shaped, enamel dish next to the jar. 'That's the stomach and this contains the contents.'

'What do you have for us, Doctor?' asked Abbs.

'The stomach contained undigested dried fruit within semi-dissolved matter. Fruit cake at a guess, there was no trace of an earlier meal remaining.'

The inspector nodded. 'We now know she was served afternoon tea before she went out. Can you get the time of death any closer?'

Dr Avery shook his head decisively. 'Not possible, I'm afraid. The state of the stomach indicates the contents were ingested about two to three hours before death and that merely corroborates your thoughts of this morning.'

'It's looking as though the murder took place roughly between six o'clock and about half-past seven,' said Abbs. Mr Biggs cleared his throat with a small cough and looked up, fixing the detectives with his shrewd, bright eyes.

'So the poor lady was meeting someone at dusk, then?' he said, softly. 'A terrible business. We estimated the lady's age at about forty, Inspector.'

'I doubt that will help the Inspector find the perpetrator,' said Dr Avery in some irritation.

'Could you learn any more from the wound?' asked Abbs, addressing his remark to the doctor.

'Again, no more than I surmised at the scene.' They bent together over the head as the doctor tilted it a little towards him. The hair had been shaved away from the edges of the wound. At such close quarters, a few greying strands could be seen, together with incipient pouches beneath the eyes and a patch of coarse skin on the cleavage. Abbs knew that back in the Exeter station, he was reputed to be a cold fish, yet he felt despicable for noticing such details even while his dispassionate mind recorded them.

'No foreign particles embedded, unfortunately. If you examine the extent of the haematoma which can be seen more clearly now, the bruising pattern indicates considerable force, applied by a smooth weapon. If it were the angular handle of a cane, I would expect to see sharp tears.' Dr Avery handed Abbs a magnifying glass. On either side of the table Reeve and Mr Biggs had moved closer as though seconds to the two principles.

'Thank you, Doctor,' said Abbs as he straightened up. 'A life preserver still looks likely, then.'

'I should say so. Lead-weighting would fit with the severity and spread of the trauma while being a smooth surfaced weapon.'

'It would fit in a coat pocket,' said Reeve.

'Yes, that's another point,' said the doctor. 'If Miss Geake was confronted by a raised weapon she would have put up her arms to protect herself. It's human instinct, but whereas a man might try to grab the weapon or hit out, a female surely would raise her arms in horror or turn to flee? The fact that there are no defensive injuries on her hands or arms, and the site of the wound to one side here, suggests she saw no danger until the impact.'

Nodding thoughtfully, the soft sound of Mr Biggs's tongue clicking behind his teeth made Abbs look across at him. The clerk looked as though he were about to polish silver in a butler's pantry, were it not for the unrecognisable stains on the dark green apron he wore.

'A terrible business, to be sure.'

'It is indeed.' He supposed it too churlish to ignore the fellow, who presumably meant well. He had little patience with obsequiousness nor those who devoured penny dreadfuls and lurid newsprint accounts of mayhem. The idea that some poor devil's horror was entertainment to the masses disgusted him. And yet, thought Abbs, as the others showed Reeve the long incision, his working life was spent peering in dark places.

Beyond the circle of light, their shadows were thrown giant-like against the cold wall. As he watched, one detached itself from the rest and loomed over him. The gas flickered and the undertaker's clerk coughed tentatively.

'It would appear, Inspector that one small mystery has been solved. Young Bram was telling the truth as he saw it, after all.'

'What's that you say, Biggs?' asked Dr Avery.

Reeve looked at Abbs and their eyes followed the clerk as he gestured to the pile of grey clothing folded on the workbench.

'Bram's ghost,' breathed Mr Biggs.

The tide had retreated a long way out and the beginning of water could be discerned only fitfully as the wind blew clouds to and fro across the pale sliver of moon. Somewhere far out a single light burned, marking a vessel. Abbs stood at the esplanade railings, relishing the cool night air after the fug in the

Anchor. Reeve had gone up to his room but he needed a few moments alone to think in the darkness before retiring to the small chamber under the eaves. A clock sounded across the streets, whether from the town-hall or the church, he knew not. His over-tired mind roamed back over the events of the long day. At this time on the previous evening, Miss Geake already lay dead. He felt a stab of pity for the needle tongued, clear-sighted woman he had met. Unhappy and not without goodness. Gone now, gutted like a fish on the mortuary table.

He rubbed a hand over his brow, knowing he should have remembered Bram's tale at once. What he most feared was happening, he was weary and missing things. The telegram from Superintendent Nicholls, there on his return from the hospital had been circumspect in its wording. Even Nicholls for all his coarse bluster would observe the proprieties. He was a great one for discipline and would not have lowly, uniformed constables in Seaborough reading a dressing-down for a senior detective. But the order had been uncompromising. One more week to solve the murders or the case would be taken from them.

Jabez Biggs, who could stitch a gaping incision in a corpse more neatly than some women could hem a sheet. He was right of course about Bram's tale of the churchyard ghost. Miss Geake had evidently taken to half-mourning since he had interviewed her. Could Mr Biggs be more involved than appearing at every opportunity? Abbs could see no motive but that was so for everyone connected with Tower House on the day Miss Chorley died. Biggs had not even been there. Philip Winton had told them of his fear that the clerk knew something about his background. How when they'd worked together, Mr Biggs had stealthily questioned him about his past. He was not a blackmailer, decided Abbs, but rather one of those people who avidly collect information, simply for the pleasure of its possession.

Miss Geake though, he believed, had tried her hand at blackmailing and paid with her life. Reeve was inclined to the view that she had been meeting a lover. Sergeant Tancock had returned, both disgruntled and triumphant with two discoveries to present. A lady's reticule had been found in the churchyard and an elderly female who lived diagonally opposite the church had seen a woman of Miss Geake's description entering the gate at approximately a quarter before six o'clock. There had been no response yet from the constabulary in Hampshire. Abbs, deciding there was no point in calling at the station again at that late hour, walked slowly back to the inn. His footsteps echoed in the empty street and the sky was as dark and clouded as his thoughts.

Twenty-four

The reticule, dark blue beadwork with a drawstring, tassel and wrist loop, lay on the desk between them. It had been found behind the heap of dead flowers in a corner of the churchyard. The few contents were spread out, a handkerchief with the initial *A* embroidered in one corner, a tiny flask of smelling salts and a key. There was no money.

'Miss Geake leaves Tower House at some time after half-past four when Sarah collects the tea things. It takes a half-hour to walk down to the town, maybe forty minutes for a woman. We don't know what time she left but a female in grey costume is seen entering the churchyard at a quarter before six o'clock, it all fits.' Abbs sat back in his chair.

'Lucky the old lady was looking from her window,' said Reeve. 'She was expecting her son to call and keeping an eye out.'

'And Bram saw his ghost on his way back from the butcher's as it was near closing. Which according to the sergeant would be about six. So it looks as though Miss Geake met someone in the churchyard at least twice, probably at six o'clock and she made sure to be there early.'

'Funny place to meet, though, sir.'

'I was giving it some thought last night. How many places are there where two people can meet without being seen, somewhere perceived as safe and respectable for a woman and dry if it rains?'

Reeve chose not to see it as a rhetorical question. 'They can't go in a public, and they don't want to use one of their homes. Let's see, they could converse while walking.'

'Too much risk of being seen,' said Abbs promptly. 'They don't want questions asked.'

'A sea-front shelter then or... the church porch. In the middle of the town, respectable with the vicarage close by and villas opposite, yet not too overlooked and sheltered from bad weather,' finished Reeve.

'I think so,' agreed Abbs, 'and at dusk they were unlikely to be disturbed. Most folk don't care to frequent graveyards then but Miss Geake was a strong-minded lady.'

'So who was she meeting and why?'

'I don't believe she was having assignations with a lover, Sergeant,' said Abbs. 'I think she was blackmailing the murderer.'

Reeve started to whistle under his breath and catching the inspector's eye, stopped. 'Putting the black on. She was taking a big risk, sir. She didn't expect to be battered over the head then.'

Abbs winced in distaste. 'No, I think we can assume Miss Geake felt safe. She thought she had a winning hand and miscalculated.'

'So we're looking for a man?'

'Dr Avery did say a woman could have managed it, though it isn't easy to imagine one female doing that to another. Blackmailers are killed from desperation, fury or fear. I think it would be a mistake to assume the murderer is male.'

'She would have felt safer with another woman.'

'That's a good point. So what do you think she could have known in order to blackmail someone, Sergeant?'

'Information about Miss Chorley's death,' said Reeve at once. 'She must have seen something which means it was at the tea party or when Mr Hicks called later. It puts Mr Winton in the clear. Miss Geake didn't go to the studio with Miss Chorley and Captain Selden.' He looked pleased with his reasoning.

'What I'd like to know is this,' said Abbs. 'Did Miss Geake know the identity of the murderer from the start or did she realise something over the days since?'

'But sir, doesn't this make it Captain Selden?' said Reeve, excitement shining on his face. 'We know from Sarah that it looks like she was blackmailing him?'

Abbs shook his head. 'I disagree. She had some hold over him, certainly, and we need to know what, but I can't see her sharing the house with a cold-blooded poisoner.' He regarded his sergeant with concealed approval. The morning sun finding its way through the small window was in Reeve's face, making his eyes crinkle. At eight-and-twenty, if he recalled correctly from the sergeant's record, his enthusiasm was still fresh. Abbs found himself hoping that the nature of their work would not turn Reeve into another Superintendent Nicholls by fifty. It was a long while since he had thought about his small brothers, dead before grown to be companions.

'Sir?' Abbs realised the sergeant had been speaking. 'Sorry, I didn't sleep well. What were you saying?'

'I wondered how many times Miss Geake had an assignation with the murderer?'

'I doubt she met him or her more than twice. Think about it, she contacts the poisoner, possibly at a social meeting but more likely by letter. Miss Shaw said she'd stopped going to the Ladies' Society though the servants said she was going out walking. They meet once, the poisoner needs to hear what she has to say and probably hands over a down payment. They stall for time so a second meeting is arranged. Miss Geake was leaving Seaborough, remember. This would have been their only chance to kill her.'

'It all makes sense. So who could Miss Geake have seen do something, so she realised they were the murderer?'

'Let's look at it logically. We're satisfied it wasn't Mr Winton and we'll leave Captain Selden to one side. I can't see any motive for the servants, Mrs Watkins, Sarah, William and ...'

'Jane,' supplied Reeve. 'And I can't believe it was Mary, the dismissed maid.'

Abbs yawned and rubbed his eyes. 'Which brings us to the guests on that day and self-invited Mr Hicks. What do you think about the Shaws and Mr Emerson?'

'Can't see it was Mr Emerson, myself. Why he's a retired JP, part of the gentry and he was keen to help us.'

'That wouldn't necessarily be a character reference,' said Abbs dryly. 'Though I agree in this case. There could be something in his past that Miss Chorley knew, I suppose but I'm blowed if I can come up with any motive for killing her now.'

'Same goes for the vicar,' continued Reeve, who was thoroughly enjoying himself. It was rare in his experience for a sergeant to be consulted almost on an equal footing. 'I'm not sure we should forget Miss Shaw though.'

Abbs looked at him in surprise. 'Go on, Sergeant.'

'Don't get me wrong, sir, I thought she seemed a very nice lady but we don't really know anything about her private life. Could Miss Chorley have come into possession of some secret about her? Something that would ruin her if made public? She could have met Miss Geake at the church porch and slipped home in minutes.'

'An enterprising theory, Sergeant. But do you really think Miss Shaw capable of hitting another woman over the head? Besides which, from what we've discovered of Miss Chorley's character, she would have revealed any misdemeanour the minute she knew of it. She would have seen it as her painful duty.'

'S'pose you're right, sir.'

'Which brings us to the others. Mr and Mrs Hicks and Mrs Halesworth. Let us take the ladies first.'

'I didn't meet Mrs Hicks, if you recall, sir, and I only saw Mrs Halesworth briefly.'

'So you did. Mrs Hicks seemed pleasant and kindly, a talkative lady and a close friend of the Shaws. I'd find it difficult to imagine her a murderess. Now Mrs Halesworth I could see as determined and tough as any man but direct, not devious, I fancy.'

'Couldn't she act on behalf of her husband?'

'Quite possibly but I can't believe she'd poison someone. I should think Alfred Halesworth is unscrupulous, dodgy dealings on the council, very likely but more than that, who knows?' Abbs shrugged and glanced down at his notes.

'That only leaves Mr Hicks.'

'As likeable as his wife. Someone must be wearing a mask, Reeve. I think we need to take a closer look at the business plans of our councillor and undertaker. Perhaps one of them had a pressing need for their building deal to happen and Miss Chorley stood in their way.'

'If we ask around, they'll get to hear about it,' said Reeve. 'And the bank manager won't tell.'

'I thought to ask the third member of their business dealings. As a medical man and police-surgeon, Dr Avery will understand the need for discretion and he shouldn't object to discussing his friends in the circumstances. In fact,' said Abbs, consulting the clock on the mantel-shelf, 'he probably has lunch at home. I think I'll try to catch him.' Seeing Reeve's expression fall, he added, 'I'll see him alone as that will make it easier for him if he feels he's breaking a confidence. Besides I need you here to await the confirmation from Hampshire.' Taking up his hat, Abbs paused at the door. 'Go through the reports again and if I'm not back, I'll meet you outside the hotel at ten minutes to three.'

Dr Avery's house proved to be a medium-sized, detached villa built in the local brick. It had decorative terracotta roof tiles, a sharply pitched gable with brown-painted barge boards and matching porch. A sign indicated *Surgery* to the left, where the path vanished in a gloomy shrubbery. As he turned into the short drive, the front door opened and Abbs saw a small white terrier spill down the steps and race excitedly towards him. Immediately behind him in the doorway were an elderly lady and the doctor.

'Gyp, to heel. Come here now,' called the latter. The dog paused in his careering in circles, glancing back to his master and then at Abbs, his tail wagging in friendly fashion.

'He won't bite you,' called Dr Avery as Abbs advanced easily. 'It's more that he'll cover you in hairs. For a short-haired coat he sheds them everywhere, don't you, sir?' The little dog having trotted obediently back to him, he bent and rubbed his head before encouraging him gently back inside with his foot.

'I'm used to dogs,' said Abbs, 'or I was when growing up. He's a fine specimen.'

'I had him from a farm,' replied the doctor. 'He was the runt of a litter so they were only going to drown him. As you say, he filled out well and he's a great ratter. Thank you, Mrs Fayter. I expect to be home this evening.' The grey-haired lady smiled at Abbs and bade him good day as he raised his hat to her.

'As you see, you've only just caught me,' said Dr Avery. 'Is it urgent?'

'I wanted to ask your help,' said Abbs. 'It's rather delicate.'

'Walk with me,' invited Dr Avery, raising his eyebrows. 'Now you have me curious. I'm on my way to see a patient but it's a duty call, gout. A few minutes won't go amiss. I keep my gig at the livery stables round the corner.'

'Thank you. I've seen your dog before, I happened to see you out ratting recently. I'd been exploring the hill-fort and saw you with several others making for a barn.'

'And you're thinking it a poor occupation for a Sunday?' said the doctor humorously, as they strolled. 'I did attend church in the morning.'

'That's more than I did,' confessed Abbs. 'I went up there to get away from Seaborough and think about the case.'

The doctor nodded. 'Life in a small town can be stultifying. I like the country air myself and a man should have exercise. I find fishing gives me a chance to think,' he added. 'My cares seem easier when I'm sitting on a river bank.'

'I used to enjoy it in boyhood,' said Abbs. 'You were accompanying Mr Halesworth and Mr Hicks when I saw you.'

Pausing to raise his hat to two ladies descending from a carriage, Dr Avery looked sharply back at Abbs. 'What is it you wish to know about them, Inspector?'

Abbs grinned briefly. 'There you have me, Doctor, I don't know myself. They are your friends yet as police-surgeon you'll see my problem. We still haven't found a motive for Miss Chorley's murder and I find myself wondering about the building land she refused to sell.'

Stopping still, Dr Avery appeared dumbstruck for a second, before breaking into a chuckle. The relaxing of his stern features shed years from his countenance, so that when he sobered, he looked all the more pallid. 'How did you find out about that? Halesworth was very anxious for it to be kept quiet.'

'Mr Hicks told me,' said Abbs. 'He hasn't mentioned it, then?'

The doctor shook his head. 'I've seen little of them lately, apart from our sporting afternoon and then we were in close company. I doubt Hicks has told Halesworth you know, for all they're old friends. I regard them more as colleagues and associates. Hicks is a good fellow but Halesworth and I have had our run-ins.'

'Mr Hicks did say that you'd been part of a previous business deal with them.'

'That's perfectly true. They approached me to put up a third and I'd recently been left a legacy to invest. It was a good deal, I know nothing of building but property will always give a sound return and you can see bricks and mortar.'

'Indeed so. What I want to ask is do you know of any problems either of them might be facing? A pressing need for money that they don't want known? Was there any reason that this prospective land deal was vital to one of them?'

The doctor listened attentively, his eyes on Abbs and his head slightly to one side. The bruise had gone on his face now and he moved with ease. Abbs suddenly wondered if he had tumbled in a river and made up a tale, not wanting to look a fool. He could imagine Halesworth guffawing and repeating it the length of a bar.

'I'm sorry, Inspector. Frankly, I can think of nothing that would help you.' Dr Avery knitted his brows in thought. 'Hicks is fairly cautious. I don't believe he would overreach himself. He's built a leading business in the town by doing it steadily and providing good service. Most people go to him if they can afford it, which is not to say he overcharges. In fact, he's well known for a soft heart. I believe him to be happily married and Mrs Hicks is in full possession of his confidence regarding money and business matters.'

'Really?'

'You look surprised. Mrs Hicks has helped her husband build their small empire. She knows the value of a pound.'

'And Mr Halesworth?'

'Now he may well overreach himself, I'm not privy to his financial dealings. He and his wife live extravagantly but his prosperity and influence always seem to be increasing. He has a shrewd eye for business or I wouldn't consider investing with him again. In fact, I haven't committed myself. Miss Chorley's parcel of land was the only one sufficiently large for Halesworth's scheme. He was extremely keen to get his hands on it but not desperate. He doesn't care to be thwarted but then, do any of us?'

'Do you happen to know where either of them were, two nights ago?'

The doctor looked at Abbs while he considered. 'Say what you mean, man. In early evening at the time Miss Geake was killed?'

Abbs nodded. 'I'm sorry to involve you but it's necessary. Time is of the essence.'

'Do you think they'll kill again?'

Taken aback, Abbs gazed down the street. A sweeper was coming gradually towards them, his task rather hopeless as the limes planted at intervals in the pavement were half-bare. Their leaves thick in the gutter, every now and then another fluttered down. He knew how the man felt.

'That hadn't occurred to me, Doctor.'

'I can't say where either of them were on that evening as I wasn't with them. More often than not, one or both will stop off at The Marine. The professional men of the town tend to congregate in the bar at the rear as a sort of informal club. You can make discreet enquiries there later. A young woman named Emily usually serves behind the bar. There wasn't a council meeting that night.'

The doctor pulled out his watch and consulted it. 'Excuse me but I must be on my way. I've told you all I can.'

'I appreciate your help,' said Abbs.

'Not at all. You'll want to know where I was. Which was by the fire in my study, immersed in a medical journal. But my housekeeper cannot vouch for me as I didn't require anything. Only Gyp could tell you.'

'Thank you, Doctor.'

'Don't have a mind to Jerrold,' said Dr Avery unexpectedly. 'Seaborough is a very small pond with more than its share of big fish.' He bowed. 'Good day, Inspector, I shall see you later at the inquest.'

'Take a pew,' said Halesworth, waving him to the chair before the desk. Mr Hicks watched his friend curiously as he stood before the window, stretching and gazing down on the Square garden they had just crossed. 'People still coming out,' he observed. 'Half the town's down there.' He laughed without humour. 'There goes your long-faced clerk trotting behind Avery. I saw he had a ring-side seat again, practically licking his lips he was.'

'We attended ourselves, to be fair,' said Mr Hicks, crossing his legs. 'Why have we come to your office, did you say? We'd have been a lot more comfortable at The Marine.'

Halesworth shot him an irritable glance over his shoulder and returned to philosophising on the scene below him. 'The policeman's a po-faced one. He'd never make a councillor, his voice is too quiet and there's his cocky young sergeant. You know Jerrold complained about the inspector's high-handedness? Don't think you were there when he was telling us.'

'I did hear something about it,' said Mr Hicks. 'The fellow has his job to do. He was all right to me. Decent to Bram too, which not everyone would have been.'

'That half-wit,' Halesworth grunted as though his mind was elsewhere. 'Don't see why you ever took him on. What good is he?'

'He makes himself useful. I can't afford to keep anyone who doesn't work.'

'You're too soft, Hicks, that's your trouble.'

'If you brought me here to quarrel, I'd rather we'd done it in the bar,' remarked Mr Hicks, easily.

'Mind, I've been too soft, myself,' muttered Halesworth.

'Eh? Nobody could accuse you of that, surely?'

'The vicar's daughter stepping in her carriage. Everyone wanted to hear the gory details. She stood up well in the box, though.'

'Yes, she was most composed. Fanny wanted to accompany her but she wouldn't hear of it.'

'No Shaw, though. Word is, he's unwell. Always looks as though a puff of wind would blow him over. He must be over sixty.' Mr Hicks made no comment.

'Who the devil is it now Selden's out of the running?'

'Murdering defenceless women? If I knew I'd be telling the police.'

'The detective must be running out of time. I thought Osborne gave him an easy ride but loss of public confidence and all that. Seems to me, he'll be taken off the investigation.'

'Then we'll have to tell it all again to someone else from Exeter,' said Mr Hicks.

Halesworth swung round. 'Can't see it, they'll send in Scotland Yard.'

Mr Hicks wondered what was on his friend's mind. Although as fond as the next man of gossip, Halesworth was not one to prevaricate. His impression was that he was making small-talk to delay his real reason for bringing them to his place of business. The fellow looked decidedly rattled.

'A man could die of thirst around here,' he said, lightly.

'Oh, beg pardon, Hicks. What'll it be?' Halesworth moved swiftly to the tantalus standing on a bureau. 'I could do with a drink, Lord knows.'

'Whisky, please. Better make it a small one, it's early yet.'

'I'll join you, small be beggared.' Pouring two hefty measures, Halesworth passed one across the desk and took his chair at last.

'You asked why I brought you over here,' he continued, after first taking a large swallow. 'The need for privacy.' Another generous mouthful. Mr Hicks began to feel somewhat alarmed. He sipped his own drink then set down the glass.

'Is something up, Halesworth? Has Captain Selden turned down our offer for the land?'

'What? No, I'd have told you. Jerrold hasn't heard back from him, yet. It's nothing to do with business. Do try and concentrate.'

There was nothing for it but to be patient. Mr Hicks looked encouragingly at him and waited.

Halesworth cleared his throat. 'Fact is, I needed to be somewhere where no one could overhear. I'm finished if this gets out and you know what an old tattler Cox is.' He subsided again. 'The thing is, old man. I could do with your advice. I'm in a spot of bother.'

After the story had been spilt, Mr Hicks considered in silence for a moment what he might say. 'It seems to me, you have it all worked out.' He stroked his beard as he thought. 'I don't know what you could have done differently in the circumstances.'

Brightening, Halesworth nodded. 'It's a relief to talk to someone sympathetic, nor do I. I've behaved very handsomely and it's not my fault if Nellie's been so careless. I can't be expected to ruin my life, can I?'

'No. There's your wife and girls to consider.'

'Exactly. Have another, old man. I knew you'd see things my way. It'll be all right, won't it? These things blow over.'

'If you can trust the lady not to make trouble.'

'She's never shown the slightest sign that way. She was perfectly amenable the first time, but you can never rely on women. My great fear is that someone's put her up to this. She's mentioned a neighbour once or twice, some shop clerk, scraped an acquaintance, invited her to a concert, obviously sniffing about.'

'She can't afford to turn down your offer. You said there's no family?'

'None, which is just as well,' said Halesworth. 'It's a pity about the boy, but it can't be helped.' Extracting a key on his chain, he unlocked his desk drawer and felt for a photograph. It landed between them, face down, the cardboard mount slightly creased from handling. Mr Hicks picked it up and studied it.

'Very pretty.'

'I daren't keep it at home. I wouldn't trust Rosa not to rifle my pocket-book or desk but she never comes here. I've been on pins lest a letter comes to the house, I can tell you.' Though Halesworth accompanied this with a grin as he clinked glasses, satisfied that all his troubles were behind him.

As they entered the bottom of the street they saw Sergeant Tancock coming out of his house, next door to the police station. He buttoned his jacket as he saw them and brushed some crumbs from his protruding front, making Abbs smile inwardly.

'Afternoon, sir. How did it go, might I ask?'

'Much as expected, Sergeant. The coroner heard the evidence of finding the body and the post-mortem, then adjourned.'

'Well, sir, your telegram from 'ampshire has come.'

'At last,' exclaimed Abbs, hurrying up the steps with Reeve at his heels. They waited impatiently for Sergeant Tancock to join them and pass through the opening in the unmanned counter. It seemed with maddening slowness he removed the communication from a docket spike and presented it to the inspector. Scanning it swiftly, he handed it to Reeve.

'What do you make of that, Sergeant?'

A grin spread over Reeve's face as he read the few lines, though he looked up questioningly as he handed back the message. He's learning not to jump to conclusions, thought Abbs in satisfaction.

'Captain Selden's unwell and not back at his desk.'

'From a Sergeant Webber,' remarked Abbs, studying the paper. 'Offers any further assistance, most cordially.'

'So no one at the military hospital has actually set eyes on him since he came back from Seaborough?'

'So it would seem. Let me have your *Bradshaw* again, would you, Tancock? Thanks.' Indicating Reeve to follow him with a jerk of his head, Abbs entered the short passage that led to their office.

'I'm going to have to do some calculating,' continued the inspector, when they were seated, 'but I think Captain Selden could have killed Miss Geake and just about returned to Hampshire that night. He could have travelled via the capital and in that case, stayed the night there. All that would be imperative would be to get away from Seaborough as fast as possible, without being recognised.'

'He wouldn't be known at the station,' said Reeve.

'No. I shall want you to ask if the station staff recall any passengers for the late train on that evening. I shall go to Hampshire tomorrow. I want to speak to the Captain again, in any event.'

'I'm to stay here, sir?'

'You are, Reeve. I need someone I can trust here, meaning no offence to Sergeant Tancock and his men.'

'Understood, sir.'

'I was telling you what Dr Avery had to say. He said something that struck a chord. I made a chance remark about running out of time and the doctor asked me if I feared the murderer killing again. It set me thinking on a different line. Poisoning is a calculated way to remove someone. People do it for two reasons. One, so they don't have to be present at the death, and two because they hope it will be passed off as natural causes. With me, so far?'

'Yes, sir. The doc admitted he'd probably have thought Miss Chorley died of gastro-enteritis. It was only Dr Miller's being awkward, brought us in.'

'Suppose we're looking at this the wrong way round? We see Miss Chorley's death as the beginning. What if the murderer had done this before and got away with it?'

Reeve scratched his ear reflectively as he turned this over in his mind. 'I don't quite get it, sir. What's made you think that?'

Abbs stood up and moved the few paces to the unlit grate. Leaning his hand on the mantle-shelf, he absently straightened a spill vase and traced his finger in the dust. 'I don't know, desperation perhaps? We have to find another angle. Why was Miss Chorley in someone's way? That's what it comes down to. Miss Geake's murder was a consequence.'

Returning to the desk, Abbs went on. 'While I'm gone, I want you to find out how many deaths there've been in Seaborough in.. say, this year. It won't hurt to look. When you have a list we'll go through it together. We'll be able to eliminate most of them at once, so it shouldn't take long. Don't bother with children. Do you know how to go about it?'

'See the Superintendent Registrar for this district,' replied Reeve instantly.

'Good man. I'll see what Captain Selden has to say for himself.' Abbs reached for the *Bradshaw* and a sheet of paper, as he spoke. 'There's something Mr Emerson said that I want to ask him about. We've no jurisdiction in Hampshire of course, so I shall take up Sergeant Webber's offer of assistance.'

Twenty-five

It had taken much of the day to travel to Hampshire, including three changes of train and a lengthy wait at the busy junction of Salisbury. The county was unknown to him and Abbs was interested to view the changing topography. The latter part of the route traversed the southern portion of the New Forest, which he found had long stretches of wild heath where ponies grazed and glinting pools lay between woodland. An elderly gentleman getting on at a halt was eager to tell him that *forest* in its original sense referred to a hunting ground; in this instance the desmesne of William the Conqueror and encompassed a variety of landscapes. Strangers were always surprised, he said. Though woods they passed in plenty, full of venerable oaks and beeches. Autumn seemed further advanced here with their branches almost bare and the ground thick with decaying leaves and beech mast.

The final change was at Southampton. It was late in the day for travellers but he could imagine the porters wheeling trunks and the bustle of passengers pushing their way between three platforms and signs directing them to the pier for the Isle of Wight steamer and the Hythe ferry. At that time the station was busy with respectable men of all description. Browsing at the large bookstall, Abbs decided they were clerks and managers on their way home to the growing suburbs and smaller towns along the line.

When the Netley train pulled out, they passed streets of identical, sooty terraces, their only colour from advertisements affixed to end walls. Every now and then, he glimpsed an expanse of water between building works. This he knew from consulting a map on the previous evening, must be the estuary. Southampton sat at its head and lay several miles from the coast, his destination was situated on its east side, about half-way down. As he stared out, the merchant city gradually gave way to wood and pasture, the land for the most part, flat and well kept.

The nights were drawing in and twilight had come on by the time he stepped down at Netley station. Several passengers had alighted though he could see no one waiting. A few went past the ticket collector at an iron gate and down a stony lane which looked to be the edge of the village. Someone had made a patch of garden behind railings where the station name was painted on white-washed rocks. The platform contained only a small waiting-room and Abbs realised that the main station building was on the opposite platform. He picked up his case and followed the greater part of passengers over the brick footbridge. As the clouds of steam dispersed and the locomotive slid beneath them, he viewed a trim station fronted in white stucco, built in the Italianate style. The station-master's house was attached and beyond lay a signal-box, wherein the signalman could be seen, a shadowy figure moving to and fro.

The others were streaming through the ticket-office with the determined familiarity of weary men going home. Most of them would do it for fifty years or more, he thought. Standing by a gay poster advertising *Sunny Southsea* was a uniformed sergeant scanning the faces. He smiled broadly as Abbs walked up to him and saluted smartly. Returning the smile, Abbs was amused at the contrast from his meeting with lackadaisical Sergeant Tancock.

'Am I right in thinking you're Inspector Abbs, sir?' Receiving confirmation, the sergeant went on. 'Sergeant Thomas Webber, sir, Netley's my patch. My superior, Inspector Ruddock presents his compliments. He's asked me to welcome you on behalf of Hampshire constabulary and he's put me at your disposal to show you round and assist in any way.'

'Thank you, Sergeant. It's a flying visit, as you know so I shouldn't take you too long from your usual duties. Please thank Inspector Ruddock for his assistance. I'll write a line, myself when I get back.'

'I'll do that, sir. Take your bag? Though it's only a step. I've taken the liberty of booking you into The Station Hotel here. It's not large but the best accommodation hereabouts, for all the soot.'

'I'm sure it will do very well, I'm obliged to you, Sergeant.'

'We've two inns in the village that let rooms, sir but they're mostly taken and one's on the mean side, in any case. Folk visiting the hospital generally stay here if they can.'

'Are we far from the military hospital?'

'No, sir, down the road there and a short walk along the shore takes you to the main gate. Though it's a fair step when you're in the grounds.'

'I did wonder if the hospital would have its own station?'

'Maybe one day, sir, they've everything else. The troops are taken off here but a good many arrive by sea and up Southampton Water.'

'I see. Sounds an interesting place.'

'We're very proud of it, sir. There's none like it but you'll see for yourself in the morning. I understand you need to visit the adjutant's office?'

'That's right. My enquiry is in connection with one of the officers in the army pay corps.'

Sergeant Webber nodded, his bald head gleaming in the lamplight, although he was a vigorous man of about his own age. 'We want the Commissariat then, that's the admin block.'

'I can see your help is going to be invaluable, Sergeant,' said Abbs.

'Do my best, sir. Step this way then, if you please.'

Having his ticket clipped, Abbs followed the sergeant through the booking office where a fire looked welcoming in the small grate. Outside was a spacious sweep of gravel with *The Station Hotel* standing on a corner.

'I'll leave you to settle in then, sir. You've had a long journey, I believe? Can I assist you in any way this evening?'

'Thank you, no. I'll be glad to wash the dust off and get something to eat,' said Abbs.

'I think you'll be suited there, Inspector. The landlord's wife does a very tasty steak and oyster pie.'

'I'd be obliged if you'd call for me straight after breakfast, Sergeant.'

'Will do, sir. The police house is straight down the road, on the left-hand side, just before the shops, should you need it. You can't miss it.'

'Thank you, I'll bid you goodnight, Wheeler.' Abbs watched him set off down the road at a sharp pace, his fellow passengers had long vanished. From what he could see, Netley looked quite a large village. The road which was lined with fairly recent villas, led slightly downhill in the direction of the water.

He would have liked to go for a walk and get his bearings after supper but found himself too weary to stir. One fact had been playing at the back of his mind since he had learnt it from Mr Emerson. Captain Selden had paid his visit to his aunt in late September but he had been expected in the weeks preceding Christmas. His leave had been brought forward.

His instinct told him that somehow this change of plan was significant. It had to be, they had found nothing unusual in Miss Chorley's life except her nephew's visit. It had to link in some way to her death, though how, he still did not know. He did not really believe that Captain Selden had stealthily returned to Seaborough and murdered his aunt's companion but he had one more chance to interview him. Selden's visit had to be the catalyst for the murders. Everything depended on his asking the right questions.

Twenty-six

A watery sun was breaking through the clouds as they turned into the main street. To the right, Abbs could see a parade of a dozen or so shops, their awnings down and quite a few people about their business but Sergeant Webber directed them left, towards a public house on the corner with a row of terraced cottages beyond.

'Netley doesn't appear to be a long-established village,' said Abbs pleasantly, as they walked.

Sergeant Webber beamed beneath his exuberant, waxed moustache. He seemed most enthusiastic about his charge. 'Why, sir, we've abbey ruins at the other end of the village,' he looked back, pointing out the way they had come. 'And there's a Tudor castle along that road, built to guard the Water but that's a private residence.' He turned forward again, touching his hat as an elderly gentleman passed them.

'Morning, Mr Collins. Though you're quite right, sir, there's nothing else old here. The parish church was built about the same time as the hospital. Netley's growing as it's considered a desirable place to settle. We've our share of folk living on their own means who come for the healthy air and there's more houses going up for professional types. They can live in the country and take the railway to town, you see.'

They were now passing the last building on their right and drawing level with a narrow, shingle beach opposite the cottages. Abbs stopped to take in the view. It was a morning of greys and silvers, the wide expanse of water almost merging with the clouds, shimmering intermittently in the weak sunlight. He could smell the salt and hear the haunting cry of a cormorant.

'How far across is it?'

'Four mile, Inspector. There's the steamer off to the Island,' added the sergeant, pointing.

'The island?'

'Isle of Wight, sir, where Her Majesty's house is. Though the royal party sail from Pompey, that's Portsmouth.' The sergeant shook his head, as though lamenting the royal household's regrettable lapse. 'We always call it The Island in these parts. Now here's the gate up ahead, sir.'

Rather wishing he could be left to himself, Abbs quickened his pace until they reached the double gates with a brick lodge at either side. Large lamps were affixed on top of the gate posts and a wide drive edged with young trees swept beyond.

'We'll need your identification now, sir, if you don't mind waiting outside. Won't keep you a minute.'

Abbs looked about him in great interest. The Royal Victoria Military Hospital was on a far grander scale than he had envisaged. The building was visible away to the left, set in expansive lawns divided by smaller drives. Red brick with rows of rounded windows embellished with white stone, it stood three storeys high and was surmounted by a white dome. A long wing stretched either side of the central block and on the corner visible from where he stood, another wing stretched behind. He guessed there were further wings around a great quadrangle. It was very like a barracks.

'All done, sir, you're expected. What do you make of it? Magnificent place, don't you think?' said the sergeant, without leaving space for an answer.

'It certainly is, Sergeant.' They set off along the main drive which took a curving route to the entrance. On their right the lawns ended in a belt of scots pines and Abbs's attention was caught by a wide iron pier. It had its own formal gate, flanked by a pair of seafront-style shelters.

'That's where they bring the wounded in, sir,' remarked the sergeant. 'That's why the pier's wider at that end. Course they can't take a ship in that close. Water's not deep enough near the shore. No, they take them off in tenders.'

'The hospital is far larger than I expected,' said Abbs. 'I remember reading about it when it opened. When was that, exactly?' Sergeant Webber was sure to know.

'Ten years ago, sir. Though the Queen came when they laid the foundation stone in '56. There's one hundred and thirty-eight wards, I do believe. Of course, they're not full in times of peace.'

'And what is that impressive memorial?' said Abbs, turning his back on Southampton Water.

'Ah, now, that's very interesting, sir. It's to the medical officers who fell in the Crimea.'

It would help to be left alone for a few minutes to arrange his thoughts. He was unclear whether Captain Selden was within the building or to be found at his home. Still, he was about to find out, he thought as they entered the reception area at last.

The adjutant proved to be brisk and efficient, a few minutes finding him rejoining Sergeant Webber who was chatting to an orderly, outside the entrance.

'I understand you're enquiring as to the whereabouts of a Captain Edwin Selden,' said the officer when they were seated. He handed back Abbs's identification which he had carefully examined.

'That's so, sir.'

'And this is in connection with a murder inquiry, the unfortunate death of his relative?'

Abbs inclined his head. The officer gave him a keen look before applying his reading spectacles and untying a manila folder. He withdrew a single sheet and studied it impassively for a moment. Waiting patiently, Abbs looked at the painting behind the desk. Unlike the photographs flanking it, the oil was not military in subject but depicted a mountainous scene with houses resembling chalets and lush greenery. Together with the officer's tunic, it made the only dash of colour in the customary brown office.

'Darjeeling,' said the adjutant, without raising his eyes.

'An interesting painting.'

'To the point.' He replaced the sheet, inked between printed columns and gave Abbs his complete attention. 'Captain Selden has had an unblemished military record throughout long service, principally in India. In the opinion of his commanding officers he is of good character.'

'That is not in dispute, sir.'

'Good. We don't want any of our men bringing Her Majesty's army into disrepute. I trust that's understood, Inspector Abbs.'

'I'm here to put further questions to Captain Selden as a witness. There has unfortunately been a second murder since his return to Netley.'

'In that case I can see you need to make certain he was on duty at the relevant time.' The adjutant removed his glasses.

'I expect that to be a formality,' replied Abbs. 'As I inferred, it isn't my main reason for travelling here to interview him.'

'Understood. Captain Selden comes under the Paymaster's department. He's responsible for an office of pay clerks, in other words accounts. They deal with payments for settling the affairs of soldiers from all over the empire, sick pay, dependents, allowances accrued, that type of thing and for the staff of course. In addition they handle all the bills from the purveyors' department for running this establishment. Although our purpose is medical, we are in effect an army base, Inspector.'

'The scale of it seems remarkable, sir.'

'I doubt civilians could run it. We can handle up to one thousand patients here with the beds at full capacity. And cases may be surgical, medical, convalescent or all three.' He smiled at Abbs. 'According to the Paymaster, to whom I spoke again earlier this morning, Captain Selden has not in fact returned to his desk since his leave in Devonshire. That was extended on compassionate grounds in the circumstances. He lives in the village and sent word that he is indisposed. Should this continue any further he will need to produce a medical certificate. Grief is all too common in my profession, Inspector Abbs, and cannot be an acceptable excuse for abandonment of duty.'

'Thank you for your help, sir. I won't take up any more of your time.' Abbs rose to his feet, holding his hat. 'One thing, is it usual for officers to live outside the hospital?'

'Not uncommon. We provide an accommodation block for all ranks but once settled, some officers do care to buy a house in the village, particularly if they have private means. One thing we are short of is privacy.'

Abbs was about to leave when the adjutant spoke again. 'Look here, Inspector, I've no personal knowledge of Selden, only what I've read. The army has room for all types and a good C.O deploys men where they're most useful. I would say he's better suited to administration than active service, if you take my meaning. Can you find your way back to the main door?'

Assuring him he could, Abbs pondered the adjutant's enigmatic comment as he emerged from the echoing corridor into a lovely autumn day. The sun had come out fully in the few minutes he had been inside and bees were working busily among a bed of fading lavender by the bench where Sergeant Webber was waiting.

'My word, that was quick. Where now, sir?' Breaking off his conversation, the sergeant sprang to his feet.

'If you could give me directions to this address, then I'll need trouble you no further, Sergeant.' Abbs held out a page in his notebook.

'Can't do that, sir. Inspector Ruddock wouldn't like that at all. My orders are to give you every facility. I'll see you to the door and see the gent with you, if you wish.'

'Thank you, Webber, that won't be necessary.' Conceding the inevitable, Abbs fell into step with the sergeant. 'Back the same way, I take it?'

'That's right, sir, two streets back from the shore road. Did you get all the information you needed, might I enquire?'

'The adjutant was most accommodating. That's a handsome chapel over there.'

'Indeed it is, sir. Now the cemetery...' here the sergeant actually lowered his voice, 'that's hidden way over the back of the grounds. It wouldn't do to have it seen from the windows.'

'No, I suppose not. Are the grounds extensive then behind the hospital?'

'Oh, they are, sir. Tell me, would you care to look? I don't suppose anyone in authority would mind.'

'I cannot spare the time, Sergeant. It's imperative I get on my way back as soon as my business here is concluded.' Abbs tried to inject a note of regret in his voice, nevertheless the sergeant's face fell.

'That's a real pity, sir. Down that way's the usual offices, you might say, stables, laundry, stores. But I don't suppose you expected them to have their own fire station and gasworks?'

'Indeed I did not.'

'They've a post office, school, brickworks, talk about equipped for anything. It's more like a town than a hospital. Why there's even a reservoir, though that's out of the grounds.' The sergeant broke off to raise a hand to the soldier on the gate.

With some further difficulty Abbs persuaded Webber to part company, assuring him he could find his way back to the railway station where he'd left his case and thanking him for his assistance. The street where Captain Selden lived was quiet and respectable; semi-detached villas with a few feet of front garden and their doors almost touching, the province of clerks and elderly ladies. Selden's was distinguishable only by its name Muree, which stood oddly between Ferndale and his next door neighbour Lomond. He rapped the knocker and after a moment when no one came, saw the lace twitch in the side of the modest bay window, close by him. Then the door opened cautiously and his quarry peered out.

'Inspector Abbs, you've come a long way to find me.' Captain Selden's voice was flat and dull.

'You don't sound surprised to see me, Captain.'

'Mr Jerrold wrote to me. I know about Miss Geake's death.' Sighing, he held the door wider. 'Do come in.'

'Thank you.'

'Through here.'

Abbs took in the small hallway at a glance as its owner showed him in the nearest door. An etched shell case was in use as a stand for sticks and umbrella. A console table held a brass tray and peacock feathers in an ugly vase. Highly-polished boots stood beneath and a glass in an oak frame hung on the patterned paper above.

'Do sit down.' Rejecting the armchairs, Abbs took a seat at the small dining table under the window. The fire was lit and the room felt unpleasantly warm on such a mild day. A rug was thrown over the arm of the chair with a footstool so perhaps Captain Selden really was unwell. Hard to say, as he was one of those men who never appeared to look robust.

'Can I offer you tea, Inspector?'

'I won't, thank you.'

'Is that because you've come to arrest me?' His tone wavered, thought Abbs, between nervous and bitter.

'It's because I've recently had some. Why should you believe you're about to be arrested?'

'I've no alibi for Miss Geake's death.'

'We require rather more grounds than that, sir. Innocent people very often don't have alibis.'

Hope sparked in Selden's eyes and went out again as Abbs watched. 'I should say at once that I did not kill the woman. I'm no murderer, Inspector.'

'Are you telling me that you left Seaborough on the morning you came looking for me and you've remained here in Netley ever since?'

'I am, yes. I've been indisposed so haven't yet resumed my duties. In fact I haven't left the house.'

'How do you manage about food?' said Abbs, conversationally. 'You'd been in Devonshire for some weeks.'

Captain Selden removed the side of the thumbnail he was biting, in order to answer. 'I have a woman who comes in, does the rough work.'

Abbs nodded. 'I've just been to the hospital and spoken to the adjutant. It was necessary to confirm your whereabouts.' The Captain looked down at his nails and placed his hands beneath the table. 'Fortunately then, you do have someone who can vouch for your presence here.' Captain Selden's head jerked up but he made no comment. Pushing his notebook across the table and holding out his pencil, Abbs continued. 'If you'll jot down your daily's address, I'll see if she's home later.'

'She only came and did my shopping on my first day back, but I'll write it if you wish.' He scribbled a direction and let the pencil fall. 'I know this won't do for an alibi.'

'Well as I said, sir, not to worry. People don't have them, more often than not.'

Captain Selden looked properly at Abbs for the first time. 'How is your investigation faring, Inspector? Are you any nearer finding who killed my aunt?'

'Yes, I think we are,' replied Abbs, quietly. 'We've cleared up one or two false leads and the murderer has made a great mistake in killing again. My belief is that we're close to a solution.'

'I've given it a great deal of thought and still can find no clue in the events of that last day.'

'Since you left, I've been told by Mr Emerson that your visit was brought forward unexpectedly. You didn't mention this in your original statement.'

'Did I not? I suppose it didn't seem relevant. It's true that my aunt asked me to stay over the Christmas season and I had accepted.' He hesitated, looking down at his hands. 'After that, I was offered hospitality more to my liking. I'm ashamed to say that renewing my acquaintance with my aunt seemed a chore. One I couldn't avoid so I thought I'd get over and done with. I told her that my leave had been cancelled over Christmas but I could visit her for a short time in September.'

'Thank you for clearing that up. What I'd like you to do now, if you please, is to go over everything Miss Chorley planned for your entertainment during your stay.'

Fingering his moustache, which looked half-hearted in its faded, sandy colour, Captain Selden considered. 'It's all slipping from my memory. The truth is, I didn't pay sufficient attention when she told me. Life can be one long, dreary round, endlessly taking your time from the things you love doing.'

'You mentioned a dinner party?' prompted Abbs.

'Oh yes, she planned that for my final evening. A different set of people from those who came to tea. I don't recall whom, except she spoke of the Jerrolds. I hadn't met him at the time. Where else? We were to tour the hospital, naturally. You know it was built in my grandfather's memory, my aunt's pet charity?' Abbs nodded, his eyes on an earlier page in his notebook. Nothing new had emerged so far. 'I was rather dreading that. Because of my work, my aunt thought I'd care to go over the hospital accounts. It seemed terribly high-handed to me. I'm afraid that was her character.' He fiddled with one of the tassels on the edge of the dark green tablecloth. 'You've been to the Hospital here. So you've probably gathered that my position in the Paymaster's office is rather more lowly than my aunt realised.'

'Can you think of anywhere else Miss Chorley intended you to visit or people you were to meet?'

'She said something about visiting people near Kempston but I don't recall their name. They were landowners, I believe. And there was talk of a concert at the Town Hall. I do care for music, particularly the Italians.' He smiled reminiscently. 'I can recall nothing else.'

'Thank you,' said Abbs. 'Moving on to Miss Geake, did you like her, Captain?'

'Liking didn't come into it. She was engaged as my aunt's companion. I scarcely noticed her.'

'Why did you change your mind suddenly about keeping Tower House open after your departure?'

The response was blustering. 'It was an act of kindness... for the staff, don't you know? They needed time to arrange their futures. I couldn't put them out on the street.'

'The servants tell me that you first intended to have the house shut up, directly the funeral was over. After all, why pay their wages to no purpose?'

'Look here, Inspector. You can't call me to account for every little decision. What business is it of yours?'

'My business is murder, Captain Selden. You know, servants see much more than people ever realise. But then, you do know that, don't you?'

To Abbs's inward horror, Selden's eyes started to glisten. He looked at random towards the curious wall plaques of Indian faces as he put his next question. 'What hold did Miss Geake have over you?'

A pop in the flames and the ticking of the domed clock on the mantel sounded unnaturally loud as he waited. He could see the resemblance in the two cousins now. It was there in the line of the profile and the same delicacy of manner. Selden did not appear to know how to begin.

'Is your friend here with you now?' asked Abbs, softly. The other's instinctive glance upwards at the ceiling was answer enough.

'How did you know?'

'The boots in the hall. Two pairs, different sizes.'

'You must understand, I have a friend staying for a few days that's all, while he finds other accommodation.'

'You must tell me about Miss Geake. I'm afraid I need to know what passed between you.'

Swallowing, his voice low, Captain Selden began to speak. 'She found a travelling frame I had. It contained a photograph of a dear friend. By day I placed it in the bedside drawer. I had nothing to hide but I value my privacy. So she searched my things, there's no other possible explanation. Indeed, she did not deny it.' He looked warily at Abbs. 'I don't need to spell out what she said, do I? She was too clever to say very much. I've no idea who killed her, Inspector, but I'd shake them by the hand. She was a vicious woman.'

'Did she ask you for money, Captain?'

Selden shook his head. 'She just remarked how inconvenient it would be for her to have to move out before it suited her. She enjoyed having power over me. I could see it in her eyes but that was all it amounted to.'

'I don't think there's much doubt that she asked your aunt's murderer for money,' murmured Abbs, almost to himself.

'That occurred to me when I received Mr Jerrold's letter. Do you think she knew who killed my aunt from the start?'

'We may never know for certain, but I think she worked it out over the subsequent days. She may have recalled some small action which seemed insignificant at the time and put two and two together.'

'Inspector, I have to ask you,' said Captain Selden, 'what are you going to do about what I've told you?'

'I'm going back to Seaborough to gather enough evidence to arrest your aunt's murderer,' said Abbs.

'About me, specifically.'

Abbs studied his notebook. 'I must thank you for your help, Captain. Interviewing you again has clarified my thoughts and perhaps being distanced from Seaborough has proved beneficial. There's a lot to be said for standing back.'

'Thank you, Inspector Abbs. I don't know what else to say. If there's ever anything I can do for you...'

'I must be on my way but since you ask, sir, there's something I should like to tell you. It concerns the young photographer you visited with Miss Chorley. You recall Mr Philip Winton?'

Twenty-seven

Reeve apparently had the knack of cultivating easy friendships. It was not a talent he had himself. As a young police constable based in a village, he had known everyone, that was essential in order to do his job yet he was apart from his neighbours. His upbringing, eldest son of a head gardener on a country estate had set him out of step with his contemporaries. Not quite one of the village children, sons of agricultural labourers for the most part, set just a little above the other estate workers' offspring after being noticed by and put to study with the rector. The unlooked for distinction had not lasted more than a year, the parents of his fellow pupils objecting to his presence among their sons and his extra tuition coming to a sudden end.

Now he could hear Reeve sharing a joke with Dean as they made tea for the four of them. The sergeant was one of those easy-going men who would make himself at home anywhere, while he would always remain an outsider. He had called in at the station, well into the previous evening to be told by Constable Prowse that the two of them were having a drink in one of the town's taverns. Declining the offer of a mug of cocoa from Prowse who was yawning over the front desk, he'd returned to *The Anchor*. When he'd caught up with Reeve, he'd glanced around his room with ill-concealed distaste. It was strewn with clothes, periodicals, the contents of pockets and even a paper bag bearing the evidence of a snack. He'd had several hours to live with his certainty on the return journey but it had seemed too late at night to give the sergeant more than an edited version of what he had realised at Netley.

He had suggested the others join them as their local knowledge would be invaluable. Sitting round the desk in Sergeant Tancock's office where there was more room, Abbs moved some folders as Constable Dean handed out their steaming tea.

'Did you have any difficulty in compiling this list, Sergeant?' Reeve answered as he took the chair nearest him.

'None at all, sir. I had to journey to Kempston where a lady clerk at the registrar's office was very helpful, once she saw my authority.'

'So these are all the deaths in Seaborough so far this year, not including the two murders.'

'There were a few infants as well, sir, as you'd expect, but you said to ignore them.'

'I can't say as I get it, sir. Why d'you want to see them?' Craning his neck, Sergeant Tancock read the list. Abbs swivelled it a little in his direction.

'A fishing expedition, Sergeant. I'm looking for anything suspicious. It struck me that our murderer might just have had reason to do it before. I thought it wouldn't hurt to go over recent deaths in case something had slipped through. He or she was driven to kill again almost certainly because Miss Geake had power of life and death over them. I'll stick with *he* for convenience. It's possible someone earlier had stood in his way and their death passed unquestioned.'

Shifting from one ample buttock to another, Sergeant Tancock looked unconvinced. Constable Dean leaned across and addressed the inspector with marked enthusiasm. 'They say murder's easier after the first time. Do you want us to tell you anything we know about these names, sir?'

'Yes, facts regarding their demise, at any rate. We'll take them in reverse order, starting with a Mrs Mary-Jane Wharton, age at death, sixty-five. Ring any bells, either of you?'

'Wharton,' said Tancock, nodding. He took a smacking mouthful and spluttered. 'Gawd, that's hot. She lived in one of those houses along Marine View.'

'According to this, she died of heart disease,' read Abbs.

'That's right. Swelled up something alarming, she did. Her daughter used to push her along the esplanade in a bath chair.'

'Do you know if there was any money?'

'She were a widow. Went to her children, a married son and the daughter.'

'Do either of you recall if she died in the hospital or at home?'

'Hospital I think,' said the sergeant.

Abbs considered it briefly. 'That seems perfectly straightforward. Elizabeth Marker, aged nineteen? Poor girl.'

They both shook their heads. 'Don't know of her, sir.'

'Cause of death, phthisis, lung disease in other words. No, there's nothing for us there. The death before that was an Albert Pardoe, aged one-and-forty, cause of death, internal injuries from fall.'

Dean and Tancock exchanged glances. 'No one poisoned him for his money,' said the latter. 'More likely he died owing.'

'Everyone knew Bert Pardoe, sir,' explained Constable Dean. 'We'd had to take him in a few times for causing a public nuisance while he was drunk, getting involved in fights, that sort of thing.'

'Didn't you mention him on the morning the cells were overflowing?' said Abbs, his face clearing.

'That's right, sir. He worked with the same lot, Halesworth's men, the builder's.'

'I recall seeing their cart outside the hospital on our first visit.'

'You see them all over the place,' continued the constable. 'They're the biggest builders in town. Bert Pardoe fell from the scaffolding on a house they were roofing.'

'Was he drunk, then?' put in Reeve.

Sergeant Tancock shook his head. 'Not at work, Caleb Halesworth wouldn't stand for that. No, I talked to them all. Turned out he'd been complaining of feeling dizzy. His missus were that shook up. I were there when they fetched her, poor body. Just shows, he used to knock her about. Not often, mind, he were a good husband to her.'

'Can a man who takes his fist to a woman be described in those terms?' said Abbs in the driest of tones.

'He was in his way, sir. You know what they say, *'A dog, a wife an' a walnut tree, the more you beat 'em, the better they be.'* Not that I hold with thrashing dogs or horses,' said Tancock, virtuously. 'We've a collecting box for dumb animals on the counter.'

'Mrs Pardoe's a decent sort,' said Constable Dean. 'She's friendly with my ma, they work together up at the hospital laundry.'

'How about Joseph Colman, aged thirty-eight when he died. Cause of death, shotgun injuries?'

'We remember that,' said Constable Dean. 'Don't we, Sergeant?'

Sergeant Tancock grunted. 'B.... fool. Shot himself. Still, that's farmers for you. Always got an easy way out to hand.'

'Why did he do it?' asked Reeve, brightly. He gave no indication of a sore head, thought Abbs, nor did Constable Dean. Whereas at not yet forty, he was feeling stiff from two days folded in a railway carriage.

'Woman trouble, what else?' said the sergeant. 'He were about to lose his tenancy. He only farmed in a small way, his missus ran off with another man and he took to drink. No one murdered him for his money, that's certain.'

'Before him was Amos Turl?' said Abbs, looking round the table.

'Sorry, sir, never heard of him.'

'It doesn't matter. Aged eighty-eight, cause of death, decline. I think we can rule him out. Perhaps I am making bricks without straw.' He saw Sergeant Tancock's face express agreement. 'However, we may as well go through the lot.'

When they finished, the sergeant stretched and got slowly to his feet. 'Anything else you need us for, Inspector?'

'Not for the present, thank you, Sergeant. You'll soon be able to have your other room back. Reeve and I are returning to Exeter in the morning.'

'Really, sir, does this mean you're giving up, then? Only what'll I say, should folks ask?'

'You can tell them our enquiries here are concluded for the present. Now I'd like to borrow Dean, if I may? The sergeant and I will pay a last call at Tower House and there's one other person we need to see. First though, Dean, can you get me the list of items removed from the house on the day after Miss Chorley's death?'

'Certainly, sir, but all the foodstuffs on it were sent for analysis and destroyed.'

'No matter, Constable, the list will suffice.'

'To think of all the times we've sat at this table and shared a pot of tea. End of an era, you might say.'

'I don't like change, it's true. I'll miss you m'dear but I wish you well in your new life, knowing you'll be happier.' Patting her old friend's arm, Hannah regarded her affectionately.

'I shall miss you, you've been a good friend, Hannah. You'll write and tell me all the news?'

'Of course and I shall want to hear all about Tunbridge Wells.'

Bertha Watkins cut herself a second slice of plum cake. 'I'll be agog to hear who did the murders, that's if they ever find out. I were certain sure Miss Geake poisoned the mistress.'

'I mind it well,' Hannah smiled at her.

'Those two detectives didn't stay above a quarter-hour. They went up to the mistress's room but I don't know what for.' She shivered between mouthfuls. 'Tisn't like the same place, you know. Mr Jerrold's had men in, rolling up the carpets and stacking the pictures against the walls. The library shelves are empty and the furniture's covered in dust-sheets. The rooms are all hollow somehow.'

'What that great place needs is a proper family to take it, with little ones running in and out of the garden. Bring a bit of life up there.'

'Captain Selden didn't want it. I s'pose he has his own life all settled. He'll want the money it'll fetch though.'

'You haven't heard if anyone's buying it?' Busily chewing, Mrs Watkins shook her head. 'So did the others get suited in the end?'

'After a fashion. Sarah's all right, o'course. That kind always fall on their feet. I daresay her parents wouldn't want her back for ever but they'll take her 'til she's wed, if she earns her keep. She's a good little lace-maker, learned at her mother's knee. William's staying on over the stables for a time, to keep an eye on the property. The gardeners have been paid off. That just leaves young Jane. Her mother will take her in on sufferance but she'll be sharing with her three sisters and you wouldn't believe how much that girl eats.'

'If you like, I could get Miss Adelaide to ask if any family needs a kitchen maid? She'd be pleased to get her a good position.'

'I'm sure Jane would take that as a great kindness and tell her she's an honest girl. She might be slow but she's ever so obliging. Doesn't mind any rough work.'

'I'll ask her directly. She can enquire at the Ladies' meeting.'

'I'm sorry to hear the vicar's no better and not to hear him preach one last time.'

'It's distressed him terribly to miss a service. And old Reverend Tomlin who steps in likes to give a good hour and a quarter's sermon. It was standing outside all that while with Miss Geake's body, God rest her, that made him worse. He talks of saying prayers and sprinkling holy water on the spot but he can't leave his bed. Who would ever have thought such a thing would come to pass in Seaborough?'

'You didn't sense it, then, Hannah? Before I go, I wonder if you'd just take a look, tell me what you see? Go on, do.'

'Very well, Bertha. I can't promise anything but you know what to do.' Finishing her tea, Mrs Watkins turned her cup upside down and rotated it three times on its saucer. Her eyes sparkled with relish as she slid it across the kitchen table.

Twenty-eight

It had been easier than he'd feared to get Superintendent Nicholls to listen. His first assumption had been that they'd 'come back with their tails between their legs,' as he put it. Bracing himself for a gruelling encounter, not at first invited to sit down, he'd put his case for an exhumation order. The contemptuous laughter had been expected. Nicholls though, was no fool. He had risen to his high rank by getting results. Known throughout the city as a formidable thief-taker, a murder of quality had rarely come his way. Eventually Abbs had seen the slow smile spread across his features, the mechanisms of his mind as predictable as those of a clock. If Abbs was right, he could contrive to take the credit. If he was wrong... after causing such trouble and expense on a 'half-baked, crackpot notion,' his career as a detective would be over.

'You realise it'll have to go all the way to the Home Secretary's office?' he'd growled. His cold gone, Nicholls's voice was back to its biting worst. Patiently he'd said yes and no in the required places until the Superintendent had agreed to make an appointment for them both to see the Chief Constable at his home outside the city. There he had reiterated his inquiry step by step and the Chief Constable, a former military man, had understood it was the only way to get the evidence that would convict.

The telegram of assent had returned from the capital and the necessary arrangements had been made. Dr Chisholm from Exeter was of their party and of the Seaborough contingent, only Sergeant Tancock and Constable Dean were to be present. The undertakers were coming from Kempston, it being imperative that Mr Hicks was unaware of their enterprise.

A dark shadow detached itself from the line of trees along the perimeter and picked its way to Abbs.

'Cold night, sir, still, it's nearly November.' Reeve thrust his hands in his jacket pocket as he spoke.

'It is but I'm hoping the wind will hold off the rain. I've been watching the clouds blow, they're moving fast. Any sign yet?'

'Not yet, sir, we should hear them soon. Sergeant Tancock sent me to ask if you'd care for a nip to keep out the chill? He's brought a flask of brandy.'

'Not for me, thank you. I trust he'll remain alert, we don't want him falling in the open grave.'

Reeve grinned. 'It'll be a nightmare for the men if it does rain.' The church clock began to chime, followed a few seconds later by the one at the town hall. As they finished, the faint clop of hooves replaced them in the darkness. 'I'll go and meet them.' Abbs remained where he was, watching the stars which were there and not there as the clouds raced across the sky.

Presently an irregular line of lights came bobbing toward him like glow-worms, as men encumbered with equipment and holding up lamps drew near. He went to have a word with them, ensuring they had their instructions. Canvas screens were positioned on two sides of the grave, even though they were a distance from the road. Lamps were hung on poles, sacking laid on the grass and the men began to dig. They worked in silence except for the odd grunt of effort. The man nearest Abbs soon broke off to remove his jacket, the flannel stale with pipe tobacco.

'This is going to take a while, sir,' murmured the undertaker, a broad-shouldered man in a heavy cape, holding his lamp aloft. 'I'd recommend a handkerchief when we unscrew the lid.' Thanking him, Abbs wandered aimlessly between the new graves. From a little distance the glow of lamplight and the shadows behind the screen looked like a campfire. He waited by a carved angel, its stone cold to the touch. His wife had a similar memorial, not his choice, it was too elaborate, but her family had wished it.

Back in Exeter he had visited Ellen's grave, reading the lines he knew by heart. He had said a kind of silent good-bye to them both. For he had finally admitted to himself that he wasn't mourning his dead wife any longer. The dull weight he carried was not grief, sorry though he was that she and the child were dead, it was guilt. He knew he wasn't the first young man to have mistaken a pretty face and winning manner for something much deeper. When he met Ellen, she a nursery-maid travelling with her employers while they visited acquaintances in Norfolk, he had wanted to make her his wife. He had transferred to the other side of the country for her and within a year he had understood his mistake. Everyone had a duty to make the best of their lot in life and so he had. He did not believe she had ever known.

The thud of pick on ground recalled him to his surroundings. The bank of earth along the side of the grave had grown considerable. Someone made an exclamation as their spade hit a different texture, followed at once by the chink of metal. Abbs moved to stand with Reeve and Sergeant Tancock, while Constable Dean had been left by the gate with the undertaker's van. They watched him now as he directed his men to scrape the lid clear of earth and held his lamp lower to read the small name-plate.

There was an unpleasant, sucking sound as the coffin, reluctant to tear free from the red Devonshire clay was lifted sufficiently to get ropes underneath. Then it was laid on trestles and the men bent over the screws.

'Wait for the stink,' muttered Sergeant Tancock. Abbs watched the moon above the spire of the chapel, his fists clenched against what they would find. If he was right, they would know at once, he thought. Reeve shivered, his eyes intent on the widening gap as the lid was moved.

There was very little odour. At first Dr Chisholm blocked their view, while the undertaker held a lamp steady for him. Straightening up, he beckoned Abbs and Reeve to come closer.

'You were right, Inspector. I shall do the tests of course but there's no doubt in my mind. Arsenic kills the bacteria in the body that would begin putrefaction. Thus where it is present, the corpse is unnaturally preserved. After six weeks or so, it should be smelling to high heaven and looking very different from this. Come, don't look so worried, see for yourself.' Abbs and Reeve moved to one side of the open coffin.

'That greenish tinge is a surface mould that's got in from outside.' The two detectives stared down at the ghastly, yet still life-like features of the former builder's labourer, Bert Pardoe.

Twenty-nine

Three more days had passed, waiting first for the test results and then for the warrant to be obtained from a city magistrate. Nicholls had not congratulated him and indeed perhaps that would have been premature before the arrest. Abbs could not rid himself of a bad feeling, a presentiment of gathering trouble. Dr Chisholm's report had confirmed what they had seen in the cemetery at Seaborough. Arsenic deposits had been found in the hair and fingernails. The powders given them by Mrs Pardoe had been innocuous but the box bore a faint trace of arsenic.

On the late afternoon of the third day Inspector Abbs and Sergeant Reeve left for Seaborough for the last time, taking with them a burly constable from the Exeter division. Dusk was falling by the time they descended from the train. They were met by a sombre-faced Sergeant Tancock and once again escorted to the small police station near the sea.

'I still can't hardly believe it, sir. There's no chance you could have it wrong?'

Patiently, Abbs shook his head, recognising that concern rather than insolence directed the sergeant's remarks. Beside him Constable Dean looked wan and uneasy. Brought face to face with the reality of detective work, it was not the swaggering adventure Reeve had described.

'No chance whatever, Sergeant. I'm certain of the chain of events. The Chief Constable and the magistrates are satisfied.'

'But why finish off Bert Pardoe? How could he gain by that?'

'Pardoe was blackmailing him. He must have seen something, either while he was working there or possibly when fetching his wife. We interviewed Mrs Pardoe on the day we left and she said her husband sometimes waited outside for her on the day she was paid. She was able to tell us enough to justify the exhumation order.'

'There's plenty in this town will be staggered. He were liked, you know.' Tancock was talking as though he were already dead, thought Abbs, his voice faded away until there was no more to say. The shadow of the rope lay on the counter between them.

'Where is he to be found, Sergeant?'

'He's not at home, Sir, nor at The Marine when we checked.'

In his office, then. Abbs rather thought they would be expected. He turned to Reeve, Dean and lastly Constable Franks, waiting stolidly by the entrance.

'It's time to go.'

It was starting to rain, making the sea invisible. A lamp-lighter was beginning his work in the square. The branches of the trees were bare now and the grass swept clear of leaves since their previous visit. They had reached the last weeks of autumn and the year was quietly dying. A sad, reflective time, it always seemed to him, before the gaiety of Christmastide.

They left Franks stationed by the main door. The police conveyance and cabman remained in a side street, unseen from the windows. Abbs directed Constable Dean to the rear of the building with instructions to watch the back exits. He had not forgotten that the office had a glass door to the outside and there would be a kitchen door.

He looked at Reeve, tense by his side as they stood just inside the entrance area. 'Remember, we need him to talk or there are things we'll never know. If I read him rightly, he's more likely to do that here than in a cell. I think he'll need to tell someone.'

'And they always like to justify themselves,' replied the sergeant, bitterly. 'What if he makes a run for it? This place is a regular warren.'

'He'll come quietly,' whispered Abbs with more confidence than he felt. 'Where could he go? Ready?'

Reeve squared his shoulders and flexed his fingers, curving them loosely as though ready to spar. The place was very quiet, lamps burning dimly on either side of the corridor, a stifled cough, the shadow of a form sitting at a table. No one challenged them. And there at the far end was the door on the left. Abbs turned the brass knob, it opened and they were inside. The gas bracket was turned down and an oil lamp on the desk threw a pool of light for writing, a dark frock coat was hung round the back of the chair. The room's occupant was standing at the other door with his back to them, looking out at the rainy night. Then Dr Gilbert Avery turned slowly towards them.

For a moment, no one spoke. Abbs was shocked at the doctor's haggard appearance, his eyes hollowed and red as though gritty with lack of sleep. He stood in his linen, his cuffs loosened and a wicked-looking surgical knife dangled from his hand. The two detectives halted by the door, which Reeve had closed behind him. He let out a hissing breath and Abbs realised that he too had been holding his.

'Well, gentlemen,' Dr Avery inclined his head. 'Do I offer you tea and assume you come to consult me?'

'It's too late for that, Doctor,' said Abbs. Lowering his eyelids in acknowledgement for a second, Avery gave a wry half-smile, little more than a twitching of the lips.

'I gathered as much. Really, Abbs, you've learnt nothing about this godforsaken town if you imagined I wouldn't hear about your late night visit to the cemetery.'

'Why not put down the knife, Doctor?'

'What a soothing voice you have, Inspector. A better bedside manner than I ever did but I don't believe I will.' Avery studied his fingertip, drawing the point of the knife along his finger. A thread of crimson sprang instantly in a line. 'Stay over there, if you please.' He pointed the knife in their direction.

'We're in no hurry,' remarked Abbs in a neutral tone.

'You know, I couldn't be sure when you would come,' said the doctor, conversationally. 'Though I reckoned on your discretion. I waited here for you last evening.'

'We needed the test results on Albert Pardoe's body.'

'Ah, of course. A greedy fool who's no loss to this world.'

'It didn't give you the right to kill him.' Reeve couldn't stop himself bursting out, glancing apologetically at Abbs, he subsided as quickly.

'Oh, I didn't kill him, Sergeant,' said Avery. His back to the window sill, he regarded them steadily, his right hand grasping the knife handle.

'We have enough evidence to see you convicted of Pardoe's murder,' said Abbs. 'His wife still had the box of powders you gave him.'

Avery shrugged. 'I may have given him a helping hand but I did him a favour, put him out of his misery as I would a dog.' He studied their uncomprehending faces and sighed. 'He was dying, anyway. All right, Abbs, I'll tell you what you want to know. It will be a relief in some ways.' Abbs sensed Reeve give a flicker of acknowledgement. The sergeant had planted himself against the door, his arms folded.

'Pardoe was snooping about outside one day, probably hoping for something left lying around or trying to spy on one of the nurses. He was a repellent individual who would lie in wait for his wife on the day she was paid for her work in the laundry here. Incidentally, Sergeant, if you'd seen the bruises on her arms, you wouldn't be so quick to defend him. He spied in this window and saw me with the safe door open and a cash box on the desk. I was removing some banknotes and folding them in my pocket-book.' Avery's eyes narrowed as though he were seeing that day again.

'He let himself in the door there and set about blackmailing me, grinning with pleasure. Naturally I tried my d.......t to convince him I was acting properly, taking the money to pay in the bank but he wouldn't have it. We'd had a fete here the previous week, raising money for the new wing and the cash box contained the proceeds. He was a thief himself, you see, and thought he'd recognised a kindred spirit. It amused him no end to see someone of my class behaving like him. He was matey...' the doctor spat out the word in disbelief.

'He said it made us equals and we could do one another a good turn. He was beyond all convincing of my innocence. What made it worse was he said he'd seen me at a card table in Kempston. He knew I was a gambler. I had to give him some money there and then to get rid of him. I couldn't allow myself to be blackmailed, you must see that? I felt like a rat cornered in a pit.'

'What did you mean by saying Pardoe was dying, anyway?' asked Abbs, quietly. He fervently willed Reeve not to do anything that would stop Avery from talking.

The doctor made a dismissive gesture with his empty hand. 'While he was taunting me and demanding money, he suddenly doubled up with the gripes, saying he had constant indigestion and blaming it on his wife's cooking. He begged me to give him something to ease the pain.' He smiled, coldly. 'He had no fear at all. He thought it was the start of an alliance. I had a paper containing arsenic compound in my drawer there. It was the work of a second to push it in a box of stomach powders so he took it at random.'

'His wife could have taken it,' said Reeve, stiff with indignation.

Avery looked indifferent. 'That didn't occur to me, I confess. It was sufficient to kill him in one dose. I knew his death would be taken for gastric trouble. Who would poison a labourer? As it turned out, the dizziness came on when he was on scaffolding and he fell to his death. But you wanted an explanation of my remark. I questioned him briefly and from his symptoms I'm fairly sure he had cancer of the stomach. So I'm not as inhumane as you think, Sergeant.'

'Had you been embezzling the hospital funds for long?' said Abbs.

'Long enough. The subscriptions for the new wing put a lot more money in my way. I thought I'd covered my tracks well.'

'Oh, you did. For a long while we had no idea.'

'So, how did you come to suspect me?' They might have been having a discussion in the bar at *The Marine Hotel.*

'We had the first intimation when Mr Emerson told us that Captain Selden's visit had been brought forward,' said Abbs. 'The visit was the only unusual event in Miss Chorley's life. Then we started wondering if the change in date could have made a difference to anyone. But we still didn't see who or how until I went to Hampshire to talk to Selden again. Ironically I needed to check his alibi for Miss Geake's murder or I might not have done so.' The small amount of colour drained from Avery's features as he listened intently, his eyes fixed on Abbs. 'We knew Miss Chorley intended showing her nephew round the hospital. Captain Selden told me that she wanted him to look over the accounts.'

'And you pieced it together? Congratulations, Inspector. That arrogant, interfering old woman signed her own death warrant. If she'd been content to leave the hospital in my hands, I'd have made good the money and she none the wiser. But she had to show off her charity. I thought I had three months but the nephew coming early forced my hand.'

Abbs shifted his weight, tension in every muscle of his body. He could feel the contempt radiating from Reeve, the greater because he had admired the police-surgeon.

'Don't come any nearer, Inspector. I find I'm in no hurry to be condemned. My mind's been in a prison these last weeks. I never set out to kill anyone, events forced it on me.' The knife wavered and a sudden spat of rain on the glass made Avery start. His wrist shook for an instant. The evening was now fully dark. Abbs watched the rivulets of water run down the window and half-glazed door. Their reflections looked back at him, the lamplight making it impossible to see outside. He wondered how close Constable Dean was. Then the doctor spoke again.

'Have you worked out how I did it?'

'Yes,' said Abbs, simply. 'For a long while we were looking in the wrong direction, concentrating on the people Miss Chorley saw that day. That was a distraction, like a conjuring trick. You poisoned one of the headache powders you prescribed for her, so you had no idea when she would die. You didn't need to. You would be called in and sign the death certificate. All that mattered was that Miss Chorley died before she could ask her nephew to look over the accounts. But your plan went wrong when you were called away on the night of her death and the servant had to fetch Dr Miller.'

'I thought she'd take the arsenic long before. It was a close run thing. I was gone hours that night, a difficult birth at one of the farms. Miller had no suspicion, he made a fuss out of pomposity and spite.'

'You claim you never set out to kill anyone yet you'd prepared arsenic, had it at hand in your desk. You cold-bloodedly planted poison among medicine for two people. That's premeditated murder.'

'I was desperate, I tell you,' the doctor's voice rang with anguish. 'Three unpleasant individuals have departed this earth. Weigh that against all the good I've done. I owed money left and right hand. Still do. My house is gone when a promissory note falls due. I've wagered everything I have and lost.'

'You had a pile of sporting papers in this room, the day we met,' said Abbs. 'It didn't seem important at the time but you swept them away hurriedly and that made me notice. Then when I saw you out ratting, you looked like a different man. What happened when your face was bruised?'

'Something you don't know?' Avery breathed audibly, his chest rising and falling in agitation. 'I'd been at a card game in Kempston and been losing heavily all day. I already owed some people there but my luck had to change.' His eyes looked feverish, thought Abbs. 'When I left The Golden Lion I was set upon by ruffians, in the yard behind. It's what happens when you can't pay your debts. I knew then my life was collapsing, just as surely as a house of cards. To confound my ill luck, Halesworth saw me on the train.'

Reeve had left the door and edged a foot forward, by his side. Abbs wondered if Avery had noticed the bulge of metal in the sergeant's jacket pocket. He wanted to stretch out a hand and warn him back but he could not. The doctor too had moved fractionally nearer the outer door. Abbs knew his willingness to talk would not last much longer.

'What about Miss Geake?' said Reeve. 'How did she know what you'd done?'

Avery's face hardened. 'Naturally she knew about the old woman's powders. She'd given her one that evening before the sickness started. Eventually she guessed. There was no proof but the accusation would have sunk me. I couldn't let her repeat her suspicions to anyone.'

'Did she threaten to tell us?'

He shook his head. 'Nothing so public-spirited, Sergeant. She wanted money of course. Doesn't everyone?' Neither of them answered him. 'Miss Geake didn't care what I'd done. She hated her employer. She offered her silence in return for enough money to set herself up. As if I had it...' The doctor gave the beginnings of a bitter laugh that died in disgust.

'What happened to the weapon?' demanded Reeve.

Dashing a hand over his brow, Avery looked exhausted, his knife hand lowering a little. 'I despatched her with my fishing priest. It's back with my tackle.' His shoulders were slumping but he raised his head and half-smiled at Abbs. 'I was minded to open the veins in my wrists. They say it's an easy death but I couldn't bring myself to begin and then I heard you coming. No more arsenic, you see.'

'I can't let you...' began Abbs, taking a step forward.

'Stay back, both of you.' Avery jerked the knife at them. 'I warn you, this is scalpel sharp and I'll use it on one of us.'

'Why the gambling, Doctor?' said Abbs. 'You had a respected position in this town.'

'Because I was bored, Abbs.' The doctor flung out his words, his voice rising. 'You couldn't understand how frustrating my life has been. I don't heal people. I've spent years patching the poor when what they need is money and lackeying to the fat, idle rich with their imaginary headaches and their gout. Everyone else is on the fiddle in this town. Why shouldn't I have money and live a little? At least risking everything on the fall of dice made me feel alive. At least I've been no hypocrite. Miss Chorley lived on rents from hovels in the filthiest rookery in Exeter.'

As his words poured out, Doctor Avery stepped to the outer door, his free hand reaching behind him for the knob. 'I'll not hang, Abbs. For pity's sake let me die in my....'

Reeve lunged at Avery, intent on disarming him, knocking Abbs almost off his feet as he flew past. As the sergeant reached Avery, one hand wrenching his free arm, the other fist raised to punch, the doctor instinctively twisted sideways, had nowhere to go and his hand holding the knife collided with Reeve's chest.

Afterwards Abbs felt as though everything had been suspended in time. As he threw himself across the intervening gap in his turn, he caught one glimpse of Avery's shocked face before he threw open the door and plunged into the night, the door banging and the rain sweeping in.

Crumpled on his side, there was a dreadful wheezing sound coming from Reeve's throat. Kneeling and desperately heaving him over, Abbs felt the dark stain spreading across his shirt. The knife was not there. Reeve's eyes were on him and he was trying to speak. Tearing off his jacket, Abbs frantically held the material hard against the wound.

'You're going to be all right, stay still. Don't try to speak. Help's on the way... Ned...'

And fumbling for his whistle, Abbs blew until Dean appeared, white-faced in the open doorway and several footsteps could be heard running along the corridor towards them.

Thirty

One month later

The impressive edifice of the cathedral loomed ahead of them, its intricately carved west front lit by the afternoon sun. The frost on the surrounding lawns had lingered all day and the sunlight, though cheerful, had no warmth about it. The man leaving the *Globe Hotel* in the middle of the old buildings flanking the Close bent his head solicitously as the lady at his side spoke to him. Though he did not offer his arm as they began to stroll slowly to the far end of the walk.

Inspector Abbs and Miss Adelaide Shaw had drunk tea and crumbled cake in company with her father, Mr Shaw having business in Exeter. They had discussed politely and cordially everything other than the deaths that had taken place in Seaborough that autumn.

'My father will miss his roses.' Adelaide halted by a flower bed where a few buds hung browned and ruined. 'It's a pity these never had a chance to flower.'

'Will you have no garden in London?'

'Only a very small one, I believe. I have never visited my Aunt Shaw's house. But we shall be happy in Bloomsbury. Papa will have his books and he intends to obtain a ticket for the reading room at the British Museum. He will enjoy seeing the antiquities,' Adelaide smiled resolutely at him.

'I do hope so,' replied Abbs. He wanted to ask if he might write to her but the words remained unspoken.

'He could not return to his parish duties as before. You saw how easily he tires now. He made light of it to you but we feared he would not come through.' He nodded gravely, thinking that the treasures in the museums of the capital were all very well but that Mr Shaw would never again explore a hill-fort or seek an arrow head on the ground.

'I'm sorry about your sergeant.' He could see the concern in her eyes as she faced him. 'He was very brave.'

It was all so unnecessary, he wanted to rage. Reeve's foolhardiness d... near got himself killed. Abbs knew that Reeve had liked Avery. He'd felt betrayed and his anger made him determined to disarm and arrest him. He blamed himself for not keeping Reeve back.

'He received a commendation last year for saving a child's life. He snatched a small girl from the path of a coach-and-four. That's why he was promoted to sergeant early.'

'How is he faring?'

'Reeve's on the mend now, though not yet returned to duty. He's needed a lot of nursing. Fortunately he's young and fit.'

'He was very kind on the day I found Miss Geake's body. Does he have family to care for him?' He shook his head, to his shame, he did not know.

'I shall always believe Dr Avery was responsible for ruining my father's health, you know. If he hadn't stayed by the body when he had a chill, it wouldn't have turned to pneumonia.' Her voice had that hard edge of someone struggling to contain their emotions. She turned away towards the passers-by, her face hidden by the edge of her bonnet. Abbs wondered if she would always associate him in her mind with bloodstains and corpses. He feared she probably would.

'I don't believe the doctor intended to stab Sergeant Reeve,' he said gently. 'It all happened in such confusion.'

'I'm sorry, it's not very Christian of me. I hope they're all at peace, including him.'

Abbs was silent, remembering that terrible evening when they thought they'd lost Reeve. Sergeant Tancock's men had searched all night. The knife had been dropped outside but it was well into the next morning before Dr Avery's mangled body had been found on the rocks at the foot of the cliffs.

An old lady was scattering seed to the pigeons and a nanny had stopped to watch them with her two charges, the children muffled against the cold. Beyond them a flurry of rooks rose from the trees in the garden of the Bishop's Palace. Adelaide lifted her head, watching them soar about the cathedral towers.

'Mr Hicks has taken Gyp, the doctor's dog. They feared he would pine but he's settled well, Fanny says.'

'That's kind of them.'

'And the Halesworths are buying Tower House.' She smiled shakily at him. 'Mrs Halesworth is very nearly, perfectly satisfied... except she would have liked to be head of the Ladies Society and that has gone to Mrs Jerrold.'

And she had her chance of a new life, though not in a way she would have wanted. She would make the best of it, he knew, and perhaps she would find someone to marry in London.

'Do you remember Mr Biggs, Mr Hicks's clerk? I'm afraid he's suffered a seizure.'

'A lot has changed in Seaborough, then.'

More than she knew, he could not tell her that he'd had a letter from a grateful Mr Winton. His premises would be to let again for he was setting up in Southampton with an investment from Captain Selden. And Constable Dean had resigned, finding the work of policing was not after all to his liking.

After reaching the end of the walk, there was nothing to be done but slowly retrace their footsteps. Reluctantly, Abbs escorted his companion back to the hotel entrance, her gloved fingers briefly in his as they shook hands and parted.

Touching his hat to an acquaintance, he walked away briskly, skirting the pigeons until he reached the arched gateway that led to the rest of his life and all the hubbub of the modern city. He would not forget Seaborough and some of the people he had met there.

Hesitating, he stood looking back, undecided.

The End

About Seaborough

Seaborough is, of course, a completely fictitious Devon seaside resort, though it uses elements – though not the people – of several coastal towns in the county. Many places along the Devon coast tried to become popular resorts during the nineteenth century – some succeeded better than others. We took the name Seaborough from a female Victorian ancestor of John's, Seaborough Care, who lived a hard life a long way from the sea shore.

ABOUT THE AUTHOR

John Bainbridge - a husband and wife writing team living in England. In their spare time they love to explore the towns and countryside of Britain.

We hope you have enjoyed reading A Seaside Mourning. If you have, we would appreciate it if you would leave a positive review on this book's page on Amazon and tell your friends. You can contact us at: gaslightcrime@yahoo.co.uk

The Gaslight Crime Blog

Visit the Gaslight Crime blog to keep up to date with our latest publications.
Click follow at www.gaslightcrime.wordpress.com

ALSO FROM GASLIGHT CRIME

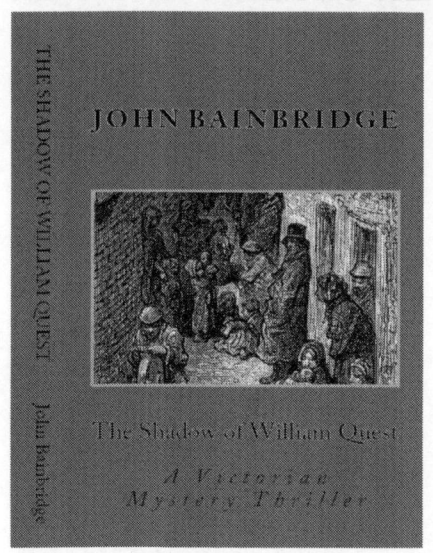

A tormented past casts long shadows. In the London of 1853, where the grand houses of the wealthy lie a stone's throw from the vilest slums and rookeries of the poor. A mysterious stranger carrying a swordstick walks the gaslit alleys and night houses seeking vengeance. A man determined to fight for justice against all the wrongs of Victorian society. Who is the secretive William Quest? Following Quest's trail from the teeming streets of London to the lonely coast of London, Inspector Anders of Scotland Yard is determined to uncover the truth.

NOW AVAILABLE IN PAPERBACK AND KINDLE EBOOK

Printed in Great Britain
by Amazon.co.uk, Ltd.,
Marston Gate.